T0349971

Also by Walter Tevis from Gollancz:

The Man Who Fell to Earth
Mockingbird

The Steps of the Sun & Far From Home

Walter Tevis

Rent Control copyright © Omni Publications International Ltd 1979
The Apotheosis of Myra copyright © Playboy Publications, Inc. 1980
Out of Luck copyright © Omni Publications International Ltd 1980
Echo copyright © Mercury Press, Inc. 1980
The Other End of the Line copyright © Mercury Press, Inc. 1961
The Big Bounce copyright © Galazy Publishing Corporation 1958
The Goldbrick, originally published as *Operation Goldbrick*,
copyright © Quinn Publishing Co. 1957
The Ifth of Ooth copyright © Galaxy Publishing Corporation 1957
The Scholar's Disciple copyright © National Council of Teachers of English 1969
Far From Home copyright © Mercury Press, Inc. 1958

This edition first published in Great Britain in 2016
by Gollancz
An imprint of the Orion Publishing Group
Carmelite House, 50 Victoria Embankment, London EC4Y 0DZ
An Hachette UK Company

5 7 9 10 8 6

A CIP catalogue record for this book is available
from the British Library

ISBN 978 1 473 21313 5

Printed and bound in Great Britain by Clays Ltd, Elcograf S.p.A.

MIX
Paper from
responsible sources
FSC
www.fsc.org   FSC® C104740

www.gollancz.co.uk
www.orionbooks.co.uk

CONTENTS

THE STEPS OF THE SUN

For Eleanora Walker, Dr. Herry Teltscher,
and Pat LoBrutto

Ah, sunflower, weary of time,
Who countest the steps of the sun,
Seeking after that sweet golden clime
Where the traveler's journey is done . . . .

William Blake
Songs of Experience

>

1

When they knocked me out I regressed like a shot to my childhood on Earth and stayed there in a kind of wakeful dream for two months. At times I would become aware of the throbbing of the ship's engine, of the sleek tubes that fed me, of the machines that exercised my body and of the soft voice of my trainer, but for most of the voyage I was back in my father's house in Ohio with the smells of his cigar smoke and of his books and the awe I had felt as a child toward the certificates and diplomas on the wallpapered wall over his desk. There were faded blue flowers on that paper; it seemed I could see them more clearly from captain's quarters on my interstellar ship than I had as a child. Forget-me-nots. There was a brownish stain near the ceiling over a framed diploma that read DOCTEUR DE L'UNIVERSITÉ HONORAIRE. I sat on the green-carpeted floor and stared silently at the stain. My father, silent also, read from an old book in German or French or Japanese, stopping every now and then to make a note on a three-by-five card or light a cigar. He never looked at me or acknowledged my presence. Mother was out; Father was stuck with keeping me. I felt guilty: Father was busy, his work was important, I was a trouble to him. I must have loved him terribly—his rare, shy smile, his quietness. I did not even hope that he would someday explain his work to me. When he died I still knew nothing about that ancient history he spent his life brooding over. I have never read his books. I had him buried in a fine cemetery, glad to be old enough and with money enough to do it right and well. I was twenty-three when he died and already rich. My father was a scholar—world-famous I was told by Mother—and his style was genteel poverty. I loved him ardently, in silence.

I nearly awoke once here on the ship, when my trainer had allowed his attention to lapse and one of the exercise machines was straining the muscles of my abdomen. I found myself for a moment lying on my back on a red leather bench, groaning upward against steel springs in the ship's gym and with hot tears flooding my face. I had just come from my dream trip to Father's study, awakened fleetingly by pain. The trainer's face was tight with anxiety. As if through a partition I heard his alarmed voice saying, 'Sorry, Captain Belson,' and I muttered something about love and fell back into my chemical sleep. The astonishing thing was the tears. I had not cried at my father's funeral. I had never mourned him. I had hardly thought of him for thirty years. And here I was at the age of fifty-two, somewhere out in the black reaches of the Milky Way, weeping copiously for him. In sleep I returned to his study and sat cross-legged on his floor, silent. I watched his concentration at his desk. Somewhere outside of me I heard the hum of the ship and exulted, propelled beyond the speed of light toward constellations totally outside my father's understanding.

They woke me two weeks before planetfall. There was a crew of seventeen. I owned the ship; I had bought it a year before. We were heading toward an unexplored planet of the star Fomalhaut, known as FBR 793. It was my first voyage away from Earth.

I have always come awake quickly. There is something feral in me and I welcome it when I awaken. I was on my back in my stateroom and the ship's doctor and navigator were standing by my bed. The doctor was holding a cup of coffee out to me. I ignored it for a moment while I looked around. The room had been painted a pale blue as I had instructed; I could dimly remember the smell of fresh paint in my sleeping nostrils. There was a porthole to my right and one crystalline star, blindingly bright against velvet black, was almost centered in it. I stretched my arms, my legs, twisted my head on my neck. There was strength in my body; I could feel it in my pectorals, my biceps, the muscles of my thighs; the sense of power went through me like a quiet euphoria. I felt my belly; the paunch was gone.

I looked back toward the doctor, reached out steadily and

took the cup. There was a white porcelain vase with red roses in it on the desk by my bed.

'Thank you for the flowers,' I said.

'Glad we could grow them,' the doctor said. 'How's your head? Any hangover?'

'Not a bit, Charlie,' I said. It was true. I felt wonderful. I sipped the coffee and felt it penetrate the raw emptiness of my stomach.

'For god's sake don't drink it fast,' Charlie said. 'Bad enough to drink it at all.'

I had told them to have coffee ready. 'I know myself well enough,' I said, and continued sipping.

'It's a new self,' the doctor said.

I looked at him over the edge of the cup, over the little red stripe that went around its porcelain edge. 'Charlie,' I said, 'it's a new self but it still likes coffee.' I finished half of it and set the cup down. Then I got out of bed, a bit slowly. I was naked and tanned. I looked good. The blond hair on my arms and legs had been bleached a pale yellow by the ultraviolet lamps. 'Let's go to the bridge,' I said.

'Okay,' the navigator said, startled.

'And while I'm dressing, see if you can find me a sandwich.'

We were still too far to see the planet. I could have slept another week, since there was very little for me to do when awake. There was little for anyone to do on the ship. But two months' sleep had been enough to get me into shape and to avoid serious boredom. I wanted to do some reading. I wanted the feel of being the owner-captain of a spaceship. I was the first man in history ever to own one and I wanted to savor the experience.

The bridge was a semicircle twenty feet across, at right angles to the ship's acceleration. The acceleration was continuous at one-fifth G even in spacewarp, and it gave us enough weight to walk. For exercise I used springs over cams—zero-gravity Nautilus equipment. There was no such thing as an intergalactic Olympics; had there been, these machines would have prepared the athletes. I felt ready to go for a gold medal.

9

The sandwich turned out to be Virginia ham and gruyère. With all the cold and the vacuum around us, food-keeping was easy and we had plenty. It was a good sandwich, but half of it filled my shrunken stomach. I gave the other half to the navigator. 'How's the uranium?' I said.

'Fine,' he said. 'Exactly as computed. We could repeat the voyage without refueling.'

The bridge was mostly empty deck, carpeted in beige. Its heart was a pair of red computer consoles and a panel of switches. Nothing more complicated than a locomotive. There were six rectangular portholes, and the stars seen through them were splendid, but after a while boring. I had seen them before my sleep and was impressed, but only briefly. The first sight is spectacular; there is no cold mountain sky on Earth that reveals the stars so brilliantly. But I find the sea on an ocean voyage more continuously interesting. It has life in it, while this interstellar panorama, however dazzling, has none. If it should really be, after all, the visible manifestation of a god, I refuse to be awed. I have no need for an inscrutable deity; my father's inscrutability was sufficient. I have enough to do with my life. I need no gods too distant to reveal themselves to me, no presence behind the star's glitter.

I am no mad Ahab. I am a businessman, looking for uranium. The Earth had wasted almost all she had. I gathered together what I could to power this old Chinese ship and was staking half my fortune on a Schliemann-like hunch that a planet of Fomalhaut would have uranium. 'Belson's Bubble' was what the Chicago *Tribune* had called it. Well, to hell with the Chicago *Tribune*.

'Captain,' the navigator said, 'a message arrived when you were asleep.'

I nodded. 'Later. How's the garden?'

'Even better than we planned. You saw the roses. It came during the third week out . . .'

I stared at his chubby body, his balding head. 'Bill. I said *later*.'

'I'm sorry.'

'Let's look at the garden.'

We went across a catwalk and down a silky ladder with skid-resistant rungs. In the low gravity and with my splendid

10

new muscles I felt like a youthful spider descending a spoke in her new web. I was wearing faded blue jeans and a gray tee-shirt, with gum-soled gym shoes. In low gravity it is easy to slip, and though your weight is slight your mass can bruise you.

It was breathtaking to see. There were tiers upon tiers of lush greens and yellow and red roses spotted among the food-bearing plants, far more dazzling to me than the stars outside. 'The hanging gardens of Babylon' my mind said, almost aloud. There were heavy avocados and oranges and grapevines and potatoes in bloom and peas with blue flowers and great trailing vines of Kentucky Wonder Beans. The air was moist and pungent, hot on my cheeks. As we walked, in floating strides, through an air-sealed doorway, warm air caressed our bodies. It was like a damp twilight in the tropics. Greenery and flowers and warm, moist air; my heart leaped up at it all. All of it mine.

I picked a tangerine from a heavy-laden tree in a copper pot, and peeled it. It was delicious.

'Okay, Bill,' I said. 'I am ready now to read that message.'

YOU ARE ORDERED HEREWITH TO PLACE YOURSELF UNDER HOUSE ARREST AND RETURN TO THE EARTH IMMEDIATELY. YOUR URANIUM FUEL IS CONFISCATED BY ORDER OF THIS COURT. YOU ARE CHARGED WITH VIOLATION OF THE ENERGY CODE OF THE UNITED STATES. YOU ARE HEREBY APPRISED THAT SPACE TRAVEL IS A HIGH CRIME AND MISDEMEANOR, PUNISHABLE BY A PRISON SENTENCE NOT TO EXCEED TWENTY YEARS, AND THAT WASTEFUL USE OF FUEL IS ALSO A HIGH CRIME AND MISDEMEANOR. YOU ARE SAID TO BE TRAVELLING WITH-OUT A VALID PASSPORT AND CONSPIRING WITH OTHERS TO VIOLATE THE LAWS OF THE UNITED STATES.

IF YOU FAIL TO APPEAR BEFORE THIS COURT BY 30 SEPTEMBER 2063, YOUR CITIZENSHIP WILL BE REVOKED AND YOUR PROPERTY CONFISCATED.

U.S. DISTRICT COURT, MIAMI

'What's the date?' I asked Bill.

'October ninth, two thousand sixty-three.'

I was seated in the Eames chair in my stateroom. Bill stood silently by, waiting to see if there would be an answer.

11

I tossed the paper on my desk. 'Tell them we're sorry but we can't turn around. Say the retros are malfunctioning.' There was a lacquered Chinese table by my chair. I set my coffee cup on it. 'Nothing from Isabel?'

'Isabel?'

'Isabel Crawford. In New York.'

Bill shook his head. 'No, Captain.'

'Thanks, Bill. I'd like to be alone for a while.'

'Sure, Captain,' he said, and left.

On my right was a deck-to-overhead bookshelf, curved with the slight curve of the ship's hull. It was filled with books: novels, histories, biographies, psychology, poems. Way up on the top shelf, bound in leather, sat the seven volumes of American history written by my father, William T. Belson, Professor of History (ret.), Ohio University. I had owned them thirty years and had opened each of them once, for about a minute. I stared at them then, from my captain's stateroom on this preposterous voyage of discovery, for a long time. But when I arose to pick a book it was *The Ambassadors* by Henry James.

FBR 793 became visible the day before planetfall. I first saw it as a small half-moon a hundred million miles from Fomalhaut. There was no real thrill; it was just there, another uninhabited celestial body, a planet called 'near-dead' on the charts. No one had ever set foot on it; it had been studied from a ship in orbit about forty years ago. The ship that photographed it lacked fuel for landing and takeoff, even back in those uranium-rich days.

FBR 793 was the twenty-third extrasolar planet discovered, and, like all the rest, it was without advanced life forms. Whatever the official reasons for the explorations conducted by the United States, the People's Republic of China and the Japanese, there had been only two real ones for sending ships out to interweave the Milky Way. One was the insane desire to find intelligent life somewhere other than on Earth—as if there wasn't enough of it on Earth, and mostly in trouble! The other was the hope of cheap fuel.

Well. Nobody found life, intelligent or otherwise. And there weren't many planets. Most stars didn't have any. And

12

nobody found uranium, or anything other than granite, lime-stone, chert, and desolation. The whole thing was a failure and it had been abandoned. I picked it up again in my middle age—in what they called a midlife crisis in the times my father wrote of. A geologist told me at a beach picnic once, while spitting watermelon seeds onto coral sand and stroking the brown arm of a languid woman, that he had seen photos of FBR 793 somewhere and they looked like safe uranium to him.

'What's this "safe uranium"?' I said.

'Somebody at M.I.T. worked it out,' he said. 'If uranium is formed under a gravity lower than Earth's it would have different characteristics. It wouldn't be radioactive except in a magnetic field.' He looked at me. 'No meltdowns.'

'Jesus!' I said, 'there'd be money in that.'

'You'd never be able to count it.'

I lay there and thought about that for a while. The tide was going out into the tranquil bay on which we lolled. It was about three in the afternoon and sunlight blazed on us. It was Jamaica, I think. I had worked at my desk in a hotel apart-ment that morning, had been unsuccessfully fellated at lunchtime, was bored with working out mergers, with pine-apples and papayas, with Caribbean music, blow jobs that didn't work, Blue Mountain coffee, counting my wealth. I was fifty and worth three billion. *What the hell,* I thought, *space travel might be more fun than this. It beats suicide too.* I started phoning geologists and the people who knew about the few mothballed spaceships that hadn't been scrapped by the governments that owned them. That was how it started—Belson's Bubble. Had that girl been more effective at lunch-time, it might not have happened.

In some ways I suppose my ambitions are stupid. I have more money than I can spend—have had that much since I was thirty-five. I own country homes, villas, a yacht, a man-sion in New York; yet I want to call no place 'home'; the last thing I want is a home. Often I stay in hotels or sleep in my car. I do not want a study like my father's, some mute terrain of intellectual combat, some preserve of self-justification. I will flee from life in my own fashion, will slip around reality in whatever ways suit my temperament. I can afford it. I make my money in coal, the stock market and real estate, and I know the realities. Money does not follow fantasies, except in show business; and I am not in show business.

I looked at the planet—my planet—half-outlined by its sun, half dark, and I said, 'We'll call it Belson.' Why not? I'm getting on in years.

Belson it is, that big, smart, spherical marvel. When we got closer I saw it had rings. That hadn't been in the reports, and was quite a surprise. My heart leaped up to see them through the windows of the bridge, red and lavender: the rings of Belson. I was really getting interested. We were a few light-hours away now, and Belson was huge on the screen, its surface a greenish-gray. I loved the rings.

The ship had begun decelerating the day before and our gravity had ceased, then reversed and increased to a little more than Earth-normal; we were slowing down fast. What had been up before was now down, since we had shifted polarities. The ship was rotated 180 degrees, while we were all strapped to cots. It was hectic for a while and a few small, unnoticed things like paperclips and the ship's cat floated around crazily while we spun in the changing gravity. That yellow cat drifted, back arched in alarm, by my face. We stared at each other. Its eyes seemed to blame me for its condition. 'Sorry,' I told it.

The other people in the crew were supposed to have been using the gym but probably hadn't. They were clearly bothered by the sudden increase in weight. But my muscles were ready for it and it felt good to have heft for a while again. I did a lot of walking that last day in transit, through the engine room, the garden, across the bridge, through the storage and equipment and research rooms. Whenever I passed a porthole I looked out to see my enlarging planet, Belson. I spoke to no one. The landing would be done by automatic equipment, with the pilot at ready to override if necessary. The pilot was a middle-aged woman with red hair; I had hired her with the possibility of sex in mind—there was something motherly about her and I am drawn to that.

I had no real ambitions for Belson, and I had come to see that. If I found uranium it would be a pleasure, but what the hell. Maybe I had really come all this way to give the place a name, to stake out an unworldly home for myself. Belson had a breathable atmosphere and mild temperatures; a man could live there if he had food and water enough. But the image of myself as the first extraterrestrial hermit had no appeal then and I shook it off.

It was my accountant, a gentle and paunchy Jew named Aaron, whom I first told of my plan to hunt uranium in space. 'What for?' he said. He was drinking a Perrier. We were at P. J. Clark's and it was November and already snowing heavily outside the windows.

I looked at him and finished my rum and Coke. 'Money.'

'You need more money?' Aaron said.

I laughed wryly. 'Adventure.'

'I don't believe it,' he said. 'A man can have adventure easier.'

'The world needs energy,' I said. 'Nobody's going to solve the nuclear-fusion problem. The oil's gone—except for what the military has stashed away. They've shut down the fission plants because the uranium's dangerous. And we may be headed into an ice age. Somebody's got to find power somewhere, Aaron, or we'll all freeze.'

'Four bad winters don't make an ice age,' Aaron said. 'There's wood enough to keep us warm. The population's going down, Ben. It'll work out.' He fished the lime from his Perrier and licked at it speculatively. 'They tried going out in ships when we were kids and they gave it up. Experts. Now they've made it against the law. There's nothing in space but grief.'

I liked Aaron. He was solid, and serious, and smart. He liked playing devil's advocate with me. And he had made me think. 'Okay,' I said, 'it isn't adventure.'

'What is it then?'

I smiled at him. 'Mischief.'

He looked at me and frowned. 'I'm having a hamburger,' he said, and waved for a waiter. 'Mischief I can believe. We'll call it exploration for mineral resources and I'll try for tax credits. Let's eat our lunch and talk about something cheerful.'

I ordered a rare steak and a chocolate mousse and a mug of beer. That night I called Isabel and took her to see *Così fan tutte* at Lincoln Center. At intermission I told her I was planning to try space travel. She took it in, but with astonishment. We were in my box on red velvet seats, and I was half drunk. The music was grand. During the second act I turned toward her, planning to reach my hand gently up her gorgeous dress, and saw that she was furious.

'What's wrong, honey?' I said.

She looked at me as though she were looking at a disorderly child. 'I think you're running away.'

I left New York the next day, to begin my search for a ship. Sometimes the city depresses me, now that there are so few taxis and cars and no trees in Central Park and half the restaurants I knew in my twenties have gone out of business. Lutèce and The Four Seasons are gone, and there's a midtown woodstand where Le Madrigal used to be. And the stores! Bergdorf-Goodman is gone, and Saks and Cartier; Bloomingdale's is a Greyhound bus depot. Everybody travels on bus or train because you can't run an airplane on coal. I've never felt that any place in this world was really my home. Why not try another world?

The landing was perfect, with only slight help needed from the pilot. We came down at a spot where it was morning, as light as a feather. Outside the portholes Belson's surface gleamed a shiny grayish-black. Obsidian. At a distance was a field of something resembling grass. The sky was a musty green and had clouds like Earth clouds. Cirrostratus and cumulonimbus, high and white. It looked good to me.

The pilot shut off the engine. The silence was overwhelming. No one spoke.

I looked across the bridge at Bill, the navigator. He was recording the landing in the ship's log. That seemed only proper; I felt traditional, and wished for a ship's orchestra to play 'The Star-Spangled Banner'.

After a few moments Bill said, 'I'll put on a helmet and step outside.'

'Hold it,' I said. '*I'm* going to be the first man to step out there. The readings on the gauges are all right by me; I'm not wearing a helmet.' I was shocked by the energy in my voice after the calm I had felt while landing.

Isabel told me that night after the opera, 'Ben, I wish you knew how to take it easy. I wish you didn't rush around so much,' and I said, 'If I didn't rush around I wouldn't have so much money and I wouldn't have you here by this marble fireplace taking off your clothes.' Isabel was wearing a blue half-slip and blue stockings. Her naked breasts were like a little girl's and my heart went out to them while the big logs flickered and I still heard Mozart tingling in my ears. We didn't live together anymore, but we were still close at times.

What I'd said made her angry. 'I'm not with you because of your money, Ben.'

'I'm sorry, honey,' I said. 'I know you're not. It's just that I'm in some kind of hurry all the time, and I don't know how to stop. Maybe this trip is what I need.'

She looked at me hard for a moment. Her face was beautiful in its concentration and her skin glowed in firelight. Isabel is a Scot and it was that Scottish skin of hers—and her lovely voice—that had drawn me to her years before. 'I hate you for wanting to risk your life,' she said. 'You don't need to risk it, Ben. There's nothing to prove.'

Oh Jesus, she was right. There was nothing to prove then and there's nothing to prove now. And I knew it. I think I'm addicted.

So I rushed out the hatch of that spaceship onto the dark obsidian surface of Belson in the morning and slipped and broke my right arm. While my seventeen subordinates watched from the big portholes on the bridge, I did a slip and a slide and a cartwheel and was flat on my ass with my right arm under me bent like a paperclip and me screaming. It hurt like hell. The air of Belson was clear and it smelled pleasantly musty; I savored the smell even over the horrible goddamned pain. 'Son of a bitch,' I said.

Charlie got to me with a hypodermic of morphine. He helped me back to the ship and into my stateroom before X-raying and then setting the arm. It was compound and broken in two places. What a fucking mess! But the morphine felt wonderful.

I hadn't thought of obsidian being slippery. The reports hadn't said anything about it. But it sure was. Belson was a glass planet. And who needed that?

17

I had a fever the next day while my six geologists and four engineers started seismic testing for uranium ore. Toward evening, huge booming explosions began to rock the ship while I lay dazed with morphine, and spooned myself full of vichyssoise and lemon mousse. Boom! My small Corot fell from the wall. After dark I invited Ruth, the pilot, to watch the movie with me. She accepted graciously enough and I kept my hands to myself. Chemical euphoria was my real companion.

I'd never had morphine before and something in me knew, the minute it began to diddle my nervous system, that this was heavy magic indeed. I felt the thrill of danger in it. There was a *sufficiency* to it, a filling of empty spaces in the soul, that had snagged my bewildered spirit instantly, right out there on the dark slippery surface of a brand-new planet. It was splendid chemistry; when I awoke the next morning not giving a damn for the world I had come to explore but only wanting my fix, I was suddenly frightened. When Charlie came into my state-room with his syringe I was even more frightened. I told him to forget it, to find me some aspirin. It took him half an hour to find some. That's the modern world for you. Here we were on a spaceship with the most advanced geologic and exploratory equipment and with a sick bay to rival Johns Hopkins. We had a drug synthesizer; we had a computer that could take out your appendix; and the doctor had to borrow aspirin from the man in charge of the engine room. I felt my destiny was trying to force me into becoming a morphine addict.

The aspirin helped the pain a bit, but I was edgy. *What the hell*, I thought, and told Charlie to give me a half dose of morphine. Oh yes.

There are few things in this world that do what they promise, and fewer still that deliver more than you expected. Morphine is one of those; it promised only relief and it carried heart's ease in its wake. It was chemical bliss for my cluttered soul. I felt the hook. What the hell. You could go the route of De Quincey and Coleridge and all those other sad losers. But I had controlled a lot of things in my life before, and I figured, *Few things are as good as this chemical. I'll ride it for a while*. I knew enough to suspect it might be riding me, but I felt I could handle that too. There would be a piper to pay. But that would be in due time.

I found soon enough I could lower the dose and still get what

I wanted. The mornings of the next three weeks I rode a low morphine euphoria and roamed Belson in a nuclear jeep, my arm in a sling and Ruth at my side, playing music on the little ball recorder. It was *Così fan tutte* mostly. I think people who record live performances are jerks; still, I do it myself sometimes for the hell of it. It gives me something to think about during the dull passages, with the little meters and the tone controls to check. I had recorded *Così fan tutte* that night with Isabel at the Met. I kept to one shot of morphine a day; in the afternoons, when it wore off, my price was a headache, for which the remaining aspirin served until it ran out. I would visit the seismic sites, driving across the slick obsidian, listening to arias composed light-years away in Austria, and even when my soul was not singing along from the alkaloid chemistry at work on my brain, it still greeted the strangeness of a new planet with thrilling of the nerves. There wasn't much to see on Belson, but I had come to love the place.

The first time I found the grass and drove on it, it screamed like a tormented woman under the jeep's tires. And when I stopped and got out I found the grass I had crushed was bleeding, bleeding on my shoes and on the tires of the car. It was the red of real blood and enough to disconcert the most euphoric of men. I was shocked deeply. I got the jeep off it as gently as possible.

That night after dinner I found out from the chief engineer, who was also a biophysicist, that the grass was nothing like Earth grass and was incomprehensible to him. It was brown, about foot high, and did not grow on the surface at all. It was the upper ends of some long, tenuous filaments that went down through the obsidian miles beneath the surface, far below our powers of investigation. No man on board and no equipment either was strong enough to uproot a blade of it. Nor could it be severed. It screamed and bled when crushed, but no one had the foggiest idea why or how. And crushing it did not kill or break it. If it was alive, that is. The biophysicist's name was Howard. He said the grass was some kind of a polymer. Big deal. So is nylon.

And then one twilight, when we were all on board ship eating leg of lamb together, we began to hear something faint and musical coming from outside. For a moment we all froze.

I got up and opened the hatchway. It was the sound of singing, coming from a field of grass that began a few hundred yards west of the ship. I went out with the doctor and we walked carefully on the slippery surface, under the light of Belson's setting sun, toward the grass. The grass was singing. It came from all around us.

And the weirdest thing, the thing that raised the small hairs on the back of my neck, was that the voice and the melody were *human*—as human as any of us. You could not distinguish words, yet what it sang sounded like words. It sang loudly and it sang softly and the melody kept changing. For a moment, startled, I thought I heard strains from *Così fan tutte*. Sometimes the grass undulated as it sang, and sometimes it was still. When it moved, the long shadows on it from the low sun rippled with the music. I had never seen anything more beautiful, had never heard anything so moving. For a moment I feared it was the effect of that morning's morphine, but I looked around me at the crew members—at the other six men and the eleven women—and I saw they were transfixed by it too. They were astonished and as moved as I.

Howard fell on his knees by the grass, holding his head close to the sound. I could see that he was crying. Ruth stood by me, staring ahead of herself. Nobody spoke. I was weeping too.

Then the sun set and a moment later the music stopped. Someone turned on a flashlight. We walked silently back to the ship, and when we got there some of us got drunk. There was little to say. It had been the most powerful esthetic experience I had ever felt and was in itself worth the voyage, if anything could be. I had my recorder with me and had had the presence of mind to record part of it, erasing most of the precious *Così fan tutte* in the process. But the grass was better than Mozart, and besides, I was tired of Italian arias. I told no one that night of my recording, since no one was talking much.

The next morning one of the engineers found a scraggly plant growing in a fissure in the obsidian near the ship. That area had been studied closely before and nothing had been found growing. The plant was not like the grass. It did not bleed and you could pick it. Howard took it to his lab for

20

analysis. I was curious; had the singing made it grow?

I played the recording in my stateroom while eating my breakfast croissant, but the music wasn't the same. It was good, but the resonance was gone. It sounded like a big choir and that was all.

By afternoon Howard had analyzed the sample as far as he could. Howard is a thin, stoop-shouldered man, with nicotine stains on his fingers. I found him in his lab, reading a printout. He was smoking a cigarette and looked tired. I asked him what he had found out.

'Well,' he said, 'it's a salicylate, like one of the organics you find in willow bark and that we've been synthesizing on Earth for centuries. But there's something I don't understand about the molecule.'

'What's a salicylate?'

'Aspirin's one,' he said. 'That's the one in willow bark. Different from this . . .' He held out a fragment of the plant. 'But close to it.'

'*Aspirin?*' I said. I was shocked. I had carried music with me, and aspirin. Last night the planet had made both.

'It would probably cure a headache.'

'Is it safe?'

'I suppose so,' he said. 'Safe as willow bark.'

'I'll take some,' I said. My head was aching anyway, since that morning's fix had worn off.

He figured out a rough dose and I took it. It was bitter, like aspirin. Howard protested that we should try it on some lab mice first, but I went on ahead.

My headache vanished in three minutes. Vanished completely and stayed vanished. It was then that I began to believe the planet was intelligent and that it had goodwill. Belson spoke my language. The music had spoken to my heart as directly as that plant had spoken to my nervous system. That kind of a fit cannot be accidental; the odds against it are too strong.

I developed my theory of an intelligent planet and tried it on Ruth. She was polite but clearly didn't buy it. I dropped the subject. Ruth had been having dinner with me since the first week on Belson, but we didn't sleep together and we didn't talk much. She was busy with her scientific thoughts and I with my

21

mystical ones. And my morphine. And I had sex problems.

I named the little shrub endolin. It turned out there was a lot of it around, growing out of cracks in the obsidian. I had come to Belson looking for power; instead I'd found music, euphoria and relief from pain. I was beginning to love this place.

2

Why did I buy this ship in the first place, this small portable universe? Well, for one thing I had gone impotent. My once enthusiastic and catholic member had become shy, sullen, and would not serve me. Would not serve my lady friends either. There were quarrels, recriminations; I tried resorting to masturbation and, to my dismay, found that was out of the question too. My joint had taken leave of its senses and my senses had taken leave of my joint. It went on like that. I began to feel disgraced. I wanted to kill someone. My therapist said Mother; he was probably right, but Mother was already dead.

Isabel was my eventual port in this storm and kept me from going completely bonkers. She worked with me physically for a few days—and it was indeed work—and then abandoned that, sensibly saying, 'It's best to wait awhile, Ben.' I moved in with her, into her little studio apartment on East Fifty-first Street, and slept with her and her two big chunky cats in the little loft bed that she had built with her own pale, esthetic hands. Isabel was a good carpenter; she had worked on theater sets for years before developing the courage to try acting. God, what a tiny place that was! And you could never escape the street sounds from the windows: the shoutings of drunks and mad bombers and all-purpose crazies at two in the morning; the steam-powered garbage wagons at four, and the screeching wood vendors at seven-thirty. Wood was seven dollars a stick in midtown, and Isabel had a fireplace. It was the worst winter in forty years; on most mornings the water in the toilet would be frozen solid. I tried enormous bribes on the super for heat; he would give me his shy Yugoslav smile and pocket my hundreds, but the heating pipes remained silent. I tried, one frostbitten morning when the weight of three blankets was suffocating me, to bring Isabel to her senses and get her to sail to Yucatan with me for the winter. But she was adamant. She held the covers up to her chin and said, 'You know I'm in a show, Ben.'

I could feel the little hairs in my nose as stiff as icicles. 'Honey,' I said, 'you've got six fucking lines in that show, and one of them is, "Hello".' I couldn't see outside because ice had formed on the windowpanes. And we had a fire in the grate; I had thrown some sticks on it at four in the morning, shaking so much from the cold that I'd almost missed. What would all the poor people downtown be doing, the ones who couldn't afford wood and insulation and storm windows? The Red Cross gave out blankets, but there were never enough. I made a mental note to give a quarter million to the Red Cross. Or maybe a sheep ranch, so they could grow their own. It was seven in the morning and I could hear the wind howling around the corner from Third Avenue.

'Sweetheart,' Isabel said, 'I'm not going to be your dependent. And I'm warm enough.' Isabel slept in long woolen underwear, hiding all that radiant skin of hers and those girlish breasts under scratchy BVDs. I slept wrapped around her warm body, dressed in a flannel nightgown and gym shorts.

We'd had that argument enough times before, so I gave it up. Isabel wasn't about to take advantage of my wealth. That afternoon I hunted around and found a big old coal stove at a blackmarket shop on Seventh Avenue and got the name of a dealer. Burning anthracite for private heat was illegal, under the Nonrenewable Resources Act; it took hard-coal trains to move the food and other essentials around the country, and the enforcement was pretty tough. But I had connections and was willing to take the chance. After all, I was in the business: Belson Mines. I managed after three phone calls to get two dozen cabbage-sized lumps of anthracite and promise of another delivery in five days. Isabel and I were warm enough after that. My dealer, a skinny little fellow in a pea coat, tried to sell me some cocaine along with those black lumps, but in those days I had no interest in drugs. It took a voyage to the stars to get me hooked.

With coal in the grate, Isabel went back to sleeping naked, but it didn't help my impotence. I remember waking up at 5 A.M. sometimes with a yearning in my groin, but if I woke Isabel—no easy task, since she slept and snored like a hibernating bear—it was no good. My scared member would retreat and I would be frustrated and feel like a fool to boot. And have Isabel furious with me for wakening her to another strikeout. 'Ben,' she'd say, 'if you want me take me. But quit waking me up for these *experiments*.' I blushed like a child and couldn't get back to sleep. It was horrible. This was after that conversation in Jamaica with the geologist; I began to have daydreams of space travel. I will say this about myself: when I sublimate I sublimate grandly.

So I bought this ship and furnished it, made sure there were a few attractive women in the crew, and set forth to the stars with a limp penis.

'Doctor,' I said to Orbach, lying on the leather couch in his office, my big lumberjack shoes resting on the arm, my head against a fat leather pillow, 'If I don't get some orgasms soon . . .'

'I wish you wouldn't pressure yourself so much,' he said. 'There are other ways to use your energies.'

'I could lie, pillage and kill. I could run for President. I could travel through space.'

His voice was wry. 'The last sounds the least destructive.' And that clinched it. The next day I told my lawyers to find a spaceship. The one I eventually got was Chinese; it was called *Flower of Heavenly Repose*. I had most of its old scientific gear junked, built a launching pad in the Keys, furnished the captain's quarters with antiques, hired a crew, and took off for Fomalhaut. This took a year. It would have been five if I hadn't been wound up like a steel spring with celibacy. If I couldn't push myself into a woman's body by an act of will, will would push my body across the galaxy. I hated the spiritual algebra of it, but I understood the equation well enough; I had been robbing Peter to pay Paul for most of my life. That's how you get rich in a world of dwindling resources, a world with its springs running down.

Somebody years before had told me about sleep bodybuilding; you could avoid the boredom of getting into shape

25

by doing it in a long chemical sleep. I hated exercise and the idea had charm, but I didn't feel then that I could disappear from the world of the awake for two months without financial risks of the worst kind. When I learned that, despite the spacewarp tricks my ship was capable of, it would still take three dull months to get across the Milky Way, I decided to grab the opportunity and I had the Nautilus machines installed. I had been developing flabby pectorals and a pot. Firming up my body might firm up its sweetest part too. Hell, maybe in a two-month nap I might have a cascade of wet dreams and get some relief that way. But as it turned out, I didn't; I spent most of my dream time with Father.

I have kept myself in transit ever since I left home at eighteen. I studied metallurgy at one college and Chinese at another, moving from hotel to hotel while I studied. My Aunt Myra in New York left me eighty thousand dollars when I was fourteen. I put it into forests at a good time, and by college I could afford a suite at any hotel I fancied and a secretary to type my term papers. I've never stayed in a plain hotel room; I always take suites. I think I fear being stuck in a single room like my father.

I realize as I write this—as I dictate it—that I am living now in a single room, as I did at Isabel's. I am the sole resident of this moonwood shack, or cabin, the only piece of architecture on the planet Belson. There are no forget-me-nots on the walls, which are the matte silver of moonwood itself, that charming mineral. Still, the thought that I have become the inhabitant of one room and that my condition therefore resembles my father's makes me uneasy. Like him, I spend hours at my desk, reading. Like him, I smoke cigars endlessly. Like him, I speak to no one.

I need to mine more moonwood and build on another room. I need a companion. I need Isabel.

I've lived here four months now, with my little morphine factory and my red computer and with the garden outside. There could hardly be a way of being more alone, except that the planet itself is my friend and lover. When I get morose I can water my garden or shoot up or do as I am doing this very moment: dictate these reflections into the red box that types them up and never makes a spelling error. My fractured life

26

comes rising from a slot, in crisp Bodoni Bold on an endless sheet of Hammermill Bond; there's enough of it now to paper this moonwood cabin, to give a celestial womb lined with the print reflections of my life.

Since the ship left, there has been no sound but my own voice and the rare singing of the grass. Sometimes the planet shows me its rings. Her rings. His rings. They are seldom visible from here below, although I don't know why. One night last month I was awakened by the grass singing and, *mirabile dictu*, had my first orgasm in years, lying there alone hearing that powerful wordless song and picturing Isabel and the warmth in her Scottish face. That one ejaculation undid a coil deep in my spirit and blew fresh air into my musty soul; I went for three days afterward without morphine. Isabel, I send you my love. I want to marry you if I ever come back to the Earth.

I've known Isabel for ten years and lived with her for five agonizing months, and only now am I coming to realize how much she means to me. Wouldn't you know I'd put twenty-three light-years between us before I would see that? Maybe the distance is necessary to see beyond the fights we had. During our last month together my impotence turned me into a godawful nag; I worked on her case endlessly, nagging her about whatever came to mind, inwardly tearing myself apart with thoughts about all the potent lovers she must have had in her life. I would imagine stupid-looking young men who mounted Isabel's slight body with the aplomb of jockeys. My stomach ached at such thoughts. Yet Isabel gave no justification for them. She was faithful to my forced celibacy while I lived with her, and there were no mementoes of other men around her place. I know because I looked.

I nagged her about her career. I told her she should try for bigger parts in plays, or quit the theater. I would complain about the time she spent shopping for clothes and about the way she seemed to fill that small apartment with shoes and dresses so there was no place for my corduroys and jeans and lumberjack shirts. And yet I knew during all this that I secretly approved, because Isabel looked splendid in her clothes.

I wasn't always that way with her. I could be pleasant

27

enough at times, and Isabel liked my sense of humor and my general disdain for the pretense of the business world. We were also both serious lovers of New York and of New York food. And Isabel knew, as women do, that I genuinely appreciated her good looks. There must have been something about me that she liked or I'd have been kicked out, if only for the messes I made on the floor with my cigar ashes. Isabel's floor was painted white; she had done the job herself not long before I moved in. Six layers, and each one rubbed down with steel wool. I managed to spill a lot of ashes from my Gueveras on that floor and then grind them in later by pacing. Hostility, I suppose. One cold Monday after her play had closed, Isabel spent the day on her knees scrubbing the floor and then giving it another coat of paint. She did this in black panties and socks, bare-breasted, with a coal fire blazing in the grate. I tried to ignore her from behind my *Wall Street Journals* and my stock reports and prospectuses, but I couldn't keep my eyes off that undulant ass and those lovely breasts that hung down and gently swung from side to side as she scrubbed with a Kiwi brush and then rubbed and then painted. But I kept my hands off her, knowing all too well I had no follow-through available. It was agonizing, and I felt guilty about having made the floor a mess in the first place. There was a big scratch in it where I had thrown and broken a coffee cup in one of my rages over not getting it up. She filled the scratch with plastic wood, sanded it and then painted over it. Bless her heart. And then that evening she bundled herself up and went off to the Morosco Theatre to try for a part in a revival of *Hamlet*. She came home to our paint-fumed apartment and announced she was going to be Gertrude, Hamlet's mother, that it was a terrific chance. Here was Isabel, forty-three years old, as happy as an ingenue with her first part. I should have married her on the spot and started having children. God what a healthy brood we could be making! But instead, I was dismayed by it all and began to think of leaving. We had lived together five months, without sexual intercourse. And I didn't want to get that beautiful floor dirty again. I didn't want to watch Isabel struggle to learn all that blank verse. I remembered *Hamlet* from college; it was a big part.

Eventually I got a suite at the Pierre. It was four rooms and a kitchen on the fourth floor for three thousand a day, plus tax and service. It was warm, since the management had good connections. I took up cooking in earnest.

My best success was pot roast. I got a real pleasure—maybe my only pleasure in those sexually bleak days—from peeling carrots and potatoes and onions, weeping through a dozen onions at a time, standing over my stainless-steel sink and blinking tearily out the window at the empty shell of the General Motors building. I browned the meat in safflower oil, the only oil Isabel would touch, after coating it with durum flour and drenching it in Java pepper. Java pepper was another of Isabel's fetishes. I had to admit she was right too. And I wasn't cooking all those roasts for her either. She never came up to that suite, with its big beige sofas and its oriental rugs; I never invited her.

Oh Isabel! What a pervert I turned out to be, when push came to shove! It's all too clear now as I speak this on Belson: I didn't move out of your place because of the cold or because you were memorizing blank verse. I moved out because I had fallen in love with you. There I would stand in that high-ceilinged old kitchen with its white walls and its wooden countertops, and all the sexual energy that your body had inspired in me—that waist, those hips, those sweet breasts—went into my doleful midafternoon peeling of carrots, my weeping over stacks of shiny brown onions! My analyst, the Great Orbach, would call it sublimation; I call it a fraud and a cheat. I should have been arrested for gross and illicit orality. (Officer, do you see that big man over there, with the glasses and the lumberjack shirt, the one with the stack of vegetables at his elbow? I want him taken into custody and charged with criminal avoidance of manhood.)

I'd had Henri Bendel's send over a set of steel cookware, but all I ever used of it was one big pot. Sometimes the small saucepan for thickening gravy. Twelve hundred dollars, plus the 12 percent New York City tax and eighty dollars for delivery, and all I used was two pans. The damned roasting pan didn't even have a rack in it; I had to balance the meat on top of the carrots and onions to keep it from boiling. But my pot roasts were terrific. I served them with strawberry jam on the side, and a Bibb and arugula salad. Chocolate mousse for dessert. If my alienated member had been less shy, I could have gotten into the pants of every actress on Broadway that season, from the quality of my pot roast and the big wood fires I had in my living room to eat them by. Not to mention my charm, good looks and money. Ah well! What really happened was that I made a lot of women furious with me for not even *trying*. What I wanted was to eat with them and look at them and talk. Sometimes I did try rolling around in bed, but I knew before I started that it would come to grief and anger. And it always did. I got some heady oral satisfactions with women whom schoolboys would have given their souls to fondle: a Belgian movie star, two leading ladies, a diva, a ballet dancer, the estranged doxy of a uranium man even richer than I, a handful of courtesans who did sex more dexterously than Chinese women assembled radios. The oral satisfactions were nice, but I'd have been better nourished eating fruit. Some very huffy women left that apartment in the mornings.

I had sense enough to realize it was a midlife crisis. I'd been studying the history of the uranium explorations and had come to feel—as a lot of well-informed people felt—that the government had stopped looking for uranium at just the wrong time. It had been the repercussions of all those wasted voyages and all the spent nuclear fuel that finally brought about the CEASE agreement, banning space travel. 'Use the fuel at home!' President Garvey had shouted in her schoolteacherly way, and a lot of politicians had breathed sighs of relief.

But the fact was that safe uranium was just around the corner. A lot of experts felt that way; but no government was willing to take the risks anymore. Just one space voyage would use about 6 percent of the Earth's entire supply of uranium. Enough to heat Shanghai for ten years. You couldn't go out into Milky Way without putting the ship into a spacewarp, and you couldn't do that without a few trillion megawatts at your disposal.

I had been toying with the idea for two or three years, ever since that conversation in Jamaica with the geologist. I did some talking around and found the thing was like ESP, a lot of knowledgeable people were believers; it was just that governments were uptight about it. And private industry was afraid to touch it—especially in those unprofitable times. Hell, the prime rate was 4 percent.

The SALT talks were still going on—SALT 17, in fact—after a hundred years. But it took exactly six months of martinis and tea in Geneva for the whole goddamned world to decide to quit looking for uranium in space. We could still bomb one another into radioactive dust at the touch of a few well-placed fingertips; but we would now sit and freeze because the gamble for energy scared the politicians more than the gamble with Armageddon did. Well. *Plus ça change, plus c'est la même chose.*

I figured it would cost me about eight hundred million to outfit a ship, hire a crew, and go to Fomalhaut. If I could find uranium and bring it back in quantity my profits would be almost beyond measure. Eight hundred million was half of what I was worth. If I lost it all I would still be rich, would still have more money than I could spend in a long lifetime. What the hell. I was getting tired of pot roasts and of angry women. I was unmarried. I hadn't used my stock exchange seats for a half-dozen years, and interest rates were abysmally low. And I am a restless man. I had been looking, unconsciously, for something big to put money into. What the hell, I might captain a spaceship off to the stars. Captain Belson. Why not?

It was insane for me to spend that cold winter in New York with temperatures at twenty below zero when I could have gone to the Yucatan in my boat. Getting coal for a boat was easy enough; transportation came under a special heading in the Energy Act. But the *Wit's End* stayed tied up in the East River that winter and got its hull cracked when the river froze solid in January. It didn't bother me much when that happened, though; I had my mind by then on other modes of transport; I had begun buying the *Flower of Heavenly Repose* and the uranium the trip would take. It was as complicated as preparing a small nation for war and I was thankful to throw my energies into it. I had six telephone lines put into my apartment in the Pierre and eventually installed a staff of five men and seven women on the two floors above mine. When the first warm day finally came, in June, we all toasted the

31

spring together in my living room and got pleasantly drunk on Moët et Chandon. One of my purchasing agents was an amiable fat lady named Alice. She wore pink coral jewelry and sipped her champagne like a bird. Alice asked me what we would call the ship. Peking had just agreed to sell. I tossed off a fizzy mouthful before I spoke. *'Isabel,'* I said. 'The ship is the *Isabel*.'

3

Belson has a diameter half that of Earth's—about four thousand miles. It is a great deal denser, though; the gravity is over half of Earth's. I weigh a hundred thirty pounds here; I'm two twenty in New York. Six feet four. Since Belson has no oceans, there is actually a lot more land area than on Earth.

There was no way we could explore it all. My experts back home had picked three sites from the old photographs and we tried each of the three. They were all in the same general vicinity on the planet, each a few hundred miles from the other. We had two jeeps for getting around. You could drive on the obsidian easily enough, although it was rough on the lower back and you had to watch out for skids. I wished I had been able to bring an airplane and the fuel to operate it; I would like to have explored more. But my geologists had assured me, after studying the pictures, that it wouldn't be worth it. If there was uranium it would be within three hundred miles of where we landed, and the rest of the planet's surface would be the same as where we were. Belson had almost no geological features—at least few were detectable. There was no food and little water.

Negative reports kept coming in from the tests. It was beginning to look bad. We had discovered moonwood—a lovely mineral material that could be sawed and hammered and had a silvery surface; but it would hardly be profitable to export it. At that distance even gold wouldn't pay its own freight. Only uranium could really justify the trip. And it was beginning to look like there wasn't any.

When I was fourteen I worked up the temerity to ask my father's advice on choosing a profession. I was a tall and gangly kid then with platinum-blond hair and muscles too weak to bold my body up properly—or so it felt anyway. I was awed by my father and by his silences. I stood in the doorway to his study for about ten minutes staring at those forget-me-nots on the wall and at the array of diplomas below them before he looked up and nodded toward me.

'Father,' I said, feeling awkward and callow, 'I need your advice.'

He nodded again, hardly seeming to see me. There was a mild scowl on his perfectly shaven face. He was wearing a brown sweater and brown flannel trousers; there was gray hair at his temples but the rest of his hair was black. I was the only blond in the family.

'I've been thinking . . .,' I said, groping. 'About what kind of work I'll do.'

He nodded again, still silent. I felt cosmic pressures in my skull.

'I mean I should study something in college . . .,' I said with a lameness that bordered paralysis, suddenly aware that college was two years away. Why was I asking such dumb questions of a man so clearly occupied with universals?

He spoke, and his voice came as if from the bottom of a well. 'What talents do you have?' he said.

I could think of nothing. I felt as ungifted as a tree stump. Actually, I could play the piano very well, was a whiz at mathematics and physics, had a passable singing voice, had written a two-act musical comedy for my high-school drama class, and could read poems in Chinese. I managed to forget all this in the presence of my father's clear unawareness of any of it. 'I don't know,' I said. Thinking of those words now, I still wince with embarrassment.

'Well,' he said, with a distance as great as that of the broad gray Atlantic, 'what can I say?' And he turned back to his book.

My mother was equally helpful. I popped the same question to her after she had just come back from a bridge party and was pouring herself a screwdriver in the kitchen. The sink was full of chipped dirty dishes; a Picasso clown hung askew over the stove, with grease on the frame. 'Benny,' she said, 'I am not a vocational counselor. And your hair needs combing.'

With that kind of help I decided to take my instructions in life from the outer world. And the outer world, shrinking into itself as it was in those sad, cold days, had this advice for me: make money. It seemed like a good idea. And it was; in the stock market I found my authentic talent.

And yet somehow here on Belson, when the *Isabel* was still my home, I didn't stop to think of what a money-maker endolin could be. It is remarkable stuff—the genuine anodyne. But I was wrapped up in my morphine highs then and in my theory of the planet's intelligence and in brooding about Isabel and in the strange soothing my spirit was given just in riding a jeep across vast plains of obsidian in the afternoons, skirting fields of Belson grass and drinking in the musty smell of the warm Belson air.

The grass never sang again for us. The seismic studies revealed no uranium but a lot of lead. I was getting out of shape again, even though I worked out on the machines every now and then. It was time to head back to Earth, to have myself put to sleep again. So I thought. We gathered a couple of crates full of endolin and about eighty large slabs of moonwood. The navigator and I worked out a route home, planning to pop out of our self-generated spacewarp at a different set of stars from the ones we had drawn energy from on the way out; I gave instructions to be awakened a day before we arrived at one called Aminidab, a never-visited star that had looked right to some people at M.I.T. I told the doctor to jettison the rest of his morphine. I would go cold turkey the easy way: unconscious. I could have wept. Not for the morphine, which I knew I would have to give up soon anyway if I didn't want to addle my life forever, but for Belson. I loved Belson and didn't want to leave.

The night before we left was a bright one, with both moons up and full. I gave myself a double injection of morphine and went out for a final barefoot stroll. I walked along the edge of the grass in a fine euphoric high for miles. The grass was silver in the moonlight, and the vast, dry, serene emptiness was like the desert in an Henri Rousseau painting. The obsidian felt warm beneath my feet. Sometimes the grass sighed gently and I sighed back at it. I felt as I had never felt before the warm spiritual presence of that lonely planet, the only one of its sun. I had become ecstatic with morphine and with my sensitivity to impending loss. My neck tingled. I began to talk to the grass. I told it how I felt. It seemed to sigh in response. I told it about Isabel and about my impotence with her and it sighed with me. I told it about my daughter Myra and her arthritis, about her poor, painful life. I talked about how my world was growing cold and empty after millennia of vigor and bounce. I became higher, more mystical, moved by what I was saying and by the splendid isolation I had here in my far corner of the Milky Way. I forgot the people back on the ship and felt alone with Belson, *my* Belson. It seemed to me then that Belson was the finest and biggest thing I had ever known. The rings came out in the night sky and glowed on my body.

After a while I lay drunkenly in ring light on the grass, gently so as not to bruise it or make it bleed. It seemed to embrace me with a million small fingers. In my head I began to hear something like words. At first they made no sense, but after a while they became clearer. It was the grass speaking to me: I could tell by the cadence, which was the same as the singing. The words were both in my head and outside, murmured by the grass. What they said was, 'I love you.'

They had to come and find me in the morning and they carried me back to the ship. The doctor said I must have overdosed. I told them nothing but asked if anyone had heard the grass speak the night before. No one had.

We delayed leaving for a day while Charlie gave me some psychological and motor tests. I did fine on them. I knew I had had no overdose and I knew that Belson had said it loved me, but I also knew to keep my mouth shut about it. The next day we brought the coils around the ship to within a half degree of zero Kelvin, and when superconduction was in effect we generated the field and slipped into our warp. We popped out fifty hours later, two light-years away, and soaked up energy from a nearby sun. You cut the uranium bill in half that way. It was a reddish sun with no planets and had none of the zip of Fomalhaut. I was already homesick for Belson. I could have cried again. I had the doctor put me to sleep. All the way to Aminidab I dreamed of New York and Isabel and of the voice of the grass saying, 'I love you.'

The way I felt about Belson's intelligence was something like the way I feel about the stock market. The market is a dumber entity; it is blown around by half-baked gusts of emotion. The way to handle it is to learn everything you can about it and then depend on intuition. The intuition may feel mystical; but, in my case anyway, it isn't. I know what I'm doing with the market and I have the bank accounts to testify to that. I never developed a profession for myself after those consultations with my parents, but I'm not a fool. I trust my mystical feelings. I believe that Belson loves me.

When I was about twelve I played an old game called Monopoly with a kid I knew. My father had given me the game for Christmas; it was something from his collection of memorabilia from the twentieth century. And maybe it was a subliminal nudge toward the robber-baron capitalism I was eventually to espouse for myself, to fill in the time. The kid's name was Toby. We played in the living room of his house for a dollar a game. Toby was a rich kid by my standards of the time. My family lived in a permoplastic bungalow near the campus; his had a fourteen-room stone mansion. Toby's father was a judge and owned an alcohol-powered car. Toby himself was a ferocious competitor, more so than I; but I always won. I picked up all the necessary principles of the game the first time around. The basic philosophy was to go for broke, take every sensible risk you could. It was a solemn lesson for me. It was that philosophy that helped send me to Belson, and it was that philosophy that made me overrule my navigator and choose a potentially wasteful stopover at Aminidab. All I knew about Aminidab was that it was a sun of the same spectral type as Sol. No one had ever gone near enough to see if it had planets, but the astronomy people at M.I.T. had picked it as a good risk. After all, for all the exploring that had been done in the twenty-first century, not one star in a million, in the Milky Way alone, had been observed closely enough to see planets. Computers had decided on the ones to look at. There are a whole lot of stars out there. They haven't been counted yet. It is gratifying to think they never will be.

Well. When they woke me up they were clearly excited. Nineteen planets had been spotted and we were still quite a distance away. You can't pop out of a warp near a star; you pull out a few thousand million miles away and then creep up on it. We were still creeping.

I felt fine and saw I was back in shape again. I drank my coffee and headed for the bridge. There was Aminidab, and there, like specks of light, were its planets. They looked like dust motes by a light bulb.

Aminidab turned out to have, all told, thirty-four. I was exultant and gave orders to work out a path for a quick photographic circuit of each.

'That'll take a lot of time,' Ruth said. 'And fuel.'

'I know it,' I said. 'But, Ruth, there's going to be uranium on one of them or more. Come one. Let's go for it.' For the time I had forgotten Earth and Isabel. I could smell success and it was turning me on. I wanted uranium. Of course I wanted uranium for the money it could make me and for the simple success of my voyage and to confound my enemies back on Earth. But I wanted, more importantly, to provide the world with safe and easy power again; in the days before leaving I had daydreamed of finding trillions of tons of it on some far-off planet. It was possible. It didn't have to be as scarce, even with its half-life, as it was on Earth. There were younger planets. There might be vast mountains of it somewhere— mountain ranges even. Yet it was, I knew, a daydream of an impotent man: endless potency.

The third planet we photographed looked so good to me and to the geologists that I ordered a landing right there. It was a dense little world, half under water and with a lavender sky. We skimmed over part of its surface, in low orbit, gawking. There was plant life all over. The oceans were pink. I liked it. Not with the deep affection I felt for Belson, but I felt sanguine about this planet. It looked young. It had energy.

We found a kind of mossy plain and landed. This time Ruth did the landing herself and made a good, simple job of it. My respect for her doubled. Ruth was a good woman; she just didn't have much to say. Her red hair had gotten very long on the trip and I liked the way it fell over her competent shoulders. But when I praised her for the landing she seemed cool when she thanked me. Something was going on there, it must have gotten worse during my long sleep.

38

Before opening up we checked the atmosphere. There was a lot of oxygen—twice that of Earth. The rest was nitrogen and traces of inert gases like argon and xenon. We had better be careful about fires, the doctor said, and not breathe too deeply. You could addle your brains with too much oxygen.

The plain we were on was about ten miles from a place that had photographed out as mildly radioactive. There was a lot of water on this world, and if the uranium turned out to be there we could stay indefinitely. I liked the idea of exploring. What the hell, it looked a little like Jamaica, except the colors were all wrong. Orange tree trunks, for instance. The gravity was eight-tenths Earth-normal and there were heavy pink clouds in the sky. We touched down in a storm of warm, tropical rain. It kept up for two days. How it all drained off I don't know. It was a furious, drenching downpour and it pounded on the ship's hull like hail on a plastic roof; the noise was almost deafening. It was frustrating. We didn't dare go out for fear of being drowned. Here we were on this lively planet, ready to get our jeeps out and throw ourselves into the explorer's dream of a lifetime, an adventure beyond the childhood imaginings of any of us, and we had to stay inside because of rain.

I finished *The Ambassadors*, had a morose and silent dinner in my stateroom with Ruth, who excused herself right after the mousse, and lay on my bunk, listened to the rain and thought about my early days in Athens, Ohio.

When I was a kid in Athens there were horses everywhere. The Energy Acts of those days classified burros and horses as solar—since they ate vegetation—and a person could have as many as he could afford. Athens was a hilly place, with its small university built two hundred years ago in the Appalachian foothills; and although people had bicycles, horses were the best way to get around. It's a lovely little town still, I suppose, although I haven't been there for twenty years. We had a sweet-tempered chestnut mare named Juno, and some nights when Father was reading in his study and Mother was asleep on the living-room couch I would go out to the garage and sleep with Juno, lying on her moist and tickly straw, soaking in her body warmth and her body smells, listening sometimes to the fluttering and groaning noises she made in her sleep. Juno died when I was fifteen, and I mourned her more than I would mourn either of my parents.

My father supplemented his professor's income by having Juno serviced and selling the foals. She never failed to produce, bless her heart. She gave birth to a succession of colts in deep, rich, glossy browns and blacks, and she nursed them with love and patience, watching them grow and urging them on. Her grief when Father sold them was, to me, palpable. I could feel her mourning. I made a special point of sleeping with her on the nights after a colt of hers had been taken away, regardless of how cold it might be in the garage, and she would nuzzle me in her sleep sometimes and the garage would fill for a moment with the resonance of her doleful, motherly voice in its sad whinnying. I knew how she felt. I would have whinnied along with her had I known how.

When Juno died she wasn't replaced. My father had taken an early retirement to do research, and the three of us were on a reduced income and couldn't afford a horse. Father hardly went anywhere anyway, and Mother had undergone two bad falls from Juno. Juno's body was sold to the recycling plant on the edge of town and I retreated farther into myself and my dreams of wealth. There was no one left in that grim household to love.

I remember my mother coming out to the garage one night when Juno was still alive and I was lying against her flank half-asleep, dreaming already of stock-market quotations and of the killings I would make. Mother was wearing a pink chenille bathrobe. She had a candle in her hand and her face was as puffy as bread dough and her hair wild. 'My God!' she said, seeing me. 'You fool. That horse could roll on you and kill you. Or kick you to death.'

I opened my eyes and stared at Mother. I could have stood up, easily, and beaten her senseless. Juno wouldn't hurt me. I stared at Mother and said nothing.

Mother suddenly seemed to weaken and become confused. She put a hand to her forehead, and even in candlelight I could see the blue veins in it and the trembling. She looked at Juno and spoke as if to her. 'What's going to become of me?' she said. Juno was silent. So was I. Mother turned and went back to the house. About a half hour later I got up from the straw and went through our vegetable garden to the living-room window and looked in. There sat Mother on the sofa with her robe open and a drink in her hand, staring at the gray floor of our living room. The study candles were out; my father was in bed. It was about three o'clock in the morning; I could tell that by the stars. In those days we still were allowed electric light until 10 P.M., but it was far later than that. Mother had lit six candles and was sitting there as though hypnotized, the flesh on her cheeks sagging, her breasts exposed, sagging, her arms sagging at her sides. Whenever I hear the phrase 'spiritual bankruptcy' I think of Mother sitting there, an empty woman.

Mother was dead within a few years, and shortly afterward my father died. I was thirty before I found out that my father was not a famous scholar at all but just another university hack, his whole lifetime worth at most a couple of footnotes in the work of a real historian. What fools they were, with their unlived lives! What cowards! I have tried to erase them from memory but I cannot completely; something in me can still, in the dark of night, ache for a parental touch that I cannot even remember, ache to be held by them. At such times I force my memory back to Juno, and Juno, as always, comforts my hungry spirit.

It was Ruth who asked me, in a kind of shy, distant way, if we shouldn't give our rainy planet a name. I didn't hesitate. 'We'll call it Juno,' I said. My heart was gratified at the thought. I looked out the window at the heavy rain and the shadows of strange trees burgeoning up from the wet soil. What a fecund place, what life!

When the rain stopped I was the first one out of the hatchway, walking more soberly this time but my heart exultant. The air smelled of wet grape leaves and was as moist as in a greenhouse. There was a breeze; I could hear rustling, paperlike, from the distant forest. The grass had a rich green hue and was spongy underfoot. What a place, what a splendid place! I was high with the thought that this could go on forever, with thirty-three more planets around this sun alone! Actually it was a pair of suns; Aminidab had a small red twin called Casca and I could see it just above the distant horizon.

41

I turned back toward the ship. Ruth was standing in the doorway looking out, her face morose.

'Come on out, Ruth!' I shouted, and she smiled faintly and walked out and stood for a minute. I jogged over, put my arms around her and gave her a hug. Then I pulled back a bit and waved at the others inside. 'Come on out!' I shouted. 'Bring some wine and we'll have a picnic!' I looked back at Ruth. She was shaking her head at me, in a kind of motherly mock-alarm. Her face had brightened considerably. It suddenly occurred to me that I had never told Ruth I was impotent, and I immediately realized she must be miffed at me for not even trying to get in her pants. Jesus, I can forget the simplest social obligations sometimes when I get wrapped up in myself, as I was on Belson.

Well, we had the picnic there in our first few hours outdoors on Juno and we had a great time—all eighteen of us. When I had awakened a few days before from my long nap, I noticed a certain coolness in the crew and interpreted it as pique at the way I could sleep away most of the trip, while they had to contend with the tedium. Probably bitching at one another too, and getting into sexual complications the way people will. The idea of a picnic was an inspired way of getting past hard feelings and inaugurating a new camaraderie in this new world of ours. It worked splendidly. One of the seismic engineers, a normally quiet woman named Mimi, produced a guitar and began singing old twentieth-century songs. 'Downtown' and 'Let it Be.' Howard and another engineer brought out bottles of red wine, a wheel of cheese, some cans of tuna fish and six loaves of rye bread; we found a dry place on the spongy ground and sat around together and sang along, with our mouths full of food. We kept passing wine bottles. It was delightful. Nobody was worried about dangerous life forms, and there really wasn't any need to worry. If there were any animals—which was very unlikely—they could hardly have *homo sapiens* on their diets. We drank the wine and watched the suns move across the sky at a merry clip—since Juno's rotation took a little less than eight Earth hours—and then were entertained by a night with five moons and the twinkling of about a dozen of our nearby fellow planets. Despite the brightness of the sky, I could spot Sol as it rose, looking nondescript, just another Spectral Type G, Main Sequence, star. That little pinpoint flicker in Juno's purple sky was the sun of my old Earth, the blazing god of its ancient religions; from here I saw it as just another distant rhinestone among handfuls of them thrown across the night sky. Ninety million miles from Sol would be Earth, too small to see, where Isabel lived. I waved toward Isabel, a bit sadly, and fell asleep for a while on the grass.

Later that night I found myself briefly alone with Ruth and almost told her about my sexual problem. I wasn't sure that I was still impotent; I just had, then, a lack of interest that might have merely been desuetude—a kind of 'solitary confinement blues', as some of my friends in prison used to call it. I spent two years in a prison in New Jersey, back when I was young and in too much of a hurry to assemble my first ten million. It had to do with price-fixing. Alleged. I managed to get market reports in my cell and found ways of sending out buy-and-sell orders. I was worth about twelve million when I got out, so the experience paid off well enough, although I did get restless in jail. When I left I had managed to corner the marijuana market in the prison; it had been done largely in a spirit of play. *That* was the only real price-fixing I ever did: I got it up to three hundred an ounce for mediocre Jamaican and passed my holdings on to a friend—a murderer and there for life—who was grateful to take over. He sends me Christmas cards and an occasional moody letter. Eduardo had murdered two wives; I knew how he felt.

Most of us didn't sleep that short night, our first in the open for some time. The first sun, the little one, was back up three hours after the big one had set, and it made a pleasantly soft light to explore by.

The forest was made up of those trees with slim orange trunks. The trunks were warm and leathery to the touch; the leaves were membranous and translucent, with a kind of ivory-colored Spanish moss hanging from some like old lace; they rustled pleasantly in the grapey wind. We looked for fruit but there was none. The forest was large and the trees were all alike. We kept on walking through it. There was little chance of getting lost, but just to be sure I marked our path occasionally with a page from *The Ambassadors*, which had

43

somehow wound up in my jacket pocket. After a while the second sun came up, the light changed from red to yellow, and it began to get warm. The spongy grass became harder underfoot as its moisture evaporated. I was getting hot and sticky and was thinking about going back to the ship for the nuclear jeep when we came up over a slight rise and Ruth, who was the first up there, shouted, 'Wow!' and we all came up alongside her and gaped. Below us stretched a broad valley all the way to the horizon, with trees and bushes and plants: brown and crimson and mauve and yellow. The small hairs on the back of my neck prickled.

We were all still a bit high from the picnic and from being up all the brief night; we rushed down the hill and started looking at the different plants, first in childish delight and then trying to find things that seemed edible. I found some long pods growing from a yellow bush and picked them; they were slippery and smelled grassy in my hand. Ruth found something that looked like an avocado, and Howard found stalks like celery. We began gathering in earnest, shouting at one another when we found something that looked good. You could move fast and easily in that gravity and we were all over the place. Nobody dared bite into anything yet; it all had to be tested first for poisons and digestibility. We loaded ourselves with this astonishing harvest laughing and joking. It was a profound release after the long trip from Belson and the days of waiting in the rain.

We found a lot of things that looked like food. Howard and Sato, our biophysicist and our physiologist, checked them out with beakers and computers and lab mice and found that half of them were indeed edible. Protein, carbohydrates, fats. Just like Earth. My yellow pods had little orange peas in them that tasted like almonds. Howard's stalk was as crisp as celery but tasted like fish. And someone had picked mushrooms that looked suspiciously like Earth mushrooms and in fact *tasted* like mushrooms. Sato muttered something about 'interstellar spores' and I shrugged. I didn't really care if they were fungoid cousins of what grew on Earth, carried here by astral winds or by the hand of God; they were nearly as good as morels and they would be splendid on steaks or in an omelet. The big orbiculate leaves of the orange-trunked trees were edible but tasted like kerosene. There was a plant that was like wheat, and I later got some kernels from it and ground them up and made a few passable loaves of bread. I had learned to bake during those morose days at the Pierre. The flavor was slightly acid but it worked out fine with the mushrooms when you fried them and made a mushroom sandwich.

I was really beginning to feel good with the crew. The picnic had begun it, and finding new foods and sharing them cemented it; we had become a family. When I saw Sato walking hand in hand with Mimi, I felt a warmth in me that I had never felt, even for my daughter Myra with her unlucky body and her doleful eyes.

I went to bed early that night and dreamed for a while of Myra.

The next morning everyone was a bit tired at breakfast. But by the second cup of coffee we were all charged up again. Within a half hour our chief engineer, Annie, was outside in her overalls supervising the unloading of the two nuclear jeeps and then having a plant wipe installed on the front of the bigger one. Mimi and Sato left their breakfasts half finished and went off to the equipment lockers to break out the uranium detection and sampling gear. The geologists started a discussion of three possible mining sites that our computers had picked from the infrared photos, taken while the ship was in orbit. The nearest site was seventeen miles away, but the likeliest was six miles farther. The basic problem was ground transportation. You could hardly use the *Isabel* for short hops.

I finished off my pancakes and bacon and stayed out of it for a bit. But when I'd had my second cup of coffee I spoke up. 'Let's go for the big one first,' I said. 'Annie can go in front with the wipe and we'll follow with the gear.'

Arturo looked up from his charts. 'What about the seismics?' Arturo was chief geologist and looked testy.

'We won't do seismics. I have a hunch we won't need them here. This first time out I'm going to put my faith in a shovel.'

Arturo looked at me with dismay for a moment. Then he said, 'Captain, with all respect, we have to zero in on a thing like this. You can't just start digging . . .'

He was sitting across the table from me. I stood up with a

cigar in one hand, reached the other hand out to his chart, and pointed to a spot where a group of computer-drawn lines converged. 'We're looking for a mineral with an atomic weight of two thirty-five,' I said. 'And there is something very heavy right there—twenty-three miles from here.'

'Captain, the photo equipment isn't capable of that kind of discrimination. It could be thorium or actinium. It could be lead.'

'We'll see what it is,' I said.

In an hour we had our two-jeep caravan set up. I sat with my Seas, Roebuck shovel in the driver's seat of Annie's jeep, and the other one followed with three geologists and their equipment. Annie had a wipe cylinder installed on each of the front fenders and she blasted while I drove at a steady five miles an hour. At first she was very careful and businesslike with the big silver tubes, but after a bit she started getting into it and operated the controls as though she were firing six-guns: *Zip!* Trees and bushes puffed away in pink bursts of cloud. *Zap!* Great lavender flowers vanished as we humped and rocked our way along the denuded ground, and stands of leaves the size of rowboats fell into dust.

I had fed Arturo's chart into the jeep's readout machine; my navigating behind all this molecular devastation consisted of keeping two little green lights on the dash superimposed. More accurately, bringing them back together every time I hit a big hump and they veered apart.

It took four and a half hours to get there and I suspected the three behind us wanted a break. But I didn't want to stop and we pushed on until the beeps of the homing device on the dash got loud enough to let me know we were very near our destination. I pulled up, turned off the ignition and got out. I was shaky from the ride but excited. I could smell uranium. Or, more precisely, money.

The other three came dragging up in a minute, looking dusty and weary, and I handed out beers from the back-seat. Then I took my shovel and pointed toward a rise just ahead. It was a kind of grassy hillock about the height of my mansion in New York. We all took long swigs of beer and then I said, 'I think that's an outcropping and I think it's what we're looking for.' I looked at Arturo, who had been in the second jeep. 'What do you think?'

He nodded a bit coldly. 'That's where the lines on the chart converge,' he said. 'But there's nothing radioactive around here. It's probably lead.' He was holding a Geiger counter.

'If it's safe uranium it won't affect a counter,' I said.

'Don't be sure,' Arturo said. 'Nobody's ever seen safe uranium. It's only an educated guess.' He looked skeptically toward my hill. 'Maybe a hopeful guess.'

'This is one hell of a time for that kind of talk,' I said. 'I'm going up.'

Before anyone could say anything, I had started up the hill. It was overgrown with some kind of matted, pinkish vegetation, with no handholds; but in the light gravity and the good shape I was in I managed to scramble my way up. I looked back and saw the rest of them beginning to climb. I turned back to the summit I stood on. It was a flat place, a bit larger than a pool table. I took a firm grip on my shovel and started digging.

By the time the others were on top and were standing, sweating and a bit annoyed, looking at me, I had dug through the top soil. I raised a shovel load now of a mustard-colored mass and held it out toward them. It was very heavy stuff, whatever it was. 'I'm no geologist,' I said. 'Can somebody tell me what this is?'

Annie was the first to reach for it. She took a pinch between her fingers and sniffed it. Then she took the equipment case from her shoulder and got some little electronic machines out. Arturo did the same. When he felt the stuff and its heaviness and then rubbed some in the palm of one hand, he showed surprise but said nothing. The four of them worked on the samples for several minutes in increasing but silent agitation. I felt excitement growing in me. It was like the feeling you get when a stock begins to move up and you sense that it's going to go through the roof.

Annie spoke first. 'My God!' she said, 'I read uranyl nitrate at eighty-six percent.'

'Unstable but not radioactive,' Arturo said in a hushed voice.

'I cannot believe this,' Mimi said, with a thrill in her voice.

47

Suddenly she stood up. My heart had begun pounding like a triphammer. She threw her thin arms around me and hugged me with astonishing strength.

I hugged her back, and then the others piled around us in a big huddle of arms and bodies. 'I believe it,' I said.

It turned out that the whole hill and the ground for acres around it were 86 percent uranyl nitrate—a U236 compound and yet as safe as buttercups. The other 14 percent would be no trouble for the *Isabel*'s refining equipment. The only problem was getting it to the ship; we had a hold capacity of sixty tons. Hauling that much ore twenty-three miles in jeeps would be a pisser. The best idea was to take the *Isabel* up into orbit and bring her back down again as close to the hill as possible.

But when I told Ruth that was what I wanted, she said, 'Look, Ben. Maybe I can jockey the ship over without all that fuss.'

And she did. We got everything back on board, strapped ourselves into our bunks, and Ruth brought the *Isabel* shuddering up to a few hundred feet of altitude, tilted her forward for a moment, and then brought her shuddering back down on her own white tail flame. It was a gorgeous maneuver; I was astonished that it could be done at all.

When we stepped out a half-hour later over smoking ground, we stood twenty yards from my hill of uranium. Ruth stood beside me looking modest but clearly pleased with herself. I turned and shook her hand warmly.

The next morning we opened the big hatchways and lowered the processing machinery to the surface. The two enjays—the nuclear jeeps—were fitted with backhoes, and Mimi and Sato each drove one while Annie had the metallurgical plowing equipment taken out and got it in place. By afternoon, fourteen people were working together and a steady stream of uranyl nitrate was moving along conveyor belts.

The *Isabel*, seated on her retros as she was, is nearly as tall as the Washington Monument, and a great deal thicker. I walked around her several times while the preparation of this cargo was getting underway, the piling-up of our bonanza, and then I stopped for a long silent look at the heavy boxes now escalating their way up to the empty holds. The thrill of discovery was gone. I watched this accumulation of potential wealth with something like weariness. It was beyond doubt the apex of my financial career and a mineral find almost beyond the dreams of Cortez in Mexico, yet I found myself without enthusiasm. *Maybe I'm just tired*, I thought. I went back on board and into my stateroom, took a bottle from the cabinet and poured myself a stiff drink. The *Isabel* was shuddering as her holds began to fill. I took a long swallow of Bourbon and sat wearily in my Eames chair. What it all meant for me then was merely more money. I had won my original gamble and was bringing off a coup that would stagger the financial communities of the world. Juno uranium could reverse the decline of New York, of the whole United States. If an ice age really was on its way, this uranium would keep the people of the world from freezing, would open up new possibilities even for the poorest. Especially for the poorest. And I could be, in a few years, the richest man alive.

I finished my whiskey and poured another. I felt weary. I felt as though I had done nothing and solved nothing.

4

I believe that in the twentieth century a person could become a billionaire on four or five correct guesses and on being in the right place at the right time three times. The United States economy underwent a steady expansion during that century. A tenacious but lucky fool could quadruple his inheritance with less skill than it took to win at Monopoly. Quite a few tenacious and lucky fools did just that, and then went on to work widespread mischief with their radio stations and their crusades for Christ—that Gentile, middle-class Christ of the Texas billionaire!—and their John Birch societies and their general loutish arrogance.

There are still men and women of that kind around and I know some of them pretty well. I don't socialize with them at their prayer breakfasts and their Permastone country-squire mansions, but I sell real estate to them from time to time. They are a rarer breed in the twenty-first century than in the last two. Ours is a dwindling economy. Energy sources and population have been shrinking for seventy years. If a person in 1940 had bought almost *anything*, from canned-soup factories to Australian ranchland, and hung on to it for twenty years, he would have enriched himself enormously and along the way gained a reputation for perspicacity. His sons and daughters would have been written about in the papers as though their lovers and their art purchases and their drug addictions were of national importance.

Well, it doesn't work that way anymore. If you hang on to what you own, it loses value. Markets keep getting smaller; there are fewer people to buy canned soup. Even with the Chinese now using armpit sprays and mascara and perfumed toilet paper, the world market keeps getting smaller.

-I have several ways I rely on for making money; the chief one is knowing when to sell and what to sell for. There are lots of things for sale out there and, as always, some are bargains but most are not. I buy the bargains and I know how and when to sell them. I am not a producer of wealth or of much that society needs or wants; most people like me are the same and always have been; we are really people who are either smart enough or powerful enough or rich enough to begin with, to be able to take advantage. Marx called us jackals, and, as usual, Marx was right. I'm worth about two billion and I sometimes hate myself for it.

When I was in my late thirties and making a lot of money in the declining real estate market, I went through a period of a few years collecting impressive-looking buildings on bankruptcies and by finding weaknesses in the networks of mortgages that were common in those days. It was easy, once you grasped that things were going bad faster than anybody else thought they were. It was the 2040s, the time of the uranium bust. Nobody was having any babies; the military had its crude hands on all the crude oil; whole industries were reeling; just taking the Mercedes limousines away from all those gray-templed hustlers who sat on their boards had thrown most U.S. corporations into tailspins. I was selling short like a mad Arab at a bazaar; I rescued real estate from the courts, spiffed up its paperwork, found ways of unloading it and then found ways of writing it off. Jolly times, if you had the nerve. During all this a lot of buildings passed through my hands and I hung on to a few that suited my fancy. I wound up owning what had once been a fine arts museum in San Francisco, which I lived in for six months because of some tax advantages. I also owned a house in Georgia, four banks in Dallas, the Japan Camera Center in Chicago, two solid blocks of Park Avenue in New York, and a baroque, five-story mansion at Sixty-third and Madison. I decided one rainy Thursday to make it my family home; I spent three months knocking out walls and redecorating—over fifty workmen would be there sweating away at any given time.

I think that place reflected my time in prison more than anything else. I had learned to shoot passable nineball in jail and I had a billiard room put in my mansion, with a fine nineteenth-century mahogany table. I almost never played anymore, but I loved looking at the way the green baize surface glowed under the Tiffany lamps. I had been claustrophobic sometimes in my cell and couldn't sleep; I had a whole floor of that place as my master bedroom, with a huge bathroom each for me and Anna and an unfinished pine floor big enough for basketball. I furnished the main living room in eighteenth century; I had fallen in love with that from a picture book at the prison library: *English Eighteenth-century Houses*. There were gold armchairs with white brocade seats and cloisonné snuffboxes and clocks with cherubs on their faces. I bought two Fragonards, and a chandelier from a French palace. But all I remember using that room for was playing three-card stud with my accountants. We didn't entertain. Anna spent most of her time in the bedroom, reading or making hooked rugs.

During the redecorating Anna was living with her parents upstate, in their parsonage in Watertown, and on the night before she and our daughter Myra were to come and make a grand attempt at living with me, I went to the place and poured myself a tumbler of Japanese Campari in the cathedral-ceilinged kitchen and walked around in a kind of euphoric daze for hours. I allowed myself to imagine being a paterfamilias on the grand scale. Since Anna and I had only one child, it would be necessary for us to start breeding fast, but that seemed okay at the time. There was a big nursery on the top floor. What the hell; we could have six or seven kids and reverse the trend. I didn't know anybody else who had children. There alone in that big spooky expensive place I visualized the bustle and warmed to it. Moonlight came through high casement windows onto the floor of my cavernous living room and glistened on the cherrywood grand piano. I sat on the bench and played 'Stardust' and 'Bridge over Troubled Waters' soulfully and drank more Campari. I got up and went to the billiard room and played myself a game of nineball. I still remember: I ran the first seven and then miscued on the eight. I walked down to the wine cellar and counted the whites, took the walnut and brass elevator up to the fourth floor and surveyed the guest suite, done in early twenty-first century, with everything pastel and puffy, even the kitchen and butler's pantry. I smoked a Japanese cigar, drank a glass of Japanese whisky, turned on my Japanese music system for a while, glanced through the Japanese section of the *Wall Street Journal* and thought briefly of buying a resort hotel near Osaka. But I wasn't really interested, and Japanese investments troubled me; I knew her depression would worsen from buying American coal, as indeed has happened. My spirit was troubled there in my mansion and I didn't know why. Yes, I did. It wasn't going to work out, and I knew it then.

I still had my methane-powered Bentley in those days, and I used it to pick up Anna at Grand Central the following morning. She had traveled second-class on a wood-burner, sitting erect on one of those plastic seats by dirty windows, and had brought exactly one small suitcase with her. Samsonite. That was Anna. It wasn't exactly religion with her and she had taken no vows of poverty. But my God, did she gall me. Yet she wasn't really stingy in the soul—just closed off somewhere. Often I would wind up spiritually on her side and cursing myself for being oafish and rich. Her suitcase was half full of books.

Anna and Myra and I lived in that mansion for eight months. Toward the end of it the student riots began. Things were bad all over and the students had decided capitalism was to blame. I had no real quarrel with that, although I felt the scarcity of fuels deserved at least equal billing. For a few days of it a lot of the sons and daughters of the upper-middle-class decided *I* was the enemy, and I got edgy when they started chanting things like 'Belson go home.' Hell, I *was* home.

They hanged me in effigy, and it was a damned good effigy too. Art students. I'll never forget that stuffed manikin with my steel-rimmed eyeglasses and my characteristic lumberjack shirt and the cigar. It looked so mournful being hanged under the gaslight there at Sixty-third and Madison, my replica head at one side as if in a daydream and my feet jumping around as drunken students jerked the rope. I stared at it a long time from my billiard-room window. Then they burned it and I gasped as it blackened. What a sensation! What a deadly preview! Still, I liked being a star of the show.

Anna saw that effigy too, I'm certain, from her bedroom window. She was a lot more cheerful the next morning. At breakfast she joined me for her Rice Krispies, and for a moment she even hummed a tune. But when I suggested we bounce around in our Louis Quinze bed for a while it was nothing doing. She wanted to finish Proust. I should have divorced her on the spot, citing cheerfulness toward effigy burning as grounds. Denial of conjugal rights. Overweening literacy.

I had never paid much attention to television, but when I moved into that mansion I decided to install the best. People told me the technology had been improved a lot and it was patriotic to patronize it. Since the death of Hollywood in the first part of the century and the demise of General Motors at about the same time, the United States had led the world in only two technologies: fast food and television. During the Depression of the 2050s holographic TV had improved enormously. So I had an RCA set installed in what had once been a third-floor sitting room. It consisted of six projection posts against the room's longest wall, and I'll never forget how I jumped when I first turned it on after the installers had left. A group of real people—dancing and singing frenetically— suddenly appeared in the room, life-sized and skimpily dressed, all of them grinning at me like idiots. The sound was real too, loud and sexy and terrible; it was Broadway synthetic music of the worst kind. It turned out they were doing a commercial for life insurance. I'd had no idea. And the whole thing only used a hundred and fifty watts. I left the set on, went to the bar in the next room, got myself some whiskey, and came back and joined my illusory guests, now a middle-class family in turmoil. A soap opera. It was quite a sensation to move among them, a drink in my hand, and hear talk of their electronic hysterectomies and multiple infidelities. They were very earnest. Things were pretty low in my life at the time. I seldom saw Anna, and Myra spent all her time with doctors and lovers. I ran my businesses pretty much from my head, and a dozen phone calls a day made up my labors. I was on hold—both financially and emotionally; I got hooked for a while on television. It was a sign that things were falling apart, that my plan of settling down in New York was unreal.

Something in me welcomed the riots when they came. I haven't watched TV since. I do believe that shooting morphine is better for the soul.

Anna was the child of an improbable marriage between a little dandy of a Presbyterian minister and a big-boned grand-lady Episcopalian. Her mother, who had never attended her father's church, was far too grand to get out of bed before noon; she had lain on satin with her quilted robe and quilted eyepads while Anna took charge of the two younger brothers.

I visited them one summer vacation, when Anna was home from Elmira College, where she studied French Literature. Her family kept her so busy, fixing this and taking care of that, that we hardly had any time together. She spent one morning preparing a Fourth of July picnic for all of us, and when the Fourth came her mother decided that Anna should put away the chickens she had roasted the day before and cook a ham instead.

'Mother,' Anna said, in despair, 'I have to hang up the wash. And where will I get a ham on the Fourth of July?' She stood there looking at her mother, trembling.

'You'll work it out, dear,' her mother said. She turned and walked back up the stairs to her bedroom.

And Anna did in fact work it out. She got the clothes dry and bought a ham and cooked it and had a picnic dinner for six people. That evening she cleaned up the kitchen, fixed the damper on the wood stove and rearranged the books in her father's library.

'That girl sure is a wonder,' her father said sweetly, puffing his pipe. At the time, I thought so too.

I spent two days after they hanged and burned me in effigy getting police protection and having steel shutters put on the windows of the bottom two floors. It was a private police firm, a subsidiary of Cosa Nostra. There already was a high wall around the building with a stand of barbed wire on top. During this activity I hadn't seen Anna or Myra, but when it was all over and I was in the billiard room one evening idly shooting the three ball around on the table, thinking things over, who should walk in but Anna. She was wearing a faded green housedress and she looked tired.

'Hi,' I said. 'Where've you been lately?'

She frowned a little. 'Around the house,' she said. 'Staying out of your way.'

'You wouldn't have been in the way. I've just been telling men where to put things.'

'You should have asked me to help.' Her voice was weary. 'Ben, pour me a beer, will you?'

She seemed so relaxed and tired and familiar that my tension dissolved. 'Sure, honey,' I said. I went to the little bar at the end of the room and got two bottles of Peruvian beer and two glasses. Anna seated herself in a big velvet easy chair. I set the glasses on the table beside her and poured them both full, with big foamy heads. I pulled a smaller chair over to face hers, took one of the glasses, and sat down. Anna seldom drank, and I took this present willingness as a good sign. I sipped my beer slowly and waited for her to start a conversation. She clearly had something on her mind.

Finally she spoke up. 'Ben,' she said, 'I think I could go crazy in this house. There's nothing here for me to do.'

I stared at her, crestfallen I guess. I had been hoping for something positive. 'You should get out more,' I said. 'Meet people. We could go to the theater or the ballet.' I felt stupid immediately, saying it. There were riots and demonstrations out in the streets of New York and I was one of the prime targets of them. My wife should hardly be out at soirées or politely applauding the ballet. I always seemed to be saying stupid things to Anna.

She just looked at me wearily. 'It's like it was when we lived at the Pierre, Ben,' she said.

'I don't drink as much as I did then. And I'm home a lot more.'

She looked at me fiercely for a moment. 'You were drunk all the time,' she said. 'Or at least whenever I saw you, which wasn't often. Now you're drunk only part of the time.'

That was her first acknowledgement that I had cut down, and I was glad to hear it. 'Look,' I said, 'we could read books together, the way we did when we were first married. We should take a trip to Europe and go back to some of those places in Florence. Or that house in Brussels.'

She just looked at me and sipped her beer thoughtfully.

'Hell,' I said. 'In a week I can be finished with these damned mergers and with a coal deal I'm trying to make. I'll have time on my hands. We can get . . . can get reacquainted.' I looked toward the big casement windows that faced Madison Avenue, where my new floodlights made the tops of the two big maples glow theatrically, as though for a stage setting. Then I looked back at Anna and saw that she was crying. 'What's wrong, honey?' I said.

She went on snuffling for a minute and then took a substantial-looking handkerchief from the pocket of her dress and blew her nose powerfully. 'Ben,' she said, 'I had a miserable time when we went to Europe. I hated that house in Brussels. I spent the time hooking rugs and trying to get some heat in that *kitschy* place while you paced around and fretted and made three-hour phone calls. It was horrible.' She blew her nose again, more softly this time, and then looked at me balefully. 'What makes you think it'll be any different if we do it again?'

'I didn't know . . .,' I said. 'I thought you liked Europe that time.'

There was hatred in her eyes now and in her voice. 'I told you a half-dozen times when we were there I wanted to go home. I told you I hated Belgium. I felt uncomfortable in the restaurants, and the movies were insipid.'

'Honey!' I said. 'I remember.' Actually I hadn't, until she spoke of it. I felt immediately guilty. But, damn it, it had been ten years before. 'And didn't I have French movies brought over and we showed them in the living room? And I got a good cook and we ate in.'

She stood up all of a sudden, with her half-finished glass of beer in her hand, and stared at me and said, levelly, 'You son of a bitch, Ben. It was just like that. *You* did this for me and *you* did that. You were telling me then how *you* were going to straighten things out and how *you* were going to change. Well, you didn't change and you're not going to and I'm ill with it. I have a sickness unto *death* of hearing about you and what you are going to do and how things are going to be different. There are only two things you do, Ben; you make

57

money and you talk about yourself. And I'm sick of both of them.' She stopped and finished her beer.

Something in me was cringing. I knew what she said was true. I was obsessed with myself and with making money. But, damn it, I did pay attention to her when she spoke up loudly enough to compete with the three-alarm fire that was sometimes going on in my head. I felt wretched. 'Anna,' I said, in all sincerity, 'what do you want?'

And then she did something I had never seen her do. She gripped her beer glass, swung her arm, and threw the glass like a hardball against the far wall. Straight as a rocket. It crashed, fell, tinkled on the floor.

'Jesus!' I said, impressed.

'What I want,' Anna said, 'is for those rioters out there to come and get you personally and hang you. And then burn you. I hate your insides, you self-centered son of a bitch.'

I just stared at her. I had sensed that she was furious for a long time—years, I think. And there it was. It seemed to clear the air in the room.

'Damn your egomaniacal *soul*,' she said, and then turned and left the room.

I sat there for about twenty minutes. Then I got up, went to the pool table, racked the balls into their triangle, broke the rack, and started shooting straight pool. I ran all fifteen of them. But my stomach was in a knot. I *was* a son of a bitch. Self-centered and money crazy.

When the Mafia first came out of the closet, merged with the Teamsters and listed itself on the New York Exchange, I stayed away from the stock. Cosa Nostra Industries. I was suspicious, despite the predictions of better shipping of goods across the country. Well, as usual, I was right; shortages got worse in New York, and the arrival of food and goods became even more whimsical. During that time in my mansion there were never any potatoes available except on the black market, but there was an abundance of pears. Damned good ones too. After I finished running that rack of balls on the pool table, I went down the elevator to the living room, where there was a big Sèvres bowl of yellow and red Bartletts. I began eating them and pacing around, dripping juice on the floor for a while until I got a plate and held it under the current pear. They were remarkable—as succulent as fruit could be—and I must have eaten a dozen of them. 'Orally deprived,' the Great Orbach had said of me, 'lacking in deep and vital nourishment inside.' It was sure true. My mother's breasts had looked like rotten turnips to me. When I drank I drank *seriously*. Planning a real estate sale or a merger I could chew my thumbs until they blistered. If I didn't have the metabolism of a Brazilian fire ant I'd be fat. But I only sleep three or four hours a night and I'm normally pretty lean.

So I gobbled down those pears in my guilt and anger and helplessness and remorse over Anna. We had been married fifteen years and it seemed to be only grief. I ate another pear, dribbling juice down my chin, striding across the living room in my lumberjack boots. *Jesus!* I thought, *what does she want?*

I said that aloud, *What does she want?*, several times, and then realized I was fighting back the answer. It was obvious: she wanted me to care about her. And the truth of it was that I didn't. Not anymore. Anna bored me. There was a sweetness in her somewhere—a kind of lost child—that appealed to me strongly. There was that intelligence that had drawn me to her in the first place. But right now it was all dust and ashes. It wasn't enough. I ate another pear, more slowly this time. It would have tasted better with a little hard cheese, but that was two floors below, in the kitchen. I pictured Anna's face as it had looked in that parsonage with her cultivated, genteel family. She had seemed so smart, straightforward and fresh. So unlike anybody else I knew. She'd had a nice round bottom then too, and big, amused eyes. Talking to her was like talking to an old friend. She didn't flirt. She wasn't devious. I felt I should grab her right then and marry her.

I proposed after we had known each other three months and she accepted. She told me the truth: she wanted to get out of that place near Canada, see the larger world. She didn't want to finish college and be a schoolteacher. She wanted something 'different' she said. Well, I never found out what that 'different' thing was—although God knows I tried to. And she never did either. She didn't know what she wanted; how in the hell was *I* supposed to?

I took her to an inn in Jamaica for our honeymoon; we

stayed in a suite with a private swimming pool and private dock and our own croquet course. The bedroom was enormous, with white furniture and beds and white walls. There were nineteenth-century British paintings of flowers and horses and landscapes on the walls and three vases of flowers in the room. We had two bathrooms, tiled and huge, with a giant bowl of hibiscus in each—pink for her and blue for me. There was a stone balcony forty feet long over the rocks where the Caribbean splashed in clear blue and foam.

It was our wedding night. I had undressed quickly in my bathroom and was lying, wearing only a pair of black briefs, on one of the two king-sized beds, my hands behind my head. I was pretty inexperienced sexually myself, and Anna was a virgin.

So much for the Fergusson pill and the 'liberation of the body'—I was as scared of sex as they had been in the Middle Ages. So was Anna. We had talked about it.

But she had not said anything to prepare me for what happened next. We had gotten off the plane still wearing the dress-up clothes from the wedding. She came abruptly out of her bathroom now, with her white blouse still on and with some kind of godawful sexless rubber girdle on her bottom. She walked over to the bed in her matter-of-fact way, planted her feet like a shortstop, turned her back to me and said, 'I can't get this thing off.' I was sort of spellbound by all this. It was Anna's way of behaving all right, but I had expected something different for a wedding night. I sat up in bed, reached over and unhooked a little steel hook at the top of the thing. It felt to my fingertips like Rubbermaid.

'That's better,' she said and then proceeded to loop her thumbs under the waistband of that damned rubbery white garment, pull it down an inch and then, abruptly, let it go with a loud *pop*. She breathed an audible sigh of relief. She took it off an inch at a time that way. Pop, pop, *pop*, I can still hear it.

I had not expected Anna to act like a courtesan. But, Jesus, she seemed to be trying to tell me something awful with this.

'Jesus Christ,' I said, 'what's going on?'

Her voice was taut. 'I just couldn't get the thing *off*,' she said.

'Why did you wear it in the first place?' She didn't need a girdle. Her ass was fine.

Then she began to cry.

'I'm sorry, honey,' I said. That must have been the first of a million times I was to say that. *I'm sorry, honey*. Christ! I should have read the handwriting on the wall right then and bolted back to New York. Let my lawyers handle the annulment. But, as usual, I thought it over and figured I was in the wrong. If only I could trust my feelings with women the way I do with money! I'd be as fulfilled as a fat Japanese Buddha floating on a lotus leaf.

'The lady at the store told me I needed something to wear under the suit, and I bought it. I wanted to look right for you.'

I shook my head. She turned to look at me, standing there with a white Synlon blouse on and that big dumb rubber thing lying on the floor like a discarded chastity belt. Chastity belt is right. I've learned since that there are nuns everywhere.

'Well, she should have sold you a pair of scissors to get it off with.' I was trying to be amusing. But it wasn't funny. Goddamn it, it was *terrible*. I felt like a son of a bitch for being angry. I had loved her for her plainness, hadn't I? What did I expect? Poor girl—how could she know how to be graceful on her bridal night?

Anna looked devastated. 'I'm sorry, Ben,' she said. 'I guess I don't know how to be a bride.'

'Honey,' I said, 'it's okay. Just throw that thing away and get yourself naked and come back. If you feel self-conscious naked, wear something. Just something that isn't made of rubber.'

She smiled. 'Okay,' she said, and went back into her bathroom.

She came back after a while wearing a white gown. She had put on perfume. She lay in bed by me and we talked and both of us got to feeling better, but something in me was apprehensive. We didn't make love until the morning, after breakfast. She bled a little on the sheets. When I walked out of the shower afterward I saw that she had the sheets off the bed and was in her bathroom grimly rinsing the blood out. My stomach sank. But I said nothing to her. *What the hell*, I thought. *She'll change*. But she didn't.

61

After two hours or so of eating pears in the living room, I went into a bathroom and threw up. Then I went to the phone and called Arthur Freed, one of my lawyers, got him out of bed, and told him I wanted to get a divorce and I was willing to pay substantial alimony.

I still felt sick and my mouth was full of a sour-sweetish taste from all the pears. But something in my heart felt lighter. I had been putting off that divorce for fifteen years.

I'd been seeing Isabel from time to time, ever since I'd backed a revival of a play she had a small part in. I waited until sunup and called her and asked her to have breakfast with me. She agreed, sleepily. By nine that morning I was in her apartment and we got into her loft bed together, while her two big, loutish pussycats watched me fumble, moan and fail, I had become impotent. Son of a bitch!

In a cover article a few years ago, *Newsweek* called me 'a scrappy child of the times' and went on to speak of those 'times' as being 'the orphan offspring of the twentieth century'. In its half-assed way *Newsweek* was right. My father buried his life in the past; I lived very much in my own century. I was born in 2012, when population in the industrial societies was plummeting. It's a wonder I was born at all. The last gas station in America closed when I was four. Faster-than-light travel was perfected when I was seven, and when I was in high school the frenetic search through the stars for uranium was on, with hundreds of ships like the *Isabel* scanning the Milky Way for what the *Tribune* called 'the galactic Klondike'. Fuel for that venture reduced the world's supply of enriched uranium by half. God knows how much was thrown into the stratosphere during the Arab Wars, blowing up those half-empty oil wells and the spanking new concrete universities that dotted the sands of the Persian Gulf.

If my century is the 'orphan' of the twentieth, it is the 1990s that conceived my times. More precisely, the year of conception was 1997, when Fergusson invented his pill.

Fergusson was a cranky old celibate whose contraceptive had all the necessary characteristics: it was cheap, easy and safe, and you didn't have to remember to take it more than once. It was also nonsexist; a man or a woman could get sterile with the same pill. The first Fergusson kits came out several years before my birth, and it is to my everlasting astonishment that neither my mother nor my father took one of the reds and prevented me and this account of them from coming into being. A kit was a small plastic bottle with two pills—one red and one green. If you swallowed the red you were sterile and you remained that way until you took the antidote—the green pill. You were sterile for a weekend in Mexico or for your lifetime, as you chose. A Fergusson kit cost almost nothing to manufacture; they sold for the price of a Pepsi-Cola—two dollars. The World Health Organization gave them out free in Latin America and India. The Roman Catholic Church nearly strangled on its apoplexy; the Pope crinkled his wise old Japanese eyes in pain. The press and pulpit were full of talk about God-given procreation and the warmth of families. People nodded agreement sagely and took the pill. Minority groups shouted 'chemical genocide' and maternity wards closed down. Bantu tribesmen gave their young reds as part of traditional puberty rites. No igloo in the Arctic was without them. And everywhere the greens were left over. They seldom got taken. 'Collective suicide' *Osservatore Romano* called it. A few dutiful Irish had broods of sulking babies; the rest of mankind breathed a sigh of relief. The price tag had finally been removed from copulation. The next generation was half the size of the previous one.

Myra was born from my deliberate taking of a green on a Friday night. At the first sign of Anna's pregnancy, I popped a red.

During the nine months I lived in that mansion and tried to be a family man I would, from time to time, feel guilty about my style of life and about all the money I had. I have always been a Communist manqué, perhaps even more so than Isabel. And Isabel was born in a Communist country and went to Maoist schools. My parents seldom spoke at the dinner table in more than grunts; when they did speak it was usually to remind me that a family of six in India could have been fed on the vegetables I didn't want to eat. I silently wished in those days that I had a postpaid jiffy bag by my plate, into which I could dump my uneaten Spam and mail it off immediately to some address in New Delhi. I still pay a dole in guilt for my affluence.

Sometimes I would roam through the long hallways and parlors of my big house and find myself thinking, 'What a waste!' I would decide glumly to turn the place into a shelter for homeless drunks or a hospital, that I myself really needed no more than a single room. But then I would console myself, as one does at such times, by thinking of worse cases. If I looked across the street from my big dining-room window I could see the facade of a mansion bigger than mine, with a brass plaque that read THE PENNY NEWTON MEMORIAL SHELTER. Penny, dead a dozen years, was the last of that family of oil barons and electronics wizards; she had put her hundreds of millions into endowing a five-story mansion to be used as a home for stray cats. There were about six thousand pussycats living across the street from me, and brigades of uniformed men searched the city for more, while a staff of veterinarians and nutritionists kept the residents glossy-coated and bright-eyed. There were still plenty of families in Harlem with rickets and frostbite. Ratbite too. What the hell, at least I had earned my money. Penny had done nothing in her entire life but attend the ballet, play whist and accumulate dividends from the fortune her father had cheated other people out of. My general feeling was that the wealth of most of my neighbors was as unearned and as trivially spent; Penny's cat home was merely more blatant. Property is theft.

After several days of it, the loading got to be routine, although some crew members continued to go around in a kind of protracted excitement. I was neither thrilled nor glum, but I realized my emotional distance from the ore that continued to pile up had separated me from the crew too, canceling the picnic as it were. I made the motions of supervising the work, but I gave no orders or instructions. It was Annie with her tanned, serious face and her quickness who ran the show. Under her supervision the raw Juno subsoil was fed into machinery that refined and compacted it and processed the pure uranium into heavy yellowish pellets about the size of a twenty-dollar coin but an inch thick. The *Isabel* had brought a supply of boron moderators just in case radioactivity had to be contended with, and these were, on Annie's orders, placed between the pellets. Stacks of twenty pellets alternating with twenty moderators were then covered with transparent, high-density sheaths. The result looked like some kind of gargantuan candy roll or parfait; it would be placed carefully in a plastic case along with nineteen others of its kind. The cases were numbered and loaded into the *Isabel*'s storage by a crane.

This was not a neat and smooth operation, as in a Japanese holovision factory. Nobody wore a white lab coat, and there was a lot of dust, noise, confusion and sweating. But the boxes, looking sturdy and potent, were stacking up in the holds at an exhilarating pace—exhilarating to the others, if not to me.

I worked out in the gym every morning during these days. I took Artaud, my trainer, off the work crew for enough time to help me get the zero-gravity springs off the machines and replace them with weights, but I didn't need his help in working out. The crew was invited to use the gym too; but I was usually in there alone, shortly after a light breakfast, putting myself through a pretty grueling sequence. It would be painful sometimes, doing repeated movements against those weights, but it accomplished something very necessary for my spirit.

After working out I showered heavily, dried off with one of the *Isabel*'s heavy towels, dressed in jeans and lumberjack shirt, and went outside to make a show of being the captain of this busy and cheerful crew. Every now and then I lent a hand if one of the conveyor belts jammed or a slowdown cropped up along the line. In the afternoons I would go to my stateroom and spend some time trying to plan out my course of action when I returned to Earth with the *Isabel*'s cargo. I would try to concentrate on some of the basic decisions: should I set up my own power plants or try merging with businesses like Con Ed? Should I merely sell uranium, confining myself to the fuel market in the way I had started out, hauling coal in a wagon? Should I buy more ships and have a fleet of them ferrying fuel to Earth? Should I go into the electric-car business or even the lighting and small-appliance business, which would be booming as electricity became abundant again? I somehow could not really focus on these questions. It lacked substance. It all seemed foregone.

At night I had supper at my desk and then played solo chess or read. I usually drank, alone.

One morning in the gym, during the second week of loading, another person came in just after I had started working out. It was Howard, dressed in yellow shorts; looking skinny and embarrassed. Howard is an intellectual, he'd been a professor of biochemistry somewhere for years, and he looked comical standing in the hatchway.

'Come on in,' I said, heaving my legs up against a hundred and fifty pounds.

He seemed heartened by that. He came over and strapped himself into the hip-and-back machine, next to mine.

'Did you warm up first?' I said.

He nodded. 'Stationary running, in the mess hall.'

I grunted and continued. For a while we both worked silently. We unstrapped and changed machines; Howard moved to the leg raise I'd just left and I moved to the leg curl. He set the weights down to sixty and we began working our machines in unison. 'Captain,' Howard suddenly said, panting, 'do you have trouble sleeping here? With the short days and the two suns?'

'No,' I said. I didn't say that I was usually drunk by the time I turned in.

He nodded. 'One of those suns is always coming up just when I'm going to sleep.'

'Close down the hatch by your bunk,' I said. 'Put a pillow over your head.'

'Yeah,' he said, unconvinced. 'I could do that.'

For a while there was silence except for the squeaking of the cams and the clunking of the weights in their tracks. When we got up to switch to the next machines he spoke again. 'I keep thinking about my wives when I go to bed.'

'Wives?' I said.

'Six.'

That was a serious number. But I didn't want to talk about women just then. 'Where are you from, Howard?'

He lay down on the leg-curl bench and awkwardly got his heels under the lifter. 'Columbus, Ohio.'

'Isn't that where Ruth's from?'

'Yes. Ruth's my sister.' He strained to lift the weights but nothing happened.

'I'll get it,' I said. He was trying to do the hundred pounds I'd been using. I set it back to forty. I was a bit shocked to think of this skinny guy as the brother of Ruth, with her hefty build. 'I didn't know that,' I said. 'You sure don't look alike.'

'I favor our mother.'

I seated myself in the overhead press and began working.

'Ruth's a smart one,' he said.

I didn't reply. Howard annoyed me, as much in his tone of voice as anything. I knew that if some part of me had given up back when I was a dirty-kneed kid I could have grown up to be like him. I pushed hard at the weights, repeating fast until I could feel the sweat pop out and hear myself groaning with the effort. If my father had seduced me into imitating his aloofness and if my mother had hidden her chaos and self-hate better, instead of letting it all hang out there in the kitchen where gin bottles outnumbered spice jars . . .

I finished, unstrapped and wiped the sweat off with a towel. The hatch was open and from outside came the muted shouts and grinding sounds of the loading operation. I waited for Howard to finish and then said, 'I've had women troubles lately myself. How do you feel about marriage, after six tries?'

He puffed heavily for a while. Then he said, 'I'm not sure. Every time I do it I have high hopes. But then the fighting starts.'

I took a towel from a hook on the bulkhead and handed it to him, for the sweat. 'Over what?'

'Money. Sex. The way she dresses. What we eat.' He dabbed at his chest and armpits. 'You know.'

'I know.' I wrapped my towel around my neck and did a few knee bends. Outside the porthole I heard Annie shouting orders to someone.

'Are you married now?' I said.

'No. But I think about trying again.'

'Maybe that's why you can't sleep.'

'Could be.'

I finished my workout in silence and showered before

Howard was through his. During my shower it occurred to me that I might not go back to Earth with the *Isabel*.

The next morning I decided to go back to the valley by our original landing site and pick some food. I wanted to get away from all the activity around the ship. Annie had worked out an improved system by then that didn't require the smaller jeep. I had the earth-moving rig taken off it and invited Ruth to go along with me. She accepted, and we took off on the long drive. We didn't talk much during the trip. I drove it at fifteen miles an hour and had to pay attention to the road.

I parked at a place where Annie's road came within a few hundreds yards of the valley. We got out, carrying buckets for the food we were going to pick, headed into the forest, and began walking along one of the lanes between orange-trunked palms. 'Ruth,' I said, 'how'd you come to be a star pilot? Is it something you dreamed about when you were a kid?'

She looked over at me. 'I took it as an elective in college.'

'An elective?' I said. 'What kind of college gives electives like that?'

'Ohio State. I was studying to be a railroad engineer. *That* was my dream when I was a kid. I wanted to pull the cord that blows the whistle.'

I knew what she meant. 'Have you ever done it?'

'Nope.' There was a hint of melancholy in her voice. 'I never have.'

I started to say something else when she went on. She seemed looser now and eager to talk. 'There was a course in astronavigation on Tuesday and Thursday afternoons, and it fit my schedule. I had thermodynamics and steam-power systems in the mornings, and I wanted something simple after lunch. I thought astronavigation would be easy, because nobody was piloting spaceships anymore.'

'Why were they teaching it at all?'

'Well, they still had the equipment. The Sony Trainer and videospheres from the days of the Uranium Bust. Their landing simulator was a dream. I made an "A" in the course, and took another. It was still a glamour course.'

'Really?' I said. 'It must have been twenty years since anybody had flown a spaceship . . .'

'You're forgetting the TV shows,' she said. 'Remember those space adventure stories?' She stopped walking for a moment and looked over at me, with her eyes just a bit wide. She looked very attractive that way. 'You know,' she said, 'we've actually *done* what they were doing in those shows. We've found *uranium!*' I thought Ruth was an unemotional type; this was the first time I had heard a thrill like that in her voice. It was a pleasure to see her like that. 'We sure have,' I said.

'How much money do you think it's worth?'

'Trillions,' I said. 'It's a fucking king's ransom.'

'Then why aren't you more excited?' she said. 'You're supposed to be a . . . a *tycoon.*'

That was a funny word for her and I had to laugh. 'Ruth, I really don't know. I think about hauling this cargo back to Chicago and New York and the things I have to buy and sell and all the wheeling and dealing I have to do and it just bores me.'

She was still looking at me. She stopped walking and bent down and pulled a blade of grass and began chewing it. We all did that every now and then; the grass on Juno had a pleasant licorice flavor. In fact, I think it's habit-forming. I thought sadly of Belson grass. And then Ruth said something that shocked me. It was as though she were reading my mind. 'Something happened to you on Belson, didn't it?' she said.

'Yes.'

'Was it morphine?'

I thought for a minute. 'No.'

She nodded. 'But it was something . . . something mystical,' she said.

I was surprised at her knowingness about me, but I remained silent.

'Come on, Ben,' she said. 'It's been written all over you since that morning we had to carry you back to the ship.'

'Even during the picnic?' The picnic had been about a month before this.

'Even during the picnic.' She smiled. 'You were very sweet then and we all loved you. But a part of you was somewhere else.'

'I was thinking about Isabel. A woman friend.'

69

She frowned. 'It was something else, Ben,'

'Yes,' I said. 'It was.' But I didn't want to talk to her about how it felt to hear the Belson grass, holding me in its thousands of gentle fingers, saying, 'I love you.'

'Come on, Ben,' Ruth said. 'What's the matter?'

I looked at her closely. She was really very good-looking. 'Well,' I said, 'sex, for one thing.' I bent down and pulled a piece of licorice grass myself. 'I've been impotent for the last couple of years.'

'Oh,' she said.

I laughed wryly. 'Yeah,' I said, suddenly feeling very relieved.

We had come to the rise and we began scrambling silently down the hill. When we were about halfway down. I stopped and let Ruth go on ahead. I stood and looked around and then up ahead at the enormous valley that stretched ahead of me to the horizon. It was as splendid a vista as a man could ever want to see. I drew a deep breath of the delicious air and thought with a profound historical thrill, as deep as my genes: if mankind ever leaves a shattered Earth to live elsewhere in the universe, it should be for Juno. This was a second chance as vast and breathtaking as the one spread before the eyes of Columbus and his sailors—those rapt men from the alleys of Barcelona and Seville. The hairs on the back of my neck prickled. Planetfall had confused me; with the heavy rain, the frustration, I had missed this thrill at the time, intent merely on exploration and discovery. It had caught me now, after my conversation with Ruth. I was staggered by this planet, its breadth and diversity—its beauty and life. A part of me had been searching, all my life, for a home; my bags had always been packed. And here it was.

I looked up. Two suns shone pleasantly down on my body. At night there would be a half-dozen moons. Everything about this place was generous, replete, fulfilling. I breathed as deeply as my lungs would allow, exhaled, and walked slowly down the rest of the hill, into the valley.

Ruth was off a bit to my right and I started to walk toward her, but then decided to stay alone for a bit. I walked to my left, toward a small field of mushrooms that grew in Juno's open suns. Ruth waved at me and I waved back and bent to picking, and after a while my exalted feelings began to leave. I began sweating. It was hot. I looked over toward Ruth; she was gathering the little red berries we had discovered a few days before. As I was looking toward her she stood up and arched her back and stretched. She was sweating too and the cloth of her blouse was clinging damply to her full breasts. How pleasant to see that!

I took my shirt off and began working in earnest, pulling up the little gray mushrooms, dusting them off, and filling my bucket.

I stopped for breath after a while and looked up. Ruth was standing near me barefoot, resting herself. Her hair was wet from perspiration. 'Remember what Charlie said about UV,' she said: 'You can get a burn from those suns.'

That annoyed me a little. 'I won't get sunburned,' I said.

'You're the boss,' she said. And then, 'Ben. I wish you weren't impotent.'

I felt relieved that she had said it. 'Thank you,' I said.

'Would you like to make love anyway?' she said.

I must have just stared at her.

'You know,' she said. 'There's a lot we could do . . .'

'Yes, I know,' I said, coming out of it. She stepped closer and laid a hand lightly on my forearm.

I was embarrassed. 'Ruth,' I said, 'you're a fine woman. But I don't think I'm ready yet . . .'

She looked hurt for a moment. She let go of my arm and blushed. 'Sure,' she said, 'I understand.'

I didn't know what to say. I felt like a fool. A part of me would like to try myself with her on a field of spongy Juno grass under the palms. I could be an effective lover sometimes without the use of the essential. It had certainly been a long time. But I didn't want to. 'I'm really sorry, Ruth,' I said.

'It's *okay*,' her words said, but her voice said it wasn't.

When we got back to the ship at first sunset, I found I was badly sunburned.

I had supper with the crew that night and they were high with excitement over the cargo, but I was miserable. I was painfully red and I felt foolish for letting myself get that way in the first place. I felt awkward about what had happened between Ruth and me.

71

I was halfway through the meal before I thought of endolin and asked Charlie where he kept it. He got up from his roast beef and went to his sick bay and got some. It was a little plastic cup of dried leaves. I took a pinch, waited several minutes for the annoying pain on my back and shoulders to go away, and nothing happened. Charlie had returned to his roast beef and to a joke he had been telling the navigator. When we had arrived at dessert, he got up and came over to my seat at the head of the table.

'How are you feeling, Captain?' he said.

I looked up at him. 'How long since I took it?'

He checked his watch. 'A dozen minutes.'

'Well, it isn't working,' I said.

'Give it a few more minutes,' he said.

I looked at him. 'It's not going to work, Charlie.'

'I'll get you some more,' he said.

I looked at him. 'Don't bother,' I said. 'Get some morphine.'

He stared at me for a minute. '*Ben*,' he said, 'you kicked it . . .'

Inside, I was as astonished as he was. As far as I knew, I had hardly missed my chemical euphoria since the trip from Belson to Juno, and yet here I was with my attention suddenly fixed on wiping out the discomfort of a goddamn *sunburn* with, as they say, morphia. I was not only astonished; on some quiet level of perception and feeling, I was terrified. But my voice was unruffled and I felt outwardly as calm as a madonna. 'Get me fifty milligrams, Charlie. I know what I'm doing.'

'Ben,' he said, 'we jettisoned what I had left. Remember?'

'I remember,' I said. 'But you can make it. Go make me some.'

The ship had a drug synthesizer. For some reason you couldn't make aspirin with it, but you could make atropine, propranolol, prednisone, and two hundred milligrams of morphine sulphate a day—enough to keep a heavy spirit permanently afloat.

Charlie shook his head. 'Ben,' he said, 'as your doctor I can't allow it.'

I stood up. I'm pretty tall and Charlie isn't; I towered over him. 'Charlie,' I said, 'I am the captain of this ship. You aren't making a house call. Get me that morphine.'

He said nothing and went and got it. I took the syringe from him right there in front of everybody at the mess table and shot myself in the throat with it, just like they do in the movies. Doing it I was outwardly calm, slightly theatrical. Inside I was astonished. I sat down again and waited. The fear went away. Euphoria settled over my unquiet spirit like a luminous dust.

So I was hooked after all. Part of me thought, with wonderment: if I was going to do this, why didn't I do it with booze back in my forties in New York City? They have spiffy hospitals there for the well-heeled lush, and a man can ricochet around with a liquor habit for years and hardly suffer from it at all. I had sure come close to going that way—close enough that Anna thought I was an alcoholic. Her position was biased, however; I was drunker than usual around her. Anyway, here I was twenty light-years away from methadone centers and rehabilitation programs and emergency rooms, turning my bloodstream into a chemical bath for my brain. I am at heart a gambler and I am drawn to the edge. I stood now at an edge I had not dreamed of visiting until I broke my arm in my puppydog rush onto the slick black surface of Belson, my namesake planet.

It was then I made the decision to stay on when the *Isabel* went back with its cargo of uranium. I would write out instructions to Aaron and to Met Luk San and to Arnie; they would start buying utilities for me, selling my six million acres of woodlands, putting me in the electric-automobile business and, most of all, into the business of selling safe uranium. The instructions could be sent the minute the ship got into spacewarp; they could get the whole thing started and when I got back to New York I would do the necessary tinkering with it. My uranium was in itself a brute fact; any bright student at the Harvard Business School—that training ground for fledgling swindlers—could work out a reasonable plan for making ten billion dollars from the *Isabel's* first cargo. There was a lot of rationalization in that; I knew I should get my ass back on Earth if I wanted things to go right, that you didn't send boys to do men's work. But down deep I didn't care. I wasn't ready to get involved. I might lose a few billion by not being there to decide whether to start buying electric clock factories or get into the highway construction business, but damn it, *everything* was going to start paying off like a gambler's dream when all that power hit the hungry world. There was no way to lose, if I sold my wood, coal, solar plants and shale oil convertors and bought everything else in sight. Anyway, I had enough money already. And the *Isabel* now had enough uranium to buzz around the cosmos forever. Meanwhile I would have my fling with euphoria. I couldn't O.D.; the synthesizer wouldn't produce it that fast. What the hell, I had planned *suicide* once, in Mexico. People do that all the time; they did it over the Dow Jones Average back in the last century, dropping themselves onto Wall Street like garbage, over margin calls. Reason would dictate that if a man is ready to kill himself he should try something outrageous first.

I think the crew would have been less shocked if they found I *had* slit my throat, when I told them I was going to stay. 'Look,' I said, 'it's nothing personal. I'm going to stay on until you people get back and I'm going to stay high on morphine while I do it. I'll kick the habit in sleep on the way back. I know what I'm doing.'

But they looked at me as though I had gone berserk.

The night before the ship was to return to Earth I went to my stateroom alone and had a thoughtful supper of veal and Juno mushrooms with a half bottle of claret. It was dark outside my porthole; none of the moons was in view. I turned on the ball recorder and played the song of the Belson grass and let a pleasant melancholy suffuse my spirit. I had a small power hypodermic filled with morphine sulphate near my bedside. It was made of glass and chromium, like a fine camera. The sight of it was a deep comfort. The claret's alcohol felt good in my veins—a shy, chaste sprinkle of euphoria; but morphine was more to the point.

I picked up the syringe speculatively, held it up to the light on my desk. The addict falls in love with the tools; I found the syringe a pleasure merely to hold lightly in my hand. Phallic. Soon I would force the drug into my neck, not far from the jugular vein, in what I had come to call the 'Dracula spot'— halfway between brain and heart.

I set it down for a moment. There was a knock at my locked door. I was startled and annoyed. I got up from my chair and opened the door. It was Ruth. She was wearing her plain khaki pilot's uniform, but her hair and skin looked fresh and bright.

'What it it?' I said.

'I'm sorry to interrupt, Ben. I want to talk to you.'

'Okay,' I said and let her come in. She seated herself on the edge of my bed and I went back to my Eames chair.

'Ben,' she said, awkwardly. 'We may not see each other again.'

That was a surprise. 'You're coming back with the ship, aren't you?'

'I don't think so,' she said. 'I only signed up for one voyage. I don't think I should be away from my eight-year-old any longer than that.'

I was impatient with this. 'I'm sorry to lose you as a pilot,' I said, 'Mel should be able to get someone else, though.'

'Ben, I want to give you my address and telephone number in Columbus, Ohio. I'd like to stay in touch.'

'Sure,' I said. 'Sure, Ruth.' She handed me a square of paper with writing on it and I slipped it into my billfold where I keep papers with such things on them as the names of Isabel's cats and last September's price of wheat in Chicago. There's a forest of random information in there waiting for me to broadcast it into my central computer in Atlanta.

I felt something else was called for from me. 'Ruth,' I began, 'it's a pity we didn't become lovers.'

She shook her head. 'That's okay now,' she said. 'But I don't think you should stay on Juno. What if you get sick or break a leg?'

'I won't get sick,' I said. 'The microorganisms for that aren't around here. And I won't break a leg in this gravity. I'll be okay.'

'Ben,' she said. 'It seems so damned foolish. You need to be on Earth, selling the uranium. Making deals.'

I was beginning to get angry. I didn't need this motherly concern. 'Damn it, Ruth, I know what I'm doing. I'm sending back enough instructions to keep my people in New York busy for a year. I need time to myself. I need to ride my

75

morphine habit, too . . .' I nodded toward the hypodermic on the table.

Her face opened a bit at this frankness. 'Are you really hooked, Ben?'

'I don't know,' I said. 'I love it a lot.'

'What's *wrong?*' she said. 'Why should a man so lively and strong and rich . . . ? Hell, Ben, there's so much *to* you. You don't need drugs.'

Somehow I became furious at this. I could have slapped her. 'How do you know what I need?' I said. 'How in hell do you know what goes on inside me?'

She stared at me. 'I'm sorry. But I think you're a fool to spend months on Juno alone. You can withdraw from your habit in a long sleep. You did it before.'

'I want to do it this way, Ruth. I'm fifty-two years old and I know what I want to do for myself. I'm not ready to go back to New York and start making money. I have a dozen people whom I trust to run my businesses. I'm on vacation.' I settled back into my chair.

She sat and looked at me for a long time. 'Okay, Ben,' she said, and stood up. 'I've said what I had to.'

I could see that she was really pretty and kindhearted and something inside me reached out to her. But I pulled back from the feeling. I did not want to make love to her and I wanted to be alone with my hypodermic. I held my hand out to her. I was shocked to see that it was trembling.

She shook it and left. There was ice in my stomach. Old, glacial ice.

I locked the cabin door behind her, picked up my syringe and lay back on the bed. I held the head of it to my neck, just below the mastoids, and gently squeezed the handle. Oh yes. Comfort came down.

And as my high settled in for the night a relay somewhere in my head clicked into place and my decision veered toward its real direction. I would not stay on Juno. It was not Juno my heart longed for, with all its abundance of life and power. Not Juno at all.

76

5

I looked at them all sitting around the table, drew in a breath and said, 'We'll activate the ship's coils at nine A.M. tomorrow. The *Isabel* should be in orbit by noon and into a warp an hour after.' My head ached, but my mind was clear.

'Terrific, Captain!' Charlie said. Ruth smiled toward me. Everyone looked cheerful. They had known we would be leaving tomorrow, but this was the first official announcement of it.

'Before you start planning your homecomings, I have some news for you that you won't like,' I said. I paused only a second. 'We are taking a detour by Belson. I'm staying there.'

They were dismayed and they fussed and fumed about it, I thought for a while they might even mutiny. But eventually they accepted it. We were, as I had said, in our warp shortly after lunchtime the next day. By suppertime I was in my chemical sleep. Twelve days. That was the time from Aminidab to Fomalhaut. It was taking them twenty-four days out of their way home, and I didn't blame them for being pissed. But there was enough fuel for it and I promised them all a bonus for the extra time.

When I came out of my sleep and went up to the bridge and looked out the window, there was Belson at about the size the moon is when seen from Earth. It looked as empty as the moon. I had awakened with cold in my gut and remembered no dreams; the sight of that planet of black glass sent a deep chill into my soul; it was all I could do not to quail at it and tell Ruth not to land. Where did these spooky feelings come from, anyway? I had never felt anything but love for Belson—even when it had broken my arm.

I steeled myself, shook off the bad feelings as well as I could, and told Ruth to pick a spot on the other side of the planet from where we were before. She was shocked to hear my voice. She had been sitting hunched over the controls when I came in and hadn't looked up. Somehow she had cut her hair. It looked nice short. She blinked at me and then frowned slightly. 'Good morning, Captain.'

'Good morning, Ruth. Find us a big plain of obsidian and come down on it. I don't want us hurting the grass.'

'Okay, Captain,' she said. And she did it. Within two hours she had set us down on the planet's day side and without even a bump. Out the portholes was Belson, looking the same here as on its other side. And my spooky feelings had evaporated. I couldn't wait to get out there and start making my homestead.

It took a week. On the first day we explored the new area just to make sure. There was a higher proportion of obsidian to grass here, but that was the only difference. On the second and third days I erected myself this shack of moonwood, with the help of five crew members.

We outfitted it from the ship. We carried out the little red computer that I use for writing this journal, four of the Nautilus machines, eighteen cases of wine and, from the ship's garden, an array of hydroponics. I have my Eames chair, a mattress, my books and a very serious voice-activated recorder for recording the song of the Belson grass. A lot of food, a lot of whiskey, the drug synthesizer, seeds and hydroponics. I am relatively happy now.

My stateroom aboard the *Isabel* was not much bigger than my bathroom at the Pierre; it barely held my narrow bed, my Eames chair and a small desk. Above the desk was a narrow bookshelf, and to the right of it a hatchway that led into my private head. Whatever Chinese had designed the head had placed things so that when I sat on the john I faced a porthole that gave a view of the Milky Way; the clarity of the view was, shortly after I arose in the mornings, breathtaking. Being in spacewarp and at an analogy travel rate of two hundred times the speed of light did not affect it. I sat on the can in the mornings and watched the starry universe.

There was a kind of anteroom to the stateroom, and it was

much larger. The Chinese had used it as a captain's mess and boardroom for staff meetings. Since I either ate with the crew or with one guest in my stateroom and since there were no staff meetings, that room was the ship's gym. During my long sleep I had been carried from my bed daily, worked out and returned; I had had the the gym installed next door to simplify that maneuver. There were five Nautilus machines in there; after I was awakened I would work out for an hour each morning and then shower back in my head. It was a good routine. It was good to be away from the Earth and without a telephone, to eat breakfast alone and then move my bowels and then build up a sweat on the equipment. I especially liked working my pectorals and quadriceps until they bulged and hardened. I still work out here on Belson and the machines are better; they have regular weights now instead of springs. But sometimes I miss that little gym on the *Isabel*; I'll be working away at leg curls, say, and my mind will go back to those days, to my scrambled eggs eaten at my stateroom desk, to the satisfactions of the journey I am still taking, into myself. Looking back on it, now I feel that my decision to come to Fomalhaut was inspired. The Belson grass and all the things that happened on Juno, even the dreams of my father's study, were important in bringing about change; and yet sometimes it seems that my mornings on the *Isabel* alone, my breakfast, my shit, the stars, the Nautilus machines and the sweat that covered my hardening body and the cold shower afterward were what really changed me and began to thaw the glacier that was crushing my soul.

Many middle-aged men can't seem to change their lives at all. The more scrubby and dour things get, the less rewarding the compensatory pleasures become, the more we tend to hang on and to fear attempting a new bargain with life. I felt that way before I bought the *Isabel*. The only thing was that I damn well knew my life was getting worse. I wasn't moving anywhere, and the price for staying where I was was going up. Much of this was invisible to me; but the same voice that could tell me to sell a company no matter what the stock was going for was telling me to pull out. Good ratios all around. Good performance record too. But time to unload nonetheless. Time to sell, move, get out.

I saw my father die. He was the age I am now—fifty-two. Somebody had taken out his false teeth and his mouth closed up like a fist; a sound, half gag and half rattle, came from somewhere inside. It was as though whatever soul he owned had shrunk like a handful of dried peas in a never-opened pod and it was rattling around inside him now. *Too late*, I thought, *too late!* He needed a shave. It was the only time I had ever seen him in need of a shave. Somehow for once he looked like a man, in that last grim spasm. The son of a bitch. That was his price for staying where he was. One long soul-shaking shudder and down the tubes. Well. If there's life after death he's probably avoiding it now.

As, come to face it, I am avoiding my own life.

Well, to hell with my life for now. That mess back on Earth. Isabel and money; money and Isabel. Anna! Some nagging voice in me tells me to feel guilty because I am lying on my ass on a barren planet and shooting dope. Because I am not *engagé*. Because I am shunning relationships. Because I have become asexual and detached. Well to hell with that voice. It's the one I ignore when I want to make money. I am going to lie on my foam mattress and listen to the grass when it chooses to speak to me or sing to me. I have been a sick man lately; I need respite. I need to do what I need to do to get well. My father decided to die when he was my age; I decided to come to Belson. It beats death. And I can go back.

And that's how I got to where I am now, tending the seedlings in my hydroponic garden, twenty-three light-years from New York and as alone as the prisoner of Chillon. The *Isabel* left for Earth three months ago and I fell into my routine here on Belson as though I were born for it. It has been a spare and nearly empty time and one my soul has needed. For some reason during the last week—I count by Earth time on my Chinese watch—each Belson day at twilight the rings have come out for about a half hour and glowed like a giant and perfect rainbow in the green sky. That is the climax of my Belson day; I feel the rings do it because I'm here. Belson's first resident. I take no morphine after ringtime; I lie on the hard foam mattress on my moonwood porch and stare up at the sky. Sometimes I look at my former sun, Sol. From here it

80

is an undistinguished speck of a star, and because of its distance I see it as it was twenty-three years ago, as I saw it when I was thirty and afraid of love.

Sometimes I fall asleep while staring at the sky. Sometimes I read by the light of a little nuclear lamp, or dictate into my red computer as I am doing now, writing this. I am never lonely here. Sometimes the grass sings to me. Often I lie on it, but it has never again said, 'I love you.'

As the ship left Belson, first trembling, then roaring and howling its way upward to and immediately beyond the clouds, great fissures appeared in the obsidian plain around me; the *Isabel* disappeared upward with an alacrity that was astonishing. I had never watched a spaceship take off before and it was spectacular to see all that power unleashed. The air smelled electric—some mixture of ozone and of the unburned residue of the *Isabel*'s solid fuel, used only for takeoff and landing. She had vanished from the sky with Ruth and Howard and Mimi and all the others aboard, and the smell remained. She would go into orbit, then go nuclear and, after a half hour or so, when her capacitors were charged, into spacewarp, somewhere both within and outside the knowable universe, shimmering, taking that nondimensional road back to Sol and Earth and her landing pad in the Florida Keys. And I was here alone, as far from home as a man had ever tried to live. For a few moments my arms and knees trembled. I was scared shitless.

I stood there and then I looked around me at the glass planet where I stood and where I had elected to live for six months completely alone. Alone without even the cockroaches famed for friendship with Devil's Island prisoners, growing their cave beards in solitary; alone without the consolation of a bird, a snake, a distant rustle of tree limbs. *What in the name of God was I doing?* What was I doing to myself? And the word jumped into my head as alive as Athena when she sprouted from the brow of the Cloudmaster himself: *masochist*. Ben Belson, masochist.

Oh, yes. The cat is out of the bag, the cards are turned face up on the dirty green cloth, and the Devil has come out from behind his disguise as Dolly the Chambermaid. I could have left Anna in a flash, with her rubber girdle at her feet. Divorce is awfully easy. I'm rich. I did not leave Anna, not for all those years of berating myself for being the wrong kind of husband for her. What a goddamned painful tango we danced. Well. You marry a woman like Anna when you're afraid.

Afraid of love. I might as well face it. That's the truth of it. I was afraid of Isabel and that's why I moved out of her apartment and into that suite at the Pierre. That's why I came chugging halfway across the cosmos in this Chinese spaceship—*Flower of Heavenly Repose*. Oh, yes. Look here, Officer, my name is Ben Belson, the celebrated millionaire financier, friend to famous and beautiful women, theater buff, prowler of the galaxy and closet Marxist. Big hands, big feet, big prick and a booming voice. And a big, throbbing, empty hole in my heart.

The day after Isabel got the part in *Hamlet* we celebrated with steaks at a neighborhood restaurant. Isabel was radiant. Her complexion was luminous against her gray sweater and silver jewelry, her curly gray hair. I was pleasant on the outside but inside sullen. She had three glasses of wine; I had club soda. I had nearly given up drinking a few years before, after spotting some handwriting on the wall about what happened to people who drank gin with their scrambled eggs. In those days I was free of bad habits—especially of fucking. I smiled as Isabel drank her wine and talked about how much the part meant to her, but inside I sulked like a child.

That evening she sat by the fire with a cat in her lap and a beat-up paperback of *Hamlet* propped on the cat. She was underlining Gertrude's speeches in red. I busied myself cleaning up the breakfast dishes, clanging pans from time to time to let my presence be felt. Fifty years old and often on the cover of the *Time* or *Peking*, a 'basic force' in world finance, as *Forbes* called me once, the terror of boardrooms and a mover and a shaker on Wall Street, and there I am in Isabel's little New York kitchen clanging the frying pan against the steel sink because I'm pissed and jealous. Because she's more interested in a play than in me. Because I can't get it up with her and haven't in the months we've lived together. *Clang* goes the pan as I set it back on the wood-burning stove, scrubbed. And from here in my self-imposed exile on Belson I can see I was angry with Isabel because she was a beautiful, smart, erotic woman who wanted me to fuck her. *The very idea*, I was saying in my heart, as I scrubbed bacon grease off that morning's breakfast plates. *Who in the hell does she think she is?* said that scared child in my mossy old rib cage. I dried the silverware with a cloth and could hear the cat purring in Isabel's lap. I wanted to wring its neck. Inside me an angry virginity smoldered, grimly loyal to a pair of miserable ghosts. I started throwing the silverware into its shallow drawer. *Take that, you goddamn knives and forks! Son of a bitching, goddamned spoons!* Isabel murmured pleasantly over her text, underlining speeches, occasionally stroking the big cat, Amagansett, in her lap. I slammed the silverware drawer shut and stated, with great control in my voice, '*Hamlet* is an overrated play.' Ben Belson, literary critic.

'Huh?' Isabel said. There was an edge in her voice; she had picked up the sound of a gauntlet falling. 'What's that, sweetheart?'

'*Hamlet*,' I said, 'is an overrated fucking play. It's too long, too wordy, and it has too many corpses on the floor.' I dried my hands off on the towel, walked over and stood by the fire. The other cat, William, saw me coming and slinked away. Those fucking beasts pick up vibrations. 'Nobody really knows what *Hamlet*'s about, either. That's a lousy recommendation for a play.'

Isabel marked her place with an ivory bookmark and then looked up at me coolly. 'T.S. Eliot said it's about a boy's disgust with his mother.'

That one stopped me for a second, but I shook it off. I was in no mood to explore my own psyche. What I wanted was to work on Isabel's. There she sat, content by the fire, happy in her career and her pussycats, warmhearted and serene. And here I stood with a rage in my otherwise empty heart and my big, calloused hands trembling. I got those callouses from chopping cords of wood, in fury, at my country home in Georgia, every time the Dow went the wrong way. Inside, there in New York, I am a complete mess, a bridge hand without a face card, a barren, angry hulk of impotence, a sick and furious motherfucker, and I say to Isabel, 'Is something bothering *you?*' She should have brained me with a lump of coal.

She looked up at me steadily before she spoke. 'Ben,' she said. 'You look ready for homicide, or worse. I don't want to talk about Shakespeare with you right now.'

A part of me recognized that she was completely right. So I counterattacked. I tried to relax my feelings into something more amiable. Plausible anyway. I went back to the kitchen —actually just a space along one wall with a small stove and a dish cabinet in it—and started heating water for tea. I looked at my watch. A little after 11 P.M. 'Isabel,' I said. 'You can get awfully snotty when you talk about the theater. Do you feel Shakespeare's something holy? Too holy for a businessman to discuss?'

The black cat leaped off her lap at that one. 'Ben,' Isabel said, 'for Christ's sake come off it. I'm not a Shakespeare snob and you know it.'

Something glowed in me. I had her there. 'What about that time we saw *Henry the Fifth*? All that talk you gave me about the audience not being able to feel the cadences.' I was standing by the fireplace again, striking a pose of sweet reasonableness. 'The fucking *cadences*.' I looked at her face. I could see I had hit home. Something inside me thrilled at it.

'Damn you, Ben,' she said. 'If you didn't have a bloody tin ear yourself you'd have known what I was talking about. Shakespeare was a poet.'

'Bullshit!' The fact was that I didn't know beans about Shakespeare but I did sense that Isabel had mixed feelings about liking him and being in one of his plays. I felt I had something there. 'Bullshit!' I said again, getting into it. 'Shakespeare was a middle-class Englishman and he sucked up to aristocrats and the only people he endowed with classy feeling were princes and generals and emperors. The rest of his characters are drunks and clowns.'

Isabel didn't even look up. 'And women,' she said. Then, 'Your tea water's boiling.'

'Thanks,' I said, and walked back to the kitchen wall with what felt like controlled dignity. Actually, my mind and heart were a muddle. One thing about impotence: you miss the clarity that comes after an orgasm. Sometimes it felt as though my unspilled semen was backed up to my brain and had short-circuited half the connections there. And what was there to do about such a muddle except to shout at Isabel? 'I hate snobbery!' I shouted. 'Goddamn it, I hate the way you want it both ways, Isabel: you want to be a Communist and bleed for the masses and you cultivate the tastes of an aristocrat. Antique English silverware'—I gestured toward the nail on which hung Isabel's safety-deposit key; she kept her Georgian service for twelve in a vault—'and antique furniture. You wouldn't let a veneer in the door. You wouldn't so much as set your pinky down on a surface that wasn't hand-rubbed by forelock-tuggers in a fucking English sweatshop. You're proud as a pumpkin of being a daughter of the People's Republic of Scotland, but the only barricade you've ever stood near had footlights on it.'

I felt a muted brotherhood with Shakespeare. *Way to talk, Bill!* I looked at Isabel and it seemed as if she were far away. Everything seemed far away. Isabel was staring into the fire, where my Mafia coal was burning. Her face was pale and drawn—impassive. Then she raised her eyes to my face silently and I saw something awfully, horribly hurt there, something that twisted me in the stomach and suddenly brought me back into the room with her. 'Why are you talking like that, Ben?' she said.

I thought suddenly of Lulu and Philippe, the two California seals at the Central Park Zoo. I would walk up there sometimes around noon to buy one of the four-dollar hot dogs that the vendors sell. I needed to get out of the apartment from time to time and I'd walk up Fifth Avenue, by all those empty stores and then, near the park, by the run-down apartment buildings. The park itself was always a bit depressing, its trees long gone to wood thieves, and the zoo was full of empty cages that nobody wanted to have heated anymore. There hadn't been an elephant in the place for forty years. But there were still some birds and an aquarium, and the big heated pool was still there with its two California sea lions. I'd buy my hot dog with sauerkraut and mustard and then go, huddled against that awful winter in my mackinaw and scarf and long underwear, and look at the seals while I ate. When they swam they rubbed their smooth bodies against one another in a kind of continuous 'Hello.' The love in this was perfectly clear and as easy as sunshine, even in what must have been for those displaced Californians a frigid environment. To say the least. Yet they were full of life and of straightforward affection for one another. Why couldn't Isabel and I, two grown *homo sapiens*, be like that? Why couldn't *I*? What the hell? What was wrong?

Isabel appeared to be on the edge of tears, and there was a grimness in her profile that moved me. There was old Scot's darkness in her eyes and heaviness in her brow. 'My God, Isabel,' I said, 'I'm sorry as hell. What am I saying?'

She looked at me quickly and then looked away.

'What do I know about Shakespeare?' I said.

She spoke quickly and her voice was soft and distant. 'That's not it, Ben. It's not Shakespeare.'

'I know,' I said, becoming explanatory now. 'I know it isn't. I don't know why I . . .'

'Don't explain, for Christ's sake,' she said. 'Just shut up. You're not talking to *me*. You haven't talked to me all evening.' She stared at me hard. 'Don't you know, Ben, that the things you say *hurt*?'

I stared at her. 'I'm sorry, honey,' I said. 'I'll fix tea.'

On her bathroom wall Isabel kept a hologram of herself as a seven-year-old, taken for her first day at Socialist Primary School in Paisley. She wears a hand-knitted sweater and a kilt and her eyes hold a look of anxiety. Isabel's father was at sea for most of her childhood, and her mother was as cold as mine. Sometimes toward the end of our stay together I would see that same anxious look in Isabel's eyes, in her early forties.

In the hologram she holds a striped cat in her lap. Something in Isabel's psyche had always drawn her toward cats, and when I moved in with her she had the two, Amagansett and William. I remember shouting at Isabel once in the middle of the night that I could probably get it up for her if she weren't so damned anxious about it and her saying, levelly, 'Don't get it up for *me*, Ben. Get it up for yourself!' and knowing with a knot in my stomach that she was right, I padded for refuge into the bathroom and found the two cats huddled behind the base of the sink. They stared up at me with pained, curious eyes. I looked at them silently a minute and then said softly, 'She knows *everything*, boys.'

My red Chinese computer also reads. I can set a book in its drawer and it will turn pages and read aloud in a pleasant, avuncular voice with a midwestern accent. Sometimes I do that with my library books when my eyes are blurred from morphine or I just don't want to open them. I set the drug synthesizer to make ethyl alcohol, mix it with grape juice from my garden vines, and drink myself into a near-coma while my computer reads the short novels of James: *The Lesson of the Master, The Beast in the Jungle, The Pupil.* I've never read them sober; I'm not sure which has the ball-less William Marcher as protagonist, but I know I see him looking like my father. Distant, lost in terminal self-regard.

I speak in this journal as though my time on Belson were spent in reading and thought; in fact, much of it is passed in the grip of an uneasy lassitude. For the last five days I have been incapable of action or reading or of amusing myself in any significant way. I merely pass time. Often I feel like a fifteen-year-old hanging around the drugstore waiting for someone to drop in. Yesterday I merely waited all day for Fomalhaut to set.

When dusk comes, the sky has a way of modulating its colors that evokes feelings I have no names for. There is nothing like it in the skies of Earth, no pinks and yellows to match these pinks and yellows, no blue-grays so somber as Belson's. Last night I felt a gentle suffocation as I watched Fomalhaut descending. As it touched the magenta horizon and reflected from the thousand acres of obsidian the suffocation was relieved and my heart expanded with my lungs and I became for a moment dizzied with happiness.

It is a terrible comment on the nature of capitalism that a man as baffled by himself as I can be so successful at it—that I could become so rich and so confused at the same time.

Three days after I moved in with Isabel the temperature dropped to eighteen below zero. It was November 1, 2061. All Saints' Day. Isabel had a matinee and an evening show and she was out of the apartment all day. I managed to get out onto the icy streets and buy enough wood to make a big fire in the fireplace; I spent most of the day huddled by it, wrapped in a blanket, reading a book called *Nuclear Fission in the U.S.: The Loss of Denver.* I don't know why I didn't find myself a warm hotel room. Yet something told me I should stick with Isabel for that winter, and I didn't really question it.

She got home a little before midnight, wrapped up in a heavy coat with artificial furs and looking like a Russian countess. Her cheeks were as red as apples. She blew steam by the doorway, stamped her boots and sang out, 'Hello, darling.' It thrilled my heart, grumpy as I was, to see her like that.

But a blast of icy air had hit me from the open door and I suddenly found myself furious. 'Shut that damned door!' I shouted. And that was the way it often went from then on.

Sometimes, walking through the park that winter, dressed in a parka and muffled like a seal hunter, I would hear Isabel suddenly break out in song:

> *I like New York in June,*
> *How about you?*
> *I like a Gershwin tune,*
> *How about you?*

Her voice was so direct and unaffected that the old child in me wanted to cry at the sound of it. We held hands a lot, squeezing hard to feel one another through mittens.

We walked every day, no matter how cold it was. Isabel is the only woman I know who shares my love for walking the streets of New York. Her gray hair glowed in winter sunlight and she would face the icy air with zip and aplomb; I think I loved her most while striding briskly up Madison or Fifth Avenue in December, seeing the stares she would get from Chinese tourists muffled in their Korean scarves.

Sometimes she would window-shop. At first this was annoying; it seemed to be the customary female dumbness. But gradually I saw that Isabel was as perceptive about clothing as she was about the paintings in museums. She knew a lot about shoes, for instance—more than some people know about life. She had a sense of the sheen and poise of a shoe and·eventually made me see it for the piece of minor sculpture it could be. But when I offered to buy she said there wasn't room in her closets.

Eating at restaurants with her was delightful, and we did it a lot that winter. I think I began to love her a dozen years ago when I first saw her eat *truite fumée*. She would cut it neatly with her knife, slide an ample slice onto her fork, push a dozen capers on top—still using the knife—and then put it into her mouth and chew with serious concentration. There was nothing prissy in this; Isabel was a formidable trencher-woman and her eating was punctuated with little sighs of pleasure. That was when I was married to Anna; I was backing a play that Isabel had a tiny part in. She had also carpentered one of the sets. I was taken by her intelligent face and her figure and asked her to lunch. Nothing developed from that meeting for a long time, but watching her eat made my heart go out to her. I love people who like to eat and don't get fat doing it. This woman ate with gusto and had a waist like a girl's. In the twelve years I've known her her hair has become grayer but her figure hasn't changed. I tingle now to think of that figure, to remember her putting away *truite fumée*.

We laughed a lot on our walks and in restaurants. We hugged each other spontaneously from time to time. I was delighted by her in hundreds of small ways. But whenever we tried to make love during those five months I found myself with a knot in my stomach and some old smoldering fury in my loins. What had been a happy afternoon of walking and chatting could become a nightmare; sometimes I became withdrawn and bitchy for hours. I should have quit trying altogether; Isabel herself told me I should quit, but I found ways to override her objections. I told her my sexual failures needn't upset her, that if she were really turned on it might help my problem, that maybe at depth it was she who was afraid of sex. For about two weeks I had her buffaloed. Everybody has sexual fears; I developed Isabel's like an impresario, trying to cover up my own.

She saw through it eventually. 'Goddamn it, Ben,' she said in the middle of a cold night in the loft bed. 'You're the one with the problem and you're trying to blame me for it.'

I fumed and blustered for a few minutes and finally fell back to sleep. In the morning I waked to see her sleepy-eyed and a bit grim-faced, and said, 'I think you're right.'

Things were better for a while after that. I left her alone and quit trying to act on every sexual tingle I felt—and I felt plenty of them. I slept better. But there was a lot of fury in me, and I felt it building. Much of the time I was good-humored and enjoyed doing what little work I needed to do—which took about three hours a day, mostly on the phone—but inside a pressure was building. I was becoming a time bomb, looking for an excuse to explode. I was scared by this and at the same time exulted in it. Living with Isabel and hating myself for impotence, I had become a sullen, angry, dangerous child.

6

My hydroponics garden stands out now in green against the gray of Belson's surface, alive against that bleak obsidian. It is remarkable what Fomalhaut can do to power a vegetable, more remarkable that plants bred to the light of Sol flourish under this blue star. They do it with chemical fertilizers recycled, and recycled water. Part of the fertilizers are recycled through me; I defecate into a hopper that feeds the system, and then add potash; I eat the same rearranged molecules over and over. Orbach would love it; it fits his thesis that my personality requires self-nourishment.

I find deep pleasure in seeing those lettuces and carrots and beets and asparagus growing in their plastic troughs. They cover a half acre of surface that for billions of years has been lifeless. I walk down the rows, encouraging my plants, rubbing their wet leaves tenderly, muttering to them sometimes, sometimes pulling a leaf of lettuce or spinach and eating it there in the rows, warmed by blue Fomalhaut, alone and happy with my vegetable companions.

Since there are no seasons here, every season is growing season; I am already on my second crop and am improving the breed. Why can't you just let things *alone?* Anna would say at times in anger. Well I can't. I don't want to. So I save the best plants for seed, sensing that the new spectrum of Fomalhaut is an evolutionary spur and that some of my varieties will thrive on the short day-night cycle. Luther Burbank Belson, prodding his bush beans into stardom. It has worked, especially with the carrots; I've never seen such big, firm, orange carrots. I had Annie pull out one of the nuclear cooking coils from the *Isabel*'s galley, and I cook my vegetables on that. It requires twenty minutes at Belson air pressure to produce a carrot *al dente*—neither crisp nor mushy. They are superb with Java pepper.

I remember now the pattern of sliced carrots on Isabel's white floor the day I cooked the leg of lamb.

It was the first time I had ever roasted a leg of lamb, but I hadn't told Isabel that. My career as a cook had begun for all practical purposes in her apartment; I knew how to scramble eggs and make a grilled cheddar sandwich when I moved in, but that was it. I started taking over the kitchen at Isabel's when I felt I had to create something for her and me, something elemental and sensual. For one orifice if not the other. Orbach pursed his lips when I told him that, but he didn't look convinced. 'Hell,' I said, 'I've got to do *something*. I can't fuck, and I'm bored with making money.'

'Benjamin,' Orbach said, 'cooking is a fine and creative thing to do. But it wouldn't be wise for you to pretend you are a woman when you're having difficulty being a man.'

'Come on!' I said. 'I'm not pretending I'm a woman. My mother opened canned spaghetti for supper. And complained about it. She spent more time in the kitchen drinking screwdrivers than she did at the stove.'

'Maybe you want to teach her to be domestic,' Orbach said.

'Isabel?' I said.

Orbach frowned. 'I'm not sure,' he said.

'I'm not sure of *anything*,' I said, 'except that I love to bring her coffee in the mornings and drink it with her.'

'Bring her coffee?' Orbach said. 'Who?'

'Isabel, goddamn it!' I said. 'If it was Mother, I'd bring her a martini.'

Orbach smiled wanly at that. 'Benjamin,' he said, 'as a child you had to nourish yourself, because there was little other nourishment around.'

I lay on the couch and looked at the water stain on Orbach's ceiling. 'I get tired sometimes,' I said. 'I get damned tired of the whole fucking *weight*.'

'Clearly,' Orbach said, with sympathy. 'I'd like to use chemical recall with you for the rest of our session today. I'd like to give you sorbate and take you back to your infancy and see if we can find out what you were thinking?'

I felt myself sweating. I hadn't used chemicals in therapy for several years. They scared me. 'Those pills pack a terrible hangover,' I said. 'I need a clear head for . . .'

'For what?'

'For cooking supper tonight,' I said.

Orbach shrugged. 'Very well. Perhaps some other time.'

The supper of which I'd spoken was the leg of lamb. I'd noticed it on sale that morning at thirty dollars a pound and bought it impulsively. I then wound up carrying it around with me while I spent a couple of hours with my lawyers, who were too polite to ask what in heaven's name I was doing with a leg of lamb in a plastic bag.

It took me awhile that evening to figure out the controls on Isabel's oven, but I managed. The combination of those electronic gadgets and a heat source of hickory wood has always seemed disorderly to me. It was a Wednesday and there would be no evening performance of Isabel's play, so I had plenty of time. I cut slits in the fat and pushed in slivers of garlic, then rubbed the whole phallic thing with rosemary and coarse pepper. I had it in the oven by the time Isabel came home from her matinee; she gave me a quick kiss and a pat and went off to take a bath. I was beginning to feel very professional about this meal. I peeled away at my carrots, happy as a clam. Since the bathroom of that little apartment was only a few yards from the stove, I could hear Isabel splashing away merrily.

After a while the cats started nosing around my ankles and looking pushy. It was time for their supper and I should have fed them, but I didn't. The black one, as heavy-looking as a bag of cement, began meowing in his choked way. The brown-and-white, shyer, looked at me reproachfully. *Get out of my way, you dumb bastards*, I thought at them, viciously, not wanting to say it aloud in Isabel's hearing. The black one croaked at me louder. I wanted to tell him to go back to cat school and learn to meow properly. I began to think I should open a can of food just to shut them up. I looked at them again, at their pushy, imploring faces, at their *insistence*, and thought, *Fuck you, boys. Your lady friend can feed you when she gets out of the bath*. They looked at me as though they

93

shared an I.Q. of 3 between them. I grabbed a saucepan and threatened them with it. They slinked away.

A minute afterward, Isabel came out of the bathroom stark naked. I wanted to take her right there, but I restrained myself. Isabel could be testy about sexual advances that led nowhere. My balls had begun to tingle at the sight of her and I really wanted to drop to my knees for a while and let the lamb be well done if need be. But I pulled back from the tingle and cut it off somehow. That, I should have known by then, is how you get blue balls. That's how you get into fights over whatever is handy—like carving a leg of lamb. I should have gone ahead with Isabel and let her decide whether she liked it or not; it would have saved a lot of grief.

Instead, I started fussing with the peas and managed to spill a third of them down into the wood fire, where they hissed at me in derision. I could feel the inanimate world gathering itself for one of its attacks on my person. I began to feel like hunting down the black cat and strangling him. I reached for the oven door and burned my hand. Instead of shouting, I gritted my teeth. Stoicism. It gives you blue balls in the soul.

But I did manage to control myself enough to get the peas into a bowl and then to get the lamb out of the stove and onto a big plate for cooling. It looked terrific. Very professional. I felt a lot better. I spooned out the carrots and circled the leg of lamb with them. It was shaping up like a sculpture. I was cheerful again despite the tight feeling in my stomach. I remembered we had fresh parsley in the bin. I got some and put it at one end of the plate. *Voilà*.

Isabel had pulled on a pair of jeans and set the table by the window. I was standing by my masterwork, waiting for praise.

And then my stomach sank. Somebody had to *carve* this fucker, and I'd never carved anything in my life. When I was a kid my mother managed to roast a turkey once a year, on Thanksgiving, with a kind of cold, hungover resentment. She always carved it herself, while my father sat around looking bored. I think that, down deep, I was waiting for Isabel to get up and carve, like Mother. She came into the kitchen, in fact, and I felt a sigh of relief in myself. But what she did was exclaim over how beautiful the lamb was. And then she said, 'Hurry up and carve it, Ben. I'm hungry!'

Jesus, did I want to throttle a cat just then! If I could have just done it—or just kicked a cat around the living room for a minute, I could have sliced up that roast the way an orchestra leader slices air with his baton. With a pinky sticking out as the slices fell with gentle plops on the serving platter, arranging themselves prettily between disks of carrot. But what did I do? I gritted my teeth, stuck a fork into the roast, took a big kitchen knife and started slicing as though the lamb were a loaf of bread. Immediately I hit a bone. I tried the other end. Another bone. I slipped the lamb, greasy now and still too fucking hot, over on its side in the plate, which was now filling with juice, soaking about half the carrots and giving them the color of wet orange socks. Burning grease was sticking to my fingers. I shook it off. Some of it landed in the peas. I began slicing at the first end of the roast, but from a different angle. There was another bone. How could a white, furry lamb walk around with so many goddamned *bones* in its legs? How could the bones be coming from so many different *directions?* My cheeks were burning as though rubbed with Brillo; Isabel was watching every move in tactful silence.

And then, as I stood ready to turn my knife against anything that lived, there was an abrupt, loud *plop* as though someone had dropped a fish on the kitchen counter. It was William, the normally shy cat. He must have jumped down off an overhead shelf where he'd been hiding since I'd scared him away with the saucepan. I stood frozen, staring. During my carving I had managed to get loose a piece of lamb the size of a poker chip. William took that piece demurely between his teeth, leaped to the floor and scampered across the room. I gripped my Sabatier, visualizing the mess in the apartment from feline decapitation. William huddled with his find in the corner, under Isabel's bronze urn of pussywillows. The black cat slinked over to join him. Clearly a coconspirator. I picked up the roast, plate and carrots and all, held it over my head the way King Kong would hold a subway car, and threw it at them with all my strength. It whammed into the bronze pot with a thud that enriched my soul with relief. The plate—Isabel's best Delft—flew apart like a comic-strip firecracker. And the carrots spread themselves over the white floor like abstract expressionism. Like the perfectly placed rocks in a Japanese garden.

But *Isabel!* The poor dear woman. She stared at me in terror, and then she began to cry great rolling tears of grief. 'My cats!' she sobbed. 'My Delft platter.' She ran into the bathroom, slammed the door and locked it. I stood motionless, staring at the carrots on the floor, at the chips of china. The cats had disappeared. I shrugged, got a can of cat food from a shelf and opened it.

We were civil with one another after that one, walking on eggshells for about three days. Once, for no apparent reason, Isabel began to cry while reading her *Hamlet*. The air of the little apartment was thick with grief; I had no idea how to cut through it. On the fourth day I told Isabel I was going to move to the Pierre. She smiled faintly and said, 'That might be best.'

It was early May when I moved out, packing up all I had lived with during the winter into one Synlon bag, paying off a few of Isabel's major bills—her rent, the telephone bill, the winter assessment—before I left. She was at a rehearsal at the time. When I signed the checks my hand shook and I cursed at it for shaking. Another goddamned unreliable member. I looked around the place, nodded with controlled civility to the sleeping cats, bent down to pick up a two-dollar piece I had dropped on the floor probably a week before, sighed melodramatically, and left.

It was a surprisingly warm day and I had my heavy mackinaw unbuttoned as I walked up Park Avenue. There was a nice sense of life and bustle, with a lot of horses and a few methane taxis in the streets and people bicycling happily. My spirits picked up. I began to whistle.

Half the people on the street were Chinese. By midsummer New York always seems to be a Chinese city, a kind of cultural suburb of Peking. The Russians are ahead of everybody else at heavy industry; the art comes from Buenos Aires and Rio de Janeiro; the political life in Aberdeen and Hangchow is far more lively than New York's; and if you want to make a really big business arrangement you go to Peking, the world's richest city. But New York is still New York, even with its elevators not working and a total of one hundred fifty taxis permitted to operate (Peking has thousands, they are electric powered and have leather upholstery). But Peking is still a stodgy businessman's city, with all the old China erased from its neoclassical architecture. The Chinese come to New York for the civilized life. New York is the major city of a second-rank power, of a country whose time is slipping away; but it still has a bounce you don't find anywhere else. There are restaurants with white tablecloths, with waiters in tuxedos that look like they came from the last century, and, however they beer-feed and hand-rub their fat old steers in Japan, the Kansas City steak served in a New York restaurant, with the dim lights and the polished wooden bar and the tuxedoed waiters, is still one of the delights of the world. And New York theater is the only theater to hold anybody's interest for long; American music is the most sophisticated in the world. The Chinese are still, behind those stuffy facades, the greatest gamblers on earth and the trickiest businessmen; they've accommodated their ideology and their asceticism of the last century to their present wealth with the ease of the Renaissance Popes; they are Communists the way Cesare Borgia was a Christian. And they love New York.

The Pierre is a grand place and I know its people well. I moved in there first when I was twenty-three and working on downhill mergers; the same man still tends bar in the afternoons and he calls me Ben. His name's Dennis. I always ask about his kids. He has a son in the wood business in North Carolina; his daughter runs the office at the Jane Fonda Theatre. The manager says they're going to name my suite the Belson Suite someday and I tell him I'm all for it, that it'll make it easier to get my mail if there's a plaque on the door. They always have fresh flowers for me when I move in. What the hell, something deep in me likes to live in hotels, to be ready to check out at any time. To live by the day and pay by the day.

I had an appointment that afternoon with Orbach, up on Eightieth Street. I looked over the suite, smelled the flowers, called Henri Bendel's to order my cooking pots, and decided to walk to Orbach's and pick up a few cookbooks on the way. Maybe there would be spring vegetables in, from the South, if the Mafia wasn't in disarray from its quarrels. I called a couple of lawyers and gave them my phone number and left.

Walking up Third Avenue, I found myself looking in store

windows, not at cookbooks but at clocks. I was doing that a lot these days, developing a fascination with timepieces, with the passing of time. I noticed birthdays as I never had, would remember trivial things that had happened on a given day a year before. This started when I turned fifty. I was becoming aware that my days are numbered, that I am going to die and rot like everybody else and that I'd better get my ass in gear if I want to live my life as Ben Belson and not as some fucked-over replica of my father. I know I've made a lot of money and fame for myself, have traveled everywhere, have bedded a lot of women and eaten a lot of the world's best food, and my father did none of those things. But for twenty years something in my soul has been on HOLD, waiting, going through the motions of having a filled and good life but inside feeling morose and sullen. And there, looking at clocks in yet another Third Avenue window, I was waiting for the time to run out, waiting to join my father in the underground brigade —to terminate, with the smell of wet earth.

And, realizing that, or some of it, I was seized with anger of a kind I hadn't felt in years. I wanted to rush into the store and smash every clock in the place. Instead, I went in and bought a Chinese wristwatch. I'm wearing it now, here on Belson. I am an eccentric in many small ways; this watch is the first I've ever owned. Now that I have time to reckon with, a voice in me cries desperately, *Hurry, Ben!*

Looking back on it, I can see that picnic on Juno was a turning point for me. I have become even more of a hermit now than ever before; but something happened there on Juno that moved a big chunk of the gray old glacier inside. In college I never sat around and drank with my classmates; if I were with two or more people at a time something became stiff in my soul. I did not hate people; I never have. But there was a coldness in me that would, to my despair at times, cut me off from my fellows. Somehow it dropped from me at that picnic and I felt an easy comfort in the presence of the crew that I had never felt before. Mimi sang 'Downtown' and 'Michigan Water Blues,' and I drank red wine from a passed-around bottle and lay back on that moist grass in the grape-flavored air; I would look at the faces of the crew and silently beam.

Sometimes between songs everybody would be silent, listening to the quiet, papery sounds of those extraterrestrial leaves blowing in that fruity breeze, feeling the rich, oxygenladen air on our cheeks. I thought from time to time of Juno herself, the original Juno who slept on hay and whose massive nostrils exhaled steamed horse breath into the Ohio night air at my side, and some of the deep old fondness I felt for her was transferred to this new generous planet and to the people, mostly young, who lay about on its spongy and inviting surface with me.

Yet here I am alone on Belson.

Still, I have my vegetables. And my morphine. The rings are out. It's time to shut off the computer that is typing this, collect the morphine from the synthesizer, and shoot up. I wish I could masturbate right now, here alone under the rings of my own namesake planet.

I first came to New York in 2025. I was thirteen. Aunt Myra had suggested I spend one of my high-school summers with her on the Upper East Side. I'd never met her. My parents sent me off on a Greyhound bus, telling me the city would help in my education. I bought my own ticket, and what Aunt Myra didn't pay for in New York I paid for myself. I had a large coal route in those days in Athens. Burning coal in home stoves was still legal, and I pulled a child's wagon around the poorer parts of town selling it by the lump: two dollars for the small ones and four for the large. My markup was 40 percent. I hauled that damned wagon up and down hills about eleven miles every day after school and my shoulders would ache from it for hours afterward, but I wound up, at fifteen, with a 5 percent interest in the mine it came out of. By the time I was thirty-five I owned most of the coal in America that the Mafia didn't. I can picture myself now on that bus in my white shirt and tie and with a half-dozen hundred-dollar bills folded up and safety-pinned inside my shirt pocket. Half a fried chicken and two hard-boiled eggs in a paper sack beside me on the seat until I had a chance to throw them away. A fresh haircut. That may have been the last time in my life I wore a necktie. Except for my wedding.

The bus was a coal-burner and there was something wrong

with the boiler; we kept losing power on hills. The trip took almost three days. I ate soy protein-and-gravy sandwiches at bus stops all along the way, and in men's rooms in Pennsylvania and New Jersey read graffiti of the rankest kind I have ever seen. I knew almost nothing about sex except that it had something to do with social class and that people like my parents were alarmed by it; those graffiti shone in my brain like neon. Many of them were illustrated, with low draftmanship but high energy. It was for me a connection, however disquieting, with an outside world in which things went on I had thought went on only in my own head. A couple of those drawings are still in my memory; they can still send a wicked thrill into my balls.

For several hours between towns in Pennsylvania an amply built young woman with glasses and dark nylons sat beside me. For a while she made bland comments on the scenery and on her job as a small-town video librarian; then she slept. As her body adjusted itself in sleep her skirt inched up her thighs. Oh Jesus, I remember those thighs! Those cheap dark stockings, the white flesh above them! She snored lightly, with her lips parted. At the first sidelong sight of inner thigh my joint rose with the mindless alacrity of a Marine's salute. The smell of her Woolworth perfume intensified in my nostrils. I had become so sensitive, so alert, that I could even smell her flesh in its genteel sweatiness from my circumspect position sitting erectly beside her. Erectly. I could have driven nails with it. I pretended to be reading a book.

It was midafternoon; there were few others on the bus. If I were on that bus now I would reach my hand out toward her open lap rather than my own closed one. But what did I know then? I looked around and saw that no one was looking. I allowed myself to turn my head slightly, enough to see what was now a dark hiatus between her thighs, parted and inclined toward me. I let my hand fall gently in my lap and in that moment discovered self-abuse. My palm, touching myself, was instantly wet. My blood circulation had become disorderly; I felt faint. The pleasure had been momentary but so intense as to open a door in my spirit that has never closed. I saw in a flash that my parents were fools and that the world had punch.

An hour later I slipped my right hand into my pants pocket and did it again, more slowly. It was ecstasy. To hell with my undershorts. I would throw them away.

I would have given my soul to slip myself inside what that pink margin hid from view, to have felt it grip my adolescent member. It did not occur to me she might have liked it too. She had said she was on vacation for a week. I could have taken her to a Hóliday Inn in some Pennsylvania coal town and we could have fucked ourselves silly. Oh Christ!

My Circe aroused herself from sleep, blushingly pulled down her skirt, and got off at New Hope, Penn. I never learned her name, nor what town she lived in.

Aunt Myra was my father's older sister and had always been a shadowy black sheep of the Belsons. I had not met her before that summer of my thirteenth year. Myra had clearly been around. I knew she'd gone to Duke with President Garvey, had played bridge with Kronstadt the demon poet, had written the lyrics for an operetta, was rumóred to have had a baby by her chauffeur, and had been the mistress of three different millionaires. The last of these had left her a small fortune in cash and an apartment hotel in the East Eighties. She had lost the cash in the depression of 2004. Myra, my mother said in icy reflection over a martini, had taken her financial advice from Arab astrologers and Roman Catholic choirboys. She had lost the apartment hotel but managed to hang on to the twelve rooms of its penthouse for her lifetime. She owned nothing else.

Aunt Myra was about sixty-five that summer. She wore faded bib overalls and walked barefoot around her apartment, smoked Black Russian cigarettes and wore gold-rimmed glasses over which she peered at me in a kind of bemusement. She popped vitamin pills continuously and laughed a lot. She was a bit under five feet tall—I towered over her, even at thirteen—and despite crow's-feet, gray hair and gray tee-shirts under her overall bibs, she looked youthful. I had never seen anyone like her. I arrived at her place about suppertime, having adjusted my tie a half-dozen times in the elevator. I was carrying my cheap suitcase. I felt awkward as hell. When I knocked on the elegant gold-and-white doorway of her penthouse I expected to be greeted by some kind of sagging debauchee with dewlaps and a gown. What met me was this pretty little person in overalls and bare feet.

'For Christ's sake. Come on in,' she said, peering up at me over the gold rims of her glasses. She held out a tiny unmanicured hand and I shook it. It felt cool and friendly and as small as a child's.

'How do you do?' I said in the reserved way I had learned from Mother.

'Let's have something to eat,' she said, and led me through a big empty hallway to a cluttered living room. But what clutter! One wall was covered with paintings and watercolors; there must have been twenty of them. Bright as an African stamp collection. Oriental rugs all over too. A black corduroy sofa. A half-dozen tables. Cats—six or seven cats. There were four cats on the window ledge, below high windows overlooking Central Park. It was a park filled with trees in those days. We passed through this astonishing room and into the kitchen. It was done in a spare way—Hungarian peasant, a turn-of-the-century style in rich people's kitchens. Crude ceramic tiles, blue and white, on the walls. A grass rug on the wooden floor. Oak countertops. A terra-cotta stove. But she had a refrigerator, the first I'd seen. In Athens we used iceboxes. When Aunt Myra opened the door of her big brown refrigerator I saw shelves with bright jars and bottles, fruits and vegetables, like a picture in an old magazine. What she fixed me for dinner that night was a thick slab of pâté de foie on Bibb lettuce, a dozen tiny cornichons and a glass of Polish lager. I'd never eaten that eccentrically before. Dessert was chocolate mousse. It was delicious. I've been eating it ever since, in extended tribute to Aunt Myra and her liberation of the spirit.

She handed me a cracked Haviland plate with the lettuce and pâté on it and then the beer in a crystal pilsner glass and I stood there stupidly holding it while she fixed herself the same. Then I followed her out of the kitchen, and it took me a minute to realize that we weren't going to sit down; this would be a peripatetic supper. I worked up the nerve eventually to set my beer glass down after one sip of the bitter stuff—it was my first taste of beer—and started eating the pâté with my fingers. Myra led me around the apartment.

She had four bedrooms, three of them empty and from which I could pick the one I wanted. I chose the one with the most windows. Its furnishings were all gray and white, and it had a little Corot on one wall—two old men at a table.

While we walked around she talked from time to time in a pleasant voice about the apartment and about her cats. She asked me about my father in a kind of offhand way, and when I said he was doing okay she sniffed and said, '*I* never could figure out that boy. He was always so goddamned *calm*.' It was strange to hear that and to realize that Aunt Myra was fifteen years older than my father and, from the tone of her voice, didn't care about him much. She was nothing like my father or mother, nothing like any adult I'd known. She may have been the last person I loved—and it was love at first sight.

That summer with Aunt Myra gave me a sense of the possibilities of a city that has never substantially diminished. I have forgotten the plays and ballets we saw, but I remember the marble floors, the high-ceilinged lobbies, the soft lighting at the bars between acts, and the expansive feeling to be in New York City at the theater. We saw holo shows and two museum openings and sky music concerts in Central Park. I remember elevators, before the Energy Acts outlawed them. I remember the lights in the upper floors of skyscrapers at night. And most of all, I remember walking down quiet streets on the East Side between rows of old brownstones, looking into the windows of brightly lit apartments, wanting to live in one more than I'd ever wanted anything before. I became a spiritual New Yorker while walking the East Seventies between Park and Second Avenue at the age of thirteen.

I also learned about eating from Aunt Myra—salads and desserts, arugula and chocolate mousse. My diet is a tribute to her memory. Myra taught me another thing—chess. After a week of shows and concerts, she announced that we were going to spend a night at home and entertain ourselves. 'Do you play chess?' she asked me, looking up over her glasses. In her hand was a plastic packet the size of a billfold.

'No,' I said. 'I play Monopoly.'

'Well, you can play that too with this thing. This electronic marvel,' she said. 'But a smart young man should know chess.'

I started to say that no one played chess anymore, for the

same reason no one ever did arithmetic: human effort had long been outclassed at that kind of thing. Luck games were what my generation played. But Aunt Myra was no dummy; she might have a point. 'Okay,' I said, 'will you teach me?'

'I'm going to roast a duck,' she said, 'and then change for dinner.' She had just come home from shopping and was wearing her striped coveralls. 'This will teach you the game. Learn it and we'll play during supper.' She handed me the thing. 'Unfold it on a table somewhere and press the red spot.' Then she went into the kitchen.

It was made of some kind of rough old plastic and it looked well-worn. I took it into one of the living rooms where a walnut refectory table sat by window, pushed a few ginger jars, paperweights and African violets aside to create a space, and then unfolded it. It turned out to be a big white square about the size of a Monopoly board with a red dot at the lower left-hand corner. I pulled up a chair, seated myself in front of the board, and pressed the dot.

The surface was immediately covered with print, like a menu. Backgammon, Checkers, Chess, Go, Monopoly, Snakes and Ladders, Bridge, Poker, Canasta, Casino and so on, were listed down the left side, with a red dot to the left of each. On the right, in capital letters, were three options: 1. RULES AND INSTRUCTIONS, 2. PLAY, and 3. OPPONENT PLAY (CHOOSE LEVEL). This last was followed by the numbers one through twelve. At the bottom right-hand corner, in gold letters, was written MYRA BELSON.

I pressed 'Chess' and 'Rules and Instructions.' The print vanished and was replaced by a large chessboard, with green and ivory squares. A soft voice from the board said, '*Voici le Jeu d'Échecs . . .*'

'English,' I said, aloud.

'Yes,' the board said. 'This is the game of chess, invented in India and modeled on warfare. It is played with thirty-two pieces, or *men*, as follows: Here is a pawn . . .' and the silhouette of a pawn appeared in the middle of the board. 'Each player has eight pawns, placed on what is called the second *rank*.' The pawns appeared, black and white, in their starting positions.

I began to get interested. I could hear Aunt Myra banging

pans around in the kitchen. I got up and went to get a beer before continuing. She had the duck in a pan and was slicing an orange for the sauce. I'd never eaten duck before. 'What do you think of chess?' she said.

'Looks interesting.'

'No sex and laser rays,' she said. She was referring to the kinds of pocket games people generally played, with 3-D visuals and all the screams and curses.

'That's all right with me.' I took a liter of Nairobi beer from the refrigerator and a glass from a cabinet.

'Enjoy it, then,' she said. 'But go easy on beer. You're young.'

'I'll never be an alcoholic,' I said, thinking of Mother.

'That's good,' Aunt Myra said, putting her sliced orange around the duck. 'Addiction is a pain for everyone concerned. I understand your mother is a lush.'

I'd never heard anyone talk that way before. 'She drinks a lot of martinis,' I said.

'Mmm,' Aunt Myra said. She took down a mixing bowl and began making some kind of dressing in it. 'I advise you to stay away from home as much as you can. Your father's a cold fish and your mother drinks.'

'I work a lot,' I said.

'Do you like money?'

'Yes.'

'Good. That's a start. You need a love affair.'

'Maybe.' I didn't say I was terrified of girls. Terrified. I also didn't say I'd discovered sex on the bus coming to New York.

I took my beer back to the table and went on with the lesson. Outside the window late sunlight shone on the facades of old mansions across the street. I thought for a while about sex and money and what Aunt Myra had said about staying away from home. I wished she would invite me to live with her; I was crazy about Aunt Myra and crazy about New York. I drank down a long glass of beer, feeling the spiritual warmth it gave my belly, and went on with chess. You moved the pieces by touching the silhouette with your finger; the piece vanished and reappeared on the square you touched next. The opponent's pieces moved on their own. The voice gave instructions and recommendations, and after a couple of

105

practice games where it showed me what I'd done wrong, I told it to be quiet and played against the board in silence. I was using the first level of the board's flexible computer—built, I suppose, into the molecular structure of the plastic—and on the third game I beat it by queening a pawn. I was playing at level two when Aunt Myra brought in her blue Spode platter with a golden duck à l'orange on it. We ate with our fingers and played chess. Myra beat me thoroughly, and gave me some advice that was a lot more helpful than the machine's. We played fast games until two or three o'clock in the morning; she won them all. It turned out Myra was a rated player and had won tournaments when young. I was hooked on chess.

I stayed with Myra six weeks that summer, and it was the finest time of my life. She was the zippiest person I'd ever met. I adored her. I could have cried when I left, even though she invited me back for the next summer. She gave me the chess set as a going-away gift, and I played against the computer at level four all the way back home. I never showed the set to my parents; they never knew I had taken up the game. As if it would have mattered.

I never saw Aunt Myra again. The following winter was the first New York was to undergo with no oil for heating. In February the temperature dropped to fourteen below zero, and Aunt Myra died of pneumonia, along with thousands of others. The world was getting grimmer.

7

For what must have been a quarter of an hour, I stared at the empty sky overhead where the ship had disappeared from view. This was months ago. My neck was stiff from craning, gawking at the sky from which humanity had just disappeared. I was the only *homo sapiens* around, yet it wasn't really a new feeling to me at all.

The cabin has a porch on it; I went over to it finally, sat down, and stared for a while at the obsidian plain in front of me with its field of Belson grass at a distance. The obsidian near the cabin is a grayish green, and evening light makes it appear blue. The sky was green, as it sometimes is at twilight. The rings were not visible. Fomalhaut was dropping toward the horizon. Feeling the silence I began to whistle.

One of the strangest things about this planet is the silence at sunset; I've never gotten used to it. Some part of me expects to hear the sounds of crickets and tree frogs in the warm air—or at least the buzzing of gnats. But the only sound I know of that Belson makes is the singing of its grass—those polymeric strands that go below the surface to some obscure molten intelligence at Belson's center, to some hot old chaos like my own.

I got up finally and went inside. The cabin interior had two pieces of furniture: the Eames chair and a big moonwood slab sitting on four posts for a table. On it sat the drug synthesizer, a nuclear lamp, a pile of plastic sheets, a stack of legal notepads, a pair of ball recorders, and the computer.

There were two large windows with shutters on them to protect me if either beasts or weather should appear, although I expected neither. The light from them was weak. I turned the lamp on low. There was a pile of morphine crystals already accumulated in the receptacle of the machine; I ignored it and walked to the back wall where a moonwood shelf was my kitchen and made myself a drink of gin and water, with a little lemon juice in it. It struck me then for the first time that the cabin was familiar. I looked around me. I could have been in Isabel's apartment in New York!

The kitchen was a space along the back wall and windowless, as hers was. The dimensions of the room were about the same. Where Isabel had a sleeping loft I had a sleeping porch. Aunt Myra's little Corot hung on a side wall exactly where Isabel had hung a Malcah Zeldis. For a moment *déjà vu* made the hairs on the back of my neck tingle. What was I trying to do here across the Milky Way from New York? Keep alive the memory of five months of fighting and impotence?

I sighed aloud at that thought and then walked across the bare floor of the room and out the door. I had spent a week building the place, cutting the balsa-light moonwood with a hot molecular wire and then fitting slabs of it together to make a cabin. Yet in all the time of construction it had never occurred to me I was making a simulacrum of Isabel's New York apartment.

I walked outside, going carefully on my gumsoled shoes, past my little cluster of wet springs with their purity meters and along my hydroponics troughs with their accelerated seeds. Those seeds were already coiling under the brown medium in the troughs, ready to spring up green in a few Earth days. I was feeling much better. I took another swallow of gin. It was getting dark now. I walked slowly across the green-gray plain, away from the setting sun and toward the grass.

There was a field of it as broad as a Kansas wheat plain, a few hundred yards from my garden-to-be. I walked slowly toward it. The surface underfoot was now striated with cloudy bands of purple.

After a moment I passed a patch with cracks. In the cracks grew endolin; I could see it there, the color of heather. I bent and pulled a pinch of it. My neck was still sore from staring at the takeoff and after. I chewed and swallowed the endolin and as I continued walking the pain eased. Wonderful stuff, when fresh. If only it could speak to the soul the way morphine does. The way the grass had done.

I stopped at the end of the field. At nighttime there is usually a breeze here; one had just sprung up. The light was weak, and the grass looked gray and silky. The sky was a deep emerald. I stood at the edge of the rippling grass, finished off my drink and said, 'Hello. I'm your new neighbor.' The grass waved silently in the wind but said nothing.

I stood there alone for a long time while the sky turned black and the stars came out. There was a pink light from the only moon up, off to my left. And then for a minute I was seized with loneliness. I missed Isabel. I wanted her looking at that black sky with me. I did not want to make love to her, not even necessarily to kiss her. I just wanted her with me.

I turned and went back to my cabin, had another drink, and played the part of *Cosí fan tutte* that was left on my recorder. I'd had the machine on the seat arm between us; at several points on the recording I could hear the rustling of Isabel's dress, there at the Metropolitan Opera.

For the next few days I busied myself making simple pieces of furniture. The moonwood came from an outcropping about a hundred yards to the south of my cabin. I cut boards from it with a hot wire slicer, much like using a cheese knife on gruyère, and then nailed them together into a chair and two small tables and a set of shelves. The nails were pieces of heavy wire cut in the *Isabel*'s machine shop and fed into a forming machine that gave them a point and a head.

Every few hours I would take a break from the carpentry, not because it was difficult but because I wanted to stretch the project out. I would shoot a little morphine and then go out looking for endolin. There was a lot of it. At least once a day I would go stand at the end of the grass and speak to it, but it never spoke back to me.

I discovered something important about endolin. I had accidentally gotten a few twigs of it wet once while checking the irrigation flow in my hydroponics. I'd set the twigs on a two-day-old lettuce plant so I could use both hands to tighten a plastic fitting. Some water sprayed the endolin. Later, when it dried out in the sun, I saw it had changed color, from heather to a dark brown. When I picked it up, a fine grayish dust sifted down from the twigs onto my hand and onto the ground.

The drug synthesizer has an electronic analysis device as a doublecheck precaution. You can read out the formula for the drug you just made. A person wouldn't want the machine to slip up and make strychnine by mistake. I used the analyzer to check out the gray dust from the endolin and found it was the pure alkaloid, just as Howard had written it down for me. The rest of the plant turned out to be mostly cellulose. So the gray dust was concentrated endolin. Very concentrated; its weight was less than a fiftieth that of the twig.

It occurred to me immediately that the stuff might keep better in this form. I spent a few hours gathering a bushel and a half of the twigs. Then I wet them down thoroughly and spread them to dry in the next day's sun. When they had dried out I picked them up a few at a time and shook them carefully over a large plastic bowl. Eventually there was a half cup of gray powder in the bowl. I checked it on the analyzer, saw that it was indeed the alkaloid, sealed it into a folded-up square of plastic, and irradiated it just as I was prepared to irradiate lettuce and peas for preservation. In the nearly two months since I tried that, it has worked perfectly. A three-milligram pinch of the dust, stirred into water and swallowed, will cure the worst morphine hangover in about a minute. There are no side effects. My health here on Belson is perfect. Ben Belson, pharmacological researcher. With a patent on this stuff, back on Earth, a smart man could get a 15 percent interest in Parke-Davis, or Lao-tzu. It's a business I've never fooled with, but what the hell.

So that added another project to my daily rounds: preparing concentrated endolin. The analyzer's scales have a beam, so that whatever gravitation I'm in, it will give constant readings. I now have fifty-three pounds, Earth weight. That's almost all the plastic bags I can spare. It's enough to cure all the hangovers in Japan. They can stir it into their tea.

What a narrow, limited life this is! And how it has grown on me, how I take to it so easily! I am not homesick and I am not lonely anymore. Or if I am lonely I don't know it. Sometimes I think I swim in loneliness the way a fish swims in water, unaware that it is wet.

In my third month I began to shoot dope in dead earnest.

My veins swelled with morphine and my brain became a hot fog, burning with euphoria. Sometimes there were nightmares. I saw in sharp detail De Quincey's three old women, constructing themselves with gold knitting needles, their bodies self-knitted and self-purled for me. One resembled Aunt Myra, but when I spoke her name she looked away. Eventually all three burst into white flame and I heard myself screaming.

At the start of the fourth month I stayed on my back in bed for over four days, until the Shartz machine's morphine reserve was gone. When I finally got out of bed I fell to one knee and thought for a while of never getting up. I might have stayed there and died if I hadn't been hungry. There was a large pail of water by my bedside, but no food. I hadn't eaten in four days. My stomach felt stuck together and my head was primarily a pulse.

I pulled myself up and slowly walked outside, like a sleepwalker. It was midday and I squinted. At first I thought I was seeing another hallucination: the plants in my garden were black. I blinked and stared and scratched my funky armpits. Hair came out and stuck under my nails. For some reason the soles of my feet were sore. It was no dream. My garden had died. Black as sin. I fell once on my way to the lettuce—my dear lettuce. The leaves were like huge flakes of ash and they became powder in my trembling hand.

I stooped to my carrots and dug three up with my fingernails; what was beneath the ash leaves were brown crumbly shafts with a sour smell to them. I sat in the center of my garden, surrounded by ash and bad smells, and I remembered lying on my bed in chemical bedazzlement and looking out the door to see a black rain falling from the lavender sky and smoke rising from my garden as the rain hit my beloved plants. I had taken it for hallucination, on a par with the three self-knitted maiden aunts—the kind of thing that goes away. It didn't go away.

I lit a cigar and continued sitting. My hands still shook but my head was beginning to clear. What I needed was a dozen raw eggs and a bottle of whiskey, but I let the cigar be my pacifier while I added it up. Clearly there was more to this planet than met the eye. It had pulled a fast one on me, with

111

its death rain. What would have happened to my body had I been outdoors during the rainfall? Would my skin have gone the way of the lettuce? Must I now escalate my imitation of Robinson Crusoe and make myself an umbrella out of what was available? I dropped that for a while and thought of food. The *Isabel* would not be back for months. I had four boxes of irradiated meat behind the cabin and two dozen cartons of dried food by my sink. There was a large supply of vitamin pills and protein tablets.

I had a frightening thought, bit down on my cigar and pushed myself up. I padded back to the cabin and then around it, to where the meat was stored in sealed plastic cartons. My premonition was right; the rain had eaten through the cartons, turning them gray. Inside each, where lamb chops and steaks and pot roasts had lain ready for cooking in molecular suspension, now lay stacks of individually wrapped hockey pucks—dark and shriveled and smelling to high heaven or whatever it was above the inscrutable Belson sky. I stepped back from the smell and stared upward for a long while with an Old Testament feeling, wondering what celestial visitation this perverse planet had prepared for me. In my mind were the words spoken to Job: 'I alone am escaped to tell thee.' Son of a bitch.

Nothing fell from the sky on me and I did not become covered from sole to crown with sore boils, although I was ready.

I thought of a fissure in the obsidian nearby and walked over to it. I grabbed a handful of endolin and crunched it down raw, without a chaser. The taste was bitter and clean in my dry mouth. Then I went back into the cabin, opened up my one window to let some of the bad air out and then washed my face with the water left in the bucket. That felt better, and by then the endolin had eased my head.

Along the far wall of the cabin was a long moonwood shelf with over a dozen plastic cartons of dried food. I took a deep breath and walked over, a part of me thinking that surely nothing could have happened to my dried beans and potatoes and synthetic protein. But another part of me knew exactly what was going to be the case. I broke the heavy seal on one of the cartons and lifted out a plastic pouch of what should have been dried eggs. Inside was a light-brown mush—a kind of compost.

I ripped open the pouch and let the stuff fall into my left hand. It felt like rotten leaves and burned my skin lightly. I touched a bit of it to my tongue. It tasted like acid. I shouted a Chinese imprecation I'd learned as a student and hurled the mess out the front door. The hairs on the back of my neck were prickling. I was going to starve to death, and soon. I was already four days into it.

It was no way to go, and I knew it. I went over to my Eames chair, trying not to think about my stomach and the way it was beginning to come back to life, and seated myself slowly. I put my naked and dirty feet up on the ottoman. There was a distant humming in my ears. I clasped my sweaty hands behind my neck the way I had learned to in the Great Orbach's office and played his sturdy old Viennese voice in my head: 'Relax, Ben. The first thing is to relax.' I concentrated on my scalp and forehead, relaxing them. It didn't work. I was tense as hell, as though I were made of stiff, vibrating wires. I looked across the room toward the drug synthesizer and saw a small white mound of fresh morphine powder sitting in its hopper. I quickly averted my eyes. There was not enough yet for an overdose anyway. I knew that I could, if push came to shove, make hydrocyanic acid—or for that matter nicotinic—and erase myself in a half minute. The modern world makes death one of the easiest things in life. If only it worked as well for sex, love and work.

I tried again to relax, concentrating on my calves and thighs. They felt in need of nourishment. There were flaky spots—my grim vegetable ashes in miniature—before my eyes. There was acid in my stomach. The humming in my ears grew louder. I remembered my near-suicide in Mexico, fifteen years before.

I was in my mid-thirties and so empty inside, so disappointed with life and with all the money I was making, that I began over a long number of sterile weeks to focus my attention on euthanasia. I'd read about it in *Scientific American* and saw a segment on it on a TV show. The new pills had been invented in Germany. Naturally. They were illegal everywhere but Mexico and Bolivia. The Life-Arrest pill put you on hold for up to a thousand years, as long as your body was encased in a box or tube. No refrigeration needed. They had places in Mexico to store you, tagged and ready for revival in the century of your choice. You popped one and you were rigid in three minutes, with no pain, no consciousness. The antidote was a brief flash of high temperature and a massive electrical shock in the chest, like the Frankenstein monster. If you didn't trust Mexican engineering—and who did?—you could be shipped back home in the suspended state without legal problems, as long as you had a birth certificate and some other I.D.—like VISA. There was a place in Brooklyn that would store you underground, safe from nuclear attack and the IRS, and bring you out of it at the appointed time. Nobody explained what course your resurrected self was to take if there had been an H- or R-Bomb attack during your sleep. Maybe there would be another pill and a glass of water on your bedside table.

The other pill was called Permanent Arrest, and differed from the pharmacopoeia of the Borgias only in its speed and lack of pain, it switched you off like a light bulb. Then they dropped you into the crematorium, or recycled you in a Mexican garden. It was the latter I had in mind when I took the train to San Miguel Allende. I had no interest in trying to resume my life in the twenty-eighth or thirtieth century; I would be happy to have my private collection of dancing molecules dance again as poinsettias.

When I got there a Oaxacan Indian in a blue jumpsuit showed me the storage chambers in an old pink church, with row after row of coffin-sized plastic cartons. 'These are our Survivors,' he explained, in oleaginous English. There was a name stenciled in dark green on each box, a good many of them were Japanese. *Hara-kiri?*

'What about the dead ones? I mean permanently dead?'

'You mean our Terminates,' he said. He led me to a stone undercroft lined with bookshelves. These were about half filled with what looked like coffee cans, a name stenciled on each. I shuddered slightly. What a small space to contain a person! What *compression* of a body that it takes so long to grow and age and get comfortable in!

'What about the others,' I said, 'the ones you plant?'

He took me up some stairs and out into a garden filled with flowers and trees, but my spirit did not rise at the sight. They were shabby trees and unkempt flowers, with a lot of insect damage and sunburn on their leaves. What a misuse of human resources! I decided immediately that I did not want to join that sad aggregation of cloistered plants. At least not yet. I would sweat it out for a few more years in human form and see what happened.

On the train back to Atlanta, where I was living at the time, I thought of how close I'd come to dying, and I felt relieved and clear in the head. I thought of how many people must kill themselves in midlife, by blade or chemical or leap, rather than give up their jobs or divorce their spouses or take up a wicked habit. It struck me that the thing to do was quit the job or slug the boss or whatever. If it didn't work out, if you really fucked it up, *then* you could commit suicide. I went back to work in real estate and took up cigars and love affairs. The real estate did well for me and I doubled my fortune in eight months; the other two were less productive, but they did fill in some empty niches in my being and I forgot about suicide. Until now, on Belson, faced with starvation. What an outcome for a man who loves eating as much as I do!

I lay back in my chair and tried to relax, but my body was stiff with fear and anger and would not let go. A part of me wanted to die and another part was terrified of dying. I tried to generate Orbach's voice in my mind, but nothing happened; there was nothing in my head but the fear of death.

And then I looked across the room and blinked. My mother was sitting near the far wall, on our old Ohio sofa. Her pink chenille gown was open at the top and her breasts were visible—waxy, shining with sweat. On each side of her, candles burned in Belson air. On her face was emptiness and despair. She looked up at me as I stared and her face broke into a weak smile.

Shockingly, I found myself drawn toward that couch, toward that ruined face and those breasts. Flesh of my flesh; that loosely tied chenille covered the belly where I had once dwelt. There was my first hotel, where I had begun as a coiled marvel of gestation. I sat and stared at her, feeling drawn toward her empty and lonely death, by alcohol and cigarette and self-hatred, wanting to throw my arms around her waist and lean my cheek against her breast. I reached a shaky hand toward her and then I heard myself shouting, *'Goddamn you, Mother!'* and I was out of my chair and running.

Where I ran to was the field of Belson grass half a mile from the shack. I stopped at the edge of it, out of breath and sweating in the noonday sun. I took off my shirt and pants, then my shorts. I was stark naked and covered with four days and nights of morphine perspiration. My muscles felt shriveled and my scalp itched powerfully with all the sweat in my hair.

The humming in my ears was loud now and it was no longer a humming in my ears. It was the grass. It was singing softly. To me. Who else? It was singing to me.

'Forgive me, Love,' I said, and walked gently on it. I looked down at my feet. The grass wasn't bleeding. I walked farther, out into the middle of the field, surrounded by song. Tears were streaming down my face and my feet seemed to be damp with cool oil as they pressed the delicate flesh of the grass beneath them.

Without difficulty I found the place that was right for me, the center of the song and the heart of the field. I sat carefully at first, feeling the soft grass like a living carpet on my bare body; then I lay down on it, looking up at the hot blue spirit of Fomalhaut. The grass moved gently beneath my body, pressing my shoulders and back, my buttocks, calves and heels with a delicate massage. I felt a sensation of rocking and closed my eyes. Fomalhaut blazed on my body. The grass held and rocked me. I passed out.

When I awoke it was night and both moons were up. It took a few moments to realize that I was not hungry. Nor was I hung over, or sore, or frightened.

It was totally silent around me; the grass had stopped singing. At least it had stopped singing aloud; I felt that it might be singing in my veins—my healed veins. I felt awake, at peace, nourished, clean.

Eventually I raised my left arm to look at my watch, and as I did so I felt a series of tiny resistances against my skin and looked over at it by the moonlight: blades of grass had fastened their tips to the length of my arm, and as I raised it they fell away. I was like Gulliver with those Lilliputian ropes, except the grass did not really restrain me. When the arm was free I looked at it closely. There were little pink marks. I knew I had been fed that way, and cleaned out that way; my beloved grass had drawn the used morphine and all its attendant poisons from my bloodstream and replaced that detritus with nutrients of its own devising. I was clean. An interplanetary molecular wedding had taken place while I slept and the chemical soup that filled my veins had been filtered, strained, purified and replenished. It must have read my DNA like a helical braille with the fingertips of its filaments. This planet was a sentient being and it loved me.

Yet if Belson loved me, just who had wiped out my food supply in the first place? For a moment a shudder passed through me and I felt like the awakened Adam, not yet aware that both God and Satan watched his moves and laid their plans for him.

Fomalhaut had begun to rise and pale lavender spread itself across the sky above me. *What the hell*, I thought. *I'm not going to die after all*

The feeding I'd received that night lasted me throughout the following day. I wanted to stay away from morphine but couldn't. Or wouldn't. I wound up shooting a half-dozen small fixes into myself during the day. I thought of taking my hammer and smashing the drug synthesizer, but I didn't do that. I kept the machine turned on and myself too.

I did nothing to clean up the mess my hydroponic garden had become. I spent the day mostly sitting on my porch reading *The Wings of the Dove*, getting fuzzier in the head as the day wore on. I speak of a Belson day, which is a bit more than nineteen hours. Beneath the fuzziness was a kind of panic at my need for morphine. The way to quell that panic, of course, was to shoot more morphine.

When I became tired I took my clothes off, washed my face and hands, and walked out toward the field of grass. Suddenly I became frightened. What if that rain should fall again while my naked body was stretched out to the night sky? I stopped, then turned and headed back to the cabin. I could get a bedsheet to throw over myself. I stopped again. What good would a bedsheet do to protect me against something that had eaten through the heavy plastic food bags? That had even gotten the food in the cabin somehow while I slept? It could have dissolved me then, in my morphine trance, had it been out to get me. I turned and headed back toward the field.

I slept on my back spread out naked. As I drifted off I felt the soft tips of grass blades caressing my body, sensed their penetration into my skin. They were finding my capillaries and veins, wedding my body's life to their own. The intimacy of this connection hushed my unquiet soul.

That night I dreamed of my father's study again, with the forget-me-nots on the wall and the silent ache in my youthful heart. I sat there in my dream for hours, waiting for my father to speak to me. He did not even look up from what he was doing.

Then, in my dream, I did something that felt monstrous and frightening. I willed it to end. I stood up and turned my back to my father and walked out of the room. I shut the door behind me. I was terribly, terribly frightened. I stood outside the room a few steps from the closed door and felt as though I were completely alone, fatherless and motherless, and I knew nothing. Nothing at all.

I awoke on Belson, with no moons up and the sky black except for stars, Sol among them. I was cold and I was crying.

I lay there and cried for hours. It seemed as though the grass were providing the fluid for my tears, that I was merely a channel for liquids that entered the skin of my back and my arms and legs and passed through my bloodstream to my eyes and then flowed out and across my face, hot and merciful. I was limp all over, as limp in my body as I have ever been, and the relief was like a muted continuous orgasm. It was a letting out of pressure that I had felt so long it seemed to be merely the human condition. I exhausted my tears. When I stopped crying there was no tension anywhere in me.

And then a remarkable thing happened. Belson's rings came out, glowing across the entire sky in vast bands of lavender and blue and red, a colossal rainbow to my tears and a sign from heaven. I stared at the sky's refulgence, the illumination this planet was providing me, and my heart leaped up with joy for a long moment. Then the rings and I both eased off into quiet darkness and I slept again.

I must have slept through the next Belson day, because it was twilight when I finally awoke. I sat up carefully, feeling the grass pull away from my body. Then I leaned forward on my face with my arms outspread and embraced the quiet grass. I held that position for several minutes in silence, and then pushed myself up and stood.

I walked to my cabin and smashed my drug synthesizer with a hammer, hitting it a dozen times with all my strength. I lifted the morphine from the hopper and carried it outside to a deep fissure in the obsidian that I used as a toilet. I threw it in. Then I made coffee, thanking Belson that my bags of coffee had remained untouched by the plague that had destroyed my food.

For weeks I kept busy. I cleaned up the mess of my garden and my ruined supplies of food. I cleaned the ash out of the hydroponic equipment, sorted through my remaining seeds —undamaged by the rain—and planted them. They sprouted and I tended them. I finished James's novels and began to read Mark Twain, starting with *Life on the Mississippi*. What a remarkable book! It populated my empty world for me. I read it twice, then set it down and read *Roughing It and A Tramp Abroad*. The lettuce and potatoes grew fast. My spirit remained preternaturally calm, except for the occasional fits of morphine lust that would creep up on me. Gradually I reduced my cigars to a half dozen a day. I began to work out again on the Nautilus machines and my body, lean from the lack of food in my diet, toughened up. I spent most of my time naked—since the air on Belson was always a bit above seventy degrees. I read in the nude and slept on the grass in the nude. I became tanned and my hair bleached itself to a very light blond. Veins bulged on my arms and legs. I felt that I was all lean meat, as tough as jerked beef and as seasoned. There was a spring in my step. I thought little and felt little.

When my lettuce matured I began to eat salads, even though I was not hungry. I kept them small and perfect, mixing Bibb and leaf lettuce equally and tossing them in the sunflower oil I got from my big coarse row of those enormous flowers. When preparing the oil I would recite Blake's poem:

119

Ah, sunflower, weary of time,
Who countest the steps of the sun,
Seeking after that sweet golden clime
Where the travéller's journey is done.
Where the youth pined away with desire
And the pale virgin shrouded in snow
Arise from their graves, and aspire
Where my sunflower wishes to go.

After a few days my peas matured and I would steam them a few minutes and add them to my lettuce. The salads grew to include onions and Kentucky Wonder Beans. I welcomed these additions, but Belson was still my primary nourishment. No words passed between us, but my planet fed me like the infant I was.

One morning I awoke from a night on the grass with bright cobwebs of sexual dreams in my head and discovered with a kind of awe that my penis was pointing skyward there in the Belson dawn, as firm and erect as it had ever been in my life. I lay there with my brain half asleep and felt strength radiating throughout myself from that red, erect, sky-pointing marvel: my loving member, my true self, risen at last. Great, tingling physical pleasure suffused me. The pleasure grew and I let it grow and grew with it. And then, almost in a swoon, I *willed* for myself an orgasm. Immediately I felt it begin to happen with that lovely sense of inevitability at the crossing of the physical threshold, and I lay there and watched myself come, jetting upward in heartrending delight into the pure air of Belson's dawn.

What glory, to relearn it. I relaxed and my whole body softened. I fell back to sleep.

When I awoke to a distant roar Fomalhaut was high in the sky and I saw descending, riding a bright silver flame, the *Isabel*. A moment later I felt the ground of my planet receiving her, with a profound subcutaneous shudder.

8

Clearly the *Isabel* had landed several miles away in order not to cook me with her retros. It would be an hour before anyone showed up at my cabin. I felt resentful, knowing it was time to reenter the ordinary world—resentful even against Belson itself, whose timing was remorselessly accurate. I did not want to leave this placental grass and the stillness of my present life. I did not disturb my physical attachment to the grass, and fell back to sleep.

I awoke to shouting from the edge of the field. The voice sounded hollow and the words were indistinct, but I shuddered myself awake to the world of men. What a pain that is! What endless complications! I wished intensely for a moment that the grass could somehow absorb me into itself and fracture my body into a million blades so that I could lie there forever under the sun of Fomalhaut and when the time came, sing.

The voices kept up. Clearly the crew members did not want to walk out to me. Finally I pulled myself upright, breaking off the connections on my arms and back with little pops, feeling all those filaments severing themselves from my body.

'Okay!' I croaked skyward, 'I'm coming.' My unused voice rasped in my throat. I sat silent for a full minute until my unease subsided.

Then I stood, slowly, and looked over toward them. Charlie the doctor, and Mimi, and three others stood by a green nuclear jeep.

I walked toward them cautiously. As I got near I saw a flicker of self-consciousness on several faces and remembered that I was nude. Wearing my birthday clothes, as they say.

'You okay, Captain?' Charlie said, with a kind of quaver.

'Did you find Isabel?' I said, hoarsely.

They just looked at me.

'Did you find her?'

'No, Captain. No we didn't.' It was Charlie speaking again and his voice was soft. 'Are you all right?'

I said nothing and walked past them toward my cabin. I could hear them following me, their gym shoes padding on the obsidian. They stopped at the cabin porch while I stepped up on it and walked in.

I crossed the room to my full-length mirror, taken from the *Isabel*'s gym. I looked at myself for the first time in months. I saw John the Baptist. My hair was wild and sweaty, and my beard was a bramble. I was all bone and sinew and deep tan—angular and as tough-looking as leather. The most startling thing was my eyes, which were piercing and prophetic—the eyes of a mad seer. My prick and balls were heavy, and the hair on my abdomen and my legs was curled like wires; my eyes were the eyes of some mad old Jew come straight from the desert with his brains permanently addled by the force of the sun and of Jehovah.

I liked the way I looked and I did not want to put on clothes. I had come into the cabin with the thought of dressing myself, but now I did not want to. I wasn't ready to don civilization with blue jeans and Adidas. I might never be ready.

I walked outside and ignored the crew members who stood there silently waiting for me. I walked between Mimi and Charlie, looking at neither of them, and across the bare surface toward my field of grass. I kept walking, crossing the field and coming back onto obsidian and then walking to another field. I turned back. I could see them standing, looking in my direction. For a moment I was furious and waved at them to go away. But of course they didn't. In agitation I lay on the grass and held myself rigid, waiting for its tendrils to take hold, waiting for the rocking motion. But nothing happened. There was no movement beneath my body. After a frustrating twenty minutes, I stood and began walking back, crossing my first grass field again. I stopped in its middle and lay down again, but there was no hope in me. I got nothing from the grass.

I got up and continued walking, a bit less angry and a bit reconciled, until I came back to the crew of the *Isabel*, still standing by the cabin porch. They looked at me strangely but no one spoke. I nodded roughly and went past them and back into the cabin. I got my jeans and put them on. I slipped my Adidas over my bare feet and then put on a gray tee-shirt. Then I went to my pitcher of water, poured some into the bowl and washed my face and the back of my sun-wrinkled neck. The skin was shockingly rough to the touch.

I ran my fingers through my hair several times, wincing as I pulled out tangles. Then I looked in the mirror again and lit a cigar. I was now John the Baptist, Chairman of the Board. I took scissors and hacked off some of the business at the sides of the beard, letting bunches of hair fall on the moonwood floor, watching myself in the mirror as I did so until what I saw was less a prophet than Ben Belson himself. Then I stopped, before all prophecy and mysticism had left my face. I did not want to forget how my bloodstream had been fed for two months, nor how my sexual self had spurted a seminal fountain that very dawn.

I stepped out onto the porch. They were standing around silently. When they saw me come out looking near-civilized and dressed again, I could see the relief on their faces. Mimi's thin features lit up and Charlie smiled gently at me, clearly glad to find me more recognizable.

Mimi was carrying what looked like a gym bag. She set it on the edge of the porch, unzipped it, and brought out two bottles of Mumm's and some champagne glasses. We all watched while she undid the wires around the corks and then blasted them out of the bottles like miniature *Isabel*s. She poured mine first and handed it to me. I held it and watched the way Fomalhaut's blue light sparkled on its fizz. When the others all had glasses I held mine aloft for a toast. 'To the United States,' I said. 'Hear, hear,' Charlie said, and we drank them off. The taste was strange to my subdued tongue, acquainted of late mostly with salads. The fizz in my throat brought back New York, the opera, and women with white shoulders.

'Well,' I said, 'how did they like our uranium?'

At first nobody answered. Finally Charlie spoke up, a little grimly. 'They didn't, Captain.'

'Call me Ben,' I said. 'What do you mean they didn't like it?'

'It's still on board.'

I stared at him.

'That's right,' Charlie said. 'They wouldn't let us take it off.'

I permitted myself a quiet explosion. 'Son of a bitch,' I said.

'The uranium was classified as a dangerous import,' Mimi said. 'We were lucky to stay out of jail.'

I could see it. The energy lobbies, and Baynes in the Senate. I tossed off the rest of my champagne and held my glass out to Mimi. As she filled it I looked over her shoulder toward the field of Belson grass and gritted my teeth. Biting the umbilical cord. It had to be.

I drank off the second glass of champagne and then I said to Charlie, 'Do you have a fresh cigar?'

'I sure do, Ben,' he said, and gave me a Sacre Fidel.

I nodded thanks to him and saw relief on his face and the faces of the others. It can be a cause of tension to find a naked madman greeting you right after planetfall. 'Still on board,' I said. 'Son of a bitch.'

'You'll be arrested when you go back, Ben,' Charlie said. 'The only reason we're not in jail is we had to come get you. They couldn't leave you out here to die.'

'Who's "they"?'

'The U.S. District Court,' Mimi said. 'In Miami. The hearing took a week.'

'Someone was on board the ship, with some experts,' Charlie said, 'while we were in court. There was talk of unloading the *Isabel* into a government warehouse, but the Sons of Denver started picketing. We were in custody awhile.'

'What about my lawyers?' I said. 'What about Mel and Met Luk . . .?'

'We couldn't even see them,' Mimi said. 'They were under an injunction.' She shook her head angrily and finished her champagne. 'I got in touch with Howard's lawyer and he told me there was nothing he could do. He said you were clearly in violation of the law. Then I got Whan and Summers on the phone . . .'

'What did they say?'

'They couldn't touch it.'

'Yeah,' I said, thinking, *Baynes got to them*. He would have plugged the holes. I lit my cigar. Things were serious. I was warming to the fight.

'What about my other people?' I said. 'I told you to call Earth the minute you got into the warp.'

'We did,' Charlie said. 'We sent your message to Dolum and Flynn and this is what we got.' He pulled a folded sheet of paper from his pocket and handed it to me:

PUBLIC LAW 229BR764 OF MARCH, 2064, FORBIDS BENJAMIN BELSON THE USE OF COUNSEL. FOREMENTIONED IS NO LONGER A CITIZEN OF THE UNITED STATES. HE HAS BEEN DECLARED A DANGEROUS ALIEN UNDER THE INTERNATIONAL LAWS OF PIRACY . . .

'Piracy!' I said. I have to admit it was kind of a thrill. I had grown a beard just in time.

But my citizenship! What in hell had happened to all my friends?

. . . AND THE FIRM OF DOLUM AND FLYNN IS UNDER INJUNCTION TO SEVER ALL TIES WITH THE STATELESS PIRATE, BENJAMIN BELSON. THIS MESSAGE CONSTITUTES A NOTICE OF THE SEVERANCE OF THIS FIRM'S TIES WITH ALL CORPORATE HOLDINGS AND ENTERPRISES ON BEHALF OF THE AFOREMENTIONED BELSON.

'Son of a bitch,' I said.

'I didn't believe it at first,' Charlie said.

'Let's go inside,' I said. 'I've got to pack.' *I* believed it. I had just underestimated Baynes and whoever was on his side.

'You know, Captain,' Charlie said, 'driving over here from the ship was . . . wonderful. Bad as our news is, it's great to be here again. Back on Earth I would think about the sky here, and the quiet . . .'

'Are you trying to tell me something?' I said.

'You could stay,' he said. 'On Earth they'll put you in prison. Belson is a whole lot better than that.'

'We could drop you off at Juno,' Mimi said. 'That place is an Eden . . .'

'Crew,' I said, 'I'm getting back to New York.' I chomped down on Charlie's cigar and inhaled deeply. I was making plans. I felt totally human again. I puffed the cigar and stroked my beard. 'Let's get my stuff back on board. Let's do it fast.'

*   *   *

Getting those Nautilus machines onto the jeep and back to the ship was a nuisance, but I wasn't going to leave them behind. I wanted to be in top shape when we landed at Islamorada. For a moment I pictured myself wearing a tee-shirt in Washington when I started knocking on doors. I wanted them to see my muscles, those whey-faced charlatans. Make the bastards walk the plank.

We got the machines bolted back in place in the ship's gym and I had Annie take charge of harvesting what she could of my corn and beans and the other stuff. It was sad to see a strange face as pilot, but Ruth was gone, along with her brother, Howard. The new pilot was a quiet little Japanese named Betty. She looked competent enough, but I missed Ruth.

After the ship was ready for takeoff, I told everyone else to stay on board and I went out of the ship one last time. I walked slowly over to my field of grass and stood by its edge. Then I squatted down and held the palms of both hands against the tips of the blades. I felt them touch me back.

'Thank you,' I said. 'Thank you for feeding me.'

The grass was silent.

'I have to leave you now, Love,' I said. 'I may never come back.'

I got up and walked to the ship.

We were strapped down and lifting off in ten minutes. I had my endolin concentrate in the little gym bag that Mimi had brought the champagne in. My red computer was back on my stateroom desk, ready to continue with this memoir. My head was clear. I felt ready to move.

126

9

We orbited a couple of times and then I gave the order to slip into warp. I began formulating messages to Earth in my head as the universe outside the portholes began to wrinkle.

Warp travel is a weird business, and although the physics of it doesn't defy comprehension it does transfix it. Trying to picture it can glaze your eyes as speedily as three martinis on an empty stomach. It's a matter of pressuring your vehicle into a place where the effects of movement are grossly exaggerated. Seven-league boots. It's called 'analogy travel' by some. When you're doing it there's a side effect that makes message-sending fast and easy; there's no speed-of-light limit because messages don't *travel* from or into spacewarp; they are, in a sense, already *there*.

From Belson there were the regular Einstein limits to contend with. I didn't even have a radio. It would take twenty-three years for an FM 'I love you, Isabel' to have gotten to New York, and another twenty-three for a geriatric 'Too late, Ben' to come back. Like impotence, only worse.

When we were settled into the warp and the sense of no-time and loose space began to come down on us like the lull at the end of a party, Charlie asked me if I wanted to log the trip in chemical sleep.

'No, Charlie,' I said. 'Let's make this flight on coffee.'

My first message was to Isabel's old address:

HONEY, I'VE BEEN A SON OF A BITCH. I'M SORRY. I LOVE YOU. WILL YOU MARRY ME?

BEN

That felt good even though it had little hope of reaching

her. Then I sent one to a friend in Chicago and told him to telephone Arnie my lawyer at his home:

TELL MEL DOLUM I WANT MY CITIZENSHIP BACK. I WANT HIM TO REPRESENT ME AND IF HE CAN'T I WANT HIM TO GET ME A LAWYER WHO CAN. TELL HIM TO CALL BELSON ENTERPRISES IN PEKING AND HAVE THEM SEND INFORMATION ABOUT THE LAWS OF PIRACY AND HOW I CAN GET TO BE A CITIZEN AGAIN.

The messages were sent scrambled. I had left decoders with the friend in Chicago, with Isabel, and with my brokers, to keep messages private in case I wanted to transmit buy-and-sell orders or do business in general.

I sent a few more messages on the line of the one to Arnie, trying to find out about my bank accounts and how long it would take to get the uranium unloading problem solved. After about twenty hours my first reply came:

MISS CRAWFORD NO LONGER AT THIS ADDRESS.

Well. What had I expected? I sent a message to Aaron, my accountant, telling him to try finding her for me.

Then I got a reply from Mel:

SORRY, BEN. I CAN'T HELP. THEY'LL DISBAR ME IF I ADVISE YOU.

I smashed my Spode coffee cup on the deck when I read that one.

And right away this came in:

THE ISABEL IS FORBIDDEN TO LAND AT THE ISLAMORADA SPACEPORT BECAUSE OF HAZARDOUS CONDITIONS. REPEAT: DO NOT LAND AT ISLAMORADA.

The sons of bitches. I added forty pounds to the spring tension of the Nautilus double shoulder machine, strapped myself in and heaved against a hundred-sixty-pound drag thirty times. Goddamn, I'm strong when I'm pissed. My muscles bulged beautifully. I felt ready for violence.

By the time we came out of the warp and could see Sol the size of a dollar in the ports from the bridge, I had received a greater accumulation of negative messages than Moses had on Sinai. All of my bank accounts were under court seizure. My apartment was sealed off and barricaded. There was a contingent of mounted police on round-the-clock vigil at Islamorada to arrest me if I landed there. Anna was suing for more alimony. My house in Georgia had been burned to the red clay under it by outraged conservationists. The U.S. Public Health Service and the Narcotics Bureau had warrants out for me as a dangerous drug addict. Isabel had gone to London in *Hamlet* in the company of the young actor who played Laertes. (I thought of trying to negotiate a Mafia hit on him when we got in orbit. It would have been a first.) *Hamlet* had closed in London; Isabel had left no address. My safe-deposit boxes, stock and bond certificates, and Aunt Myra's set of Haviland china were all under government seals. As far as my legal status was concerned, any thug could probably knife me on the streets and not be prosecuted. Belson Enterprises in Peking, Belson Ltd. in Montreal, and Belson and Co. in New York were all shut down and their directors strapped by court orders. My wood lots stood idle. My car had been sold. The Pierre couldn't take me.

'Let's go into an orbit,' I said to Betty. 'East to west.' She bobbed her head down over the console and began punching figures in. 'I want to make a few passes over New York and Los Angeles while I decide where to set down.'

Don't ever trim your beard in free fall. While we were getting into orbit I grabbed a pair of scissors and tried it. It was like leveling a table by sawing the legs: I wound up with a lopsided effect, but stopped in time.

We circled at a hundred twenty miles up; it was nighttime in North America, and although there was little cloud cover it was shocking how few lights there were to see, compared with the photographs taken fifty years ago from the weapons carriers and spacelabs that used to coast around up there. You could barely make out New York, Chicago and Los Angeles; they looked like small towns. Well, they were on their way to *being* small towns.

I sat at one of the tables on the bridge puffing a cigar and watching a dark North America go by, saw the penumbra of dawn over the Pacific and then morning and then noon over Australia and South China. What a lovely blue ball that Earth is! You can't beat it for a place to live. Even with all those bastards down there trying to do me in.

After our fourth orbit I made my decision. 'Betty,' I said, 'can you find Washington and bring us down there?'

She didn't look up from the console. 'Washington, D.C.?'

'Yes.'

'Certainly, Captain. On the White House lawn?'

'We don't want that kind of attention. How bad a hole would the *Isabel* make in a football field?'

'Pretty bad. More crater than hole.'

I thought about that for a minute. 'If there's anybody there—a night football game or something—can you change your mind and pull back up into orbit?'

She turned her rice-paper face up to me and said, 'Are you out of your *mind*, Captain?'

'I was afraid of that.' I looked at my watch. August 23, a little past midnight. Well, there wouldn't be any ball games. 'Get out your Washington map and bring us down in Aynsley Field. How long will it take?'

'One hour twenty-three minutes after we leave orbit.'

She was very sharp. 'How many G's?'

'Twelve at maximum, for thirty seconds.'

'Okay,' I said. 'Let's do it after one more time around. I've got some things to pack.'

'Yes sir, Captain.'

Bill put Washington into the course console and brought a map of the city onto the screen. He turned lacquered knobs. The two coordinate lines appeared and jiggled a bit and then settled on a black rectangle not far from the Congressional Shelter Complex. Then he pushed a lever in slowly and the map expanded until the rectangles filled the screen and the outlines of Aynsley Field were recognizable. You could see the grid lines of the football field, and the end zones. He gripped a handle and a clear black dot appeared on the screen; he twisted the handle, pushed it forward and the dot found the center of the field. Then he threw the 'Lock' switch and the dot locked itself in place. 'All set, Betty,' he said.

Betty threw a couple of switches and said, 'We have our trajectory, Captain, and our atmosphere entry point.'

I really loved all this. Like Ruth, I'd watched spaceship shows on TV as a kid. Even though the actual doing of it—determining a point to drop out of orbit and a trajectory to ride down on—was no more difficult than getting a manicure, there was *panache* to it. Especially with our bright-red Chinese equipment.

I flipped on the intercom. 'This is the Captain. We'll drop out of orbit next time around, in about two hours. Tie everything down for twelve G's.' Then I drew a breath. 'I'll be the first person off the ship, and I'm going to run for it. You people are all still citizens and they won't give you too hard a time. I'm the one they want. I'll get you your salaries and bonuses as soon as I'm able. For God's sake don't tell anyone we've been to Aminidab. The important thing is to get the uranium out of here. We'll all be rich. I'll be in touch.'

The endolin packets were still in Mimi's gym bag in my stateroom. The gym had a first-aid cabinet; I got a handful of big stretch-Synlon bandages out and, winding them around myself, managed to tape about eight pounds of concentrated endolin to my chest and two or three pounds to each arm. Enough for all the hangovers in Los Angeles. I left my legs free, for running.

Surprise was clearly the thing. They would be expecting me, but they'd be expecting a middle-aged, potbellied billionaire like one of those Texas fatties. Hell, *past* middle age; I turned fifty-three the day before we landed.

They'd know I was there and they'd have a half hour to be ready. Their radar would have picked up the *Isabel* even before we entered our orbit, but they had no way of knowing where I'd try to set down. Once we left orbit, it would take about three minutes for them to get a fix on our trajectory and conclude I was coming down over Washington; that was the scary part for me, since Washington sure had the wherewithal to blow the *Isabel* out of the sky as if she were an ICBM hot from Aberdeen. That was unlikely, though, since they weren't dumb enough to think I'd attack the United States. What they would do, in the half hour they had after they'd figured we'd come down at Aynsley Field, would be to surround the ship with military police, wait for the landing area to cool, and arrest me. Then into the Chateau d'If with me, while Baynes and his cronies figured out what to do with my uranium.

Thinking all this out calmed my spirit immensely. With a

few minutes left before touchdown, the G forces had leveled off. I got out of my landing seat, grabbed the scissors and finished trimming my beard, steady as a rock this time. By then the touchdown counter had started and a red light was blinking over the mirror in the head where I'd been doing this barbering. I set the scissors down, got back into my chair and belted myself in with about three seconds to spare before the *Isabel* burned herself into Aynsley's midfield. I could see nothing through the porthole; rippling heat from our retros crimped the outside air. Suddenly the shudder of the landing began to massage my spine like a demon chiropractor, yet the effect was soothing. I literally *felt* the *Isabel* burn her way twenty feet into topsoil and bedrock like a white-hot coin dropped onto butter. She trembled, gave a sigh, settled in, and came to rest back on the planet where she was made— where we were all made.

I undid my belt and lit a cigar. I looked out the stateroom window and son of a bitch if I didn't see a goalpost! Judging by the distance, Betty must have brought us down right on the fifty-yard line. What an encouraging thing for a first sight on Earth in nine months! What an emblem for my plans! Ben Belson, broken-field runner. I bent over and retied my shoes. Outside, the ground was smoking; there were spotlights bearing down on us and smoke rose foggily into the beams.

The *Isabel* has two exit hatches. On Belson and Juno, where low gravity and a hard surface had made for less devastating set-downs, we could merely walk out the bottom one, and down a short stairway to the terrain. But for landings like this there was a hatchway thirty feet up, just off the mess hall. And the *Isabel*, being Chinese, had a special gimmick; I was counting on it to add to the surprise. I'd studied spaceships before buying this one and knew that a U.S. or Russian craft might have to wait eight hours for the ground to cool after Betty's hot-pilot landing, before anybody tried getting out and walking. But the *Isabel* had a foldout, magnesium-alloy footbridge that could arch its way over the hot circle of earth the engines had made; it could be sent out thirty feet away from the upper hatch. The only thing was I'd never tested it. On the blueprints it looked flimsy. And I'm no compact Chinese astronaut.

There was no time to sit agonizing about that one. I checked the tapes that held the endolin to my body, made sure I had my billfold, which held exactly forty dollars, some credit cards and a photograph. I patted the pocket of my plaid lumberjack shirt, my basic space-travel shirt; there were three cigars and a lighter. I checked my wristwatch; it was 2:43 A.M., Wednesday. August 23, 2064. I left my cabin, chugging with adrenalin, and scrambled up the ladder to the messroom. The hatchway was just past the dining table.

There was a porthole in the door about a foot across; I had to stoop to look out. There wasn't much to be seen: white vapor rising from the ground, and searchlights. Near the door-release handle was a switch that controlled the foot-bridge. I flipped its safety off, took a breath, and pulled it. A servo motor began whirring. I looked out the porthole again but could see nothing. The glass had steamed over. I waited, chomping my cigar and feeling my heart beat like a rubber mallet, until the whirring stopped. I grabbed the lug wheel in both hands and spun it. The hatchway lugs pulled in and there was a hiss as the Belson pressure inside the ship equalized with the 14.7 Earth pressure; I could feel warm Earth air rushing in to mingle. I heaved the hatchway open into the breeze; some papers on the table behind me rippled and swooshed to the deck. I looked out. Searchlights. Warm night air. *Earth!* I looked down. There was my narrow, shiny bridge, looking as if made of aluminum foil, as if the weight of a teddy bear would collapse it. Up ahead were lights, steam, the shadows of some kind of equipment. I stuck my head out and looked straight down, to one side of the bridge. Heat from molten ground hit my face. A siren was going somewhere in the distance. Right at the base of the ship was the rim of a serious crater; it actually glowed with a muted crimson. Black, acrid smoke was rising from it. It looked like Dante's hell and smelled like it too. I pulled my head back in the doorway, took a deep breath, and hit the bridge running. It swayed and bobbed sickeningly under my feet. I could hear it creak; a vision of myself being dropped into liquid stone pierced my mind like a spear. I ran on, trying to soften the pounding of my Adidas. Halfway across I looked up ahead. I could see the end of the bridge, swaying from side to side. The

133

fucker had never lowered itself on the turf! It was about fifteen feet above the ground! For a moment I almost turned to go back aboard the *Isabel*, to wait till everything cooled. But if I did there would be at least four men with adamant-steel handcuffs to hold me till the warrants arrived. To hell with that. I did not want to continue my spiritual growth in a federal prison. I kept on going. At a distance I heard someone shouting, but I could see no one. Past the midmark on that Japanese Garden bridgeway my weight started pushing it down. It fell about three feet and stuck, jarring the teeth in my jaws and vibrating like a drumhead. I could feel heat from the walking surface penetrating the soles of my shoes; if I stood there long my feet would start cooking. Life gets that way at times. *The wise man profits from the hot foot.* I was thinking like a fortune-cookie, but I'll stick by it still. I ran on to the end of the bridge, stopped, and began to jump up and down, shouting, 'Goddamn you, you Chinese puzzle, you fucking aluminum chopstick! Get your ass *down.'* *Thump, thump!* It was like Anna taking off her girdle. That goddamned thing! And hot as blazes by now too. The sirens got louder. The bridge dropped another couple of feet and stuck again. I saw two men in uniform suddenly emerge from the shadows below me, looking up puzzled. A searchlight fanned across my chest and face. What the hell. I jumped.

I landed on what must have been Astroturf, fell forward, and rolled. No pain, The surface felt springy, a little like Belson grass. I sat for a moment and shook my addled brains clear. In front of me was a goalpost! I had landed in the end zone! Six points. From my right the two men were approaching me. They were about ten feet away. Cops. But no guns—or none in sight. They seemed a bit dumbfounded. I stood up, looked quickly around. Lots of bleachers. To one side were a couple of trucks, one of which had headlights pointing toward me. Clearly the Army, since only the Army had trucks. Some women with rifles stood by them. Near them were men in business suits. No one was moving in my direction. They were all just watching the show.

The cops walked up, a little more composed by now. One of them came very close to me and put his face in mine. I suddenly realized I was still smoking my cigar, had held it in my teeth through the whole jump, tumble and roll act. 'Are you Mr. Belson?' he said, just a shade impolitely.

I'd never hit anyone before in my life. What I did was just extend my right arm the way you do in the Nautilus pectoral machine; in the back of my head was the memory that I'd increased the drag in that machine to a hundred eighty pounds the Thursday before. I caught him in the neck with my forearm and he fell like a stone. Jesus Christ, I'd no idea it was so easy!

The other cop seemed undissuaded by this display of muscle, or he was too confused by it all to react properly. Maybe he had lost heart when he looked up to see me jumping up and down, with my lumberjack shirtsleeves rolled up and a cigar in my mouth, on the end of that flimsy Chinese cantilever. Strong men could quail at such a sight. Anyway, he was not forewarned by his partner's sudden drop and I punched him out with a right cross to the jaw. Then I took off running. I doubled back past the *Isabel*'s crater, looked around and saw an open place in the grandstand facing the fifty-yard line. There were no people or vehicles that I could see in that direction. I poured it on and ran that way, through a gate that, *mirabile dictu*, was open, and out onto a sidewalk. I looked up and down an avenue; it was deserted. Down the street was the Washington Monument, big and clean in the moonlight. I ran that way. Back at the stadium I heard trucks moving up, and people shouting. I ran on, took a left at the bottom of the street and a right at the end of the next one, to confuse the trail. I really stretched my legs. I ran like a night wind down those dark Washington streets, past the shells of old slum houses and then down the Mall, where I ran even more gaily on grass. If you could sing while running, with your chest at the bursting, I would have sung a hallelujah chorus of my own devising. Goddamn, it was good to be home!

10

There was a chance Baynes was back at the stadium, but I didn't think it likely. If I was right he'd be at home and in touch with them by phone. It was his house I was headed for.

I stopped running at the far end of New Mall, across the street from the Mendoza Monument, and sat on the grass for a while to get my breath. It was a warm night; the ground was faintly damp and had that good Earth-grass smell. This grass was not going to say it loved me or feed me, but right now silence was all I wanted. The monument was lit and I lay on my elbow in the quiet for a while panting heavily and contemplated the heroic bronze of Guadelupe Mendoza, the first woman Chief Justice and one of my favorite people in history. When I was a kid I saved bubble-gum cards with her picture; I had always liked her motherly ways and her liberal decisions.

Baynes's house was three blocks from Lupe, a fairly modest mansion—considering its owner's wealth and power—at the eastern edge of the Congressional Compound. I was wary of guards, but there was no need to be, none were around. The place was lit up with the kind of candlepower only a senator could command; even the pair of metal deer on the front lawn had a spotlight.

I considered climbing through a bedroom window but rejected the idea. I hadn't been reborn on Belson to get shot as a burglar. So I walked up the brickwork path and climbed the stairs to the broad porch. I knocked loudly on the door and then checked my watch. It was two-thirty. I knocked again.

The door opened and a young man was standing there blinking at me. I recognized him from a visit I'd paid Baynes a few years before. I gave him my steely, no-nonsense look. 'Good evening,' I said. 'I'm Ben Belson and I'm here to see the

Senator.' I paused a second and then pushed past him into the enormous living room. On the floor at one end of the room a couple of small black boys wearing pajamas were playing with a modern rarity, an electric train. At the other end, half lying on a Chesterfield sofa, was a thin, elderly black man. He was smiling warmly at me. 'Son of a bitch!' he said with a grin. He rose sleepily to his feet, jammed his hands into his bathrobe pockets, and looked at me as friendly as you please. 'If it isn't Benjamin Belson!' he said.

'Hello, L'Ouverture,' I said, not smiling. I have to admit that he's a charming bastard. And nobody is going to outpoise him.

'They called me a few hours ago, Ben, when they found your ship on the radar.' He gestured toward the children and yawned. 'Woke up my grandchildren too.'

There was a blue viddiphone on the table by the sofa. Just then it began to hum. 'L'Ouverture,' I said. 'Turn the video off and don't tell them I'm here. It'll be in your interest.'

He nodded, flicked off the camera switch and answered the phone. After a moment he said, explosively, 'Ran away? How is it that thirty MPs can't catch a running billionaire?' He smiled at me, and listened for a bit. Finally he said, 'Well, he won't get far. I'm going to bed. And for heaven's sake don't shoot him.' He hung up the phone.

'Thanks,' I said.

He smiled. 'Nothing to thank me for, Ben. I'm curious to know why you came here.'

'Sure,' I said. 'How about some coffee first?'

'Get us some coffee, Morton,' he said, 'and something light to eat. Melba toast.'

Morton left for the kitchen and I looked around me for a moment. It was a homey place, sort of shabby-genteel, with beige corduroy-covered sofas and unmatching overstuffed armchairs. There were a couple of acrylic landscapes on the walls. Baynes was as rich as Croesus, but he lived like a college president. People said he had more opulent digs tucked away in the sun, that he didn't want to put on a show in Washington. Maybe that was it. But I've known other rich people who won't spend serious money on themselves, and I distrust them.

I seated myself in one of the overstuffed chairs and leaned back. I hadn't realized until then how tired I was. Baynes remained standing, stretching now as if trying to wake up. He'd probably spent the evening berating his captive Energy Committee, gone to bed late and then was wakened by being told I was on my way to Washington. Would he have had cops sent to his home? I didn't think so; he had no way of knowing I was coming.

'L'Ouverture,' I said, 'what in heaven's name made you do me that way? Taking away my *citizenship*. Why do a thing like that?'

'Nobody's trying to hurt you, Ben,' he said. 'And you're a rich man. You have friends.'

I just stared at him. Such a cool son of a bitch. L'Ouverture is very good-looking. He is cheap about his household furnishings and I can't remember his ever picking up a check in a restaurant, but he dresses gorgeously. He looked like an expensive whiskey advertisement in that bathrobe with the monogram over the pocket. The kids in the corner kept buzzing their little green train around its track; through silvery draperies I could see the ghosts of L'Ouverture's lawn deer in frozen grazing; two miles away the *Isabel* was sitting, packed with uranium, waiting for the ground to cool. And here I was in this dumpy living room talking to this elegant man like an angry son just back from college. Somewhere in that sky out there, down south in Pisces Austrinus, shone Fomalhaut, no bigger than a bright pinhead. And Belson? Obsidian Belson, my heart's quiet home? Too small to see from here. Too small and far away. I looked back to L'Ouverture.

Baynes was born in the twentieth century and is a fine grandfatherly figure of a man. Tall, purplish-black and shiny. In his seventies. He must be six feet six—nearly as tall as his celebrated father, one of the finest basketball players who ever lived.

I'm tall enough to be unused to looking *up* at the person I'm talking to. Napoleon claimed that being short was an advantage, it made others feel awkward to bend down to him. But I didn't feel that way with Baynes. A part of me was like a kid with him and I didn't like it. 'Being a pirate has style,' I said. 'It

138

goes with my beard. But I resent the rest of it. And think of the money the government will lose on taxes alone if I don't get my uranium to work.'

Baynes seated himself on the sofa and leaned forward, elbows on knees and chin on those big fists of his. It made our heads at the same level. 'The Committee discussed that, Benjamin. The loss in revenue will be considerable.'

There was a clatter behind me as the toy train derailed. 'Motherfucker!' squeaked one of the kids. Neither of them seemed to be more than five years old.

Baynes spoke sharply. 'You ought to say "Goodness!" when a thing like that happens.'

'*You* don't,' said the kid, matter-of-factly, and set the engine back on its track.

Baynes shrugged and spoke to me. 'You went off to wherever it was you went in violation of the law. An act of Congress forbids space travel as wasteful of energy. You attempted to import a dangerous extraterrestrial substance . . .'

'Come on, L'Ouverture,' I said. 'Why in hell did you throw the book at me? Are you afraid I'll ruin you in the wood business?' I pulled a cigar from my shirt pocket and started getting it ready to light. 'Are you still mad at me for bankrupting Exxon?' I'd bought what was left of some energy corporations a few years back, put them into receivership, and made a fortune on the tax losses. Baynes had put his money on the other side and lost.

He laughed pleasantly. 'Not at all. Revenge is a waste of time. The Committee just can't let you have a monopoly. There's a delicate balance of energy use in the United States, Benjamin. We won't have any one person disrupting it . . .'

'Goddamn it!' I said. 'That "delicate balance" means the military gets the oil, the Mafia gets most of the coal, and people like you and me get rich off the leftover coal and wood. It means that what little uranium there is is being saved for bombs. People are *freezing* out there and it may get worse. What if the temperature drops again next winter?' I puffed my cigar furiously for a moment, staring into Baynes's grandfatherly look, into his pose of bemused patience. 'You charlatans in Congress have campaigned on the word "crisis"

139

for so long you think it's only meaningful in TV spots.'

'Your concern for the ordinary citizen is touching.'

'Oh, come off it!' I said. 'That uranium out there is a gift from the heavens. Everybody can profit from it. It'll run the elevators in New York and heat houses in Omaha, enrich the U.S. Treasury and give me a lot of money. What in hell's wrong with that, L'Ouverture?'

'You make it sound idyllic,' Baynes said. 'A TV spot in its own right. You're ignoring some things, Benjamin, in your polemic. There is currently a forty percent *surplus* of wood in the country. Talk of an ice age is premature. There is enough coal in Wyoming alone to run all the elevators in the world, continuously, until the good Lord sees fit to blink this planet back into chaos. The U.S. has tidal engines, windmills and solar plants. And uranium has a bad reputation. Very bad. Consider what the conservationists did to your country home in Georgia.'

'Nonsense!' I said. 'The conservationists are being paid by the Mafia; everybody knows that. Uranium's unsafe, but so is coal. Look at the Chinese. They run their whole industrial plant on U235. The U.S. was trying to find safe uranium in space, just like me, back when I was a kid. You can't have elevators and fast cars on solar power, L'Ouverture.'

'*Benjamin,*' he said, in his gravelly, soothing way. 'Benjamin, who needs cars? They had all that in the twentieth century, and all they did was kill and maim one another on the highways.'

'In the twenty-first century they stay home and watch TV,' I said, 'and freeze in winter. There's a price for everything. The Chinese have big bank accounts and their cuisine's deteriorated; you can't buy a Peking duck in Peking. Soyaburgers and fries. They have to come to New York to spend all that money. What kind of civilization is that?'

'The Chinese are known the world over for the quality of their family life.'

'Hogwash, L'Ouverture. They watch TV together and send their kids to business colleges. There's more revolutionary zeal in Aberdeen than in all of China.' I thought of Isabel, of her sad capitalist love for communism. We should join the Communist Party together and start a revolution somewhere. I'd finance it and she'd write the slogans.

140

Just then Morton came back in the room with a tray. 'Let's have our coffee now,' Baynes said. He nodded toward a permoplastic table by the marble fireplace and Morton set the tray there. 'Why don't you put the children back to bed, Morton?'

'Shit!' one of the kids said, *sotto voce*.

'Go to *bed*,' Baynes said wearily. That seemed to work, and they followed Morton upstairs like lambs. Baynes turned his attention back to me. He was still smiling but clearly tired. It was about four in the morning. 'I don't really care about the Chinese,' he said. 'They're admirable in their way, but East is East . . .'

I leaned forward. It was time to make my pitch. I could feel the intensity in my voice. 'L'Ouverture,' I said, 'there's more safe uranium where that came from.' I gestured toward the general direction of Aynsley Field. 'A billion tons of it. We can beat those Chinese hustlers at their own game. We can be the richest nation on Earth again, L'Ouverture.' I leaned back and chewed my cigar a minute. 'And this time we're mellower. We'll do it right. We won't kill ourselves in our cars anymore. No more big horsepower. We won't bully the little countries.' I paused a moment, overwhelmed myself by what I was going to say. 'We can build a great civilization, L'Ouverture, a great, humane, and beautiful civilization. We can be an electronic Byzantium, a holy city. We can be the Age of Pericles and light up the world. Think of the *talent* in this country! Think of the architecture we can build with cheap power!'

I sat back, moved by my own words. I really believed it. America is a magnificent, fertile place, and in decline it has lost much of its grossness. What a comeback we could have, with all that power from Juno!

Baynes walked over to the table. 'The coffee is ready,' he said coolly.

I stared at him, miffed at his ignoring my rhetoric. 'Come *on*,' I said. 'Where's your patriotism, for Christ's sake?'

He began pouring the coffee with a steady hand. 'My daddy used to say to me at Fourth of July parades in Louisville, "Whitey talks pretty, but listen to him closely." '

I stared at him and almost screamed, *Bullshit*. But I didn't. I remembered the black guys in prison. The U.S. has had two black presidents and a dozen black justices in the Supreme Court; a third of Congress is black—mostly women. But the black prisoners at Leavenworth still had to fight to get shoes that fit, had to pay bigger bribes to get the easy jobs in the prison factory. I shrugged and seated myself at the coffee table.

'Your father made ten times the money my father made,' I said.

His face became arctic, just for a second. 'What in hell was your father good for?'

There was one final ploy to try, a pretty drastic one, to give myself some operating room. I must at all costs get time and money and stay out of jail. The months on Belson, self-willed though they were, were jail enough. I needed action.

Wouldn't you know the coffee cups were plastic? Here was a man who could afford anything and he used coffee cups like these. I took a deep breath, tried to dismiss things like that from my mind, and said, 'L'Ouverture, I'll give you half my share of that uranium outright if you'll get me back my citizenship and my money and drop those charges.'

He took a sip of his coffee. 'A bribe?'

'What else?' I said. 'Draw up papers and I'll sign them around noon, right after I get back my citizenship and the courts cancel that mumbo-jumbo.'

He went on sipping his coffee in silence. I leaned back in the little plastic chair by the mantelpiece, feeling at last relaxed. L'Ouverture looked thoughtful and grandfatherly. I felt a part of me yielding to his spell and I didn't mind, now that I'd played my cards. I knew Baynes: he would rather make a quiet deal like this than fool around. I looked at his contemplative, intelligent old face; this was turning out to be a pleasant welcome home. It was as good in its way as finding Isabel would have been. Maybe better, because with Baynes I wouldn't be breaking crockery or screaming at cats. Yet I knew well enough that he could be an authentic blacksnake and a threat to life and limb. *He who sups with the devil must eat with a long spoon.* Oh yes. This man could have me clapped in irons. Still, I let myself love him a bit, dangerously, for his charm. Christ, do I ever want a father! And at my age! What a charming old son of a bitch, with his shiny black head and yellowing teeth and steady hands—so manicured, so well manicured. I wanted to lean across the table and hug him.

He was looking at me. 'Have some coffee, Ben,' he said.

That reminded me of where I was. I took a sip of the coffee and almost spat it out. Instant coffee. Garbage! What kind of a father was he anyway? Somewhere in his soul was the demon that had dominated my real father: Low Rent. If Western Civilization dies it will drown in instant coffee, processed cheese and TV specials. Men and women in America have been born, lived, and gone to quickly dug graves without ever tasting real coffee, a real hamburger, or a real glass of lemonade. What right did this billionaire, the sharpest man in the Senate, have to drink powdered coffee out of plastic cups? Genghis Khan would have known better.

'L'Ouverture,' I said, even though I could go to jail for it, 'you should make your coffee with a Chemex. And I need fifty thousand in cash. I mean right away.'

'Benjamin,' he said, a bit sternly, 'I *like* instant coffee. I embrace the modern world and live happily in it. The nineteenth and twentieth centuries do not interest me. Instant coffee is the drink of the times and I drink it with pleasure. I don't keep cash around.'

'That's a pity,' I said, and tried the coffee again. I needed the caffeine.

L'Ouverture shrugged, still smiling, and spoke in his honey-eyed old voice, 'Snobbery is a waste of energy. The past is dead, Ben. Your father was an historian; mine was a basketball player. Father adapted the crane dance of his ancestors to varnished oak floors and sent me to Harvard, where I learned to prosper even as he had. He hated sports, hated the Olympics, hated abstractions. Sometimes he slept with a basketball beside him. I too delight in the real, the contemporary.'

It was seductive, but I knew Baynes too well to believe it. *You're a power jack-off*, I wanted to shout, *and the past is alive! Solipsist!* The son of a bitch probably counted the votes of his Energy Committee with a hard on. 'Look,' I said, 'I'd like to go to a bank in the morning and get some cash. When can you have my accounts released?'

He smiled benignly. 'Just have an extra croissant for

breakfast, Benjamin, and go to your bank at ten. I'll have Justice Flaherty call in a reversal. Where did you bring the uranium from? Fomalhaut?'

Jesus Christ! I thought, *How does he know?* It wasn't Fomalhaut, thank God; it was Aminidab. Juno. But how did he know about *Fomalhaut?* From that geologist in Jamaica? Anyway, I didn't fall for it. 'Come on, L'Ouverture,' I said. 'That's not the deal.'

He shrugged and set his coffee cup down with an air of finality. 'If you won't tell me where the uranium comes from, there is no deal. I'm going to get some sleep.' He turned his face toward a doorway and called out, 'All right out there.'

At first I thought he was hailing Morton, but I realized that was unlikely just as two men in brown suits came in the doorway, each holding a pair of handcuffs. The chair I was sitting on was low, in a sort of semi-Japanese way, and when I tried to jump to my feet I knocked over the table. L'Ouverture got out of the way just in time and I didn't even get the pleasure of splashing him with hot coffee. They had me by the time I'd recovered my balance and was, ignominiously, in a semicrouch like a small boy with a stubbed toe. The cuffs were of steel; I had one wrist cuffed to a wrist of each of those bastards in what seemed to be a single motion. They pulled me upright from my crouch. Private cops, probably. Cheap ones too.

One of them began to recite, 'You have the right to remain silent . . .'

Baynes interrupted him. 'No need,' he said. 'Mr. Belson has no rights. He is not a citizen.'

'You son of a bitch,' I said.

'Take him to the Reagan Detention Center and book him for illegal entry.'

My stomach sank. From rebirth to the Reagan Stir. I checked the two out. Poker-faced. But one of them, the fatter, seemed under his stern patriot look to be troubled by something.

'Okay,' I said, 'let's get out of here.' And then to L'Ouverture, who was still smiling amiably, who had almost certainly never stopped smiling, 'You are one deceitful son of a bitch.'

He went on smiling. 'Have a good day,' he said.

144

11

The Reagan Stir is way out past Arlington Cemetery, and a long haul. The cops ushered me out the door of Baynes's house and down the block to where they had a little methane-powered Honda with D.C. plates. Twenty miles per hour, maximum. We all squeezed together in the front seat, which forced me to put my knees under my chin. But I didn't feel as uncomfortable as the fat guy looked, sitting on my right with one arm and half his head out the window. We chugged along under the moonlight for about ten minutes, until we were approaching a woodshop, clearly an all-night one, at the corner of Constitution Avenue and D Street.

The fat guy with some effort pulled his head back in the car and I felt his soft belly mash against my side. The thinner one was driving with his left hand, his right being cuffed to my wrist. I really didn't like this kind of physical intimacy one bit and I'd been repeating my mantra for the last two or three minutes. 'Billy Bob,' the fat one said, 'pull over at that store. I gotta use the restroom.'

'Can't you *wait?*' Billy Bob said, sounding a whole lot like my mother.

'Hell, no,' the fat one said. 'I've been waiting back at that house for an hour and a half.'

'*Shit,*' Billy Bob said. I figured he was going to stop but, like mothers everywhere, was going to exact payment for it. 'You might have used the toilet back there.'

'Billy Bob,' Fatty said, 'pull over.'

Billy Bob drove up to the woodshop and parked. It took us a minute to get out the same door that we had all gotten in. I felt God had sent me this opportunity. I'd bet a million that whatever cops were at the stadium hadn't told Baynes on the

145

phone that I'd decked two of their number. As far as Fatty and Billy Bob were concerned, I was just an aging tycoon.

There was an old Chinese woman at the cash register inside who looked as if she had seen all there was to see and had built no small part of the Great Wall with her own rough hands. When the three of us came in as a conjoined trio, as it were, she was reading a comic book. She looked up, laid her cigarette on the edge of an overflowing ashtray, and waited.

'I need to use the restroom,' Fatty said, clearly ill at ease.

She nodded toward the far wall. A faded print of Mao surrounded by awed children hung there, and under it on a small hook a key.

There was no room for the three of us to walk abreast, but we managed to make it single file with a little shoving around and Fatty got his key. Getting back out the door was a bit confusing, but we made it. The shop was clearly an ancient gas station, with the restroom in back.

'Why don't you piss against a tree, for Christ's sake?' Billy Bob said.

'If I only needed to piss I'd a done it a quarter hour ago.' I was surprised at the uncowed quality in Fatty's voice. He had apparently developed a sense of mission over this middle-of-the-night B.M. and he was riding it. Well, I was developing a sense of mission too, although not a cloacal one.

'How in hell you going to stay handcuffed and do that?' Billy Bob said.

'Let's look it over,' Fatty said.

In back was a room with MEN on its door. Fatty unlocked it easily enough and flipped on a little ten-watt light inside. What a grubby-looking place, with wet newspaper on the cracked linoleum floor! And what a smell! The Chinese have one of the most admirable cultural histories in the world. Their cuisine—where it still exists—is right up there with the French. Hell, they make a fine spaceship. But they're in the Middle Ages when it comes to toilets.

As a partner in this venture, so to speak, I could see right away that it was going to be a problem for Fatty. Had I been he, I would have found a dark lawn somewhere, dropped my pants and made the best of it. But either that hadn't occurred to Fatty and Billy Bob, or it was far beyond Fatty's sense of propriety.

146

The room wasn't big enough for the three of us. The toilet faced the doorway. Fatty tried to cool it. He walked in, dragging me by my wrist halfway into the door, which opened outward. He turned around facing me and began to loosen his belt with his free hand, while getting himself into kind of a crouch. For a moment I panicked; if I had to watch this I would rather do a month in solitary.

But as I had hoped, Fatty suddenly gave up. 'Look, Billy Bob,' he said, nodding toward the handcuff that joined us, 'undo this thing for a minute.'

Billy Bob looked doubtful. 'What in hell . . .?' he said.

'Come *on!*' Fatty said, in desperation. 'He ain't going nowhere with you attached.'

'Okay,' Billy Bob said. He got the little magnetic key out of his pants pocket, walked in front of me and undid the cuff from Fatty's wrist, letting it dangle from mine. Then he stepped back out the door and I followed him for a step, so that I was now all the way outside.

'Close the door,' Fatty said. He was standing in the doorway. I had already seen there was no bolt latch on the inside. Only a knob.

'Sure,' I said, casually. I took the knob firmly in my now free right hand, felt the steel heft of the door, and slammed it powerfully right into Fatty's face. The door clicked shut and I could hear a thud. The strength in my pectorals felt like a triphammer. Then I jerked my left arm toward me with everything I had and Billy Bob's head shot past my face and into the door. I smashed into the back of his head with my closed fist and felt him go slack. Then I turned the bolt on the men's room door. It clicked into place beautifully.

Billy Bob was out cold with his face bloody enough that I could see the mess even by moonlight. I had no pity for him just then; he had chosen a violent profession for himself and should have been more alert. I bent down and examined his left hand for the key. It wasn't there. I'd been afraid of that. He'd probably dropped it when I'd jerked him. I began looking around the grass as well as I could by moonlight. No luck. I dragged him over a few feet and looked where he'd been standing after he'd unlocked Fatty. Still no luck. It was just too *dark*. From inside the restroom came Fatty's voice now, shouting, 'Get me out of here!' He began banging on the door.

I was getting worried. I had just about made up my mind to pick up Billy Bob and carry him back to the car with me when a small miracle occurred: a light over the men's room came on. I looked back toward the front of the building and, sure enough, Chinese Mama stood there, with her cigarette and comic book in one hand and her other on a light switch. She must have heard the commotion.

'Thank you, ma'am,' I said politely and began searching the grass with my eyes. And there it was, about a foot the other side of where Billy Bob had been standing when I'd decked him. I dragged him a bit farther, stretched out and got it. I was astonished at how steady my hand was when I unlocked us.

I looked back at Mama. Inscrutable, unperturbed. Billy Bob and I could have been discussing the weather. And the louder Fatty shouted and banged the door the calmer she looked, a genuine flower of heavenly repose all by herself. I could have kissed her. I checked out Billy Bob and figured he'd be all right in a few minutes, since his neck wasn't twisted in any serious way. The poor son of a bitch.

I started walking toward the front of the store, where I'd seen a cigar-and-candy rack. When I came up to Mama. I said, 'What's your name, ma'am?'

She took a puff from her cigarette. 'Arabella Kim,' she said. 'Are you Captain Belson from outer space?'

I grinned at her. 'Oh yes.' And then, 'I'd like to buy some cigars.' I gave her my whole forty dollars for ten cigars—cheap two-dollar ones, but what the hell—and six Mars bars. Mars seemed appropriate for a space pirate. 'Keep the change,' I told her, 'and I'd be obliged if you didn't help these two for a few minutes.' I was still out of breath a bit and my voice was husky.

'Many people are on your side, Captain Belson,' she said. 'People write letters to the Washington *Post* and say we should have your uranium. I think so.'

'Why, bless your heart,' I said, stuffing the cigars in my shirt pockets and the candy bars in my pants. There was no telephone at the store. I went over to Billy Bob's car, lifted the hood, took out the distributor, and threw it into some bushes.

Then I stood there in the moonlight for a minute and a powerful realization dawned on me: I was flat broke. Here I was reborn into the world after nine months in the sky, and I had come back to be indeed naked and helpless. I took a deep breath of the night air and felt my heart speed up with it and the small hairs at the back of my neck tingle.

I had to begin somewhere. I turned and walked back into the shop and said, 'Arabella, I need some cash.'

She just looked at me imperturbably. 'How much?'

'I'll sell you my watch for five hundred dollars,' I said. It had cost me eight thousand.

'One needs a watch,' she said. 'I'll see what I can do.'

She got up from her chair, went to a closed door at the back of the little shop, and opened it. I peered in. There was a small room filled with tobacco smoke, with Chinese revolutionary posters on the wall, some of them in tatters. At the back of the room was a cot with a wrinkled red coverlet on it and a tiny, wizened Chinese man lying on it reading *Sports Illustrated*. Probably Mr. Kim. She spoke to him in Chinese in a no-nonsense kind of way. He mumbled something that sounded surly but got off the cot meekly enough. She reached under the mattress and pulled out a little red plastic purse, opened it and took out six hundred-dollar coins. She handed them to me, smiled faintly, and said, 'Keep your watch and pay me back when you sell the uranium.'

I glanced out the window to where the stacks of cordwood lay piled and said, 'That uranium will put you out of business, you know.'

'It's a dull business,' she said.

I nodded and put the coins in my pocket. 'You're a good woman, Arabella,' I said. Then I left the shop and took off toward Union Station.

I got about five minutes of exultation out of overcoming my arrest before I remembered that remark L'Ouverture had made about snobbery. The son of a bitch had a way of getting under my skin. In a sense I am a snob about good food, good china and good theater. I like Shakespeare immensely, as a matter of fact, now that I'm not trying to win points with Isabel. Bless her heart, she never knew the competition she entered when she took me on as a lover! But I like the good things of the modern world too. I thought of my running shoes. I'd bought them at a place on Forty-sixth Street a few weeks before the *Isabel* took off. You put your feet in a pretty little device called a Contour Reader, and the son of a bitch makes you a pair of Adidas right there. I mean right on your *feet*. It's weird to watch but it feels good to have the warm polymers and rubber molded to your personal arches and to the ball and the heel and then up over the great toe. Like a Japanese massage. The machine even puts laces in, a sight more interesting to watch than most contemporary movies. And Jesus, do I love those gym shoes! Sky blue and made by electronic wizardry right before my eyes, between Madison and Fifth. Five hundred dollars. Eighty more if monogrammed. Mine have a white 'B.B.' where the rubber disk used to be on a pair of Converse.

But I was pissed at L'Ouverture. Maybe because he'd pulled racism on me. I pounded along the predawn pavements, through silent suburbs and then along the 'Ghost town' where all the poor blacks who did the paperwork for the U.S. Government used to live. Empty high-rise housing glowing dully by moonlight, emptier and spookier than Belson. I felt lucky to have been born in rural Ohio; those places, filled with the smells and sighs of government clerks and their dazed families, back when I was sleeping with Juno, were authentic anger factories. They used to defecate in the elevators in places like that, and do casual rapes on the staircases. No proper life for man at all.

Still, I'd picked up a lot of anger myself in my own loveless home. Anger and hunger—I could hardly tell them apart. *Slap, slap* went my shoes, the products of electronic sorcery and of my unique, large feet. *Whump, whump* went my substantial, furious heart; I could feel my quadriceps bulging against my jeans.

I began to think about railroad schedules. One thing about being a coal and wood tycoon: you learn when the trains run. A half-empty freight would be leaving Washington for New York at 5:15 A.M., and it was usually on time. I looked at my watch. I had twenty minutes.

Sometimes I think God sent me to Belson and Juno.

Twenty years of space exploration by three countries had yielded nothing worth having. I, a rank amateur, had found two paradises with hardly any effort. One was a genuine Eden with food and trees and pleasant air; the other its reverse, made for the likes of St. Simeon Stylites, Origen, Cotton Mather and me. Oh, the varieties of religious experience! I had five minutes to find myself a comfortable freight car and get aboard.

The station, being electronic, had nobody around. The train was there when I arrived; it hissed a bit, made those endearing heavy clangs that trains make, and looked energetic. I found a big open car with BELSON MINES clearly stenciled on it—one of my very own. I climbed up the ladder at the side, slipped over, and let myself down. There was some coal dust at the bottom and nothing else. No way to see outside. But what the hell.

I was still panting from the run and had a godawful stitch in my side. My left wrist was painfully swollen from the handcuff when I'd jerked Billy Bob. My feet hurt like hell. Suddenly I remembered that I was a human bomb of endolin! There was no need to feel pain. I got one of the plastic packs from around my left arm, took a pinch, swallowed it with a bite of a Mars bar, and in a few minutes I felt terrific. So much for pain.

After the train got started, with more noise and vibration than the *Isabel* made landing on Belson, I slept for about an hour. When I awoke the sky was beginning to lighten over-head. I climbed up the ladder and was able to perch somewhat uncomfortably on the side of the slow-moving car and watch the sun coming up over misty fields. Now that I had something to compare our Earth with, I enjoyed it even more. Only one sun and one moon and no rings either, but a beautiful planet and one to treasure. Where else would you find a Canyon de Chelly or a Pacific Ocean, a Florida Keys or an India? My heart leaped to see that sweet green of summer grass on Earth, and maple trees in leaf, cattle out in fields, and birds everywhere, determined busybodies in the morning air!

The train had a forty-minute stop in Philadelphia, at a power plant. There were a couple of railroad people there to refuel the engine and oversee the unloading of some coal, but I was able to get out for a break without their noticing me. I left the terminal and did a few simple exercises. My body was stiff and sore and I added a bit of endolin to my Mars bar breakfast. There was a water fountain outside the station—my first Earth water in nine months. The sun was well up, and warm on my face.

I found myself in a shabby part of Philadelphia—one of those 'Big House Slums' you read about. Population falls so fast these days that there is ample space for the poor in solar-house suburbs and town houses in the cities. The problem is they can't heat the places in the wintertime and the solars don't work, and the houses were so cheaply made in the first place that they were now, there among the pacified hills of a former suburb, a tatterdemalion aggregate of fallen plastic shingles, ruined lawns, cracked glass roofs and vine-clotted breezeways. It beats sleeping in doorways, but it's a depressing sight.

I found an open drugstore and bought a six-pack of club soda, some beef jerky, a box of cookies and a pack of brown hair dye. Sixty dollars and change. As I was starting to leave the store I saw a pile of *Enquirers*, and sure enough, there I was on the front page. But without the beard, thank God. No one had taken a picture of me with the beard. And in the picture I looked rather well-groomed and serious. The headline read BILLIONAIRE OUTLAW FOILS COPS. I gave the man at the counter his two dollars for the paper. He didn't even look at me. I left, reading.

It was comic in its way. I was called a 'berserk eccentric' and a 'financial maverick'. I especially liked 'berserk eccentric,' which suited my mood: John the Baptist still slept in me.

Back in my coal car I proceeded to dye my hair, using a couple of the cans of club soda and wishing I had bought a mirror at that drugstore. What I did was pour half the liquid dye into the plastic can of soda, shake it up, and then work it into my hair and beard with my fingertips. I left it there for twenty minutes, while the train chugged its way across the border into New Jersey, and then rinsed it off with another canful. I'd have given a hundred dollars for a pocket mirror. I'd dyed a spot the size of a five-dollar piece on my left forearm, where it was at its hairiest, and I used that for a kind of control; when I rinsed it off after twenty minutes there was a patch of convincing-looking brown on my arm. I hoped that on my head and beard the results were as good.

The day was uneventful and warm. I lay around in the bottom of the car like Huckleberry Finn on his raft, or rode up on the side and watched the countryside go by and ate my beef jerky and Mars bars and drank the four other cans of club soda and had a pretty good time of it. It seemed more of a real journey than traveling halfway across the Milky Way had been.

Close to dusk, the train gave me my first view of the Manhattan skyline. It was breathtaking, as it always is to me. Yet I could have wept to know that the upper floors of all the tall buildings were vacant. It is saddening to see the city at such times and know that it was once a powerhouse and isn't anymore, although those tall old buildings still stand there quiet and aloof from the streets below them. I'm crazy about the *idea* of New York. It's one of the great inventions of the human spirit, like the fugue or the Pythagorean Theorem or the airplane—the apotheosis of the *polis* and still to me the world's greatest city.

We came into Manhattan through the old Pennsylvania Railroad tunnel and climbed back above ground at Thirty-fourth and Seventh Avenue, at the Coal Dock. What a dusty, smelly place to see New York from! Almost all the fuel for the entire city came in at that point, and there were heaps of coal the size of small mountains, with the dust from them penetrating the air everywhere; I felt I could get black lung in ten minutes.

There used to be a department store—Macy's, I think—on Thirty-fourth Street; the old building was now used for coal storage. My train stopped there and I was able to climb down from the car unobserved. There were a lot of guards around, but they were there to keep coal thieves out; I merely nodded and walked past them. It was a quarter to eight and there was still some light in the sky. I found Fifth Avenue and headed uptown. A good many people were on the street but nobody paid attention to me. I felt fine—loose and easy in the body and pleasantly tight in the stomach. It was something like my first trip to the city that time I'd come to stay with Aunt Myra; I was an anonymous and rootless tourist, starting a new life, on my own in the world's best place to be on your own.

There was a mirror in the window of a videosphere store at Thirty-ninth Street, and I stopped to see myself at full length. I looked like hell—like a raunchy and flagrant derelict-rapist. The dyed hair and beard were a shock, as was the coal dust smeared on my face. I was something to scare children with. One elbow of my shirt was ripped open; my pants were baggy and filthy with coal and soot; there was a stain from hair dye on my shirt collar; and the dye on my beard and hair was uneven, with dark and light clumps sticking out crazily. I could have slept on park benches for the next twenty years and nobody would have noticed me.

When I was a teenager a fine old skyscraper sat at Forty-second Street between Lexington and Third. It was Aunt Myra's favorite piece of hopeful architecture and she was the first person to name it to me: the Chrysler Building. They tore it down a few years after the elevators were stopped by the legislature in Albany. Elevators have counterweights and the whole thing wasn't really necessary, but Albany wanted to show the world it was energy conscious. Its decree changed New York in a horrifying way, making the upper floors of all those unconscionably tall buildings inaccessible. Above the eighth it was all emptiness, derelicts and the odd fugitive.

Now where the Chrysler Building had once been there was the Heating Emporium, an open market for coal, wood, and alcohol, together with a few more exotic combustibles; I was glad to see the Belson Fuels corner well stocked and it pleased me to stand there a moment, looking like the raunchiest and most flagrant of bums, and see that each stick of neatly stacked cordwood had the name BELSON stamped on it in purple letters. Next to it was a heap of my coal, and that was not so pleasing. It was all bituminous, and you could tell it would be foul stuff by the color. But the Mafia had all the anthracite, and they weren't about to let go of it in a controlled market.

I walked up Fifth to Fifty-third Street and turned over toward Madison. A couple of cops gave me a hostile eye, and a family of Chinese tourists seemed as boggled by me as a Chinese permits himself to be. A member of the capitalist underclass—one of the dregs. *We do these things better in Hangchow.* Well, in Hangchow I'd be wearing a gray uniform and sweeping the streets with a plastic broom and touching my forelock to the fat Communist bourgeois as they daintily strolled the streets with their chubby families. I liked being a disheveled bum in New York better, with my newfound pirate's soul.

There was no doorman at the building and I walked up to the third floor. The apartment door had three locks. I banged loudly. After a minute the locks began clicking and, finally, the door opened. There was a small Japanese maid standing there, in uniform, staring up at me in shock.

I spoke softly to her, but with authority in my voice. 'Tell Miss Belson it's her father,' I said.

The maid nodded, shut the door and locked it. I waited. After several minutes it opened again and there was Myra, tall as ever, on crutches, looking at me quizzically for a moment. Finally she said, 'Jesus Christ! *Daddy.*' She opened the door wider. 'Jesus!' she said again.

I came in and hugged her. Gently, because Myra could be hurting almost anywhere. 'It's good to see you, honey,' I said. I was crying. I hadn't thought about Myra much in the past few years—thinking about her could make me feel terrible—but I really loved her.

'Jesus, Daddy,' she said, 'did you fall in?'

I shook my head. 'Something like that.'

She laughed in that sort of childish way she has. Myra is almost thirty. 'Let's sit in the living room.' I followed her as she walked with care on her aluminum crutches into the big living room with windows looking down on Fifty-third Street. Myra had never met my Aunt Myra but she had somehow arrived, as if by reincarnation, at Aunt Myra's style in interior decoration. I seated myself on a black velvet sofa, leaned back, and lit up a cigar. 'I'll wash up after a bit,' I said. She nodded and there was an embarrassed silence for a minute. There usually is, when I see her. 'How about some coffee?' she said, 'or whiskey?'

'Coffee.'

'Sure,' she said, with relief. 'Martha, can you fix coffee for my father, with cream and sugar. I'll have whiskey and soda.'

She turned back toward me and seated herself carefully in an armchair that faced the sofa I was sitting on. 'You were on the TV news last night.' She laughed a bit uneasily. 'They showed some old holos and called you the "billionaire fugitive," but it wasn't clear what the police wanted you for.'

'The bastards,' I said. '*They* don't know what they want me for. It's that son of a bitch Baynes, and probably the Mafia too.'

'I thought it was something like that. Is that uranium dangerous, Daddy?'

'No,' I said. 'Hell, no. On the contrary. It's the safest uranium in the universe. I feel like Galileo when those cardinals were after his ass. Have they bothered you?',

'No. Do they know you're in New York?'

'I don't think so,' I said. 'I've been sly about it. How's your arthritis?'

She shrugged. 'Same as always.'

'Hurts like hell?'

'Yes, Daddy. It hurts like hell.' She smiled at me in a way that might be described as 'bravely' except that I sensed a hidden edge of blame in it. If only I had been around more during her childhood, had not been off in hotel suites dissolving corporations on paper in the middle of the night or bouncing around in bed with actresses or—let's face it—finding ways of staying away from Anna and her fortitude, her unflinching zeal to be undeceived by the fripperies and fantasies of the world. If I hadn't drunk so much when I *was* at home. If I hadn't fought so much with Myra's mother, bellowing my space pirate's voice down the hallways and across the kitchens of whatever houses and apartments—in California or New York or Atlanta, or wherever my geographical yearnings took us . . .

Well, now I had endolin. 'Myra,' I said, 'I've got something for you.'

'Daddy.' She frowned. 'I don't need any more presents. Not even from outer space.'

'Honey,' I said, 'this is no present.' I began unbuttoning my shirt, for a moment embarrassed by the sexual implications of what I was doing, being about to transfer that endolin wrapped to my sweating body to the body of my daughter sitting there in her stiff, arthritic way.

'What the hell . . .?' Myra said.

'It *is* something from another planet,' I said, pulling one of the bags filled with powder out from under the bandage that held it to my chest. I pushed aside a group of ivory netsuke and a Venetian-glass ashtray on Myra's coffee table and set the packet of endolin down. Then I began opening the clear plastic carefully. My fingers trembled a little. 'I have great hopes for you and this, Myra,' I said. I was shocked to hear my voice: *vibrato*, on the edge of tears. 'I think it may be your anodyne . . .' I couldn't finish. I got the bag open and looked at the powder sitting there, like some kind of super fix, a mainline for King Kong, that destructive fellow pirate in New York. *Come on, Kong,* I said to myself, *do something good for someone you love, for a change.*

'I'll need to get a glass of water,' I said aloud, holding back tears. I stood up and barged into the kitchen, where Martha was putting ice in Myra's drink of whiskey. I got a glass from a shelf and half-filled it with water. Then I grabbed a silver spoon from the sonic dishwasher and went into the living room again. I put a pinch of endolin into the water and stirred it, shakily.

'What in hell is going *on*, Daddy?' Myra was saying. She really was beginning to look alarmed. 'You come in looking like a crazed derelict and then you pull out this Baggie of what looks like dope. They said on TV that you were a drug addict . . .'

I let the glass sit there on the table and leaned back. I began buttoning up my shirt, less shaky now. 'Well, there's some truth in what they say, honey. I used morphine quite a bit. Got hooked on it in fact, trying to feed some dumb craving, but this isn't morphine. No high comes with it. It's only a painkiller.'

'I'll try it,' she said matter-of-factly.

I stared at her. Was it this easy after all?

'Daddy,' she said, 'I trust you. And I've tried more painkillers than you have any idea of. Believe me, I've swallowed a lot of chemicals in my time.' She leaned forward, somewhat stiffly, and picked up the glass. Her hand was far steadier, despite the pain, than mine had been. 'What do you call this stuff?'

'Endolin,' I said. 'Just drink it off. There's no special taste.'

157

She nodded and downed the glassful the way a sailor downs a beer. 'Endolin, eh?' she said, with an edge of cynicism in her voice. Well I couldn't blame her for being cynical, considering the number of things she must have tried. It was a testimony to her strength that, having used morphine and probably heavier stuff, she wasn't a junkie herself.

I said nothing. It takes endolin about three minutes to work and there was no point in talking it up. I felt nervous and got up just in time to take my coffee from Martha's tray as she came in the swinging door from the kitchen. I looked at a couple of contemporary holographic etchings on the wall for a moment; but those damned 3-D things always hurt my eyes. I looked out the window down to the street, which was now empty. It was one of those phosphorescent sidewalks that glow green in the dark and it eased my eyes to stare at it for minute. I was itching in several places. I should take a bath.

Just then Myra said softly, 'My God, Daddy!' and I turned around. She was still seated. Her face was strange and her mouth was half open in astonishment. As I looked at her she shook her head a couple of times.

'Is something wrong?' I said, alarmed.

She shook her head again, more violently, staring at me. I took a step toward her. She was beginning to cry. 'Are you all right?' I said.

Her face was very serious and the expression was one I'd never seen before. 'How long does it last?' she asked.

'About six hours.'

'Will I have a hangover?'

'Nothing, honey,' I said. 'No hangover.'

'*Oh my God,*' she said and burst into tears. I squatted somewhat awkwardly by her chair and put my arms around her and hugged her. I could feel some of that pain that had just gone out of her, feel the shock of it. After a moment she pulled gently away and stood up, not using her crutches. She began walking around the room slowly and taking an occasional little two-step. 'I used to take morphine sometimes, or shoot myself full of procaine and dance for an hour or so. But the thing was I couldn't really *feel* my body. And my head would be fuzzy.'

'It just takes the pain away,' I said.

Myra went over to a bookcase, put a steel ball into a box and Chinese dance music filled the room. She began dancing more confidently, her face open and surprised still. I seated myself and watched. It was overwhelming to see her moving easily like that, still a bit careful in her movements because of her long history of pain.

After a while she stopped, perspiring and smiling now. She turned the box off and came and sat beside me. She let herself cry again for a minute, very openly and easily, holding her hands in front of her and flexing her fingers. We used to play chess with ivory pieces every now and then and sometimes it would make her wince in pain just to pick up a pawn. Now her fingers seemed completely easy and supple. After a moment she stopped crying and said, 'How about that, Daddy? I think I always knew you'd come through for me.'

'I wish I could have had it twenty years ago . . .'

'Now is good enough,' she said. 'When the pain is over it's over.' She smiled a little wistfully. 'Where did it come from?'

'From the heavens,' I said. 'From a star.' I pointed downtown. 'A star in Pisces Austrinus, called Fomalhaut. It has a planet with only two living things on it: a kind of wonderful grass and the little, ugly plant endolin comes from.'

'What's the planet called? Or does it have a name?'

'It's named Belson, honey.'

Myra laughed. 'Just like you and me, Daddy.'

I looked at her. 'And your Great-Aunt Myra.'

I took a long, hot shower after that. Myra was able to find some men's clothes that fit well enough, and I picked a denim work shirt and a pair of jeans that were a little loose in the waist. It gave me a tinge of pride to find my waist was smaller than whatever lover of Myra's had left his pants behind. I brushed off my electronic running shoes and put them on over a pair of clean white socks. There is nothing quite like a shower followed by clean white socks. I was becoming a small fugue of good feelings; what I needed now was Isabel. And a few million dollars.

After showering and putting on clean clothes I had a quiet drink with Myra in her living room. She had come down a bit from her high, but she smiled a lot. She asked me about my travels in space and I told her about Belson and Juno, although I didn't mention Juno's star. It was fun to talk with Myra that easily, leaning back into a soft couch with a drink of good whiskey, seeing her face for once relaxed and her body at ease. From time to time she would flex the fingers of a hand or work a shoulder joint just a bit, with a pleasant surprise. She wanted to know everything about endolin, and I told her everything I knew about it. How we had found it growing in fissures in Belson's impenetrable obsidian, how I'd learned to concentrate it and preserve it. It was wonderful to sit there with the windows open in Myra's big living room with the barely luminous New York street outside the window hushed with an August hush, and me with my clean white socks, my skin clean, my hair still dyed and my beard dyed and combed and a fresh shirt on my strong chest, letting the old guilt seep out of my pores and away into the nighttime, off to Fomalhaut and beyond, into the outer reaches.

When I went off to bed a little before midnight, the moon was shining as full as a hundred-dollar silver coin into the bedroom window. On the night before, I had been its fellow orbiter, in a kind of sublunar funk; here I was now, a fugitive, a pirate, dispossessed, but tired and happy going to bed in a New York apartment, ready to sing hymns to the joy of my new life. 'For he on honey dew hath fed, and drunk the milk of paradise.' Coleridge. Another junkie. What the hell. I slept like a baby for a dozen hours.

Birds were singing when I awoke. Myra was up and had found *Pain Chocolat* and espresso for me and three fresh Havana cigars. Gueveras.

I dressed in jeans and a gray tee-shirt and went barefoot into the kitchen and began making an omelet with a fried banana on the side. There was coffee on the wood stove. Yellow morning sunshine came in the kitchen window as still and humane as in a Vermeer. The cup I drank my coffee from was Spode and had a decoration of two small green frogs, facing each other amiably; my heart glowed warmly to see such frogs, and on such china. Myra was wearing a blue denim smock, and walked as if on air, as if she had never gone to sleep with fire in her joints, as if she had had a childhood of skipping rope and tag and dancing. Her hair was tied loosely in back in a bun, her hazel eyes smiled. 'Let me pour you more coffee,' she said, and I remembered her as a bright-eyed two-year-old, as lovely and heartwarming a thing as nature ever made. I had forgotten how much I loved my child.

'Honey,' I said to Myra, 'do you know of an actress named Isabel Crawford? She was in the last *Hamlet*, playing the mother.'

Myra pursed her lips a moment and then nodded slowly. 'British?'

'Scottish. In her forties. Very good-looking.'

'She's a friend of yours then?'

'Sure. Do you know anything about her? I need clues. I can't find her.'

'No, Dad, I'm sorry. I haven't any idea at all. You could call her agent.'

'I tried that last night on your phone. Called her director too, and her hairdresser. No luck at all. They'd like to know where she is too.'

Myra nodded politely while I told her this. When I'd finished she tried to be casual, but I could tell she was picking her words with care. 'Dad. Why don't you give Mom a call? She's in New York.'

Something went tight in my stomach at that. I tried to sound casual too. It was beginning to feel like acting school. 'Oh?' I said. 'Where's she staying?'

'At your old place, Dad. The Pierre.'

Jesus! I thought, *Anna at the Pierre?* It didn't sound like her at all. 'What in hell is your mother doing in New York?' I said. 'She always claimed to hate it here.'

'She was over for dinner a few nights ago, Dad. She said she was getting bored upstate and came down to do some shopping.' She looked at me. 'Why don't you ask her for lunch or something?'

For a moment it was a seductive idea. Whatever Anna might possess of a longshoreman's spirit, she was a hell of a person to talk with. I've never really enjoyed *talking* with a woman as much as I did with her. And I'd never had any trouble getting it up with her—maybe because her sexuality was no threat. I thought, standing there with Myra, of how nice sex with Anna would be—a spell of rain after a three-year drought. But then I thought of that damnable popping girdle and that righteous anger and I said, 'Myra, it just wouldn't be smart. Not now. I know what you have in mind, bless your heart, and I admit there might be something to it. But I don't need the trauma right now. There's something fragile in my spirit, and seeing Anna might shatter it.'

Myra pursed her lips. 'Okay, Dad. It's your life.'

'Oh yes, honey,' I said. 'It sure is.'

12

Isabel was not to be found in New York. I called everyone I dared call and learned nothing but what I had learned from orbit: Isabel had left for London six months before, in *Hamlet*. *Hamlet* closed four months later and no one had heard from her since, not her agent and not her friends. The agent was trying to get her to do the mother in *Mourning Becomes Elektra*—crazy typecasting for childless Isabel, with her teenage figure. She could be in Istanbul or Santa Fe or Aberdeen. I gave up temporarily and concentrated on business.

It's taken over fifty years of living to get my priorities right and to learn that love is more important than money. What fortune-cookie wisdom to spend a lifetime acquiring! But now that I knew it, circumstances forced me to put money first anyway. It was time to peddle endolin.

First I found my friend Millie Shapiro in a little studio apartment on West Fifty-seventh. Millie is a retired makeup artist, once at the top of her profession. I knew her through Isabel; they were both cat fanatics. Millie was grumpy and shaky, but she expertly washed the cheap hair dye out of my hair and redyed it dark brown, with gray at the temples. Her breath was horrible, but when I looked in her cracked vanity mirror afterward I had to whistle. She also trimmed my hair and beard for me in a kind of movie-star way that was far different from my usual rough-and-ready. She gave me a pair of black-rimmed glasses to wear and suggested I shift from cigars to a pipe and that I wear rings. I dismissed the pipe idea immediately; I have a hearty distrust of pipe smokers and tweedy people in general.

Myra had managed to put together sixty thousand dollars in cash and had bought me a money belt at an Army-Navy store to keep it in. I paid Millie, asked her one more time if she had any notion of where Isabel might be, enjoined her to silence, and life. Good woman, Millie, and I trusted her.

I did as she suggested and bought a couple of classy-looking rings at a costume-jewelry place. At a men's store I finished my metamorphosis: tight Western jeans, army boots and a red silk shirt. In the clothing-store mirror I looked as if I'd been sent from central casting to play an ageing gigolo—which was something of a laugh considering my recent troubles. Anyway, most people knew me from the covers of *Time* and *Newsweek*, and on those I'd been beardless and dressed in one of my famous lumberjack shirts. I was known as a 'boyish eccentric': the beard, red shirt and rings should throw people off as long as I could stand to go on looking that way.

Actually, I figured they weren't searching very hard for me. Baynes had the *Isabel* and the uranium and he knew there was no way I was going to get another spaceship. The next move was mine. The move I had in mind was checkmate. I went to Grand Central and bought a Pullman ticket to Columbus, Ohio.

The train had a parlor car, with armchairs and magazines and little tables to set your scotch and soda on. The furnishings were shabby—frayed green curtains on streaked windows, a peeling mural on one wall—and the upholstery was that woeful green that is one of the perversions of U.S. railroading. But I felt at home instantly in that car. I was the first passenger there and I chose a window seat in the chair with the least-worn upholstery. It was ten-thirty in the morning; I ordered a pot of coffee and toast and settled back, clicking the rings together on my left hand, occasionally stroking my freshly trimmed beard and feeling a pleasant anticipation in my stomach.

After a bit, a couple of priests came into the car and seated themselves prissily at the other end from me. And then a small, sexy woman came in and sat down alone. I began changing plans. Ever since that sight of the thighs of my fantasy sweetie who left my life in New Hope, Penn., I travel with the unconscious expectation of sex. It's an expectation that, up to the point I'm writing about, had never been fulfilled. I'd had opportunities when I was younger and on my way to check out a coal mine or a merger or a commodities possibility—taking a firsthand look at Kansas wheat, say, or North Carolina firewood—but I'd always somehow fumbled or lost out or had gone horribly, maddeningly shy at the sight of a crossed pair of legs under the hem of a skirt. The awful truth is that women turn me on so goddamned much I feel powerless with them. Jesus, do I like asses and breasts and pubic hair and the sweet pungency of vaginal lips! Thighs. The backs of knees.

All this response to a small, pretty woman entering a parlor car! Well. It had been a long time. I'd just got back from outer space and from a stretch as solo gardener on a slippery planet. A stint at impotence before that. It had been three years since I'd genuinely experienced a woman. Seeing her there, about forty, with splendid legs and an intelligent face and light-brown hair and a white blouse draping so nicely over her ample breasts, I immediately lost any notions I'd had of catching up on world news on my trip across country. I no longer cared about what had happened in politics or war or energy or show business or acts of God during my absence; I wanted to share my bed with that woman. She had been in the car about thirty seconds and I was in love with her.

Little wrinkles at the corners of her eyes. How nice! Her back straight and her ass neat and firm under her skirt. Splendid! L&M marijuana cigarettes in the gold pack and a gold lighter to match, set with assurance on the little table by her seat. *Quel délicatesse!* She ordered pernod and water in a soft voice, flitted her eyes quickly around the car, passing over me with just the hint of a pause. Oh my God, how I love all those things women do! How I love a civilized New York woman who dresses right and talks warmly and knows how to order a drink on a train! Monuments should be built to such women. To hell with generals, admirals, presidents, artists, messiahs; a civilized, grown-up woman with an education and a firm ass is worth the whole lot of them.

I was scared too. Fifty-three years old, a pirate, and I was beginning to panic at the realization that if I wanted something to happen between us I would have to make it happen. I have lost beautiful women to nobodies because of this fear, have sat stupidly by because I was afraid, down deep, that I

wasn't wanted and let some dumb, balding insurance salesman walk off arm in arm with a woman I'd been admiring for an
hour. Oh yes. As easy as I may be with actresses and showgirls,
I can turn prepubescent and unintelligible in a flash, out in the
real world. And damn it, I am a good-looking billionaire and a
lamb at love-making—a gentle and affectionate lover when
not plagued by psychosomatic wilt.

All this whizzed around in me before my coffee came, before
the train started moving. A minute at most. I knew I'd better act
fast before things got even more complicated. Before that
insurance man came in and plopped down beside her.

I got up and walked over, fast enough so I wouldn't feel my
lack of poise. 'Hello,' I said, 'I'd like to have my coffee with you.
It's coming in a minute.' I tried not to think about my red shirt,
my rings, my dyed beard.

She looked at me with no alarm at all and my heart immediately grew lighter. 'Okay,' she said.

I sat down with surprising ease and introduced myself as
Ben Jonson, using the name of my favorite Benjamin in the
arts. She was Sue Kranefeld and a professor of history at
Berkeley.

'That's terrific!' I said. 'You can tell me about the Punic Wars
and why Alexander the Great didn't live longer.'

'I'm in American history,' she said, which seemed to end
that. Maybe she thought I was being facetious, but I meant it. I
learned a lot about Scottish communism from Isabel.

Her pernod and my coffee came at the same time, and just as
I was pouring, the train pulled out of Grand Central.

'I really love this,' I said. 'I love starting a trip. I think I could
spend my life doing it.'

'Do you travel much?' She poured the water on her pernod
and we watched it cloud up.

I wanted to say I had just got back from the stars, zooming
through light-years of void, but I replied that I traveled whenever I could and that I was in the coal-and-wood business, as a
power-plant designer. Normally I don't like telling lies, but on
a train it's part of the ambience.

She brightened. 'That's interesting to me,' she said. 'I've
been in New York researching the greenhouse panic of the
twenties, and that has a lot to do with coal.'

'Yes,' I said, glad we had something in common to talk about for a while. She was wearing a perfume that smelled of camellias. That soft voice was really splendid, as relaxed as an oatmeal cookie. Something a bit of the schoolteacher about her, but how pleasant she was! And how turned on I was. What I of course wanted to say was, 'I'd sure like to *fuck*, right this minute if you don't mind.' I'd have said it too, if I thought it had a prayer of working. Since it didn't, I had to say *something*, and what I chose was, 'The coal business would be a lot different if they'd planned it right. There was no need to pump all that black soup into the air.' Talk, talk.

'They were greedy,' she said. 'When they started heating with coal and running elevators with it in the twenty-teens it was on a huge scale. People died. Crops died. They tried scrubbers and precipitators and cattle keeled over in fields. Then the greenhouse effect began.'

I was getting nervous with this and was unsure how to stop her. She had adopted the professor mode and was lecturing me. I could see the three-by-five cards in her head flipping over. 'Uranium would have been safer,' I said somewhat lamely, hoping she didn't know anything about uranium. 'Even plutonium.'

'Of *course*,' she said, as though I were a backward student, 'but Denver came at the worst possible time.'

'Just before an election,' I said.

'Do you work for the Mafia?'

'I work for Belson Mines.'

'Oh,' she said. 'Have you met him?' Her voice, thank God, left the classroom and came back to our parlor car. Outside, behind her lovely head of brown hair, were more and more trees and fewer crumbling apartment buildings.

'Sure,' I said, 'a dozen times.'

'What do you think of him?'

'I think his heart's in the right place.'

She thought about that a minute and finished her drink.

'Want some of my coffee?' I said. I had a big pot of it between us.

She shook her head 'No' and flagged down the waiter for a pernod. I poured myself another cup of coffee. 'What do you think of Mr. Belson?' I said, as casually as I could.

She lit a joint and looked out the window. 'He's an attractive man, but he seems . . . frenetic, from what I've read. And foolish.'

'That sounds accurate enough,' I said. 'I know him to be warmhearted.'

She turned and looked at me. 'I think he looks a bit like you, judging from the pictures. Are you related?'

'Cousins,' I said. 'I'd like to take you to lunch at twelve. Okay?'

'Sure.' She smiled pleasantly at me.

Beyond the window it was fields now and trees and a blue sky. The train swayed erotically, as did my loins. *What the hell*, I thought, and said what I wanted to say. 'You sure are a beautiful woman,' I said. *Isabel, I'm sorry.*

'Thank you,' Sue said.

There were light freckles on her upper arms, and not a wrinkle anywhere. I could have kissed every freckle. I vowed then I would, perhaps while crossing Pennsylvania.

I glanced over at the priests; one had his hand on the other's knee and they were bent toward each other in intimacy. What the hell. What are trains really for anyway?

She had another drink before lunch and I worried that the booze in her might get to be a problem, but she only drank a single glass of wine with her spinach quiche. We had the dining car to ourselves, and over dessert I reached out and took her hand. She leaned toward me and said, 'I can't wait until tonight to go to bed with you.'

'What a darling you are!' I said. But I was suddenly nervous. How horrible it would be not to get it up after all this. The thought of how a shot of morphine might help came to mind. But with it there was a flash of unaccustomed clarity: the only way to save this was to tell her the truth and tell it right now.

There was no one seated anywhere near us. I leaned forward a bit and said, 'Sue, I'm embarrassed to say this, but I have a sexual problem.'

She looked at me.

'The last time I went to bed with a woman was over a year ago,' I said, 'and I was impotent.'

She had become a shade distant and she lit up a cigarette now. 'Ben,' she said, 'you're a very attractive man and I like you. But I don't like complications, or embarrassments.'

'Sue,' I said, 'neither do I. But it won't be complicated and it won't be embarrassing.' She must have heard the joyfulness in my voice. Sitting right there in the dining car with a pair of dessert plates between us and watching her light a green marijuana cigarette and click her little lighter shut afterward, watching the freckles on her upper arms and the sweet curve of her neck and smelling her perfume, I felt the unmistakable and joyful response.

I leaned forward and said, 'Hallelujah, Sue! I've got an erection!'

She smiled distantly. 'It's only a little past noon, Ben. I've brought a book with me I need to read . . .'

'Come on, Sue.' I got up carefully—a bit bent over at first. 'I'll be back for you in about two minutes.'

I found a porter and gave her a fifty-dollar piece and told her to make the bed in my compartment. Then I went back to the diner. Sue was drinking what looked like a double Bourbon. For a moment the memory of my mother standing at the sink with a martini, with her ruined face, almost withered me in my tracks. But I pulled myself together. My member, though chastened by the necessity of my walking up and down train aisles, was still alive and well and ready to rejoin the rest of me. I walked up to Sue and bent down to where she was sitting and kissed her warmly on the cheek. Then on the mouth. She kissed me back, a bit warily. I was right; it was Bourbon. Her mouth was full of the taste and it sent a special electricity into my balls. I was ready for rape, ecstasy, tears. Yes, she got up and walked with me the length of two railroad cars and into my compartment. And yes, the sheet was turned down as white and crisp as you ever saw. There was a little vase with three pink carnations sitting on the wash-stand; lace curtains softened the light from the windows. We were out of our clothes in no time. I could have shouted with pride for my dear old member; I could have hung our clothes on it.

All I can say is the whole thing was as easy as anything I've ever done in my life, as easy as drinking cold water on a hot day. God what a lovely, relaxed woman. A little drunk, but I thought: *so what, if that's what she needed*. We did everything in bed we could think of doing. Weight fell from my troubled spirit—some of it was weight I hadn't even known was there —and it was like zero-gravity on the bed afterward. Free fall. If only we could live our whole lives in moments like those. I pulled the curtains open, finally, after we had both napped, and we copulated in twilight as the hills of Pennsylvania rolled by under an August moon.

The next morning she was hung over and threw up in the little sink. It seems she'd gone to the parlor car while I was sleeping and had drunk for three or four hours before coming to bed.

'What a crazy thing to do!' I said, exasperated at the way she looked and the way she sounded at the washstand. Her hair was sweaty, and in the morning light I could see a roll of fat at her waist. There were blue veins behind her knees.

'I'm an alcoholic, Ben,' she said, washing her face.

'I can't believe that,' I said. 'You're in too good shape for a boozer.'

'I only started about a year ago. After my divorce.'

'How do you feel?' I said.

'I've got a terrible headache.'

'I can fix that,' I said, and got one of the little packets out of my briefcase. 'Here. Dissolve this in a glass of water.'

She did as I told her. She dried her face and went on talking. 'I never had an orgasm with my husband until I started getting drunk.'

I just looked at her. After a minute she sat on the bed and sighed. We were both silent. Then she said, 'Hey! my headache's gone.' Her voice was brighter, and with her face freshly scrubbed and her hair combed she was beginning to look good again.

I washed myself up, got dressed and had a silent breakfast while she drank a bloody mary. The morning scenery outside the window began to restore my spirits. Sue's problems were Sue's problems; she had been no problem to me where it counted. I ordered extra toast and coffee and sent a silent prayer of thanks toward Fomalhaut.

At noon she ordered a couple of drinks—martinis this time—and by one we were back in the sack again. I feared failure for one bad moment, thinking that maybe I needed the force of abstinence to impel me. But the fear was dispelled by the salute of my comfortable member. It is a remarkable and wonderful thing to be a man.

During lunch at two-thirty she talked of how coal could supply the world with all its energy, if only it was mined and distributed right. I nodded agreement with her, not going into what I knew about it—considerably more than what any professor knew. That greenhouse effect was only an inconvenience compared to the fights among Mafia families. This was the twenty-first century, for Christ's sake. But the Mafia was run the way General Motors and the Roman Catholic Church had been run in the twentieth. It was an assemblage of bureaucrats whose only loyalty was to the institution.

Well, people like that ran the world in the Middle Ages. The people who run it now are little different. The laws of the Church meant more to the Church than the happiness of mankind. Ditto the Mafia. Ditto General Motors. Ditto Belson Industries? Yes, sometimes. A corporation is more intelligible than life; one can more easily learn its rules and live by them.

I began talking. 'The trouble with coal, Sue, is that it's heavy and dirty. It's hard to get it out of the ground and hard to ship it where you want it. You can gasify it or grind it up and mix it with water and send it through pipes, but the pipes are an invitation to sabotage. They chopped pipes like Christmas ribbons during the gang wars thirty years ago.'

I realized I was talking more heatedly about this than I had planned to. What in hell was I angry with?

She had listened attentively, with an opened book primly in her lap. I was leaning against the green back of my chair, making gestures with my cigar. I wasn't wearing the rings, since I was already heartily sick of them.

When I finished, Sue leaned forward and spoke quietly. 'Ben,' she said, 'you're Ben Belson, aren't you?'

I stared at her. 'What makes you say that?'

'Well, your hair's dyed for one thing. I noticed that last night. And you *talk* like a tycoon.'

I thought about that for a moment and almost said I was more pirate than tycoon. But what the hell was the use of being defensive about it? 'Okay,' I said. 'But for Christ's sake don't tell anybody. I'm on the lam.'

She laughed. 'On the *lam?* That's a quaint way to talk. Didn't the government make you an outlaw or something?'

'A pirate. They took away my citizenship and made me a pirate. Or L'Ouverture Baynes did, the son of a bitch.'

'I voted for Baynes when he ran for President,' she said.

'He's still a son of a bitch.' I drank some coffee angrily. 'I voted for him too. Set a thief to catch a thief.'

'Exactly.'

'Yeah,' I said, looking at the drink in front of her. I had been mulling over an idea ever since breakfast. 'Look,' I said, 'why are you going back to California anyway?'

She closed her book and took a sip from her drink. 'To write up my research. I need to publish.'

'Do you have to teach?'

'I'm on leave for six months.'

'Well, look,' I said, 'I have two interests in life: spiritual growth and financial resurrection. I'm going to Columbus to make money, so I can take my spaceship away from Baynes. If you'd stay with me I'd be able to continue my spiritual growth.'

She raised her eyebrows. 'Let me mull it over, Ben.'

'Sure,' I said.

Well, I needed to mull, myself. One problem was Ruth, my motherly redheaded spaceship pilot. I'd chosen Columbus and Lao-tzu Pharmaceuticals partly because Ruth lived there and I had some idea of staying with her awhile. And Ruth's brother was Howard the biophysicist, whose help I would need before I saw any of those wily Chinese. Ruth was fond of me, and I was fond of her. I was concerned with how things would work out if I showed up in Columbus with a new sweetie.

Why do I complicate things so much—as Anna would say. As Isabel would say. As Sue would be saying soon enough. Orbach didn't ask that question; he answered it. The reason you complicate things so much, Ben Belson, is that you are trying to get your mother's love and your father's attention. Since they are both dead, it's a complicated thing to do. I had to admit there was truth in that; there are simpler goals in life than jarring the dead loose from their sleep.

Sue suddenly spoke up. 'Sure, Ben,' she said. 'I'd like to stay in Columbus with you.'

*   *   *

By mutual consent Sue and I split up for a while. I found a *Newsweek* and read its Energy section. There was another of those pieces about plutonium—that malign transuranite stuff. *Newsweek* did acknowledge that Buenos Aires had been lost to it but claimed plutonium was now safely under lock and key. They talked about the Chinese breeder reactors and about all the cheap energy available in the stockpiles, but they didn't mention what a microgram of plutonium could do to a human lung.

There was another *Newsweek* piece, about coal distribution, full of false hope. I knew far too much about the way coal was moved around to have any faith in it at all. If the United States was going to revive, it was going to be with Juno uranium making steam for the next millennium and beyond. I could feel the straightforward power of it the way I felt my sexual power.

That brought me back to thinking about Sue. I looked at my watch. We were due in Columbus in twenty minutes. I set my magazine down and went back to the parlor car to look for her. I'd been reading in the diner. She wasn't there. The place was empty except for the two priests still in murmured conversation, still with the hand of one on the knee of the other.

I headed briskly toward the sleeping car, pushing my way past a couple of porters, already beginning to feel angry at what I was sure I'd find. And find it I did.

When I opened the door to our bedroom I could smell her. I felt like picking up her fallen-off shoe and beating her in the face with the heel of it. She was sprawled out in the easy chair in a rumpled, red-faced mess, passed out drunk. I might have been able to wake her, but I didn't try.

173

13

I left Sue on the train and felt no guilt in doing it. If that was
what she wanted her life to be like, it was her business; I
wasn't prepared to dance her loser's dance and get involved
in waking her up and feeding her endolin and dragging her
into Columbus with me and then hearing the apologies. She
knew what *I* wanted with her, and I was beginning to see
what *she* wanted. A few years ago I would have become
involved, but not now.

In the station I walked directly to a pay phone, got the
dollar for a local call and Ruth's telephone number out of my
billfold, and stood there for a long moment holding in my
hand my worn old billfold and the paper Ruth had given me
aboard the *Isabel* with her phone number and address. The
little brass dollar was in the other hand. What was I doing,
leaving one woman behind me and rushing to another?
There in that badly lit train station in Columbus, Ohio, about
seventy miles from the little town where I was born, I began to
remember my nights on Belson. My shoulders and the backs
of my legs tingled with the memory of the grass making its
interstellar connection with my physical self. My heels felt
sensitive; they remembered the tendrils that had penetrated
them. A sigh arose from my soul, and I heard an old woman
who stood at the viddiphone next to mine gasp softly, and I
saw her turn to stare at me for a moment in alarm. Did I look
like John the Baptist again? Had I sighed like a drunken beast,
as Isabel claimed that I sighed in my sleep?

Here I was about to embark on another dubious sexual
adventure, about to diddle with the life of a person who had
shown more concern for me than I had ever shown for her—
who might secretly love me, for all I knew—and I was going to

174

do this questionable diddling while involved in whatever steps were necessary to find Isabel, make money, and get the uranium off my spaceship and away from L'Ouverture Baynes. All of this while staying out of prison. *What was I doing?* Where was my Belson calm, my Belson peace? I looked down at my hand. It was trembling. I jammed it, together with the billfold, Ruth's paper and the dollar, back into my pocket. I turned away from the phone, walked out of the station and into an Ohio drizzle.

It was a five-block walk to the John Glenn Hotel. I was soaked by the time I got there and I dripped water onto the blue carpet at the desk while I registered. The clerk stared at me. I ignored him and signed, thinking of Belson nights.

I came for a moment out of this reverie when he asked if I would prefer a heated room, explaining crisply that the John Glenn had a splendid new coal furnace. There was an implication in his voice that I couldn't afford it. Not exactly a stupid inference, considering my bedraggled state and lack of luggage; but bastards like that have no business trying to make their customers feel uncomfortable.

When I didn't reply immediately he said, 'Perhaps you would prefer one of our unheated singles, with the heavy blankets?'

I blinked at him. 'Come off it,' I said. 'I want a suite and I want it heated.' My voice was hoarse.

He just looked at me.

'What's your best suite?'

'We have the Neil Armstrong Gallery on the third floor . . .'

'What's a gallery?'

'Three rooms and a terrace.'

'Is it heated?'

'Every room.'

'I'll take it.'

It was overpriced, and the gray sofa in the parlor had coffee stains on its arms. But there was space to move around in, and a combination kitchen and dining room of the kind that is dear to my heart. I christened it the Belson Grass Room and decided to use it for meditation.

I had to get out of my wet clothes and I didn't have any dry ones. The suite was warm, so I undressed, wrung out my

175

clothes, hung them on the shower rod in the bathroom and padded around naked. That turned out to be a good thing; it brought me back to my nights on Belson.

There was an oriental carpet under the table in the dining room. I pushed the table over against the wall and lay down naked on my back on the rug. The floor was warm and the carpet thick, with a slightly musty smell. After I had lain there awhile I began again to feel the tingling down my back, neck to heels, that I'd felt in the train station. The confused voices in my head, and the anger that had begun to gather in me while I was registering in the hotel, began to leave me. Eventually I dozed off.

I woke up late in the afternoon and just lay there and contemplated the state of my affairs for a while. What I needed first was money. More cash to supplement what Myra had given me and then some real money. I pushed myself up from the floor, padded into the bathroom to check my clothes. They were still damp. I went to the viddiphone by the living-room sofa and set its lens for a head shot, so my nakedness wouldn't show. I seated myself, touched the switch on the phone, and told it to get me a banker I knew. His home phone. In fact he worked for me, since I owned about 40 percent of his savings and loan. And he owed me a favor.

He didn't recognize me with the dyed hair and the beard. I identified myself, told him to keep quiet about my presence in Ohio and to have his savings and loan lend me a half million, in large bills. To fit my money belt. 'I'll think of something to give you a mortgage on, Gordon,' I told him. 'Bring papers.'

He cleared his throat and looked humble. 'Mr. Belson,' he said, with some of the soft-mouthed arrogance the hotel clerk had tried on me, 'I'm not certain it would be within my authority. As much as I'd like to accommodate you . . .'

'I'll accommodate your ass out of the loan business for the rest of your life,' I said. 'You dumb son of a bitch. You have those bills here tomorrow morning or you'll be sweeping streets for a living.' The pompous little fart. He was one of those Warren G. Harding types, with the silver hair at the temples and the grandfatherly ways. Probably younger than I. Ask him to break a law and he turns Sunday school. 'Bring

176

that money personally. If you don't you're a fiscal ruin.'

There was silence for a moment. I stared at him and let myself float on my rage.

'I'm sorry, Mr. Belson . . .' His voice was creaky.

'Forget it,' I said. 'I'll see you tomorrow at ten.' I felt righteous, ready to excoriate greedy foolishness and malfeasance in general.

Gordon looked dazed; I felt suddenly a little dazed myself. 'See you in the morning,' I said and hung up. Then I walked back through the dining room and out onto the terrace. This turned out to be a six-by-eight-foot permoplastic apron with an Astroturf rug on it. So much for Neil Armstrong. So much for his dumb remark about that first step. No feeling in it. No more life than Astroturf. At least I had announced the first human steps on Belson with a yelp and a broken arm.

But where was my peace—my Belson peace? My hands were trembling with anger.

The drizzle had lightened but I didn't stay on the terrace. I had begun thinking of Neil Armstrong and of those bland, tightly smiling descendants of people like him, who were more and more coming to rule the world. The John Glenn Hotel, indeed. John Glenn had been orbited like a fetus a hundred years ago, crouched in the belly of the hurtling whale more for publicity reasons than for engineering ones, and the people of Ohio had allowed him to make laws for all of us because of it. What folly. What an omen! I'd have voted for him maybe, for his being a sound, middle-aged test pilot before the razzmatazz of NASA, but never for his orbits, those pawn moves in the unholy game my country was playing with Russia at the time. What dangerous idiots we were in those days, with our weapons and our paranoia!

These thoughts about the United States and its long tradition of folly were doing me no good. Why was I so *angry?* My nose was itching. I was catching cold.

My shorts in the bathroom, a sky-blue pair I'd worn halfway across the Milky Way and back, were dry enough to put on, since I'd draped them over a hissing radiator. I took a quick shower, got into the shorts, and with a restored sense of purpose went to the viddiphone in the parlor. For a moment I wanted to call Ruth, but I put that out of my mind. I told the machine to give me her brother's number. I got him on the first try. 'Howard,' I told him, 'I need to see you and for God's sake don't tell anyone I'm in Columbus.'

I'd quieted down a bit by the time Gordon got to my room with the money. He tried to be hearty and companionable about it, but I wasn't buying. I signed first-mortgage papers with him for a house I own in Key West and sent him on his way. Then I put what I could of the money into my belt, rolled the rest into a crapshooter's roll and stuffed it in my jeans. When I put the belt on it was like putting a bicycle chain around my waist, but it's the best way I know to carry liquid assets. They'd have to sever me to get at it.

Howard arrived a few minutes after Gordon left and I greeted him with a hug. It was good to see someone from the *Isabel* again.

'Well, Captain,' he said, 'you look healthy. But I liked you as a blond.'

'Me too,' I said. 'Let me get you a drink.'

I poured us both some Chinese wine. The living room had a fake fireplace with a pair of high-backed red armchairs by it; we sat in these facing each other. 'Did you marry again, Howard?' I asked.

He shook his head slowly. 'After the ship landed in Florida and the court let us go I was excited about finding a new wife. I felt . . .' He was sitting hunched over his wineglass and holding it in both hands. 'I felt like a sailor in port, if you know what I mean.' He finished his wine. 'But nothing happened.'

'You didn't meet any women?'

'It seemed like a lot of trouble for nothing, once I got down to it. I took the bus to Columbus.' He smiled shamefacedly. 'I suppose I'm getting older.'

I stared at him.

'I'm forty-four.'

I could have hit him with one of the artificial logs. But I didn't do anything. The man had six divorces behind him. Maybe he knew something.

I got up and went to the bedroom. When I came back to my chair I handed him a packet. 'Howard,' I said, 'I need to have this analyzed by somebody who's really good at it.'

'It looks like dope,' he said.

'It's endolin. I want to find out if it can be duplicated.'

'I know just the man. A professor at Ohio State.' He held the packet in his hand as though weighing it. 'Endolin didn't look like this on Belson.'

'I learned a way to concentrate it.' I found myself getting more irritated with this conversation. Also, I was beginning to get a serious cold. I excused myself again and went to the bedroom for a handkerchief and blew my nose violently. My throat was sore and my skin felt prickly. I got out another pack of endolin and took a pinch, chasing it with the rest of my wine.

'Captain,' Howard shouted from the other room, 'did the grass sing anymore?'

I felt annoyed with the question. 'Yes,' I said, 'once.'

He nodded. 'Wasn't the grass why you stayed? So you could hear it again?'

'I wanted to consolidate myself.'

'You could have done that on Juno.'

'I can be very self-defeating in how I live.'

He laughed as though I was joking, although I certainly wasn't. 'You know,' he said. 'I wanted to stay myself.'

I stood in the doorway and looked at him awhile—at his sad face and stooped shoulders. He did look old. Then I said, 'On Juno or on Belson?'

'Belson,' he said.

Oh yes, I thought, furious. *There's a lot of it going around.*

I woke before dawn with my bedsheet wet from sweat and my nose and throat feeling stuffed with steel wool. My head throbbed. I got up shakily, feeling wretched, took some endolin and a glass of warm water and then got back in bed and waited. After a few minutes the throbbing stopped and I felt the fever abate, but the baroque world of predawn sickness was enveloping my spirit.

Eventually I fell asleep again, or something like asleep, with twisting around and fighting with the sheets, which would not seem to get straight and smooth no matter what I did. I remember sitting up in bed sometime that morning after the sun had risen and shouting, 'Motherfuckers

motherfuckers motherfuckers!' and trying to get the top sheet to cover my toes. *'Motherfuckers!'* Someone below me pounded on the ceiling and, fuming, I became quiet again.

I slept till ten and felt better when I awoke, again, to wet sheets. I called room service and got four soft-boiled eggs and a bloody mary. Then I put on my jeans and my red shirt, went to the living room and called Lao-tzu Pharmaceuticals.

It took about an hour of switching around from office to office before I could get anybody important—which really meant anybody Chinese. She was a junior vice-president in charge of Development and clearly a fan of the National Cultural Revival: Pear Blossom Loo. A young woman of about thirty, with black bangs above a face as inscrutable as a cue ball. Nice teeth, though, as well as I could see. I was sitting with the shades down and in dim light to make sure I wasn't recognized.

'Miss Loo,' I said, 'my name is Ben Jonson. I'm a professor of biochemistry at Stanford and I've developed an analgesic substance that should be of interest to you.'

'I see,' she said. 'The Research Division of Lao-tzu International is not here. Not in Columbus. Bogotá.'

My fever was coming back and for a minute I just wanted to hang up and go back to bed and drink bloody marys. Damn these uptight Chinese women! Damn doing business anyway! But I pulled myself together as well as I could and tried to sound charming. 'Of course,' I said, 'but the research is done. What you need to do is test it out. That's not really research.'

'I'm sorry, Mr. Jonson,' she said, 'we do not have the personnel or the equipment in Columbus to do what you say.'

'Look,' I said, 'you have a Shartz Analyzer, don't you?'

'We have several.'

'That's all you need for now.' I sneezed suddenly. 'We've run tests for a year at the University. It kills pain as well as morphine and it's not a narcotic.'

'I'm not certain, Mr. Jonson, that Lao-tzu . . .'

'Come *on*, Miss Loo!' I said. 'You look like a smart woman to me. This will take a half hour of your time and it can give you the most profitable pill since Glandol, or time-release Valium. Since Fergusson, for Christ's sake. Do I sound like a lunatic?'

'Yes you do, Mr. Jonson,' Pear Blossom said crisply. I found myself staring at a blank viddiphone screen. She had hung up on me. 'Son of a bitch!' I said and began sneezing. Then the sneeze turned into a cough. I got up and went to the bathroom and coughed and sneezed and spat voluminously into the toilet, occasionally stopping long enough to shout, 'Mother-fucker!' Whoever was below me pounded the ceiling again. I could picture some chubby, balding druggist hitting upward with a broom handle. I went on coughing, bent over and holding my belly. My nose was running.

Eventually the coughing stopped. I called room service for two bloody marys and then reached out for the Repeat button on the phone to get Pear Blossom back, but interrupted myself with another fit of coughing. *What the hell*, I thought, and called Ruth.

She came on looking sweet and chubby and a little dis-heveled. *Good old Ruth!* I thought, and my heart warmed at the sight of her there in front of me.

She was staring at me, apparently not sure who it was. 'Ben'? she said.

'That's right, Ruth,' I said warmly, with the cold now in my voice, since my nose was plugged up. 'I'm in Columbus.'

She kept staring. Then suddenly she looked almost awed. 'Oh *Ben*,' she said, 'I thought I'd never see you . . .'

'I'm at the John Glenn, Ruth.' Just then a knock came on the door. 'Wait a minute,' I said. I left the phone and walked over, opened the door and took the tray with the drinks from the waiter. I pulled a fifty from my jeans pocket, handed it to him and went back to the phone. 'Ruth,' I said, 'you don't know how much good it does just to see your face.' I guzzled one of the bloody marys and snorted.

Ruth looked worried. 'Are you drunk, Ben?'

'I'm sick, Ruth honey. I've got a cold. It feels . . . inter-stellar.'

She looked relieved. 'Do you want me to bring you some hot soup? I go to work in twenty minutes, and I could drop by . . .'

'Ruth,' I said, interrupting, 'I want more than soup. I'd like to move in with you for a week or two, while I get over this thing. I need to get a World Viddiphone Line and I need a set of barbells . . .' I sneezed again. 'How about it?'

She hesitated, started to say something. Then she said, 'Are you all right, Ben? Weren't the police . . .?'

'I eluded them, Ruth, as the papers said.'

'Oh,' she said. 'Ben, you look *strange*. Did you kick it? Morphine?'

I was starting to feel angry again. 'Yes. I changed a lot, on Belson. Can I come and stay for a week?'

She looked at me silently for a moment. Then she shook her head. 'Ben, it's too late for that. I have a man living with me. I can bring you some food, and a doctor if you need one . . .'

It was a setback for my vanity, but I managed to hide it well enough. 'I'll be all right, Ruth.'

She smiled sadly. 'Sorry, Ben.'

After talking with Ruth I sipped another bloody mary and permitted myself the old childhood gloom, then shook it off. What the hell, it was time to be grown-up about it. I'd tried the alternative enough in my life. There was business to take care of, and Isabel to locate. I pressed the Repeat button on the phone twice and got Lao-tzu again.

'Pear Blossom Loo, please,' I said.

The head on the screen disappeared and was replaced by that of Pear Blossom's secretary. He put me through to Pear Blossom with some reluctance.

When she saw me she looked ready to hang up again. 'The Research Division of Lao-tzu is in Bogotá, Colombia, Mr. Jonson.'

I kept my composure, although I felt like throwing an ashtray at her disembodied head. 'Miss Loo,' I said, 'I'll be in your office tomorrow afternoon. Do you really want me going to Parke-Davis first?'

'I will be in conference all day tomorrow.' Her face was a study in blank dislike.

'I'll be there anyway,' I said, and hung up. Her head and shoulders disappeared from the screen.

I fumed around the room for a while after that, cursing China in general and Chinese bureaucrats in particular. What Lao-tzu Pharmaceuticals needed was somebody like Arabella

Kim to run it, with her good wrinkled face and tobacco-stained teeth. It was about noon, and there were things I wanted to do in Columbus—like getting a set of barbells—before going out to Lao-tzu in the morning, but I was beginning to feel as if I wouldn't be able to do any of it. This cold, or whatever it was I had, was *bad*. I was sticky from sweat and my nose and throat were stinging. I took endolin and it kept down the pain, but it didn't do anything for the cold itself. I knew what I needed was a transfusion from Belson grass, but that was out of the question. I climbed into bed, jabbed out my cigar in an ashtray, put a pillow over my head, and passed out. Falling asleep, I wondered briefly about Sue—about where the train would have been when she came to and found me gone.

I awoke late in the afternoon feeling feverish, dazed and unworldly. I knew I was sick, but I also knew it was only a cold. Something deeper was troubling me, some old loneliness. I'd had a Private World Line installed in the room and could talk through scrambled microwaves with considerable security to any phone in the world. I could do therapy this way. I sat up in bed, adjusted the sheets, relit my cigar, and called Orbach.

Orbach came on with his usual somberness. 'Hello, Benjamin,' he said. 'Welcome back into the world.'

'Orbach,' I said, 'can you spare me an hour? Things are happening.'

He shook his head. 'I'm sorry. I have a patient arriving. I can connect you with my surrogate . . .'

'*Orbach!*' I said, desperate. 'I don't want to talk to a computer. Give me twenty minutes.'

Orbach looked at me sadly. 'I'm truly sorry, Benjamin,' he said. 'I can give you the noon hour on Thursday.'

'I don't want Thursday,' I said. 'Give me your computer.'

'It's good to see you back safely, Benjamin,' the Great Orbach said. There was a slight click and the screen went milky white. Then Orbach's synthesized voice came from the speaker. 'Hello, Benjamin,' it said. 'We can talk if you'd like.'

'Hell yes, I'd like,' I said.

'You sound angry,' the voice said.

'I'd like to talk to my mother,' I said grimly. What the hell.

'Your mother is dead, Benjamin.'

'I've heard that your machines can fake it.'

183

'I don't know the voice,' the machine said. 'I know parts of the personality, from your remarks in the office. Perhaps you can help me.'

I nodded. I'd been offered the chance to do this before but refused it as being too contrived. 'First, she was a woman. Of sorts.'

'Yes,' said Orbach's voice, now female.

'I want you to be her at about thirty-five, when I was a teenager. There was a nervous quaver in her voice. She was born in Columbus, Ohio, in 1987 and she spoke with an Ohio accent. She was a narcissistic drunk and she tried to be casual in her speech, but the self-regard and worry were always there.'

There was a pause and then the machine said, in a genteel, quavering female voice, 'Do I sound like your mother now, Benjamin?'

'That's pretty good,' I said grimly.

'If you have a picture I'll put it on the screen and animate it.'

'I'm not sure . . .' I said. But I was sure. I was faking it for the benefit of the machine. I did have my mother's picture in my billfold; I'd carried it for over thirty years and never told a soul. I reached over to the table beside the bed, took my billfold, opened it, slipped out a polychrome holo card and squeezed it on. And there sat Mother with a glass in one hand and a cigarette in the other, looking at the camera in a patronizing way. Her brow was furrowed half in irony and half anxiety. Her hair needed combing. I stared at her for a long time, unsure what I was feeling.

'Hold it toward the viewing lens, please.' It was the machine speaking but I almost jumped; it had come to seem very like Mother's voice.

I held the picture toward the tiny lens at the bottom of the set, and a moment later the face reappeared on the screen. I leaned back in bed, my head propped slightly against the wall, and puffed my cigar. My palms were sweating and my mouth was dry. 'Hello, Mother,' I said.

The face moved, quite naturally, talking. 'Hello, Benny,' it said. It was uncanny. I felt frightened.

'Are you drunk, Mother?' I said.

'Hardly,' she said. 'It's ten in the morning.'

'Oh,' I said. Somehow the wind had all gone out of my sails. 'What year is it?'

She looked down toward her watch. Mother always wore a watch, which may be why I'd never worn one until recently. Until leaving Isabel. 'It's June 8, 2024,' she said. 'And I feel like hell.'

'I hate to see you drinking and smoking like that, Mother,' I said. 'It makes me nervous.'

She looked at me and then puffed her cigarette. 'You're just a child, Benny,' she said. 'You have no idea how badly I feel. And your father's no help . . .'

Some of my anger was coming back. 'Have you ever asked him for help?' I said.

'What good would that do? You have no conception of what it's like to deal with that man . . .'

Damn it, Mother!' I shouted. 'You've never noticed, have you? You've never seen me trying to get him to talk to *me* . . .' And I broke off, startled to hear the quaver in my voice like that in the voice of the woman in front of me.

'He used to hold you on his lap when you were a baby. It was only after you got loud and had dirty fingernails all the time . . .'

'Mother,' I said, 'you're trying to blame me. Damn your soul.'

She laughed, a cruel little self-regarding laugh. 'You were hyperactive, Benny. And loud. A real pain in the neck . . .'

I stared at her, telling myself, *It's only a machine, a computer in an analyst's office on Third Avenue in New York. It isn't even her voice. It doesn't really sound like her.* Yet I saw myself as a small boy, dirty-nailed and loud and squirming and I felt hatred toward the child I saw, toward what that mechanical voice had sketched for me so blithely. 'Mother!' I said. 'Stop it!'

She looked at me and then took a knowing sip from the glass in her hand.

'Mother.' I could hear the pain in my voice as though it were someone else's. 'I was only a little kid.'

She seemed not to hear me. 'I never should have had a child.'

'I didn't ask you to,' I said.

185

She laughed a little more easily this time and finished her drink. 'You were a trial to me even before you were born, Benny. You almost tore out my liver with your feet.' She looked meditative. 'That's all you were when I was pregnant with you: elbows and feet.'

'Goddamn it!' I said, sitting upright in bed. The sheet fell away from me. I was naked there in front of her, exposed. 'Goddamn it, you were supposed to be my *mother*.'

Somehow she had gotten another glass of what must have been gin and she took a long swallow from it. 'To tell the truth, Benny, you were a mistake,' she said. 'I had too much to drink at the wedding, and took the wrong Fergusson.'

'*Orbach!*' I shouted at the machine, 'how can you know that? You're not *her*.'

Mother's picture remained on the screen, motionless now, and Orbach's voice came on, mechanically synthesized. 'It is inferable,' the voice said gravely, 'from your memories and dreams. You are not being toyed with in therapy. You hear from your mother what you yourself believe to be true.'

I lay back in bed again and started to pull the sheet over my body, but did not. I puffed my cigar deeply for a moment, nursing myself as always, and said, 'Bring her back and let her talk.'

'Benny,' she said, more brightly now, 'you were sweet enough in your way, but you never knew what *I* was going through. You would slobber kisses on me when I was hung over, and try to crawl in bed with me in the mornings, and when you were two you kept hugging your father's leg until I had to pull you away. You weren't like other children, with good manners and an ability to entertain themselves. You wanted attention all the time, and I was having problems myself. Your father ignored me. The other faculty wives made me a pariah. Life was very difficult for me.'

I watched her with appalled fascination, remembering every phrase of it from one time or another. As she went on drinking and talking her face became more relaxed and pleasant. She looked younger and I saw, suddenly, that her breasts were still high under her pale-blue housedress and not the sagging old woman's breasts of the night she had sat with the candles going. 'I know I have drunk a bit too much to be the best of mothers,' she was saying, 'but other mothers get some help from their husbands.'

Now you're blaming him, I thought. *You'll blame anybody. Like me with Isabel.* I writhed with this for a moment, lost in a confusion of myself and my chattering mother there on the screen. It wasn't really Mother anyway, only a simulacrum. *And neither am I*, I thought. *I am not my mother either, but only a likeness when it comes to love.*

'I had the whole work of rearing you,' she said. 'He did not lift one finger. Not one.'

'*Mother,*' I shouted from the bed. 'You goddamned fraud. You could have loved me anyway. You could have let me love you . . .'

'Benjamin,' she said sternly, 'you are getting an erection. Cover yourself.'

I looked down. It was true. I stared at myself for a long moment, bedazzled. I was shameless; I kept getting harder.

'Well,' she said in some kind of crazy voice that was half coy and half reproachful, 'I'm glad to see that you're normal. It's more than I can say for your father in there.'

I stared at her on the screen. 'Shut up!' I said. 'Won't you please just shut up?'

Her eyes began to glaze. 'Benny,' she said, 'you'll never know what it's been like for me all these years. God knows I've tried. I've tried to be a good wife and mother and nobody cares anything for me.'

'*Mother,*' I said, 'I cared. I tried to love you and you pushed me away, just like Daddy. The two of you were a fucking *team* . . .'

'You don't have to use that language,' she snapped. 'You've forgotten how I nursed you, and fed you . . .'

'That's not how it was, Mother,' I said. 'You used to feed me Franco-American spaghetti out of a can. Half the time you didn't trouble yourself to heat it.' I stared at her. 'You were too drunk, Mother.'

She looked down at her lap a moment and then took another drink. Her voice had become low and her eyes seemed to look inward as they had that night on the couch, with the candles. 'You can abuse me all you like, Benjamin, with your gutter language. But the truth is I'm your mother and I did my best for you.'

I sat up in bed, feeling something about to burst in my head. 'It

187

wasn't your best and it wasn't enough,' I said.

For a long moment we were both silent, staring at one another. I realized, with a shock, that she was much younger than I. Prettiness and weakness met in her face, already showing incipient ruin. My hatred for that face was insatiable; I wanted to crush it like a rotten grapefruit between my hands.

During all this my prick had remained erect. Mother looked at me awhile in a kind of crazy, muted contemplation. Then she said. 'I used to wash your thing for you, Benny, when you were little, and cute. You always enjoyed it.'

'*Mother,*' I said, '*I was not a toy.* God did not give you something to fool around with when you had me.'

She smiled a faint, smug smile. 'Why is your penis so hard, Benny?'

'*Why do you think?*' I found myself shouting. 'And you aren't worth it. You're nothing.'

I was sitting straight up in bed. I reached forward abruptly and slammed the telephone's 'off' switch with the heel of my hand. Her face, with its smug, flirtatious smile, vanished into the electronic limbo it had been generated from.

I finished my cigar slowly and got Orbach's machine on the phone again. This time the screen was blank. 'I hope you are better, Benjamin,' the machine said in Orbach's normal voice.

'I don't know. I'm not as angry.'

'And things are clearer?'

'Things are,' I said. 'I had an erection while I was looking at her.'

'Congratulations!' the machine said. 'Would you like to talk with your father?'

I reached for another cigar and held it for a while in my hand. Then I shook my head. 'My father's dead,' I said.

'Yes,' the machine said, 'he is dead.'

'Then I've done enough,' I said.

In an hour the fever was down and my head was clear. It was getting dark outside, and the rain had stopped. I looked at my watch. Eight o'clock. I would be going out to Lao-tzu in the morning and I needed to do some research first. And I was hungry.

I phoned room service for a hamburger and a glass of ginger

188

ale. Then I called the one local taxi and reserved him for eight in the morning. I hung up, pushed the 'Library' button on the viddiphone and began tracking down what was available on Lao-tzu. There was a good deal, much of it in the Shanghai People's Library.

I found two histories of the company, going back to its origins on a Nanking back street in the nineteenth century, and books about the founder. There were annual reports and stock prospectuses in English and Chinese, and a lot of miscellaneous works on the drug business in China. I put it all on 'Hold.'

On a hunch I checked U.S. Political Science and struck it rich there too: a holo movie called *L'Ouverture Baynes—Man of the Times*, and a book from the University of Kentucky Press, *Kentucky Political Campaigns in the 2050s*. I had texts of these printed out.

My hamburger arrived on a pewter plate with grapes and cheese cubes and Roquefort dressing and piles of evil-looking lettuce: clearly a Renaissance Pope Sandwich. I signed the bill and turned on the TV, switching it to play the material I had on 'Hold' on the viddiphone. I threw away the lettuce and began eating, as an introduction to the Chinese ethical drug business came on. There was a panoramic shot of Chang An in Peking and crowds of healthy, prosperous Chinese. 'Welcome to China!' a saccharine voice proclaimed. I sighed, had a drink of ginger ale, and called room service again for a pot of coffee. It was going to take a lot of caffeine to get through all this.

About the time my pitcher of coffee arrived, Howard called to say he'd gotten the report on endolin. There was no way to analyze it completely and no way whatever to synthesize it. I was delighted. I thanked him for his help and told him I had to get busy. Then I instructed the viddiphone to select out for me all the information on analgesics and to read it aloud, in English. I poured a cup of coffee and settled back in my chair.

At Lao-tzu in the morning Pear Blossom's secretary told me icily that she was in conference. I told him I'd wait, plumped myself into an armchair and opened my Kentucky Politics printout, brought along for just this purpose. I lit a cigar. It

189

must have been thirty years since anybody had made me wait in an outer office, cooling my heels like a porno-videosphere salesman, but I managed it all right. Pear Blossom came in a little over an hour later dressed in a gorgeous lavender shift and high heels. She saw me sitting there and looked away coolly, about to hurry into her office. Nice legs.

I played my ace in the hole immediately: I spoke to her in Chinese, using the Tradition-Revival forms. 'Gracious flower of the arching pear tree,' I said, freezing her in her tracks. 'I address you unworthily and my outlander's tongue is lame with its mockery of yours.' In fact, I was speaking Chinese beautifully and Pear Blossom, judging from her face, knew it. '. . . yet even my poor discourse might add treasure to the bursting storehouse of the exalted Lao-tzu.'

'I'll give you ten minutes,' Pear Blossom said.

I followed her into her office, a packet of endolin in my hand.

It took them four days to make the first offer. It was absurdly low, as I explained to Pear Blossom and her boss. By that time they had figured out who I was and had come to take me seriously. They also knew, of course, what endolin could do. They wanted it. Oh yes. It tingled my capitalist balls to sense that.

They doubled the offer the next day, and I told them again what I wanted. Three hundred million for the fifty pounds I had and for a 40 percent option on imports.

They walked out on that, as I thought they might.

The following day we met in a bigger room, with gray silk wall hangings. There was a new person among them, a very old woman in a blue robe, just arrived by plane from Peking. Pear Blossom introduced her to me as Mourning Dove Soong and I knew immediately who she was.

I spoke to her in Chinese. 'I am filled with pride to address the distinguished chairperson of the world's most formidable drug company.'

She nodded without smiling. 'You ask too much for your endolin. A headache is a headache. Aspirin is a fine drug.'

This was just what I wanted. My heart felt light. It is exhilarating to see research pay off.

'I agree heartily,' I said. 'I often buy aspirin from Bayer—a fine company—or Norwich, though that firm tediously outsells Lao-tzu throughout Europe, Scandinavia, and the Gold Coast. Upjohn also purveys a fine U.S.P. aspirin, to be found in twice as many American stores as the Lao-tzu product, unquestionably worthy though the latter is. One might weep at the thought.'

Mourning Dove was looking at me thoughtfully, holding a glass of plum wine. Pear Blossom and her boss were on the sofa. I sat in an armchair.

'One must also regard,' I said, 'those merciful aids to the arthritic which are made with an analgesic as a component. Tao, the illustrious nine-way arthritis remedy, has sadly lost millions of dollars to Anacin alone over the past seven quarters. The new plant in Rio de Janeiro for the manufacturing of Tao will be forced to close, at embarrassing cost, if this tendency is not reversed. Worker riots are spoken of publicly. One wonders what the addition of endolin, in trace amounts, might do to this unhappy competition with Anacin. Then we must consider light anesthesia for minor surgery, and the hospital market . . .'

Mourning Dove was lighting a cigarette, much as Humphrey Bogart might have. 'We'll buy it,' she said.

I could have hugged her. 'Splendid!' I said, in English. 'Let's sign the papers here tomorrow.'

Mourning Dove nodded, and sipped her wine. 'I understand you have no present citizenship, Mr. Belson,' she said.

'All too true,' I said in English, still feeling some of the Chinese way of speaking in my head. 'I have no nationality whatever at present.' I hesitated. 'Perhaps you and I are sharing a thought.' My research had told me Mourning Dove was not only Chairperson of Lao-tzu International; she also sat on the Committee for the Enlargement of the People. The Immigration Bureau.

'Perhaps. Would you like to be Chinese?'

'Mourning Dove, you are marvelous!' I said. 'You and I understand each other very well.'

'Yes,' she said, unsmiling, in her soft, gravelly voice. 'I'm certain it will help with your plans, to be free of legal encumbrances. Our embassies protect the People, Mr. Belson.'

'Oh, don't I know it,' I said, exuberant. I had planned to go for this but hadn't been sure it would work. As a Chinese I could have lawyers; I could use the whole string of multinational and world courts to go after the *Isabel*.

'Yes,' Mourning Dove said. 'It will make our contract safe from red tape. And from publicity.'

'I'm right with you, Mourning Dove,' I said. 'Do I need to pass any tests? I've read Confucius and the sayings of Chairman Mao. I have a pair of Qin horses by my croquet court in Atlanta, and my sweetheart, Isabel Crawford, is a Maoist.' I was high and feeling a bit silly. And I was really liking Mourning Dove, in whose eyes I had begun to detect amusement.

'None of that will be necessary,' Pear Blossom said coolly. 'It's a matter of form with the Committee for Enlargement, in Peking. The People's Republic does not require performances from prospective citizens.'

Mourning Dove ignored her and smiled faintly at me. 'Many of the Qin horses are exquisite,' she said. 'I am pleased with your judgement.'

'Thank you,' I said. 'Thank you for coming all the way from China.'

The forms were sent to Columbus by Transpacific Xerox, and by the next afternoon I was Chinese. I signed three papers in the presence of witnesses, made a ceremonial bow, and promised to be orderly in the arrangement of my household. Why not? I could have signed my name in script, but my professor of Chinese had shown me the calligraphic way and I did it like that, using a brush:

本
鏢
信

I became a compatriot of Confucius and Mao with a few strokes. A small world, if you know the right people. Chinese Belson.

I remained undeceived, however, aware that my being Chinese made the endolin contract safer for them. The papers were ready right after the naturalization papers. I signed them briskly. I was now not only a Chinese, but a rich Chinese.

After I left Lao-tzu with a plastic card that identified me as a Chinese national, my taxi took me to The People's Bank of Shanghai, Columbus Branch, where I set up some accounts. I'd taken a check for ten million from Lao-tzu, for good faith and to tide me over until the transfer of funds was finished. The only possible snag was in Lao-tzu's getting the endolin from the *Isabel*. I wouldn't have any more cash from them until that was brought off. Since the People's Republic maintained a big staff in Washington, and since even L'Ouverture couldn't buck the State Department where Chinese relations were concerned, I hoped they'd have it within a week. I'd told Pear Blossom how to find it in the *Isabel*'s cabin. Pear Blossom was clearly the sort of person who got hold of what was rightfully hers.

Back at the hotel I called London; first a retired actor I knew and then a theatrical agency. No luck from either. There was a subsidiary of Belson Tile and Marble in Fleet Street. I called its director and told him to find out what he could about an actress named Isabel Crawford. I'd call him back next week. His eyes bulged out to see his actual boss talking to him. 'Certainly, Mr. Belson,' he said. 'We shall put our shoulders to the wheel.'

When I'd done what I could about finding Isabel, I called the Lieutenant Governor of Kentucky, George Kavanaugh. I'd known him when he was a coal broker. We talked about Baynes, who was up for election in November. 'Is he unbeatable?' I asked, after we'd finished the amenities.

'Maybe,' George said. 'He won strongly last time.'

'Who's running against him?'

'Mattie Hinkle. Liberal democrat.'

'What chance?'

'A Chinaman's.'

'Watch your language, George,' I said. 'I'm no person to talk to about Orientals that way.'

'Some of my best friends are Chinese,' George said.

'I believe it. What's Hinkle's program? What's she promising?'

George scratched his head. 'Shit, Ben, I don't know. Reform, I suppose. She should try to get him from the Left.' Suddenly he looked at me hard. 'Didn't you escape from the Marines or something, Ben? In Florida?'

'It was two private cops, George, and it was Washington. You said from the Left?'

'Unemployment might work.' He paused and grinned. 'God, Ben, you always were a live one. Betty says you ought to be in movies.'

'I don't have the time, George. How can I get in touch with this Mattie Hinkle?'

'Try Miyagawa and Sumo in Louisville.'

'Okay, George,' I said. 'Thanks for the information. And don't tell anyone I called you.'

'Mum's the word, Benny. Where are you calling from anyway?'

'I'm staying at a hotel,' I said. 'In Los Angeles.'

Miyagawa and Sumo was an ad agency. I told them I was Aaron Fine, borrowing the name of my friend and accountant. I said I represented an organization backing liberal causes. The man on the phone was a clerk in the agency and clearly bored by all this. 'We have impressive sums at our disposal, for key candidates,' I said levelly.

'Oh?' He looked more interested. 'May I ask the name of your organization?'

'Something in the order of fifty million dollars,' I said.

He stared at me and set down his coffee cup. 'That figure is hard to believe.'

'Do I look crazy?'

'No, sir . . .'

'Look,' I said, 'I'd like to talk to either Miyagawa or Sumo.'

'They're both in conference,' he said, for the second time. This time he seemed less sure.

'Well,' I said, 'I'm going to hang up and have my bank send a million for the campaign to show good faith. Then I'll call back and I want to speak to *both* of them.' I hung up.

I called the People's Bank and told them to phone a million to Louisville. A certified check would pop out of a slot in the agency's phone in a half minute. I called back and, sure enough, I was talking to two polite Japanese. By that time I'd invented an organization. 'I represent the Friends of the Poor. We have been taking an interest in the campaign of Mattie Hinkle.'

They both nodded sagely and the smaller of them spoke. 'Ms. Hinkle thanks you for sharing.'

'That's fine,' I said. 'What Friends of the Poor is concerned with right now is Ms. Hinkle's stand on safe uranium.'

'Safe uranium?' the smaller one said. I took him to be Sumo.

'The uranium aboard the spaceship in Washington. The uranium Senator Baynes won't release for use in power plants.'

'You say it's *safe* uranium?'

'I can explain later. The main issue now, for Friends of the Poor, is Ms. Hinkle's stand on that uranium.'

They hemmed and hawed for a bit and then admitted Ms. Hinkle had no opinion on the *Isabel*'s uranium. They would be glad for me to enlighten them both on the issue.

'I'll call you back,' I said, and hung up.

The next morning Pear Blossom called to say the endolin was off the *Isabel* and in the Chinese Embassy in Washington. I asked about Baynes.

'He did not involve himself,' Pear Blossom told me coolly. She was a shade more civil, now that I was Chinese myself, but she still could project a lot of dislike.

'Baynes didn't try to interfere?'

'He was out of town. My colleagues went through the Department of State.'

'Pear Blossom,' I said, 'can I come out this afternoon for my three hundred million?'

'Two hundred ninety million dollars,' she said.

'Okay,' I said. 'Can I get it today?'

Pear Blossom looked petulant about it. I could see how it hurt her actuarial soul to part with that kind of money. She'd been boggled when Mourning Dove agreed to my terms, even though she must understand the drug market well enough to appreciate the impact endolin would make. 'Mr. Belson,' she said, 'Lao-tzu is paying you over sixty thousand dollars an ounce for endolin. I feel we should attempt to market before . . .'

'Come on, Pear Blossom,' I said. 'You know I get the money when your embassy gets the endolin. *Our* embassy. There are forty-five thousand milligrams in a pound. You'll recover half your investment in six months. You have an exclusive on imports. You've got a bargain.'

She shrugged wearily. It was the first human gesture I'd seen her make and my heart warmed to her. 'Come on, Pear Blossom, honey. It's going to double the business for you. You'll be a company hero. Don't weaken.'

And suddenly I was astonished to see her, there on my big viddiscreen, smiling at me. 'Okay, Mr. Belson. I'll have your check ready.' What nice teeth she had!

Pear Blossom had thawed enough to be downright agreeable. She congratulated me in Chinese and gave a demure bow as I took the little plastic check. The weather was getting cool and she wore a tight lavender sweater and Synlon jeans. 'Pear Blossom,' I said, 'how'd you like to join me for breakfast?' We were sitting in her big antiseptic office. Behind her desk was a huge photograph of the Chinese Olympic Soccer Team.

'That would be pleasant,' she said, almost bowling me over. I really hadn't expected it. 'There's a cafeteria on the second floor.'

It was about ten-thirty in the morning and we had the room to ourselves. I had figs and a pot of green tea; Pear Blossom had coffee and a danish. After we'd finished I looked for a few moments at the array of photos of bright pill bottles on the walls and then smiled at her. 'You really look good in that sweater,' I said.

Insensitive as Pear Blossom might seem, she appeared to be alert to the vibrations in my words. 'Oh?' she said, coolly.

What the hell? I thought. 'You're really a very dandy looking young lady,' I said. 'It's a nice fall day outside. Why don't you let me take you for a spin in my taxi?' Pear Blossom was probably in her late twenties; it occurred to me I hadn't touched the firm skin of a really young woman in a coon's age. Her jet-black Chinese hair shone in the fluorescent lights and her skin was flawlessly white.

Unfortunately, at my question her eyes had turned to something resembling Belson obsidian. 'Mr. Belson,' she said, in the voice you use for lunatics, 'what do you have in mind?'

I almost backed off, but I felt I'd be damned if I would. 'Sex,' I said.

She put her little white hands firmly on the table and leaned toward me, speaking very distinctly. *'You old man,'* she said in the crispest English I'd ever heard. 'You crazy, arrogant old man. I don't want your body touching mine.'

'I'm sorry to hear that,' I said, grabbing what composure I could from what was flying out every window in the big room. I could see myself in her eyes: a clumsy old Caucasian wanting to soil her body with lecherous hands.

'I'm going back to my office, Mr. Belson,' she said, as distant as Fomalhaut. She got up and walked off, paying my check as she left the cafeteria.

I guess humility is good for you, if it can be kept to short bursts. It took me about three minutes to recover and remember how I really wasn't a dirty old man and that my body was in terrific shape. Besides, I was rich, and gentle, and good with children. I was helpful to the downtrodden. I made excellent fettuccine. Ruth liked me. Anna probably loved me. Isabel ditto, if she still remembered me. I'd cured Myra.

I took the check out of my shirt pocket and read the figures again. I began to feel better.

I hadn't bought Chinese securities for years, had never held a seat on the Peking exchange, and knew next to nothing about how to beat Chinese income taxes. But I didn't want to put my money in anything American, for fear of Baynes's tying it up. I'd have to get a Chinese lawyer, a Chinese broker and a Chinese accountant, for openers, and I didn't want to spend the time right then doing research. I'd done a thorough study of gold about five years before, and there is nothing more comfortably international. What I did was take a quick look at current prices, sigh a little, and buy two hundred fifty million worth of Chinese gold. That meant a new number would be placed on a list in Zurich. The simplicity of gold always scares me. Thirteen thousand four hundred a troy ounce. All it's really good for is filling teeth.

The other forty-eight million went into three bank accounts: one Chinese, one Japanese, and one—for sentiment —Scottish. Using the Chinese account and my Chinese name, I bought a five hundred thousand, paid-up American Express card, for traveling.

Back at the hotel that afternoon my passport card was already in the phone slot, with a scowling hologram of my face on one side and the crimson symbols for the People's Republic on the other, together with the usual date and place-of-birth information and warnings against travel in Russia, Cuba or Brazil. I slipped the card into my billfold, called Miyagawa and Sumo, and told them I wanted to speak to Mattie.

They put her on immediately. She came on the screen as a stocky, no-nonsense type in her mid-fifties, with glasses and closely cut hair. There was a matronly toughness to her, but her voice was soft. 'My agency finds no record of a Friends of the Poor,' she said, straight-out. 'How do you account for that, Mr. Fine?'

I'd figured that might happen, since Miyagawa and Sumo had time to check it out.

'Look, Ms. Hinkle,' I said, 'I'll be straight with you. I'm not Aaron Fine, I'm Ben Belson. I want you to beat L'Ouverture Baynes so I can get my spaceship back.'

She peered at me through her glasses for a moment, impassively, and then said, 'That's pretty blatant, Mr. Belson.'

'You're absolutely right,' I said. 'Illegal in every way.'

'I understand you're not even an American citizen.'

'That's right, too,' I said. 'They took it away from me.' I decided the best defense was no defense at all. She'd have to make up her own mind, if she wanted me to buy her the election.

She pursed her lips and thought about it a moment. 'Mr. Miyagawa said you spoke of several millions.'

'Fifty. I can let you have it in gold. Five million at a time. I'll

198

give you a number of an account in Zurich; you have it transferred where you want it.'

'People get long prison terms for less,' she said.

'That's the truth,' I said.

'How can I know you aren't setting me up for just that? How can I know this phone call isn't being recorded?'

I was lighting a cigar as she said these things. I took a big puff and then set it in a hotel ashtray. 'Well,' I said, 'you can never be sure. Anyway, I don't think *my* phone is tapped. To answer your first question, why would I want to set you up for anything? So Baynes could beat you? You know as well as I do he's already got you beat.'

She pursed her lips again, in a schoolteacherly way. 'I have other enemies,' she said.

'I don't doubt it. You'll just have to assess the risks. You know who your enemies are; you'll have to figure out why I would be working for them.'

She nodded. 'May I call you back?'

'No,' I said. 'Sorry. I'm keeping my whereabouts a secret. I'll call back at noon tomorrow. Shall I go ahead and set up that Swiss account?'

'Don't do that,' she said. 'Just call. I'm addressing a D.A.C. meeting at noon, so make it at eleven.'

'What's D.A.C.?' I said.

'The Daughters of the American Confederacy,' Mattie Hinkle said.

I sat there and fidgeted for a minute. Then I decided to go ahead with it despite Mattie. I punched my Bank Dispatch code into the phone and had Shanghai send a twenty-million credit to Geneva under the rubric FRIENDS OF THE POOR FOR MATTIE HINKLE and a notification to Miyagawa and Sumo.

If I didn't hear anything for a week I'd send the rest of it.

I slept well that night and dreamed beatifically of money. Not of graphs on production charts or shorts in corn futures or even of bank accounts, but of crisp green beautifully engraved bills and brightly minted coins. For a while during the night I was a baby wrapped in new thousand-dollar bills, as though in swaddling clothes. I gurgled with the joy of

199

contact with all that sweet money while older folk moved slowly by me, their steps taken as if in a sea of molasses, themselves dressed soberly in gray and brown suits, disdaining my infantile garment of cash. I smiled at them all.

14

Some part of me must have been expecting it all along. When I saw the four Marines the next morning standing in the lobby at the foot of the stairs, it had some of the quality of *déjà vu*. Big sons of bitches. I stared at them and froze. When one of them took me by the right arm I came out of it and tried to pull away from him. It didn't work. I suppose I'd been imagining myself as one of the strongest men in America; this was a rude brush with reality. This youth with the perfect shave was bigger than I in every way. His fingers on my forearm felt like rocks. The other three looked about the same.

When they took me past the desk to the door the clerk looked away, busying himself with some records. Outside the hotel was a gasoline-powered military jeep. I sat in back with a Marine on each side of me and we drove off down Broad Street while people on the sidewalk stared.

I got back a bit of my composure in the jeep. 'Men,' I said, 'where are you taking me?'

'Air base' was all I could get, from the only one who seemed to know how to talk. He had sergeant stripes. 'You're not supposed to do this,' I said, 'I'm a Chinese national.' I might as well have been speaking to the wind.

They took me about twenty miles to Kissinger Air Force Base, put me on an F-611 jet fighter, and flew me to Washington at four times the speed of sound. Those military sons of bitches; they burn jet fuel as if it were seawater.

It's quite an experience to fly like that, let me tell you. The *Isabel* could zip through her warp at two hundred times the speed of light, and light goes fast enough to circle the earth seven times in a second; but even so, that little white jet felt a hundred times faster. *Zoom*, Pennsylvania! *Zoom, zoom*,

New Jersey! *Zoom*, Maryland! *Zip*, Washington! Good afternoon, Senator.

I wore one of those white spacesuits for altitude and was handcuffed to my seat, feeling like a nailed-down snowman skimming the stratosphere in this military frisbee. When we slowed for a landing the G forces pressed my body like the hand of death. I sat strapped in a tiny cockpit, feeling like hell, feeling like a childish fool, and unable to say a thing to anybody. I couldn't even hear my own voice the roar of those fuel-wasting jets. Damn the military. They could have sent me back on a Pullman and saved everybody a lot of grief. But I grudgingly had to admit what they were doing made Baynes look good, the son of a bitch. There was class to this operation.

Four MPs at the Washington Air Base got me out of the white suit and into another jeep. They drove me straight to the Reagan Detention Center, where Baynes was waiting, dressed elegantly in gray tweeds. I checked my watch; less than two hours since they'd picked me up. If only they could handle mail like that. 'Hello, L'Ouverture,' I said, rubbing my wrists where a cop had just taken off the cuffs. We were in a steel-walled room without windows, sitting on wooden benches facing one another through plastic; our voices came through speakers. There was no humanity to this; I'd have felt closer talking to him by viddiphone.

'Ben!' L'Ouverture said, shaking his head in mock dismay. 'What a nuisance! What a waste of taxpayers' money!'

'That's exactly what I've been thinking,' I said. 'How did you find me?'

Baynes shook his head again. 'Ben,' he said, 'it was simplicity itself. You left clues everywhere. People recognized you in Philadelphia and called the FBI. The Chinese Embassy filed a report.' He looked at me in a kind of bemusement. 'Ben,' he said, 'I don't see how a man so careless could be so rich.'

I felt myself blushing. Caught in my fool's paradise again, playing games. Tom Sawyer Wins An Election.

'Quit rubbing it in,' I said. 'What is it you want from me?'

'I want to know where that uranium came from, Ben.'

'I figured as much,' I said, 'and I'm not going to tell you.'

202

L'Ouverture leaned toward me, with his elbows on his knees. He was wearing a pale-blue oxford-cloth shirt and I could see silver cufflinks. He folded his long black fingers together. 'That's no way to talk, Ben,' he said. He smiled amiably. 'If you don't tell me, you'll spend the rest of your days in this building.'

'The Chinese Government . . .'

'The Chinese Government doesn't know where you are, Benjamin, and I don't think they care. Mourning Dove Soong is a busy woman. She has more to do than keep up with your whereabouts.' He smiled again.

'What are the charges against me?'

He threw back his head and laughed, stretching out his long arms from his body. Then he shot his cuffs and set his bony elbows on his knees again. 'Oh my my!' he said. 'Resisting arrest, twice. Assaulting a police officer, four times. Illicitly importing dangerous drugs. Using same. Telephone fraud. Crossing state lines as an unregistered alien.' He laughed again. 'There are friends of mine on the bench who would give you ten years at hard labor just for burning up Aynsley Field.'

I just looked at him. What was there to say? I knew he was at least partly wrong about Mourning Dove, if only because Lao-tzu needed me for future supplies of endolin; but I wasn't going to tell Baynes that. I wasn't going to tell Baynes *anything* this time.

'Well, L'Ouverture,' I said, 'you seem to have all the cards.'

He nodded and smiled grimly. 'You dealt them to me, Ben.'

'L'Ouverture,' I said, 'I don't need this. I'll give you sixty percent of my uranium . . .'

He looked at me very coolly. 'I don't want it.'

'You don't *want* it? My God, it's worth a king's ransom.'

He shook his head. 'I'm a king already, Benjamin.'

I looked at him. He was certainly *dressed* like a king. 'It'll triple your wealth, L'Ouverture. It'll put America back on top of the heap.'

He looked at me calmly. 'Who are you to talk that way?' he said. 'You're Chinese.'

'Come off it,' I said. 'That's an expedient, not a political choice. We can be partners. Belson and Baynes.'

He sat there awhile, looking very collected, very urbane. Finally he spoke. 'I like things the way they are. I enjoy my work, Benjamin. The United States is doing very well under its energy laws, and I helped frame them.'

'And you profit from them.'

'They are good laws, for the resources we have.'

I just looked at him, feeling nothing. There was no way to get through to this man, and I knew it. He did not want to be partners with anyone, and the only way I could bargain with him now would be to tell him about Juno and how to get there. But then, thinking about that, I realized something I had missed before: if he really wanted to know where my uranium came from he would have found out from the crew. He could have locked them up as conspirators, or pirates, and pressured them until someone told him. And he hadn't done that. 'You don't really want to know where I got that uranium,' I said.

He looked at me and smiled tiredly. 'How perceptive you are, Benjamin.'

'You just want to keep things the way they are.'

'In a nutshell.'

I sat there awhile. Finally I said, wearily, 'Can you get me some cigars?'

He smiled. 'I'll have a dozen boxes sent.' He stood up to his full height on the other side of the plastic. What a hugely tall man he was, and how light on his feet and flexible for his age! The goddamned devious son of a bitch.

'Sacre Fidels,' I said. And then, 'Do you ever use Nautilus machines, L'Ouverture?'

He smiled down at me. 'Daily.' He straightened his jacket and patted the pockets with his huge hands, smoothing them. 'I have to go now,' he said.

I stood up. 'What will you do with the *Isabel*?'

'It can stay where it is. Its hatch has been welded shut. And the portholes are covered. It is under perpetual guard.'

'Like the Tomb of the Unknown Soldier?'

'Exactly.'

'And it'll just stay at Aynsley?'

'I have no interest in football.' He turned to leave.

'L'Ouverture,' I said, 'when am I going to get out of this place?'

He turned back to me and shook his head sympathetically. 'Benjamin,' he said, 'I'd tell you if I knew.'

I nodded. It all seemed eerily natural, this conversation with the thick transparent plastic between us. 'I know I was spotted in Philadelphia,' I said. 'But how did you find out I was in Columbus?'

He stood silent for a minute before speaking. Then he said, 'Sue Kranefeld. She called my office.'

The Reagan Stir is a wretched place—a kind of flophouse of prisons. I was given a cell with a tiny TV and a cold-water shower. There was a library and, thank God, a gym. I worked out with weights and an LAT machine twice a day and sometimes did pushups in my cell. They had me in Diplomatic Isolation, which meant no visitors and no newspapers and no news shows on my TV. I was in Washington, but I didn't know if the public at large knew where I was. After a week I quit caring.

I hate to admit this, but a part of me warmed up to prison. I shifted into the psychic gear I had been in on Belson and all I really missed was my vegetables. I got the complete short stories of Henry James out of the prison library and spent my days between working out, reading and playing chess. At level eight. There was a UV booth in the gym; I added to my Belson suntan, which had faded a good deal. I wasn't allowed to talk to other prisoners—although I always nodded at a woeful Arab who worked out on the LAT machine next to me—and that suited me fine. Ever since Father's forget-me-nots I had known the game of spiritual Robinson Crusoe; I found sweet sadness in playing it yet again.

Sometimes at night I would watch TV, after getting weary with Henry James's games of ethical chess and of people who responded to moral crises by not finishing sentences. The Chinese TV channel was doing a thirty-part dramatization of European history, shot in Peking, and I got hooked on it. It wasn't the European history I had been taught and it was amusing to see it from a Chinese perspective. One Sunday night after a supper of frankfurters and beans I sat on my bunk drinking coffee from a plastic cup and idly watching a segment of the sixteenth century in England, when something about Queen Elizabeth caught my attention. Her walk seemed eerily familiar. I stared. It looked like Isabel in a red wig. I sat upright and turned up the volume. It *was* Isabel, in lace, pearls and heavy silk, looking like an authentic queen, even though it was ludicrous to hear her voice dubbed in high-pitched Chinese.

The Chinese view of Elizabeth was as a kind of virginal nymphomaniac. She was shown turning on Essex, and Cecil and Raleigh. Drake was trying to get into her pants. All of this was very disturbing, and when a scene came on where she was lying in bed with Essex, both of them naked, and she fending him off with chatter, I nearly choked. I wanted to kick the idiot who was playing Essex, grab Isabel by her lovely waist and demonstrate the folly of coyness. I could have pounded my head against the wall for the waste of my five months' impotence with her. There I sat in my cell, staring at her electronic image with an erection—the only erection the sight of her body had ever given me and as useless, now as an airplane on the moon.

I'd been happy enough with Henry James, chess and weight-lifting before that, but it changed everything. I wanted to get out of prison and back to life again. It was toward the end of October; I'd been in stir six weeks, with no trial scheduled and no word from anybody. I stepped out of my Robinson Crusoe daze like stepping out of a pair of dirty socks and found myself in reality. It was awful. I was in prison, horny, angry, and ready to go, but I couldn't get out. Four walls. Bars on the windows. Guards. Frankfurters, beans and instant coffee.

This kept up for two weeks and would have been the death of me if they hadn't, suddenly and without notice, let me out. The eighth of November. Two guards came into my cell after breakfast and told me to pack. That took three minutes, including brushing my teeth. They took me to a desk where I signed papers, got back my billfold, was admonished to 'watch my step' and taken to a coal-gas black Maria. I didn't know what in hell was going on, but suspected it had something to do with the election. My prison had been well heated if nothing else; it was icy and gray outside. Glad as I was to get out, a part of me was sorry to leave the warmth of jail. We drove past the Washington Monument, looking bleak in the winter air, and then a few blocks later I looked down a side street and saw sticking up proudly into the sky above tall buildings, covered with snow, the *Isabel!* That cheered me up. I blew her a kiss as we went by.

They pulled up at the Chinese Embassy and the guards ushered me into a back door, where four Chinese soldiers took me into a room with painted screens and modern furniture. Two Chinese ladies fingerprinted me, in red. A tall, thirtyish one who seemed in charge handed me rice paper forms to sign.

'What's all this about?' I asked, in English.

She pulled a cigarette from her robe, lit it and blew smoke toward me. 'I am taking you home, Mr. Kwoo.'

'Kwoo?' I almost jumped out of my skin. 'What the hell is this *Kwoo?'* I still hadn't signed the papers. 'Let me have one of your cigarettes if you don't mind, and then explain to me what going home means and about this Mr. Kwoo.'

She gave me a cigarette and lit it with a little red electronic. 'Mr. Kwoo is your Chinese name,' she said.

'That's not what's on my passport,' I said.

'We have a new passport. It seemed expedient to change your identity.' Her face was hard-looking but the voice pleasant enough. Except for the hardness she was a beautiful woman. 'The United States does not want you to leave its shores. Senator Baynes would like to keep you under lock and key until . . . how do you say it in America?'

'The cows come home. Hell freezes over.' I began to pace around the room, hands in my jeans pockets. 'I wasn't planning to leave any shores, anyway.' But it had already dawned on me; they were going to take me to China. What the hell; it beat prison. And Isabel might be there. 'Is "home" China?' I said.

She nodded.

'Okay,' I said, 'okay. I'll need some clothes.' The prison jeans and dungaree shirt I was wearing were all I had. 'Does this have to do with endolin?'

'Our interest in you, Mr. Kwoo, is not pharmacological. It is your other cargo that occupies our attention. It has caused us to go to some lengths to take you from prison.'

Shit. They wanted the Juno uranium fields. For a moment I chilled with the image of a Chinese dungeon somewhere. What if they had revived the water torture? Meltdowns were a scandal to the People's Republic and the old ladies who ran it; there were radioactive villages and ruined rice paddies sprinkled all over that ancient geography. My well-being, in that context, would mean very little.

'Is Mourning Dove Soong behind this?' I said.

'Madame Soong is Deputy Chairman for the Honshu District. I do not know her position with respect to your case.'

'Okay,' I said. 'I'll go to China. How do we get there?'

She took another cigarette and lit it from the butt of the first. 'We'll go by ship, Mr. Kwoo.'

'All right,' I said. I stubbed my cigarette out in a little jade dish. 'But tell me. What does "Kwoo" mean?'

The shorter woman spoke up, in a quiet voice. 'It's an old Mandarin word. It denotes an ancient coin. You could translate it as "cash".'

I looked down at her and fingered my beard. 'Well,' I said, 'you people do know how to name the newborn. I accept Kwoo.' *Ben Kwoo*.

It was a Chinese jet that took us to the Embarcadero in San Francisco. This time my stratosphere suit was crimson. There was a valve in the mask, so I could sip oolong through a straw during the two-hour flight. My cigarette-smoking friend was seated behind me, but had little to say on our intercom. I tried to get her to talk about her family, but she wasn't interested. I sipped my tea and brooded a bit. Then I did some knee bends just as we were zooming over the Rockies and started figuring out ways of getting back into the search for Isabel from wherever we were going in China.

A gray Mercedes was waiting for us; we drove in silence from the airfield to a dock. The car pulled up at the gangway to a coal-burner with rusty sides. On the forepeak lettered in red was PRS KEIR HARDIE. It was a Scottish ship! 'What the hell?' I said to my chain-smoking companion. She was climbing the gangway alongside me with her short black hair blowing in the offshore wind. 'Why aren't we sailing Chinese?'

'This was available,' she said, stepping briskly aboard.

My stateroom was ready and she ushered me right to it. My heart lifted when I walked in. The parlor had a screen painted with blue morning glories; there were walnut tables and blue silk poufs. Along one bulkhead was a galley with a refrigerator, a molecular cooker and a freezer. 'How long will the trip take?' I looked at her. 'And what's your name?'

'My name is White Heron. Many call me Jane. It will take us two weeks to cross the Pacific.'

There was a bar with relief carvings of birds on its front and two crystal decanters and glasses. I crossed over to it and sniffed one of the decanters. Scotch, sure enough. I started to pour. 'Would you like a drink, White Heron?'

'Jane,' she said. 'I'm on duty.'

'Suit yourself,' I said and made mine larger. I went to the refrigerator, filled my glass with ice and clinked it around. I was still wearing my red stratosphere suit. I took a drink and a ship's whistle blew, loud, clear and thrilling. Nothing in this world sounds better than a ship's whistle. 'Are we leaving?'

Jane nodded and the deck beneath our feet began to vibrate. I drank another musty slug of scotch, spreading out my big feet into a seaman's stance. 'Jane,' I said, 'who assigned me to these quarters? It wasn't you, was it?'

She looked at me coldly. She'd have had me in the bilges if she'd been in charge. Then she shrugged. 'It was Mourning Dove Soong,' she said. 'Your partner at Lao-tzu Pharmaceuticals.'

'Yes,' I said, and drank off my scotch. 'Bless her heart.' I thought of Arabella Kim and her woodlot in Washington. Old Chinese mothers, the two of them, as good as gold. Maybe there was something in matriarchy after all.

I played a lot of solo chess during the next few days and then began to suntan myself on deck when we got far enough into the South Pacific. I read a few twenty-first-century Chinese novels, but their vigor wore me out. Everybody was productive and brave in those books, and nobody made love except after a Confucianist wedding, and then they did it solemnly and in the dark. Puritanism is like the wheel; if it ever got lost it would be reinvented fast.

I was allowed no access to the ship's communications equipment, which was probably just as well. I wasn't ready to do business just yet. I managed to borrow some recent Scottish magazines from one of the mates and entertained myself with stories of love among the fens or brawls on collective farms in the lowlands. Still dull stuff, but better than the Chinese. More balls.

The ship plowed across the blue Pacific as if in a dream, leaving a wake like a glory in that awe-inspiring surface. At night the stars were magnificent—nearly as bright as from my toilet seat on the *Isabel*. When we got to our southernmost point I could see Fomalhaut, near the horizon.

Nobody talked to me much and I didn't try to make friends. They were probably under orders anyway. There were some other passengers, all well-to-do Chinese families. It seemed the *Keir Hardie* was used by the higher ranks of the Party. As much as they officially excoriated one another, the Chinese and the Scots could work things out when it came to luxury. There's nothing new in that.

I took my meals alone and ate with chopsticks. The officers' mess supplied what I ordered, and once offered a haggis if I wanted to try one. I declined politely. I had no television and no newspapers and didn't care. It was shipboard lull and fine with me. But I worked out in the ship's gym daily and did pushups in between, coiling up for whatever lay ahead.

I would see families sometimes standing in a row along the gunwale, wrapped in their heavy overcoats, staring out to sea. The children were touching—so solemn and oriental, with their bangs and quiet black eyes. Sometimes a beautiful child would peek toward me as I stood nearby, in one of my crazy capitalist outfits, but there was never any conversation. I'd like to have adopted about six of those kids. I'd have loved to cook pot roast for a bunch of them and taught them how to play chess.

Well. Children are hostages to fortune, as Bacon said. But what else is there to do with your time?

I can see myself dying by coronary in a parlor suite, clutching my throbbing shoulder and mumbling, 'Hey! I need time to think about this!' I would be ninety and still in good shape but without a home or family, without a profession. Tycoon is no profession. All I do is make money and chase women. And travel. *I haven't done anything with my life!* I would say in that hotel suite, thrashing about in the kitchen in terminal anguish, falling dead over the *truite fumée*.

One evening at the beginning of my second week there was a knock on my door. I was at the table, playing king's gambit against Myra's board. I got up and opened the door. It was Jane, wearing a pink silk dress. She was lighting a cigarette.

'Hello,' I said.

'Hello. I've come for that drink.'

'Sure,' I said. 'Come in.'

It was one of those tight traditional dresses with a slit down the side. The amount of leg she displayed coming in the door was alarming; a voice in me immediately said, *Watch it.*

'I'm in the middle of a game,' I said.

She nodded and seated herself on my lavender pouf. Her black hair shone and she wore scarlet lipstick; her face was dead white and Chinese-round with perfect Mongolian eyefolds. She looked like a poster ad for a twentieth-century movie. The Dragon Lady. She watched me silently. I returned to the sofa and lit a cigar. I was in my prison dungarees—comfortably faded now since I washed them at nights and hung them on deck to dry. If they got rained on I wore my red silk stratosphere pants and went barechested, like an Italian trapeze artist. She was looking me over the way Fu Manchu might look over a captive American spy. *We have ways of making you talk, Mr. Belson.* 'I like big men,' she said.

'You're a tall person yourself,' I said. 'What will happen when we dock in China? To me, I mean.'

'You'll be interrogated and given living quarters. Much depends on your cooperation.' She lit another cigarette from the butt of the first, and then ground the old one out in one of my jade ashtrays. There was silence for a while, except for the rumble of ship's engines. I turned back to my game.

I was going for a back-rank checkmate with my queen's rook, but I couldn't get the proper file cleared of pawns. I leaned forward and tried to concentrate. Just as I found the

211

move I wanted, she spoke. 'I've never had an American lover,' she said.

I brought a knight to bishop five and looked over the board at her. 'I'm not American anymore.'

'Nonsense. You're the most American person I've ever seen. Like Abraham Lincoln.'

'That's good company,' I said, 'and I thank you for putting me in it. Lincoln was a genius and a man of heart.'

She looked at me as though appraising a minor artwork. 'A big American man with a big sad soul.' She crossed her legs with the sound tight silk makes. 'Just like you.'

'I feel more affinity with Billy the Kid,' I said, nervously. 'But thanks anyway. If that actor hadn't plugged Lincoln at the play it would be a different world. What if Chairman Mao had been gunned down in the fifties?'

'Chairman Mao made many errors.'

'Maybe,' I said. 'But Mao was what China needed. You were lucky to have him all those years.'

'If one didn't spend one's time being rehabilitated.'

'Okay,' I said. 'Okay. Where is this ship going to dock?'

'At the Port of Celestial Winds, District Four.'

'I never heard of it.'

'Newly built by the People.' She looked me over silently again. I turned back to Myra's board and tried to concentrate. Abruptly she said, 'I'd like sex.'

'Jane, honey,' I looked up again, 'I've got other things to think about. My heart wouldn't be in it.'

She ignored that and stood up languidly. Then she arched her arms behind her back and unfastened the neck of her dress. I have a great weakness for the upper arms of beautiful women and I could hardly not see how fine hers were. Firm and perfectly white. While I watched in reluctant fascination, she let the dress drop to her ankles and stepped out of it. She kicked off her sandals. She was wearing scarlet panties and a thin gold necklace. Her body was as white as snow and without a flaw. Tiny white breasts and tiny white feet. I was getting hard. 'Come on, Jane,' I said. 'I'm not in the mood for this kind of thing. I'm fifty-three years old and well past my prime and I'm in love with a Scottish actress.'

She walked over to the sofa and sat beside me. 'Take off your pants.'

'Come *on*, Jane,' I said, panicking. The tops of her shoulders were the best I'd ever seen. I blinked with unease.

'There's nothing to be afraid of,' she said. And then, 'Is your pubic hair blond too?'

'It's got a lot of gray,' I said.

'You can lie back on the couch and I'll undress you.'

'I tell you, Jane, you're a splendid-looking woman. Enough to drive a man right out of his skull. But I wasn't cut out for this . . . this gigolo thing. I have to pick my own times.'

She laughed at the word 'gigolo.' 'There's nothing wrong with your servicing me. Chinese men enjoy the opportunity. Many of them are trained for it, in schools.'

At the word 'servicing' I stiffened. I could run out onto the deck, or lock myself in the bathroom. Except that my perverse member was now so rigid there was no way I could stand up in those tight prison jeans.

'Mr. Kwoo,' Jane said, coolly, 'you'll need a good report from me when we arrive in China. If I say your thinking is confused it could cause you hardship.'

Jesus Christ! I thought. Am I going to have to do this like a whore? Can a man really do that and satisfy the lady in a state of panic? My member was answering this silent inquiry in the affirmative; it was undaunted. The eager son of a bitch. I felt betrayed by the same partner who had betrayed me the other way with Isabel.

I looked her over. She sure had a fine body, even though it looked as cold as ice. And I loved the red panties. *What the hell*, I thought. *I used to sleep with a horse.* 'Okay, Jane,' I said. 'But let's go into the bedroom and do it right.'

'Here is adequate,' she said. She began to unzip my pants.

'Look,' I said, pushing her hands away, 'I'll do this myself.' I unzipped with care and freed myself. I slipped the pants off, and then my shorts. I was already barefoot. I started to get up.

She had already stood. Now she pushed on my chest, with alarming strength from a smallish person, and I sat back. 'Just lie back, Mr. Kwoo,' she said. 'I think your pubic hair is charming, with all those curls.'

'Jesus Christ, Jane, I'm no *courtesan*. I can't just . . .'

213

'Yes you can. Clearly. Just lie back and relax.'

I think I was blushing. She was aroused to where she looked dangerous. Her nipples stood out like little Marines. 'Okay,' I said, defeated. 'Okay.' I lay back awkwardly, bending my knees to fit my frame to the couch.

She had peeled off her panties by the time I got there, and then she mounted me in a gung-ho way, as though she were a sailor and I a B-girl. I didn't like it at all, but my sexuality was in another world, doing its business in the dark like an Old Testament fanatic. I wriggled despite myself and ground up into her with a twist. 'That's it!' she whispered and began pumping in earnest. I pumped back. She began kissing me open-mouthed, smelling of booze. Her nipples pushed into my chest. I began to feel smothered. She pulled back just in time and I could see her face twisted in some kind of unearthly concentration, her eyes upward and sweat on her porcelain forehead, with the bangs now sticking to it. I froze at the sight.

'Don't stop now,' she said.

I started pumping again. From the waist down I was a satyr. But my better part was watching in alarmed detachment.

'Yes!' Jane hissed—not to me but to the ceiling. She grabbed my shoulders and I winced when her nails dug in. Then she went slack and fell across my chest.

I don't know why that orgasm of hers didn't provoke one on my part, but it didn't. Suddenly I felt a physical need that was as potent as the need for air when you find it cut off. I started pumping against her limp body.

Abruptly she grew rigid, and then pushed off of me. 'What the hell . . .?' I said, throbbing.

'I'm finished,' she said.

'Well, I'm not,' I said and reached out to grab her. She stepped back nimbly. I sat up, furious. My groin was beginning to ache. 'I can rape you,' I said.

'I'd kick you first. You'd never forget it.'

She stood there sweating like an Olympic gymnast and I believed her. I leaned back on the sofa. I'd had a lot of practice at sexual frustration—at Isabel's and at the Pierre afterward—and for a moment I gave up. 'Suit yourself, White Heron,' I said.

'I have suited m‚ ‚lf,' she said. She bent elegantly to the table by the pouf and took a cigarette. Her back was to me.

I was off the couch and had her around the waist before she could straighten up. I was careful not to hurt her or break a bone; but I had her on the floor in ten seconds. I looked down at her face. It was flushed but composed.

'If you rape me,' she said. 'I'll put you in prison.'

'Mourning Dove Soong likes me,' I said, breathing hard. 'If you try that, she'll have you in front of the Central Committee.' That was mostly bluffing, but it seemed to work. Her face for the first time lost some of its composure. 'Then enjoy yourself, Mr. Kwoo.'

'I'm Ben Belson,' I said, 'and I'm not going to rape you.' And I wasn't. My member had finally bowed out of the fray.

Jane stayed out of my cabin for the rest of the trip. I didn't see her again until a cold morning when I passed her on deck after coffee and then looked through mists over the port bow to see the coast of China. Right over there. Despite apprehensions and uncertainties, the thrill was exquisite; to sail the Pacific and then see China distant in the mist is an experience that goes right to the marrow of your bones and tingles the back of your skull like a morphine rush. I stared for a moment and then started doing side-straddle hops by the gunwale, wearing my red spaceman's pantaloons, barefoot on the slippery metal deck. Jumping jacks, some people call them. I slapped my hands together over my head and hopped my legs out and in, saying hello to China. The ship's whistle blew. I stopped and held my breath. We were turning starboard and I felt a heartrending throb as the screws adjusted to a new course. We steamed straight toward the China Coast.

The *Keir Hardie* docked at a long gray pier late that afternoon. The rain had changed to sleet and it was freezing cold. I had no coat. The dock city looked like Cleveland in the nineteenth century—dark satanic mills and grit in the air. Coolie longshoremen lounged on barrels at dockside, in Ghengis Khan hats and overcoats, smoking what might have been opium. The ship was docked by computer; and when it was done a huge red display suddenly lit up on the side of a plastic

215

warehouse, spelling out in neon-like letters: WELCOME TO THE PEOPLE'S REPUBLIC OF CHINA. My teeth chattered. I had thrown a blanket over my shoulders and was wearing my electronic running shoes, but I had no socks, having lost them sometime before in the Reagan Stir, and my toes were freezing.

One of the female crew members found me like this, swigging from my decanter. She approached me warily, as one might examine a sick grizzly.

'If you don't watch out,' she said, pronouncing the word 'oot,' 'you'll have pneumonia in the lungs.'

'Honey,' I said, 'I have no coat or socks. This is it.'

'I'll bring you something against it,' she said. 'Hold on now.'

She jogged back to a stairway and down. A minute later she came back with a jacket, two pairs of socks, a pair of mittens and a tam. 'The mate had these put by,' she said, handing them to me. The coat looked pretty small, but I thanked her from the bottom of my heart, went into my cabin again, and managed to get it all on—although my wrists stuck out of the sleeves of the mackinaw and it wouldn't button over my chest. But the mittens were stretchy enough and the tam fit. It had a damn-fool red pom-pom on the top, which I managed to bite off and stuff in my pocket. I looked at myself in a closet mirror before going back out again. It was terrible, with the red silk pants and the rest of it. But what the hell; I stepped back out on deck, head high.

Jane was waiting for me, wearing an army uniform this time with the long gray overcoat and epaulets. A major's insignia and a gray garrison cap. She looked like the Empress of Austria, or a Chinese Greta Garbo in *Ninotchka*.

'Well,' I said, holding my composure pretty well, considering my outfit and hers. 'So you're a soldier. I had no idea.'

'You look a fool,' she said, not without some pleasure.

'White Heron,' I said, 'use your sadism on the troops. I'm not afraid of you.'

She lit a cigarette and said nothing. A moment later the gangway went down and the First Officer left the ship. There were four male noncoms with rifles standing at dockside. They must have marched up while I was changing clothes.

216

One signed a paper the officer handed them, returned it, shouted something to the others and then led them up the gangway to where we stood. The leader saluted Jane, who returned it casually, her cigarette between the fingers of the saluting hand.

We marched down the gangway and onto the ancient soil of China. I didn't exactly march, but stumped along because of the two pairs of wool socks stuffed into my running shoes. I was arriving in China even more clownishly than I'd arrived at Aynsley Field by spaceship. Well. Dignity was never my object in life.

They had a staff limousine—an actual nineteen-nineties black Cadillac with power windows and a glass partition; as far as I knew, the only one like it in America was under glass at the Smithsonian. Two flags of the People's Army flew from fenders. A sergeant opened the door and I got in. It was a billionaire's car if there ever was one; I felt immediately at home.

Two soldiers got in back with Jane and me, and sat on the jump seats. We drove in silence away from dockside. The coolie loafers puffed their long pipes and stared at us through the sleet. I relaxed against glove-leather upholstery and lit a cigar. Willy-nilly, I had my dignity back.

We drove about five miles past industrial buildings before hitting open country. The sleet had lessened; it was getting late in the day. There were houses surrounded by perfectly groomed fields. Pink tile roofs glistened wetly. I saw children playing in front of a barn; they stopped to wave as we drove by. I waved back. Old men drove gray steam tractors or red nuclear jeeps; there were vehicles everywhere. We passed a house with a table in its front yard where four old women sat at tea, their heads together in gossip. Pigs rooted at the edge of the house. An old man sat on the porch in an overcoat, reading a newspaper. *Everybody was Chinese. A whole country full of Chinese!*

A few miles later we drove by a four-story factory building painted bright blue. The sun was setting behind it. There were hundreds of electric cars in a lot near the gate, a sight America hadn't seen for sixty years.

'What do they make there?' I asked Jane.

'Toy airplanes,' she said. 'For export.' *My God*, I thought, *Myra has one of those. I bought it at F.A.O. Schwartz.*

Our destination turned out to be another airport. In a grim, institutional waiting room I changed into a fresh stratosphere suit—yellow this time—and was taken without ceremony to a Confucius 433 jet. Jane was my fellow passenger again. She stubbed out her cigarette while the pilot zipped down the runway; she covered her bangs with her helmet as we shot up for altitude like an arrow of Apollo, leaving behind us a plain that stretched twenty miles from the sea and ended in a vast range of blue mountains, now glowing in the setting sun.

'Where to?' I said into the intercom.

'Peking,' Jane said. 'The Imperial City.'

We landed in darkness a few hours later. I was drowsy now and in need of food and rest. My seat on the plane was designed for a smaller race of person than I, and my ass was sore from it. I hadn't had anything to eat since that breakfast coffee. When we started coming down I asked Jane if I could get a sandwich at the airport.

'No time for that, Mr. Kwoo,' she said as we banked into a landing curve.

Two girl soldiers marched us from the plane to a black electric Mercedes. My stomach growled. I lit a cigar. We drove down a dimly lit airport road and then through suburbs of row houses with an occasional corner grocery lighted brightly, where old people shopped. Where were the young? We crossed Chang An Avenue and came into a downtown district with a few bright lights but not many people. It was only nine-thirty, and this appeared to be Peace Blooms Square right in the heart of down-town. A few blocks from Tien An Men. Everybody must be at home watching television. I was gratified to see what appeared to be a drunk, asleep on a bench near a closed book-store. An American tourist? We drove on. A few blocks from the square we stopped in front of what appeared to be a hotel.

'Where are we?' I said.

Jane answered in Chinese. 'You will be a guest in the House of Comradely Love.'

218

I was marched past a grim lobby with four male clerks at a desk. We went into a gritty freight elevator and stared straight ahead as we went up eighteen floors and creaked to a stop. The door opened. The hallway had a gray linoleum floor, with cigarette butts. A dead geranium sat in a cracked pot near a barred window to my right; we turned left, past metal doorways to the end of the hall. There were four locks on the door. The girl who had brought us here produced four electronic keys and unlocked them one by one without getting any of the locks wrong. She stepped aside. Jane pushed open the door into a single room. A bare twenty-watt bulb hung from the ceiling, illuminating the ugliest hotel room I had ever seen. A cockroach scurried along a broken baseboard; the air smelled of cabbage.

'What the hell are you trying to do to me, White Heron?' I said.

She looked at me a moment and then spoke in English. 'You should have been more cooperative. Aboard the ship.'

'Wait till Mourning Dove hears about this.'

'Mourning Dove Soong,' White Heron said, 'is enjoying a long vacation in Tibet, at a monastery without viddiphone. She will be there meditating, indefinitely. I have been given charge of your case.'

I stared at her.

'Welcome to China,' Jane said, and clanged the door behind me. I stood transfixed in that cold, cabbagey room. In dim light I saw an oak dresser, a straight-backed chair and a sagging bed. A toilet without a seat was in one corner, and a dirty washstand with one tap at the other. There was no telephone, no TV, no bathtub or shower. There was no food. The one window had bars an inch thick.

I managed to sleep anyway, with my clothes on. There was a cake of rough yellow soap and I got fairly clean with it in the morning and then used the wet towel to wash some of the grit off the window. I looked down between bars eighteen stories to a park. It looked like Gramercy Park, in fact. I was stiff as a board and frightened. My joints ached and I was trembling with cold. I did situps and knee bends for ten minutes, trying not to think about breakfast. Trying not to think at all. They would hardly bring me to China just to starve me.

When I'd finished and was wiping off the sweat with my one other towel the door started unlocking. This time two men were waiting for me, in noncom uniforms. They escorted me silently to the elevator and punched the up button. We arrived at a kind of penthouse on the twenty-sixth floor, which turned out to be the cafeteria. A few old people were sitting at tables, drinking tea.

The guards continued to flank me while I went to the serving counter. The food was piled in steel trays and lit by flickering light bulbs. I got six hard-boiled eggs, a cup of soggy rice and a mug of black tea. There was no cream or sugar.

I took a seat by the balcony with a view of Gramercy Park, and cracked my eggs while the guards watched. The eggs were awfully dry in my mouth, and when I tried to wash them down with tea I spilled some on my beard because my hand was shaking. *Don't weaken, Belson*, I told myself. But there was a gnawing going on at the roots of my soul. I knew what it was I had begun to want the minute I saw that room, that scurrying roach, that awful bed. Morphine.

When I finished, the men marched me back to the elevator. In the lobby two other soldiers met us, both with rifles, and the four of them escorted me out the door and across the street to a building with a big sign that read PEOPLE'S CLOTHING AND AIDS TO HEALTH.

Inside, a chubby middle-aged man looked me over. 'Mr. Kwoo?' he said.

'That's right.'

'Well, we can certainly make you more fashionable than *that*.' He frowned at my yellow spacesuit.

'You're going to make me an outfit?' I said.

'Absolutely!' he said in English. 'The very best. We know about you from the newspapers, Mr. Kwoo, and we know your importance.'

Thanks a lot, I thought, remembering my hotel room.

The five of them took me to a back room where a big metal box stood, like an upright coffin.

'Just step inside,' the man said. 'It works like a dream. An absolute dream.'

I stepped in. He threw a switch and I heard a hum. An

invisible beam must be scanning my body, doing a contour map. 'All right now,' he said and turned it off.

'How long does it take?' I said.

'About ten minutes. Do you like midnight blue? For the trousers, I mean?'

'How about blue jeans?' I said.

'Sorry,' he said. 'This isn't Los Angeles. I was planning flannels. We'll cut four or five shirts in different pastels, and then, to cap it all, a simple down jacket in gray silk.'

'Don't make it look Italian. And I'll need shoes.'

'I'm sorry, Mr. Kwoo,' he said, 'but our shoemaking equipment isn't working. We can give you fresh hose for those . . .' He looked at my feet with distaste.

'Adidas,' I said.

'I'm sure they're *marvelous* for speed.' He turned and walked over to a wall where bolts of fabric hung above one another, reached his short arms up, and with some dexterity pulled down a heavy bolt of gray cloth. He smiled benignly toward me and then lugged the fabric over to a large gray machine, slid it into a hopper at one end and delicately pressed a green button on the side. There was a low whirr for about fifteen seconds, a click, and then another louder whirr. A folded pair of pants slid out onto a red enameled tray. He walked over and picked them up. 'Perfect,' he said. 'It's really a superb piece of equipment. Japanese.' He handed them to me.

I slipped out of my spacepants right there and pulled on the flannels. They were of good fabric, but they fit over my narrow ass like a glove. 'Jesus!' I said, 'they're *tight.*'

He looked me over, pursing his lips. 'Well,' he said, 'this machine does make them snug. That's the truth of it.'

'Isn't it working right?' I said. 'I haven't seen anybody on the streets wearing anything like this. The men outside are wearing good Communist baggy pants.'

He blushed a little. 'To be frank,' he said, 'I'm under orders from the Army. From Major Feng.'

I stared at him. 'White Heron?'

He looked up at me helplessly. 'Yes, Mr. Kwoo. White Heron Feng. You are to be dressed as a . . . as a courtesan.'

'Jesus Christ!' I said. Inwardly I had a sense of my life—my

221

tired and crazy life—coming full circle, with a kind of preordained click. *Okay*, I thought, *I can follow this out to the end.*

They made me a down-filled gray jacket and one of those Ghengis Khan caps, with the earflaps. It all fit well and looked good. They were far better clothes than you could buy in New York. The truth of it is there's nothing first-class made in America except television and French fries. Television *equipment*, that is; the shows are for cretins.

Outside, it was bitter cold and I tucked my head down and started toward the hotel. One of the guards grabbed me by the arm and stopped me. 'We go elsewhere,' he said in English.

'That's a good thing,' I said.

They walked me four blocks through streets crowded with Chinese. Men, women and children, and they all stared at me politely. Most of them looked well-dressed and well-fed. Some carried gold-headed walking canes. There were occasional groups of Japanese among them, in business suits and double-breasted Chicago overcoats, with lapel cameras. I got snapped a half-dozen times, standing out because of my height and my clothes and my rifle-carrying escort. The street we walked along was full of black passenger cars and red taxis. Vendors sold *dim sum* and tea at street corners. There were bookstores and news-stands on every block. Some people walked along reading. The bustle enlivened me, brought back my love of cities. I strode with bounce in my feet and made my escorts scurry to keep up with me in their heavy overcoats and rifles and short legs. The sun was out fully now and the streets were clean, lined with trees, and busy. I began to whistle. *Così fan tutte*. We passed a park with grandmothers and children and swings. Trees everywhere—so unlike New York. Bright theater posters adorned a fence. A big one for *Macbeth* caught my eye, but I didn't stop to read it. The architecture was dreary Old Stalinist, but the feel of Peking was lively—far more so than I'd remembered it. There were soldiers and sailors of both sexes, pretty girls, old Arabella Kim types with shopping bags full of celery and tomatoes, lovers. From time to time electric limousines passed in the street with red flags, carrying Party members. We walked by a *shu mai* vendor with a stack of books on his little wheeled stand. Looking closely I saw *The Complete Works of Leo Tolstoy* and *The Novels of James M. Cain* next to the dumplings. I still had a few American dollars in my billfold; I bought a copy of *Mildred Pierce* in Chinese and stuck it in my shopping bag.

After that, we turned a corner by a construction site and came upon an enormous white marble building, set back in a park where a dozen armed soldiers were patrolling. The building was about thirty stories high, with an entrance like a Turkish mausoleum. Over the doorway hung a huge silk banner with black ideograms: THE DEFENSE OF THE PEOPLE IS THE DUTY OF THE PARTY. Ten-foot-high statues of Mao and a dozen of his successors stood on the grass, surrounding an ICBM of the kind that carries a dozen R-bombs. *My God*, I thought, *this is the Chinese Pentagon*. The headquarters of the most powerful military force in history.

The fence was of wrought iron and twenty feet tall. We stopped at a guard box where four dour matrons in army uniform checked out the papers of my guards and then, steely-eyed, let us pass. They looked at me as though I had been found in a slag heap somewhere. I took a cigar from my pocket and started to light it. One of the women snatched it from my hand. 'No smoking,' she said, in a bullfrog voice, in Chinese.

'Let me have that back,' I said. 'I won't light it.' My voice sounded hostile as hell; I'd have slugged her if I hadn't been surrounded by rifle butts.

'When you leave,' she bullfrogged back, and put the cigar on a metal table in the guard box.

Shit, I thought. I had only one more left, and the Chinese didn't trade with Cuban deviationists.

We crunched our way down a gravel path bordered in peonies, blooming crazily here in winter. I bent down and felt the ground. Warm. *My God, they must use electric wires to heat it*. I'd never seen such profligate use of power in my life. The path was about five hundred yards long, and not a candy wrapper in sight. Bright-green grass all around in the compound too, and no pigeons on the statues. They gleamed in the sun.

Two workmen were polishing the brass on the doorway

when we came up. They stood aside, nodding deferentially to my guards, and we went into an enormous Romanesque anteroom with groined arches. This led into a still larger room, a foyer with a ceiling eight stories high, and narrow windows that let light slant in and glow on pink marble columns that seemed to be everywhere, like a forest. It was as vulgar as hell, but impressive. A kind of junk cathedral with pink marble floors and crystal chandeliers and the echoing sounds of officers striding around in military boots. A crew of men was polishing the floor over at one side, while men and women officers, natty in uniform, strode from hallway to hallway like Prussian officers under Frederick Wilhelm. About six corridors fed into this grand room and the traffic was heavy.

We took a left and entered a long hall, only three stories high this time but still lit by crystal chandeliers. We walked down it, past posters celebrating victories: the Urals Campaign of 2007, where the Chinese had routed half the Russian Army in a week; the Japanese Peace Mission of 2037, where the Great Fleet of the People had sailed into Tokyo Bay to explain to the Diet that Japan must stop rearming. At the end of this hall was something that stopped me in my tracks. A simple old realistic painting of young Mao, almost slim, squatting by a hut with a pitifully small bowl of rice in his hand and his eyes dark with fatigue. Near him sat Lin Piao. The caption read 'The Long March.' I could have cried. What men—what men they were!

My guards took me by the arms and led me to an elevator. 'You sons of bitches,' I said, 'don't you have any respect?' But I said it in English and nobody tried to answer me.

The elevator was an express; it shot us right to the top of the building; we stepped out onto a red-carpeted hallway where two female guards checked us out again before taking me from my male ones. The men who brought me were awed by their surroundings. They were told to go back and return to their base. I would be watched over from here. The two new guards took me down the red carpet to a simple teakwood doorway and knocked. A male orderly let me in.

I looked around. I was in some kind of outer office, something like a doctor's waiting room, with Scandinavian-style chairs and magazines on coffee tables. The orderly took me across the room to a teakwood door and knocked softly. We waited a minute until it opened. A middle-aged woman, with a general's star on her collar, stared at me. 'My God,' she said, in English, 'it's Belson.'

Thus began one of the strangest episodes of my bewildered life: my five weeks as a Chinese whore. There was a certain fascination to it. They weren't monsters; they were hard-working and competent army officers—the Underchiefs of Staff of the Army of the People's Republic. Several were very attractive. There was a bedroom down the hall from one of their conference rooms; it was decorated in a Chinese idea of Western Macho. There was a giant fieldstone fireplace at one end with a moose head over it and crossed dummy rifles by the hearth. A huge brass bed sat in the middle of the room. The place was ludicrous, but a lot more pleasant than the House of Comradely Love, and the steaks sent up from the senior officers' mess were splendid. As long as I behaved myself with these ladies I could stay there and be left alone at night. Nobody asked me about uranium, the *Isabel*, or endolin. We had little conversation; all they told me was that White Heron had recommended me to their attention.

So I tried to accommodate myself to it as best I could. They must have had erection pills ground up in my food and drink; I had a hard on whether I liked it or not at almost all times. My physical health was excellent and I found myself on my back for hours a day, my mind often totally divorced from the movement of my hips and the sensations of my bruised penis—pleasuring one general or the other, with my eyes squeezed shut and lines of Shakespeare in my head:

For God's sake, let us sit upon the ground
And tell sad stories of the death of kings . . .

Sometimes my thoughts would be jarred by the orgasm of my partner. I had become a thinking dildo, a mournful captive of my adolescent dreams.

Sometimes when alone in the room I would stand back from the bar, a drink in my hand, and look at myself in the big mirror. My work had narrowed my waist and firmed my abdomen even more than the Nautilus machines could, and I was still tanned. The smell of jasmine and of just-departed flesh might be in my nostrils. A line from Yeats would sometimes come into my head:

'In dreams begin responsibilities . . .'

and then I would wonder how long it would go on. In a fashion time-honored in the trade of prostitution, I found myself going to sleep drunk every night and so hung over in the mornings that my first two or three tricks might have been a continuation of the night's unpleasant dreams. My God—tricks! I had no endolin and no morphine. I ate, drank, slept and copulated. I had quit exercising, since my work was vigorous enough. No. I had quit exercising because I didn't feel like a man anymore. My underwear was always returned to me perfumed, and sometimes flowers were sent to the room by one of my lovers. When we drank together the woman would pour the drinks. The oldest of them—a wiry brigadier in her fifties—liked to feed me my desserts with a spoon. I ate them greedily.

It ended as quickly as it had begun. One Thursday morning, in the week before Christmas, my first visitors were a pair of policemen in gray uniforms and red armbands. They were polite and clearly intelligent. I had no idea where they were going to take me and didn't particularly care; my main feeling was relief that I didn't have an erection when they woke me. I dressed and left without breakfast.

The day was horribly raw, a Chicago-in-January day in Peking, with ice everywhere in the streets. Everybody but me was wearing puffy overcoats and boots and enormous caps. Fortunately, the limousine was parked near the building and I made it inside without frostbite. It felt like thirty below. In the car I was glad to be in the company of men again; I felt I could live without women forever. I leaned back in the middle of my seat.

It was a long trip. It took an hour to get out of Peking, and we followed a winding road through bare, ice-covered trees for another hour before turning down a narrow path and beginning to climb a series of hills. At first there were scrubby bushes flanking the narrow road, then snow. The gray pavement had been plowed flawlessly, although there was no sign of habitation. After an hour the snow was high on each side of us and we were humming at a smooth thirty miles an hour through what felt like a cloud tunnel. I was shockingly hungry. Little spots whirred in front of my eyes against the dead white of the world outside. It was spooky and peaceful, like a shared dream, and no one spoke for over an hour. The driver was a wiry old Chinese with a chauffeur's cap; he kept both hands on the wheel and both eyes on the road. Once I cried out when a jackrabbit shot across in front of us like an apparition. The car was very warm; after a while I fell asleep.

I was awakened by a stop. Outside the driver's window two guards, so muffled around the faces I couldn't tell whether they were men or women, were standing like huge chessmen. The driver opened the back door with a switch; icy air stung my face; one of the guards bent down toward me, staring over a high collar and muffler and from under an enormous furry cap. Sunlight glinted on a bayonet. I stared back into sharp, ambiguous eyes; the guard nodded, said something to the driver and closed the door. We drove on.

We were on top of the hills now, rumbling through plowed snow along a flat plain. There were no features, no sign of life. It was like a snow-covered Belsen. I stretched and rubbed my eyes. Somehow my hunger had gone. The sun was out; we drove through streamers of mist that were now lambent, along a perfectly straight road across the plain. After ten minutes I could see in the distance a red pagoda roof.

As we came closer and slowed, I made out a house or temple about the size of my parents' home in Ohio, with a few wooden steps and a simple door in front. Snow had been cleared away from all around for a radius of about fifty feet. The roof was bright in the sun. On it sat a large bird or the image of a bird, head tucked under its wing. A dove.

Our car pulled up to the front steps. A tall, muffled guard was waiting, with no rifle this time. He held an enormous greatcoat open for me. I stepped from the warm car into it, pulling its huge collar around my ears. The guard took me firmly by the elbow and led me up the steps. The door opened. I walked inside, the weight of the coat giving gravity to my movement. I felt astonishingly calm, and the wearing of that coat for only a minute conferred dignity on my spirit as well as heft, as though it had been the robe of a Manchu emperor or Prospero's magic cloak.

I was in a small room with no furniture. The bare floor was teak; ink brush drawings of birds hung on the walls.

There was a wide, green-lacquered door at the far side of the room. I walked toward it and as it swung open I saw daylight and green foliage. I heard the sound of falling water. Standing in the doorway I looked up at a skylight, with a willow tree brushing its top against it. Through ferns, light sparkled on water. I took a step forward and saw the surface of a pool. A gravelly, womanly voice said, 'Come in, Mr. Belson.'

'Mourning Dove!' I said. 'I hoped it would be you.'

I stepped forward onto gravel, turned at the feathery stand of ferns, walked around the pond and its small waterfall. A couple of abrupt *chunks* startled me; frogs had jumped into the water at my approach and were now peering at me from wet bubble eyes, the rest of their dark bodies floating below the surface in subaqueous murk.

At the other side of the pond on a raised wooden dais between willow trees sat Mourning Dove Soong in a white wicker chair. Her hair was white and she wore a plain black robe. She looked much older and terribly frail. Her face was chalky and, as I came closer, massively wrinkled around the intelligent black eyes. She was looking at me steadily. On her lap slept a gray cat. I walked to the chair across from her and took it.

She looked at me for several moments. Then she said, in English, 'You are calm now, Mr. Belson.'

'Yes. A lot has happened since we first met. Some of the experiences have been calming.' I wondered if she knew what I had been doing in that room back in Peking. 'I hope your life has been a pleasure for you.'

'It has not been,' she said.

'I'm sorry,' I said, truly feeling sorry. 'Is it the endolin?'

'I am not concerned with endolin,' she said. 'Would you like tea?'

'Yes. And food too, if I may?'

'You were not fed in Peking?'

'Not since last night.'

She nodded. 'That would be Major Feng. I told her to treat you well, but she believes I do not care anymore. I will remind her eventually.' She pressed a button on the arm of her chair, and I heard a soft buzz in another room. A boy of about twelve came in, dressed in a black robe like Mourning Dove's. He stood before her and bowed slightly.

'Bring us food from the kitchen, Deng,' she said gently, in Chinese. Then to me, in English, 'There will be no meat, Mr. Belson, since I do not eat it. But what we have is good.'

I said nothing and watched Deng as he walked across the gravel and left. When he was gone I said, 'Mourning Dove, I am very seldom calm. All my life I have been in a hurry and I'm not even sure what for.'

'You make the simple difficult,' she said. 'Perhaps because the difficult is simple for you.'

A voice in me was saying *Fortune-cookie wisdom*. Yet if anyone on Earth was wise, it was this woman. I could feel wisdom around her presence like a magnetic field. 'I've been bored with making money,' I said. 'But when I stop I just seem to crash around and hurt other people, like Isabel.'

'Miss Crawford is a strong person and can profit from the experience.'

'You know Isabel!'

'I had your history examined when I learned of your cargo.'

'The uranium?'

'Yes.'

'And you know where Isabel is now?'

Mourning Dove nodded, stroking her cat. The cat stretched itself and yawned.

'Mourning Dove,' I said in agitation, 'I'd be relieved if you'd tell me where she is.'

'Mr. Belson,' she said, 'I do not wish to play cat and mouse with you and I wish you well in life. But I am not ready to tell you that. Maybe later.'

I stared at her. 'Mourning Dove, I love her. I need to know where she is.'

She looked at me calmly. 'Mr. Belson,' she said, 'China needs safe uranium. Our sources of power have caused far more pain than you feel for your Isabel.'

The way she said it gave me pause. 'Has something happened?' I said.

She took her hand from the back of the cat and laid her thin arms on the arms of the chair. 'While you were crossing the Pacific there was an accident in the North, near the village of Wu. Thousands of cubic feet of radioactive gas were emitted and many died. Wu is my home village and it was I who ordered the reactor built forty years ago, to show good faith in my policy.'

'Your policy?'

'I am one of the sponsors of the use of nuclear fission in China, Mr. Belson. I agreed that the price in lives would be worth the profit—in the contribution to China's future.'

I could feel her pain, even though her face didn't show it. 'And you had family members in Wu?'

'Yes. My daughter and three sons. Seven grandchildren. They are dead now, or in hospitals dying.'

'That's unbearable,' I said. I wanted to hold her and try to comfort her. 'Do you blame yourself?'

She looked at me. 'Who else is to blame?' she said. 'I championed nuclear fission. I had the plant built near Wu.'

I just looked at her. What could I say? 'What are you going to do?' I said, eventually.

'I am going to have lunch,' she said.

Deng had come back from the kitchen carrying a flat basket and a low table. He set the table between us and put the basket on it. It was full of fruit and vegetables. Another boy, who might have been Deng's brother, followed with a ceramic teapot and two cups. He set the cups down and poured.

'I don't see how you stand it,' I said, watching the boy pour the steaming tea and thinking of those corpses and of a provincial hospital somewhere, with the ruined faces of the dying.

'The big things are simpler than the small. One doesn't complicate them. I went to a monastery in Tibet and fasted. Necessities arrive unbidden, like dreams. It was necessary to grieve properly and I have grieved.' She handed me a cup of tea. 'I planned to greet you in Peking, Mr. Belson, to buy your uranium. I am sorry to have caused you a long wait.'

'That's unimportant. I too underwent a kind of . . . purgation. I hope your pain will relent. I wish I could help.'

'I see that you do,' she said calmly and sipped her tea. 'The broccoli is nourishing. It has been steamed in ginseng.'

I took a bite. It was delicious and my appetite returned in a flash. 'Did you visit Wu afterward?'

'Yes,' she said, drinking tea. 'I took endolin to the survivors. They are not in pain.'

'I'm glad it helped,' I said. I finished a floret of broccoli and then took a big peach and ate in silence, looking at the water of the pond and at the green ferns that surrounded it. I thought of Juno, of all that safe uranium there, enough to power our world forever. 'Mourning Dove,' I said, 'I still love America, even though it has treated me badly. And I'm crazy about New York. I don't want my country to be an outpost of a Chinese empire.'

'Your country is China now.'

'By adoption. And I think I could be a Confucianist. But right now I would like to settle in New York, with Isabel if she'll have me, and devote the rest of my life to making it into a great city again.'

She was silent for a moment. Then she said, 'Crashing around?'

'Maybe I can do it calmly.' I said this with surprising passion. 'I've learned a lot in the last year, Mourning Dove. I may be ready to enjoy the rest of my life.' My head was feeling very clear, and there were no more spots in front of my eyes. This was one of the loveliest rooms I had ever been in and I felt I was with the oldest and best of friends.

She nodded. ' "The road of excess leads to the palace of wisdom." '

'That's William Blake!' I said. 'I hope it's true.'

'It is true. I was excessive when young, as you are, Mr. Belson, and I have become wise. I believe that in my case one brought about the other.' She returned her attention to the cat. 'I read Blake in college, in London. I desired to know everything when I was young, and to be infinitely rich and to become a member of the Central Committee of the Party. I have had four husbands and alienated them all. They are all dead now and I have forgotten them. But I got what I desired.'

She looked at me. 'I have not forgotten my mother and my father. My mother would beat me for nothing . . .' Suddenly her old face tightened alarmingly. '*For nothing*, Mr. Belson. She has been dead fifty years and I hate her still. I hate my father for letting her do it, and he too is long dead.'

'Jesus!' I said. 'It sounds familiar.'

'It is not uncommon. The thing is to rule it and not to let it rule.' She paused. 'One cannot attract the attention of the dead, though many try.'

'Oh yes,' I said, blinking, 'many try.' My voice sounded strange.

'You are crying,' Mourning Dove said. 'As much as I hate my mother I also love her. With a mother it is hard to do otherwise. Perhaps you love yours still.'

Orbach had tried to tell me that, but I wouldn't listen—not in my stomach or heart or wherever it is. I looked at Mourning Dove through tears. They were pouring out, some of them slopping down on my big hairy right hand that held a half-eaten peach. I could see my mother's face, lost in self-regard. Grief suffused my body, starting in my stomach and spreading to my chest and shoulders and heaving the muscles of my abdomen and my face.

Gradually it subsided. I heard the pond waterfall again. I leaned back and stretched. I could feel the strength of my limbs, the soundness of my heart. My beard was wet. I took a bite from the peach, letting the juice mix with tears.

'You are a remarkable man, Mr. Belson,' Mourning Dove said.

I nodded and swallowed. 'Would you call me Benjamin?'

'Benjamin,' she said, 'I want your uranium.'

I nodded. 'You can have half of it.'

Her voice was quiet. 'No. All. China needs it.'

I looked at her. Her face was unshakable. 'I can't do that. There will be enough to go around. I can send the *Isabel* back.'

She just looked at me. 'You can be made to tell us where it is from. Chemicals . . .'

'I know. But they aren't reliable.'

'Torture,' she said, as if mentioning a stock option.

I shuddered. 'Oh, I know. You could do that and it would

work. But it wouldn't give you what's on the *Isabel*. That's in Washington, and L'Ouverture Baynes is no fool.'

She had finished her tea but was still holding the cup. She leaned over now and set it on the table beside the basket. 'L'Ouverture Baynes will be out of office next week. He was defeated in November, Benjamin.'

I stared at her and said, 'Mattie . . .?'

'Miss Hinkle campaigned with tales of the *Isabel*'s uranium, claiming the needs of employment in Kentucky. She will be sworn in in January. You will be able to recover the *Isabel*. I want it brought to Honshu.'

'Mourning Dove,' I said. 'I can't do that. I can let you have half of it. That's thirty tons. You can replace all the U235 in China with thirty tons and it will keep you till I get more.' My heart had begun beating wildly again, thinking of how L'Ouverture had been defeated and that I could get hold of my spaceship again.

'Why would I want the United States to be powerful?'

I stared at her. 'Oh Jesus, Mourning Dove,' I said. 'Don't do to us what the British did to you, with the opium and all that bullying. The world doesn't have to be run that way.'

'There is danger in a house without a master.'

'Oh, come off it,' I said, exasperated with her. 'That's fortune-cookie wisdom and it sounds fascist.'

'It's Confucius.'

'I'm sorry, but it's still no good. Remember your mother? She was a master, wasn't she? Who needs that?'

That seemed to touch her. She pursed her lips silently for a moment. I waited. 'America will waste the fuel,' she said, 'as it wasted the oil of Texas and of the Persian Gulf. America built tall buildings with sealed windows and burned oil to cool them in summer.'

'You sound like L'Ouverture. It doesn't have to be that way anymore. America has changed. We're more civilized, less crazy about dumb toys. Cheap power can permit a beautiful life as easily as a crass one.'

Her face had softened a bit, but now it hardened. 'Benjamin,' she said, 'the person who supported me as a child and comforted me after Mother's beatings was my great-uncle, Too Moy. The boys who served us are his

233

great-great-grandsons and my nephews. They are all the family I have left.'

'I'm glad you had someone to comfort you,' I said. 'With me it was a horse named Juno.'

'One takes what one can find. Too Moy was very old and crippled. He had seen Mao himself. He was a peasant. In Wu our water power came from the power of human legs. A man or a woman sat astride a device like a wooden bicycle, across a stream, and pedaled the water into rice paddies. Sometimes for ten or twelve hours a day. There is slight fulfillment in such work and a great deal of pain. My great-uncle walked little and took much aspirin for the cramps in his legs. I was able to get medication for him, and it helped, but at times he would lie on his pallet in the room behind my mother's house and groan. Paddling was all he ever did, and he did it for over fifty years. Yet he was an intelligent man, with a loving heart. I might have been a cruel person without his love.'

'It's awful to spend a life like that,' I said.

Her face was rigid. 'Yes,' she said. 'All the labor that Too Moy did in his lifetime could have been done better by one of the motors Americans were cutting their lawns with when he was young.'

I nodded. I had nothing to say.

'You Americans did not create that oil you used for your cars, your air conditioners, your lawn mowers, or for the plastic films you wrapped toys and pens and vegetables in. The oil was made by the world itself, when great ferns covered Texas and the Persian Gulf. It took millions of years to make it. You and the Arabs threw it away in a century, on foolishness. With that oil, my great-uncle could have had a happier life. There were many like him all over China. When my great-uncle was young, people like you in America called such people the "yellow peril" or "faceless millions".' She leaned over toward me in quiet fury. 'My Great-Uncle Too Moy was not a peril, was not faceless. He did not mope in impotence. He was a better man than you, Mr. Belson.'

I sat there stunned for a long while. I stared at the water, trying to spot the frogs. But they were out of sight now. Minutes passed in silence. I thought of counterarguments, thought of mentioning the cars and jets the Chinese had transported me in, the luxurious life that Party members like Mourning Dove herself lived, the red flag limousines and the graft in the military. But I could not get that great-uncle out of my mind. My vision had somehow become very clear; on an impulse I took off my glasses and slid them into my shirt pocket. I could see everything with a preternatural sharpness, every wrinkle in Mourning Dove's impassive face, every leaf of the willow. Back at the other end of the pond were the eyes of a frog, just on the still surface of the gray water, looking toward me.

'Mourning Dove,' I said, 'I would like to be your son.'

She did not look at me. 'I have no son now.'

'I know. I would like you to adopt me.'

She raised her eyes slowly. 'Why?'

'I need a mother.'

She kept looking at me for a long while. 'Perhaps you are only trying to win an argument.'

'God, *no!*' I said passionately. 'I have let that go for now. I truly love you and want you to be my parent, the way Too Moy was yours and saved your soul for you.' I paused and looked at her, not crying now but feeling as though the slightest breath of air could bring tears. 'I want my soul to be like yours. I want you in my memory to drive away the drunken fool who lives in there.' I kept looking at her.

She remained impassive for a long time. Then she reached out a fragile white hand and placed it on the back of mine, on the arm of the wicker chair. 'Benjamin,' she said. 'Benjamin. You may keep half of the uranium.'

I felt as I had felt when, naked to Fomalhaut, I had slept on the grass that fed me and awakened to the magnificent yet distant rings of Belson.

15

The theater occupied the bottom floors of a hideous new office building—one of dozens along Chang An Avenue a mile east of Tien An Men Square. We drove up to it in a chauffeured limousine. It was I who arranged the demolition of Mitsubishi Tower in New York twenty years before; this Chinese abomination resembled that Japanese one, except for the statues. Flanking the doorway were massive bronzes of a peasant and a soldier, shirt-sleeves rolled, staring tight-lipped toward the future. What in hell is so holy about the future? Anyone who feels that way about it should be forced to read history at gunpoint. The crowd was mostly young; they wore blue jeans or quilted Synlon pants, and bright foul-weather jackets. They were probably students from the Institute of Life Enrichment and Managerial Skills, a few blocks away. Some stared as the theater manager led us past the ticket queue and into the lobby. Conspicuous as I was with my height and blond beard, it was Mourning Dove who attracted the stares; she responded with a thoughtful frown.

A flunky had rushed ahead of us, and when we were ushered into our box he was hanging a painting of Chairwoman Chu, arms folded in her turn-of-the-century black jacket. He left the picture crooked for a moment, held Mourning Dove's chair for her obsequiously, murmuring praises as she seated herself, then quickly straightened Madame Chu and left.

When we were alone I said, "Some of those looks downstairs were mean.'

She lit a Lucky Strike with a stainless-steel Zippo and held the closed lighter in her frail hand for a moment. I saw with surprise that the hand was trembling. She put the lighter in the pocket of her gown and said, 'The accident near Wu has affected my standing with the people.'

I remembered my agitation at being hanged in effigy on Madison Avenue. 'Are you in any danger, Mourning Dove?'

'I have enemies.'

'I bet you have.' I thought of White Heron.

The play had been running for two months; it would close in a week. We had been driven into Peking that afternoon, had gone to the People's Hall of Records for a brief ceremony and then, at Mourning Dove's instructions, were driven here.

While we waited for the curtain, people kept looking up at us from time to time. Some seemed only curious to see a Party official and her blond escort, but some showed open hostility. I settled back into my Victorian opera chair, rested my elbow on one of its little antimacassars, and lit a cigar. It was like a box in a movie Western; the chairs were upholstered in dark-purple velvet; the oil painting of China's first Party Chairwoman hung over velvet draperies behind us; there was a brass railing in front of us with yet more purple velvet hanging from the rail to the floor. But it was comfortable and spacious. And I knew that what you pay for in China is privacy and space. China may be down to half a billion souls, but it still teems. I chewed nervously on my cigar and left Mourning Dove to her thoughts, almost bursting with impatience for the curtain to rise. By the time it went up I had cleaned my glasses twice and my cigar was a mess. I ground it out in the ashtray and leaned forward toward the stage below.

The witches were adequate but no thrill. They were got up as Japanese Shinto priests and their English was more comical than scary. But their old faces did look like something to be reckoned with, and the blasted heath they stood on made me think of those vast acres of obsidian I had lived on so long:

Fair is foul, and foul is fair;
Hover through the fog and filthy air.

Macbeth was a big Australian named Wellfleet Close, with an Aussie's red face and a bellowing voice; he looked as if he had the required gift for murder. Duncan and Banquo were South-east Asians. I know the play pretty well, having a certain spiritual familiarity with that dangerous couple; I knew

237

when to expect her first appearance. But when the scene abruptly cut to Lady Macbeth with a big letter in her hands, I was startled. There she was, and yet not really. She wore a long russet gown and no wig; the bright lights made her gray hair shine and her eyes seem large and commanding. I knew it was Isabel, yet it was Lady Macbeth too.

She began reading the letter aloud,

They met me in the day of success and I have learned . . .

Even while pouring tea Isabel could dazzle with her voice. Here in Peking, after all the uncertain accents that preceded her entrance, the sound of her own Scottish speech, the real English language, was electrifying. Even these Chinese became hushed at the authentic ring of it. The play went on through its blood and dreams, and Isabel took every scene she was in, dominating the stage. She was a first-rate actress. I'd had no idea. When it ended with Macbeth's head on the pole, I glanced over at Mourning Dove. She seemed lost in thought. Applause filled the theater.

During the curtain calls I stood and shouted, 'Isabel!' and she looked up to stare at me a moment. I could have climbed down to the stage, but something in her look made me keep my distance. Maybe Lady Macbeth was still in there, and I didn't want any part of that.

When she looked away from me I sat and leaned back in my seat, trying to calm myself. Mourning Dove was lighting a cigarette. The sound of the applause became fragmentary. Voices began calling out. Men and women in the front rows were standing, not facing the stage now but facing our box, staring up in anger, shouting, 'Comrade Soong. Comrade Soong.'

Mourning Dove rose, stepped to the front of the box and held the rail with both hands. She looked very old and frail, but her voice was steady. She spoke in Chinese. 'I am Mourning Dove Soong. What is wanted of me?'

'An accounting,' someone shouted, 'an accounting of the Death Tax for Electricity. An explanation of Wu.' More shouts repeated this. I came over beside her for moral support, but she seemed not to need any. I was in more need of help than she, with emotions flying around in my stomach like leaves in a monsoon.

'I will come to the stage,' Mourning Dove said. I stared at her, shocked. She put her hand on my arm and said, 'One is accountable to the People.'

'Let me go down there with you, Mourning Dove,' I said.

'If you wish.' We left the box, went down a staircase and through a small door that led backstage. I looked around for Isabel. She was not in sight.

Then suddenly I was onstage with the curtain up, blinking out across bright lights at a bunch of angry Chinese, most of them standing. Beside me stood Mourning Dove, only as high as the middle of my chest, with a cigarette in her hand and her eyes straight ahead.

'Nine hundred seventy died at Wu,' Mourning Dove said. 'Another thousand will die before this winter is a memory. It was I who ordered the reactor built.'

They were silent for a moment. Then someone shouted out, 'Murderess.' And someone else shouted, 'Lady Macbeth! Bloody hands!' I began to be afraid for her.

'This theater is well-lighted and warm,' Mourning Dove said. 'China has power everywhere because of uranium. You do not labor on foot in rice paddies, nor do your mothers or fathers. You study at universities and attend the theater. Your homes are warm. A price is paid for this.'

'Too high,' someone shouted—a young woman with traditional bangs and an army jacket. 'It is too high a price.'

'Have you considered the alternative?' Mourning Dove said.

There was silence for a moment, and then a lean young man in the third row shouted, 'China has coal, and wind, and tides.'

Mourning Dove was lighting another cigarette. When she closed her Zippo she looked at the man who had spoken and said, 'Coal blackens the skies and the lungs. It is dangerous to mine. The wind and tide are a perpetual delight, but they will not power the factories of Hangchow nor warm the hearths of Shanghai. That is a dream.'

The young man only looked more furious. 'Coal may be burned with precision and the skies made safe from its breath. One must take pains.'

Before Mourning Dove could speak I said, in English, 'Coal

239

has its own tax of death, its own blight. I am a merchant of coal and speak from experience.'

A heavy man with a Charlie Chan mustache sat in the second row, wearing a business suit. 'Who speaks?' he said loudly. 'Who is this pale devil with the voice of a bear?'

'I'm Benjamin Belson,' I said. 'I do not endorse Mourning Dove's decision to build reactors. I cannot speak for the dead. But the decision was not a foolish one and Madame Soong has taken responsibility for it.'

Several voices cried out, 'Foreign devil!' And then Charlie Chan stood and said, 'Your English tongue is that of the killer Macbeth. Take your English and go home.'

I remembered those student rioters who had burned my effigy and told me to go home. I am proud of my Chinese; it was a thrill to use it. *'I am home,'* I said in Chinese. 'I am a citizen of the People's Republic, and Mourning Dove Soong is my foster mother. I bring a new uranium, star-born, that will not destroy life.'

At my first words in their own language, many of them were clearly shocked. Several seated themselves, as if mulling it over. But the older man was relentless. 'I cannot accept your professed gift to China. China has been promised gifts from white devils before. Opium was such a gift.'

'I am not British,' I said angrily. 'I love China. I am dismayed to see its ancient culture discarded and its men become soft. But China's greatness is everywhere manifest, as was that of America in the time of my grandfathers. I too mourn the accident at Wu and know the cost of China's wealth is incalculable. In this case the dead speak.'

The old man was adamant. 'Only the devil calculates with lives.'

Mourning Dove was watching his face. She spoke directly to him. 'Someone must,' she said.

They stared at each other for a long moment. Finally he said, between his teeth, 'Murderess,' and sat down. Another voice, from the back, picked up the cry of 'Murderess' and then another. I heard a man shout, 'Capitalist!'

And then a voice rang out from behind me and I turned to see Isabel standing by me with her hands on her hips, facing the audience. The part in the curtain was still moving from where she had just stepped through. She was in Lady Macbeth's russet gown, but the stage makeup was gone from her face and it looked pale under the lights.

'*What kind of Communists are you?*' she said.

'*English,*' someone hissed.

Isabel's voice could have waked the dead. 'I am *not* English,' she said, spacing the words out. 'And you are hypocrites. You make me ashamed for the great Mao and for his discipline.' She pointed at the old man. 'Your jacket is from Saks. Solar power cannot make such jackets.'

Several of the more thoughtful ones had become quietly attentive. Finally a young woman who had been silent spoke up from about twenty rows back. 'Yes, we live well. Must others die for that?'

Mourning Dove answered. 'Yes.'

And immediately I said, 'Not anymore.'

The anger was still in the air, but less powerfully. For a long minute everyone was silent, wondering if it would start up again. Then a couple in the back row got up and left the theater. More followed, and after a while the three of us were alone onstage with the footlights still blazing on us.

'Mother,' I said, 'I'd like you to meet Isabel.'

In the gutters of Chang An Avenue lay occasional clumps of left-over red confetti, from some parade or other that afternoon. It was bitterly cold and halos of frozen mist surrounded the street-lamps. An occasional official car droned by under electric power, its red fender flags flapping. Party officials were on their way to meet sweethearts or were coming back from gambling clubs. A sleek electric bus hummed past us, with most of its seats empty.

'Did you mean that, Ben? That China was wise to use nuclear power?' Isabel said.

'I did at the time,' I said. 'But I was defending Mourning Dove. God knows how many have died of leukemia alone.'

'I've thought of that.'

'Isabel,' I said, 'I'm not impotent anymore.'

'That should ease your temper.'

'Yes.' There was a lighted skyscraper between us and Tien An Men Square and we were heading toward it. It looked a bit like the Empire State Building. 'They've lost a quarter million people,' I said. 'Maybe twice that. If they'd burned it right, coal would have been more humane. But they were in a hurry, and they had all that uranium at Sinkiang and Kiangsi . . .' I felt a sudden wave of sadness.

'Mourning Dove didn't need your help,' Isabel said.

Two Mercedes limousines hummed past us, down the middle of the broad old avenue. From one of them came the muffled sound of Broadway music, a new musical called *Oriental Blues*. What strange transactions the modern world conducted!

'Anyway, it's over. I'll have my ship back in three weeks, and they'll start changing cores.'

Isabel was wearing an enormous down-filled coat and a black watchcap pulled over her ears. I had my hands jammed in my pockets against the cold. Expert opinion said it was not an ice age, but here we were in another horror of a winter. 'You were magnificent in the play,' I said, for the second time. 'I've never seen a Lady Macbeth like you.'

'Ben,' she said, 'it's a fine play, but sometimes it felt like Fifty-first Street, with you.'

That annoyed me. 'I'm no murderer.'

'That's not what I mean. You can be awfully bombastic.'

'I've changed,' I said.

'I hope you have,' she said, a bit grimly. We walked in silence for a while. Abruptly she stopped and turned to me. 'Ben,' she said, 'I don't want to be a supporting actress in your melodrama.'

That hit home, and I said nothing. We were coming up to the skyscraper. There were ideographs incised on an arch over its entrance. We stopped and looked at them.

'I can't read Chinese,' Isabel said.

'It says INSTITUTE FOR THE ADVANCEMENT OF HAPPINESS BETWEEN MEN AND WOMEN.'

She hesitated. 'You weren't the only cause of those fights,' she said. 'When I let you move in, my life felt empty and I expected you to fill it.'

'And did I?'

'With a vengeance.'

'Look,' I said, 'that's all past. You've got a career that's

242

clearly taking off. Fieler wants you to do Ibsen in New York. I have to buy into Con Ed or start up my own company. I've got to mount another voyage for endolin and uranium. We won't be focusing on each other all the time. Besides, I can get it up now. Sometimes I can't get it down.'

She looked at me closely. Under the lights by the building I could see the redness of her cheeks and the red tip of her nose. 'I gave up my apartment in New York,' she said, 'and my sister has Amagansett and William.' She hesitated. 'You won't be going after the uranium yourself?'

I shook my head. 'There's a new captain.' She hesitated and I said, 'I'll be moving back into my mansion and I want you with me. I want the cats too. I'd like you to marry me.'

'Things have gone very well since you left,' she said. 'The *Times* ran my picture during *Hamlet* and I did television here in Peking before *Macbeth* . . .' She stopped. 'Ben, you require more attention than I want to give.'

'Honey,' I said, 'don't forget the good times. We used to take walks and eat in restaurants and go to concerts. We really enjoyed each other.'

'Sometimes.'

I shrugged. 'I'll take you home,' I said. 'Where are you staying?'

'I have an apartment near Tien An Men. We can walk.'

I started walking and suddenly I felt Isabel's arm interlink itself with mine. I remembered how we used to hold each other on those cold nights in her apartment, sleeping wrapped up with one another.

She must have been thinking of the same thing because she said, 'You can spend the night with me, if you'd like.'

The apartment was quiet and warm. There were no cats. We made love easily, in silence, and then lay on Isabel's blue Chinese bed holding each other as tightly as yang and yin. Gradually we separated enough that we could lie on our backs with our feet touching.

I lit a cigar. 'How long does the play run?' I said, breathing easily and as relaxed in the body as on Belson grass.

'Eight more performances.' She rolled over and kissed my

243

neck. 'Oh my, Ben,' she said. 'It was about time.'

'We could get married in Peking,' I said.

She rolled over, stretched her arms out and yawned. 'New York, Ben. We ought to get married in New York.'

The elevator had been double-checked. Workmen had taken it up and down a dozen times. But there was a lot of embarrassed tension among us. Then there were rumblings beneath our feet, a sturdy whine overhead, and we began moving upward.

'Well, for one thing,' the Deputy Mayor said, trying to break the tension, 'the Maintenance Workers' Union is solidly Democratic.'

The rest of us said nothing, but as we approached the top floors the ride began to smooth out and I started feeling an exhilaration like blasting off for Fomalhaut two years before. I stood with the four of them silent in the middle of that freshly painted car with its polished brass handrails and its gray floor, and the old rush of fast travel expanded my soul for a moment. As we slowed near the top I felt Isabel's hand take mine and squeeze it. The car stopped, the door hummed open and we stepped out onto a red carpet laid on a floor still covered with scuffmarks from the last group of tourists to leave, thirty years before. Someone had opened a few windows, but the air was still musty. There were graffiti on the walls—one could have been an imprecation from a hidden tomb. DEATH TO INTERLOPERS it read, in spray-paint orange under a veil of dust. There was a crew of a half-dozen workmen cleaning up. I hoped they would get that one off soon. Heavy blinds covered the windows we faced; it was west that way, and the late-afternoon sun in June would be blinding. I started to head back around to where I could look out to the east, but Isabel put her hand on my arm and said, 'Take it easy, Ben. Let's wait a few minutes.'

'Okay,' I said, remembering my breakneck rush onto

Belson. 'Let's get a drink.' A bar was being set up under the shaded windows and several bottles and some glasses were already out.

Isabel was looking around her, at the long-closed souvenir stand, the grimy coffee urns, the high-ceilinged room with metal girders overhead, and the yellowing photograph of Manhattan on the wall above the elevator—Manhattan as it was around 2025, with all the Japanese skyscrapers. Above this was written in faded letters: OBSERVATION DECK.

We went to the bar and she handed me a canapé. As I gave her a drink I noticed the light on the window blinds wasn't so bright anymore; the sun must be hidden by another tall building. I walked a few steps over and pulled the cord. There had been a lot of talking in the room, with the laborers and two foremen and the Deputy Mayor and his secretary and a holovision crew that was just getting their equipment out of the elevator. But when the blind began to go up a hush spread itself around me. Before I looked out myself I glanced around the room. Everyone was staring toward the window.

I turned and there it was: the New York skyline. The sun glowed from behind the cylinder of the Bank of Hangchow, and its light made quasi-silhouettes of the giant old buildings of the West Side—all of them empty but still astounding to see from this solid old masterpiece of a skyscraper: those solemn black shapes, pushed skyward in turn-of-the-century confidence, almost all of them taller than the one we stood on.

'My God,' Isabel said finally. 'It's New York City!'

Somebody laughed softly and the silence was swallowed again in chatter. More people kept coming from the elevator. Ice tinkled all over now. A five-piece band was setting up a in a room behind us; above the other hubbub came the occasional spurt of a trumpet, the nervous clang of a cymbal. I walked around the tower several times, looking out toward the Hudson and the East River and the southern tip of the island. A few weak lights down near street level came on—the twenty-watt fluorescents we had all lived with for a third of a century, but all the upper stories remained dark. At the northern end of the deck, facing uptown, was a table draped with red, white and blue bunting and faced by rows of chairs. On it sat the black switchbox and a microwave transmitter dish like a tea saucer aimed toward New Jersey. The switch had been locked into the 'off' position with a key. I looked at my watch; fifty more minutes. Booming male laughter was coming from the anteroom. I turned and walked in. Sticking up over the crowd was L'Ouverture's shiny black head, his big toothy smile. He was stretching his long arms out and laughing while several other people looked up admiringly. He did look beautiful, in a pale-blue seersucker suit with a crisp white shirt and red tie.

Just then he saw me coming. *'Benjamin!'* he shouted. 'Benjamin Belson, Intergalactic Pirate.'

People pulled away to let me pass. I walked up to him. 'Piracy is as piracy does, L'Ouverture,' I said. I heard my voice. It sounded dangerous.

'Ben,' he said, his arms still out above heads, 'I'm not even a senator anymore. You've got your spaceship and I'm in commerce. Let me congratulate you.'

I was right up to him now, looking up at his flawlessly shaved face, the bright silk of his necktie, smelling his cologne and hearing the rustle of his suit as he now brought his grotesquely long arms down from the gesture my arrival had attracted. 'L'Ouverture,' I said, 'I accept your congratulations.' Then I thought, *What the hell.* I handed my drink to someone and put my arms around Baynes. His arms came around me. We hugged hard for a long time and I could feel the warmth of his enormous hands across my shoulders. 'Ben,' he whispered in my ear, lowering his head to say it, 'you are a child of mine after all.'

I pulled back and looked up at him. 'If I am,' I said, 'I've left home for good.'

He smiled benignly. 'What could be more in tune with the order of things?'

'I'll get you a drink,' I said.

The Mayor arrived and the holo filming began. During a lull in that he handed me a pair of Xerograms and I pressed them on. One was a formal thank you from President Weinberg with a White House logo glowing in gold on its projection; the other was in strong calligraphy: 'I am pleased with my son,' it said. 'Your journey has relighted the world.' The Mayor tapped my arm, ready to begin his speech. I followed him to the dais and stood at the bunting-draped table. Someone had unlocked the power switch. Isabel sat in the front row in her blue dress; she looked smart and strong.

The Mayor went on longer than I had expected and I began to get impatient. He talked about the simultaneous ceremonies in Boston, Dallas and Chicago, about the new electric heating that would soon be flowing into Montreal and Vancouver, about Juno uranium plants scheduled for Zimbabwe and Rio and Paris, about the new reciprocity in U.S. relations with China, while I stood with impatience, wanting to get on with it and occasionally slipping a look at my watch. For a moment I became appalled at myself. Did the road of excesses lead only back to this? Had I lost my impotence and quieted my rages only to become another impatient rich man with a distended ego? I looked down at myself. There was my Ralph Lauren cotton jacket of midnight blue, my Bert Pulitzer shirt, my blue silk Marley tie, my gray trousers gently resting their cuffs on English shoes. Under all this a body still firm and a set of genitals no longer in spiritual orbit. I looked up and there was Isabel with a light smile on her lips, looking not at me but at the dull man at my side. Had it all only come to this, then: the speech of a politician, expensive clothes, and boredom?

In a seat behind Isabel a relaxed-looking man whom I didn't recognize shifted his weight in his chair. He glanced down toward his watch. I looked around the room, from well-dressed person to well-dressed person: others were restless too. L'Ouverture, the biggest man there, sat in the back row looking bored out of his skull.

My discomfort subsided and I became easy again with my clothes and my life. I thought of how well Isabel's career was going, how she worked at her acting and at getting our home in order. I thought of the *Isabel*, now in the limbo of analogy travel from Belson with a load of endolin aboard and a crew ready to fill the empty holds on Juno. Ruth was captain this time, sleeping in my old suite with the porthole in the bathroom, but the Nautilus machines were at our home on Madison Avenue in the room with the pool table. Mourning Dove was presiding over installing new cores in the reactors of the Middle Kingdom. The world was not ready to wind down yet, and New York was not ready to become a memory like Samarkand or Constantinople.

While this verbal fugue was playing in my head, a part of my attention was picking up Mayor Wharton's speech. He was praising the work of the *Isabel* and the abundance it had brought. Then he paused, turned to me and said, 'With us now to close the circuit is the captain of the *Isabel*.' I took a step forward and spoke. 'I am an impatient man and I want to throw this switch, but I want my wife with me when I do it.' I looked at Isabel. She stood up, walked around the table and took my arm. We gripped the heavy handle, hesitated a moment and pulled it together, looking toward the window behind the rows of chairs. The switch clicked into place and the microwave blipped its signal off to the power plants across the river. No more than a dozen windows lighted up outside. Isabel looked up at me. 'Is that all?' she said. 'Is something wrong?' People were standing and looking out and a few were murmuring; the ceremoniousness had evaporated.

'As we know,' Mayor Wharton was saying, 'there will be a delay while the elevators are going up and people are entering the high floors.' I could picture those old offices and apartments. People with flashlights, people who were part of this big Manhattan party just now beginning, would be wandering about on dusty floors, putting bulbs into sockets and finding long-disused switches and trying to get them to work. The elevators had been checked out over the past months, but there had not been enough professionals to climb all the stairs and get all the rooms open. Now it would be mostly volunteers: clerks, actors, bankers and sanitation workers and their lovers. Children too. People with martinis or beer bumping around in musty old rooms and hallways, in executive washrooms with rusted plumbing and office suites with peeling walls and dust-covered light fixtures and musty carpets. Elevator shafts would be groaning and rumbling again with their cables, so long slack, now going suddenly taut. I thought of the remnants of final office parties, the empty champagne bottles and the uneaten cheese and canapés sitting on empty desks, there since the last office workers had left in 2031, when the legislators in Albany had stopped the use of elevators. In some rooms there would be napkins strewn about, unemptied wastebaskets, an occasional umbrella or a forgotten purse.

Isabel brought me out of this reverie. 'Ben,' she whispered, 'follow me.'

People had broken up into groups and were chattering, glancing from time to time toward the windows. A few more lights had come on in the lower stories, but the city was still dark. Isabel had me by the hand. She led me away from the crowd and out into the anteroom with the elevator. Behind us the band had started playing. To the right of the elevator was a door with a small table in front to keep it from being opened. Isabel pulled the table aside. 'I checked this out a while back,' she said. She turned the knob and opened the door. Fresh air hit my face. 'Come on!' she said.

We walked down a short hall into a cool breeze. It was dark and I nearly stumbled, but we had left the doorway open and enough light came from the room behind us that I could find my way with Isabel leading. The noise of the band behind us faded. I felt I was in a windy tunnel, now hearing only the purposeful clicking of Isabel's heels. I was just starting to protest when I saw her stop in front of me by a black staircase. I blinked. It was an old escalator, not working. I looked up and saw a rectangle of black, with stars. 'Come on up,' Isabel said, leading the way. I followed her and the starry rectangle above grew larger and the air windier.

We stepped out onto a dark metallic surface. I looked up; the mooring mast of the building that useless tower intended as a home for dirigibles, loomed up over us. I looked outward. The panorama of a dark Manhattan was in front of us. We walked a few steps toward the edge of the platform, our steps clanging, and just as we arrived at the steel railings, with wind now blowing strongly in our faces, just as Isabel took my hand, a horizontal row of lights came on in a building in front of us. I caught my breath. More lights came on, to our left. Then to our right. We stood silently in the night air, staring.

Landing on Belson the first time, Ruth had slid the *Isabel* into a single orbit under the rings and I, standing on the bridge in gym shorts in my newly strong body, had felt my heart stop at the sight that wheeled before us: those magnificent rings in airless rainbow above a circle of void. Below them hung the gray curve of Belson itself. The *Isabel* moved from the sunless side of the rings of their illuminated side, and light suddenly filled the windows of the bridge and bathed our faces in a refulgence beyond all knowing. A small pale moon hung poised between the rings and the planets, shimmering as the *Isabel* must be shimmering in that splendor, poised in Newtonian certainty of hurl and granitic heft, floodlit by magic as we ourselves were. There is beauty in our galaxy that the human mind can only reach out for and brush against before recoiling. There is a sweep and color that our history upward from warm amoebic seas has hardly prepared eyes and nerves for. I had to look away.

Here in New York, as the lights of its own metropolitan scale came winking on randomly at left, at center, at right and up and down and middle in scrambled array, with the pale, limited incandescence of tungsten and of phosphors, filling in the pieces of the great architectural jigsaw, I did not this time turn away. I am not able to forget the Belson rings, nor do I ever want to. I am not one to forget either that this human world of ours has beauty that can stun the mind—the rain forests, the canyons, coasts, the gray skin of deep ocean, the grim antarctic mists. New York was built by pressure and noise, yet its beauty—far beyond the human noise that made it—penetrates to the marrow. I felt Isabel's warm body beside me and heard her breath catch in her throat as we watched Manhattan create itself before us. I would have given my whole lovely fortune for Aunt Myra to be there with us and to have heard her own breath catch as she saw New York reawaken. I hugged Isabel to my side. It was good to be home.

THE END

FAR FROM HOME

FAR FROM HOME

For Eleanora, Mimi, Stan, Rosemary, Bette, Frank,
Amy, Lynn, Merle and Herry

CONTENTS

Part One

Close to Home

RENT CONTROL

"My God," Edith said, "that was the most *real* experience of my life." She put her arms around him, put her cheek against his naked chest, and pulled him tightly to her. She was crying.

He was crying too. "Me too, darling," he said, and held his arms around her. They were in the loft bed of her studio apartment on the East Side. They had just had orgasms together. Now they were sweaty, relaxed, blissful. It had been a perfect day.

Their orgasms had been foreshadowed by their therapy. That evening, after supper, they had gone to Harry's group as always on Wednesdays and somehow everything had focused for them. He had at last shouted the heartfelt anger he bore against his incompetent parents; she had screamed her hatred of her sadistic mother, her gutless father. And their relief had come together there on the floor of a New York psychiatrist's office. After the screaming and pounding of fists, after the real and potent old rage in both of them was spent, their smiles at one another had been radiant. They had gone afterward to her apartment, where they had lived together half a year, climbed up the ladder into her bed, and begun to make love slowly, carefully. Then frenetically. They had been picked up bodily by it and carried to a place they had never been before.

Now, afterward, they were settling down in that place, huddled together. They lay silently for a long time. Idly she looked toward the ledge by the mattress where she kept cigarettes, a mason jar with miniature roses, a Japanese ashtray, and an alarm clock.

"The clock must have stopped," she said.

He mumbled something inarticulate. His eyes were closed.

"It says nine twenty," she said, "and we left Harry's at nine."

"Hmmm," he said, without interest.

She was silent for a while, musing. Then she said, "Terry? What time does your watch say?"

"Time, time," he said. "Watch, watch." He shifted his arm and looked. "Nine twenty," he said.

"Is the second hand moving?" she said. His watch was an Accutron, not given to being wrong or stopping.

He looked again. "Nope. Not moving." He let his hand fall on her naked behind, now cool to his touch. Then he said, "That *is* funny. Both stopping at once." He leaned over her body toward the window, pried open a space in her Levelor blinds, looked out. It was dark out, with an odd shimmer to the air. Nothing was moving. There was a pile of plastic garbage bags on the sidewalk opposite. "It can't be eleven yet. They haven't taken the garbage from the Toreador." The Toreador was a Spanish restaurant across the street; they kept promising they would eat there sometime but never had.

"It's probably about ten thirty," she said. "Why don't you make us an omelet and turn the TV on?"

"Sure, honey," he said. He slipped on his bikini shorts and eased himself down the ladder. Barefoot and undressed, he went to the tiny Sony by the fireplace, turned it on, and padded over to the stove and sink at the other end of the room. He heard the TV come on while finding the omelet pan that he had bought her, under the sink, nestling between the Bon Ami and the Windex. He got eggs out, cracked one, looked at his watch. It was running. It said nine twenty-six. "Hey, honey," he called out. "My watch is running."

After a pause she said, her voice slightly hushed, "So is the clock up here."

He shrugged and put butter in the pan and finished cracking the eggs, throwing the shells into the sink. He whipped them with a fork, then turned on the fire under the pan and walked back to the TV for a moment. A voice was saying, ". . . nine thirty." He looked at his watch. Nine thirty. *"Jesus Christ!"* he said.

But he had forgotten about it by the time he cooked the omelets. His omelets had been from the beginning one of the things that made them close. He had learned to cook them before leaving his wife and it meant independence to him. He made omelets beautifully—tender and moist—and Edith was impressed. They had fallen in love over omelets. He cooked lamb chops too, and bought things like frozen capelletti from expensive shops; but omelets were central.

They were both thirty-five years old, both youthful, good-looking, smart. They were both Pisces, with birthdays three days apart. Both had good complexions, healthy dark hair, clear eyes. They both bought clothes at Bergdorf-Goodman and Bonwit's and Bloomingdale's; they both spoke fair French, watched *Nova* on TV, read *The Stories of John Cheever* and the Sunday *Times*. He was a magazine illustrator, she a lawyer; they could have afforded a bigger place, but hers was rent-controlled and at a terrific midtown address. It was too much of a bargain to give up. *"Nobody* ever leaves a rent-controlled apartment," she told him. So they lived in one and a half rooms together and money piled up in their bank accounts.

They were terribly nervous lovers at first, too unsure of everything to enjoy it, full of explanations and self-recriminations. He had trouble staying hard; she would not lubricate. She was afraid of him and made love dutifully, often with resentment. He was embarrassed at his unreliable member, sensed her withdrawal from his ardor, was afraid to tell her so. Often they were miserable.

But she had the good sense to take him to her therapist and he had the good sense to go. Finally, after six months of private sessions and of group, it had worked. They had the perfect orgasm, the perfect release from tension, the perfect intimacy.

Now they ate their omelets in bed from Spode plates, using his mother's silver forks. Sea salt and Java pepper. Their legs were twined as they ate.

They lay silent for a while afterward. He looked out the window. The garbage was still there; there was no movement in the street; no one was on the sidewalk. There was a flatness to the way the light shone on the buildings across from them, as though they were painted—some kind of a backdrop.

He looked at his watch. It said nine forty-one. The second hand wasn't moving. "Shit!" he said, puzzled.

"What's that, honey?" Edith said. "Did I do something wrong?"

"No, sweetie," he said. "You're the best thing that ever happened. I'm crazy about you." He patted her ass with one hand, gave her his empty plate with the other.

She set the two plates on the ledge, which was barely wide enough for them. She glanced at the clock. "Jesus," she said. "That sure is strange . . ."

"Let's go to sleep," he said. "I'll explain the Theory of Relativity in the morning."

But when he woke up it wasn't morning. He felt refreshed, thoroughly rested; he had the sense of a long and absolutely silent sleep, with no noises intruding from the world outside, no dreams, no complications. He had never felt better.

But when he looked out the window the light from the streetlamp was the same and the garbage bags were still piled in front of the Toreador and—he saw now—what appeared to be the same taxi was motionless in front of the same green station wagon in the middle of Fifty-first Street. He looked at his watch. It said nine forty-one.

Edith was still asleep, on her stomach, with her arm across his waist, her hip against his. Not waking her, he pulled away and started to climb down from the bed. On an impulse he looked again at his watch. It was nine forty-one still, but now the second hand was moving.

He reached out and turned the electric clock on the ledge to where he could see its face. It said nine forty-one also, and when he held it to his ear he could hear its gears turning quietly inside. His heart began to beat more strongly, and he found himself catching his breath.

He climbed down and went to the television set, turned it on again. The same face appeared as before he had slept, wearing the same oversized glasses, the same bland smile.

Terry turned the sound up, seated himself on the sofa, lit a cigarette, and waited.

It seemed a long time before the news program ended and a voice said, "It's ten o'clock."

He looked at his watch. It said ten o'clock. He looked out the window; it was dark—evening. There was no way it could be ten in the morning. But he knew he had slept a whole night. He knew it. His hand holding the second cigarette was trembling.

Slowly and carefully he put out his cigarette, climbed back up the ladder to the loft bed. Edith was still asleep. Somehow he knew what to do. He laid his hand on her leg and looked at his watch. As he touched her the second hand stopped. For a long moment he did not breathe.

Still holding her leg, he looked out the window. This time there were a group of people outside; they had just left the restaurant. None of them moved. The taxi had gone and with it the station wagon; but the garbage was still there. One of the people from the Toreador was in the process of putting on

265

his raincoat. One arm was in a sleeve and the other wasn't. There was a frown on his face visible from the third-story apartment where Terry lay looking at him. Everything was frozen. The light was peculiar, unreal. The man's frown did not change.

Terry let go of Edith and the man finished putting on his coat. Two cars drove by in the street. The light became normal.

Terry touched Edith again, this time laying his hand gently on her bare back. Outside the window everything stopped, as when a switch is thrown on a projector to arrest the movement. Terry let out his breath audibly. Then he said, "Wake up, Edith. I've got something to show you."

They never understood it, and they told nobody. It was relativity, they decided. They had found, indeed, a perfect place together, where subjective time raced and the world did not.

It did not work anywhere but in her loft bed and only when they touched. They could stay together there for hours or days, although there was no way they could tell how long the "time" had really been; they could make love, sleep, read, talk, and no time passed whatever.

They discovered, after a while, that only if they quarreled did it fail and the clock and watch would run even though they were touching. It required intimacy—even of a slight kind, the intimacy of casual touching—for it to work.

They adapted their lives to it quickly and at first it extended their sense of life's possibilities enormously. It bathed them in a perfection of the lovers' sense of being apart from the rest of the world and better than it.

Their careers improved; they had more time for work and for play than anyone else. If one of them was ever under serious pressure—of job competition, of the need to make a quick decision—they could get in bed together and have all the time necessary to decide, to think up the speech, to plan the magazine cover or the case in court.

Sometimes they took what they called "weekends," buying and cooking enough food for five or six meals, and just staying in the loft bed, touching, while reading and meditating and making love and working. He had his art supplies in shelves over the bed now, and she had reference books and note pads on the ledge. He had put mirrors on two of the walls and on the ceiling, partly for sex, partly to make the small place seem bigger, less confining.

The food was always hot, unspoiled; no time had passed for it between their meals. They could not watch television or listen to records while in suspended time; no machinery worked while they touched.

Sometimes for fun they would watch people out the window and stop and start them up again comically; but that soon grew tiresome.

They both got richer and richer, with promotions and higher pay and the low rent. And of course there was now truly no question of leaving the apartment; there was no other bed in which they could stop time, no other place. Besides, this one was rent-controlled.

For a year or so they would always stay later at parties than anyone else, would taunt acquaintances and colleagues when they were too tired to accompany them to all-night places for scrambled eggs or a final drink. Sometimes they annoyed colleagues by showing up bright-eyed and rested in the morning, no matter how late the party had gone on, no matter how many drinks had been drunk, no matter how loud and fatiguing the revelry. They were always buoyant, healthy, awake, and just a bit smug.

But after the first year they tired of partying, grew bored with friends, and went out less. Somehow they had come to a place where they were never bored with, as Edith called it, "our little loft bed." The center of their lives had become a king-sized foam mattress with a foot-wide ledge and a few inches of head and foot room at each end. They were never bored when in that small space.

What they had to learn was not to quarrel, not to lose the modicum of intimacy that their relativity phenomenon required. But that came easily too; without discussing it each learned to give only a small part of himself to intimacy with the other, to cultivate a state of mind remote enough to be safe from conflict, yet with a controlled closeness. They did yoga for body and spirit and Transcendental Meditation. Neither told the other his mantra. Often they found themselves staring at different mirrors. Now they seldom looked out the window.

It was Edith who made the second major intuition. One day when he was in the bathroom shaving, and his watch was running, he heard her shout to him, in a kind of cool playfulness, "Quit dawdling in there, Terry. I'm getting older for nothing." There was some kind of urgency in her voice, and he caught it. He rinsed his face off in a hurry, dried, walked to the bedroom and looked up at her. "What do you mean?" he said.

She didn't look at him. "Get on up here, Dum-dum," she said, still in that controlled-playful voice. "I want you to touch me."

He climbed up, laid a hand on her shoulder. Outside the window a walking man froze in mid-stride and the sunlight darkened as though a shutter had been placed over it.

"What do you mean, 'older for nothing'?" he said.

She looked at him thoughtfully. "It's been about five years now, in the real world," she said. "The real world" for them meant the time lived by other people. "But we must have spent five years in suspended time here in bed. More than that. And we haven't been aged by it."

He looked at her. "How could . . . ?"

"I don't know," she said. "But I know we're not any older than anybody else."

He turned toward the mirror at her feet, stared at himself in it. He was still youthful, firm, clear complexioned. Suddenly he smiled at himself. "Jesus," he said. "Maybe I can fix it so I can shave in bed."

Their "weekends" became longer. Although they could not measure their special time, the number of times they slept and the times they made love could be counted; and both those numbers increased once they realized the time in bed together was "free"—that they did not age while touching, in the loft bed, while the world outside was motionless and the sun neither rose nor set.

Sometimes they would pick a time of day and a quality of light they both liked and stop their time there. At twilight, with empty streets and a soft ambience of light, they would allow for the slight darkening effect, and then touch and stay touching for eight or ten sleeping periods, six or eight orgasms, fifteen meals.

They had stopped the omelets because of the real time it took to prepare them. Now they bought pizzas and prepared chickens and ready-made desserts and quarts of milk and coffee and bottles of good wine and cartons of cigarettes and cases of Perrier water and filled shelves at each side of the window with them. The hot food would never cool as long as Edith and Terry were touching each other in the controlled intimacy they now had learned as second nature. Each could look at himself in his own mirror and not even think about the other in a conscious way, but if their fingertips were so much as touching and if the remote sense of the other was unruffled by anger or anxiety then the pizzas on the shelf would remain hot, the Perrier cold, the cars in the street motionless, and the sky and weather without change forever. No love was needed now, no feeling whatever—only the lack of unpleasantness and the slightest of physical contact.

The world outside became less interesting for them. They both had large bank accounts and both had good yet undemanding jobs; her legal briefs were prepared by assistants; three young men in his studio made the illustrations that he designed, on drawing pads, in the loft bed. Often the nights were a terrible bore to them when they had to let go of each other if they wanted morning to come, just so they could go to work, have a change of pace.

But less and less did either of them want the pace to change. Each had learned to spend "hours" motionless, staring at the mirror or out the window, preserving his youth against the ravages of real time and real movement. Each became obsessed, without sharing the obsession, with a single idea: immortality. They could live forever, young and healthy and fully awake, in this loft bed. There was no question of interestingness or of boredom; they had moved, deeply in their separate souls, far beyond that distinction, that rhythm of life. Deep in themselves they had become a Pharaoh's dream of endless time; they had found the pyramid that kept the flow of the world away.

On one autumn morning that had been like two weeks for them he looked at her, after waking, and said, "I don't want to leave this place. I don't want to get old."

She looked at him before she spoke. Then she said, "There's nothing I want to do outside."

He looked away from her, smiling. "We'll need a lot of food," he said.

They had already had the apartment filled with shelves and a bathroom was installed beneath the bed. Using the bathroom was the only concession to real time; to make the water flow it was necessary for them not to touch.

They filled the shelves, that autumn afternoon, with hundreds of pounds of food—cheeses and hot chickens and sausage and milk and butter and big loaves of bread and precooked steaks and pork chops and hams and bowls of cooked vegetables, all prepared and delivered by a wondering caterer and five assistants. They had cases of wine and beer and cigarettes. It was like an efficient, miniature warehouse.

When they got into bed and touched she said, "What if we quarrel? The food will all spoil."

"I know," he said. And then, taking a deep breath, "What if we just don't talk?"

She looked at him for a long moment. Then she said, "I've been thinking that too."

So they stopped talking. And each turned toward his own mirror and thought of living forever. They were back to back, touching.

No friend found them, for they had no friends. But when the landlord came in through the empty shelves on what was for him the next day he found them in the loft bed, back to back, each staring into a different mirror. They were perfectly beautiful, with healthy, clear complexions, youthful figures, dark and glistening hair; but they had no minds at all. They were not even like beautiful children; there was nothing there but prettiness.

The landlord was shocked at what he saw. But he recognized soon afterward that they would be sent somewhere and that he would be able to charge a profitable rent, at last, with someone new.

A VISIT FROM MOTHER

(for Herry O. Teltcher)

By the marble fireplace in the main bedroom a discreet television set was playing. It sat on a Regency stool with inlaid legs. The program was a videotape of a ballet.

"My God," Mother said, as he brought her and Daddy in. "It's in *color!*"

Barney was flustered. They had been dead a dozen years and for a moment he had forgotten. "Sure, Mom," he said. "Color TV's been around for years . . ."

Mother's face, bright for a moment, became wistful. "It's a pity," she said. "Your father would have enjoyed it so . . ."

Barney glanced at his father shyly, then glanced away. His father's face was impassive; as always, he neither confirmed nor denied what Mother had said about him.

"Would you like something to drink?" Barney said to her. "Coffee maybe?" It was eleven in the morning.

"You go ahead, Barney," Mother said, pronouncing his name with a kind of sigh. "I don't want anything for myself."

She was wearing the same J. C. Penney dress she had worn to Daddy's funeral, the same black patent shoes. Daddy was wearing a blue serge Nixon suit and brown shoes. His hair was pale gray; his face was pained, as though his false teeth were hurting.

They were both Midwesterners and they looked out of

273

place in this New York apartment. Somehow, Barney remembered, they had even looked out of place in their own Ohio ranch house, however much Mother had tried to possess the space of it by endless dusting of furniture, by the covering of its cheap parquet floors with her own hooked rugs. Daddy alone had filled and held one corner of the living room of that airless house with its pastel walls, its Currier and Ives prints, the hooked rugs everywhere, Grandmother's sofa, Aunt Millie Dean's cherry table, the coat of arms on the kitchen wall by the never-used copper molds—the curved fish, the decorated ring, the gingerbread man that might have formed mousses or cakes but never had. Daddy had made that dark corner his, sitting grimly in the overstuffed armchair with his *Time* or his crosswords or staring out beyond the pale curtained window at the nothing at all that surrounded them. As a child, Barney's heart had moved toward that silent and frightened man with inarticulate love, unable to look him in the eyes.

Later, after his coronary, Daddy's place had become the painted brass bed in the corner bedroom, where he lay and smoked Viceroys in a holder and continued his grim solutions to crossword puzzles in magazines and almost never spoke. Mother had completely become his voice: "Your father doesn't think much of the fall programs, Barney," or "Your father believes the economy is headed for a slump." But he never heard Daddy say anything.

Barney led the ghosts out onto the terrace. Mother gave a polite gasp at the view of the Hotel Pierre, rising to the right of the General Motors building. Two pigeons flew up from the floor of the cedar decking. The terrace was splendid on this June morning; the ivy on its fence glistened in the bright sun; its scarlet geraniums glowed.

"You certainly have a lovely apartment, Barney," Mother said. As usual her voice held back somehow in the praise. There was a "Yes, but . . ." in it, if only by inflection.

For years he had ignored the way Mother gave with her words and took away with her voice. But now he said, "What's wrong with it, Mother?"

Daddy was seating himself carefully in one of the lava gray deck chairs, as though, even dead, he had to protect himself from exertion.

Mother looked shocked, then reproachful. "I didn't say there was anything *wrong,* Barney . . ."

Anger hit him suddenly and unexpectedly. "Damn it, Mother!" he said, astonished at the strength in his voice. "I *heard* the way you said it."

She looked powerless but she came back instantly. "I wish you wouldn't use that kind of language, Barney. I know that times have changed since we passed on, but your father . . ."

"Fuck my father," Barney said. "It's you I'm talking to, Mother."

At the word "fuck" his mother gasped and fluttered her hand over her heart. For a moment she became Blanche DuBois, raped by Stanley Kowalski.

Barney glanced toward Daddy and saw his face frozen in pain. "I'm sorry, Mother," he said. "I shouldn't have said that."

Mother's relief was immediate. She became Lady Bountiful at once. "Oh, I suppose people talk that way all the time now," she said, as if her absence from the living had produced the degeneration in standards she had always expected it would. "It's just that we're not used to it is all."

He was wondering how she could know how people talked nowadays when she said, "Some things do come through to us, you know. Not a whole lot."

"Where are you when you're not here?" he asked. "Is it Purgatory?"

"Oh, no," she said. "It's not Purgatory. Your father and I don't even know if there *is* a Purgatory. We're in a quiet place," she said, with the old hint of a whine in her voice, as if she were trying to tell him something too painful for words. That he didn't write to her often enough?

He had shown them the whole apartment now, in the ten minutes since he had prayed to see them and they had, surprisingly, stepped out of the elevator. He had had no idea such things were possible, yet accepted it easily enough. There had been a lot of new and surprising things in his life lately and this was another of them.

He had only lived in the apartment six weeks, here on the Upper East Side between Fifth and Madison, with skylights and high ceilings and marble fireplaces. A year before he had been living in an old house near a small Ohio town, wishing he were dead. Now he had an $1,800-a-month apartment, was a slim fifty-one years old, had grown a beard. The folk art paintings on his walls alone had cost more than his annual salary as a professor. The apartment was the top floor of what had once been a millionaire's mansion. Barney had made the money by writing a book about viruses that had, wildly, become a best seller for thirty-seven months. Two Nobel laureates had pronounced it the best work on the subject ever written.

"It certainly is nice to have a terrace," Mother was saying. "If only Gwen were here to enjoy it. Gwen always liked being outdoors."

So that had been it. The "but." "Gwen can go outdoors in Ohio any time she wants to, Mother," he said. "She has three acres all to herself."

Mother looked hurt. "You know what I mean, Barney."

Immediately he felt the stab of guilt that Mother had clearly wanted him to feel. He buried it. "Gwen is well rid of me," he said. "And I'm happy with Isabel."

"It's too bad we can't meet Isabel. I suppose that when a woman goes out to a job . . ."

He could have brained her with a two-by-four. "Can you stay for an hour?" he said.

That caught her by surprise and she turned to Daddy. "I don't really know. What do you think, Allston?"

Daddy grunted some sort of assent, his first vocalization since arriving. Mother turned back to Barney and said, "Well, I suppose it'll be all right. No more than an hour."

"Good," Barney said, with triumph. "I'll call Isabel and tell her to jump in a cab. We can all have lunch together."

"Barney!" Mother said. "You're such a child. We don't need lunch. We're dead."

Isabel arrived breathless but poised. In her tight Sasson jeans and T-shirt her figure was stunning; her face, without makeup, framed by curly gray hair that matched her gray eyes, was luminous. Gwen's waist was thick, her face solid and plain; she had a comforting look to her, domestic and tranquil. Isabel looked like a movie star on a day off. Gwen dyed her hair; Isabel glowed in gray.

"Mother and Daddy," Barney said, "I'd like you to meet Isabel." Isabel looked at their faces wonderingly. She had seen photographs of them. "Jesus!" she said. She held out a hand to Mother.

Mother was cool. "I'm sorry, dear, but there's no touching."

Isabel looked up to his face. "What's going on, love?"

"It's real, honey," he said. "Hard to believe. But you get used to it."

"I'd like a glass of wine," Isabel said.

The four of them sat on the terrace. A blue jay perched itself on one corner of the fence, facing itself toward Central Park. The sky was a perfect blue. There was no breeze. Mother's hands were folded in her lap, over the pleats of the blue rayon dress. Daddy stared at the middle distance. Isabel sipped her wine, Barney his coffee. The black cat, Amagansett, came to the open French doors and crouched himself toward the jay, motionless.

"Is your accent British?" Mother said at last to Isabel. It was a fencing question; if Isabel's accent were *not* British de Gaulle had been Japanese.

Isabel nodded over her wine. "Scottish."

"Such a civilized country," Mother said. "With the lochs." She pronounced it *lox*.

"Mmmm," Isabel said and set her wineglass down on the deck.

"Yes," Mother said, somehow satisfied by the exchange. She had managed to remove for herself any threats that Scotland might have for her and was ready to get down to business. "Are the two of you married? I don't want to be rude."

"No, Mother," Barney said. "We have no plans to be married."

Mother pursed her lips. "You're very . . . liberated," she said.

"Oh, come on, Mother. It's no big deal and you know it."

"*Barney,*" Mother said. "I'm not thinking about what other people do. And God knows you're *old* enough to do as you like."

He looked at her. She was Mother all right, with the dewlaps at her neck—or wattles, or whatever they were—and the pink-painted and wrinkled lips in a kind of pout. He had seen that pout a hundred times on the streets of New York. She sat now in the deck chair with her knees a foot apart and the hem of her rayon dress pulled back. He could see the sagging white flesh of her inner thighs above her rolled-down beige nylons. He turned his head away, pretending to look at the blue jay. "Then what are you thinking of, Mother?" he said.

"Of your health, Barney," she said, and he looked back at her own rampant unhealthiness. "Of the doctors who told me you should take it easy, should not excite yourself . . ."

My God, he thought. *That again.* "Mother," he said aloud, "I've had cardiograms yearly for thirty years. I don't have rheumatic heart anymore." Yet in her presence he hardly believed it. "I'm not a sick child." But the words lacked conviction.

Isabel stood up and stretched. "I've got to get back to work at the museum," she said. Isabel was a director of the American Museum of Folk Art; Barney had been in love with her for nearly a year. She was forty-three, twice divorced, with a Ph.D. in Art History from Glasgow and a perfect bottom. "Good-bye, Mrs. Witt and Mr. Witt," she said. "Your son's a terrific lover." She finished off her wine at a gulp and left. No one had eaten lunch.

"Well," Mother said, "she certainly is up-to-date. I see she feels comfortable without a bra."

"Come off it, Mother," he said. "Are you trying to tell me she's a whore?"

Mother looked away with a grimace. "Times change, Barney," she said, as though they didn't. "I just hope you're sure she's what you really want."

"I hear you, Mother," he said. "You said that about my first bicycle, the red one."

"It's just that your father and I want you to make up your own mind about what's right for you . . ."

"My father hasn't said anything about Isabel," he said. It was something new for him to speak like that and he felt a sense of exceeding proper limits. But he did not look at his father, the pathetic and silent figure in the chair.

"I know how your father feels about you," she said. "We've been married a long time."

"How are your . . . your existences, now?" he said, changing the subject.

She brightened a bit. "Your father rests well," she said. "I still seem to have my old difficulty sleeping." As far as he could remember, his mother slept all right. She only liked complaining about not sleeping, about "tossing and turning." "You know, Barney," she went on, "where we stay now sometimes our forms change and we become different ages of our lives. Sometimes I'm the age I was before you were born. And sometimes your father and I become babies, just little fat things with diapers on. When that happens I just sleep and sleep."

"Wow!" he said, genuinely astonished. "Do you have any control over it?"

"Well, yes. It's more or less a matter of willing it."

"But, my God," he said, "then how can you have a sleeping problem? You can make yourself an infant whenever you want to and just sleep." He shook his head in exasperation. "Like a baby."

She pursed her lips. "It just doesn't seem *right*, Barney. For a grown-up person . . ." Her voice trailed off in a way he recognized, a way that meant, *Don't pry into my sorrows, Barney. I have sensitivities you wouldn't understand.*

When she was living he wouldn't have persisted, but things were different now. "Come on, Mother," he said. "If you really wanted to sleep it certainly wouldn't strain your dignity to be a baby." Then the stupidity, the narrowness of her struck him and he said, "Jesus, there's something terrific about being a baby for a while."

She shook her head adamantly, giving the look that meant, "I knew you wouldn't understand." Finally she said, in a confidential and pained voice, "Barney. There's no one to change the diaper. It's . . . humiliating."

He stared at her in disbelief. *Of course. All those matches in the bathroom, those bottles of Air Wick.* The way she made him run the lavatory tap when he peed, and aim for the edge of the toilet, so she couldn't hear it. The horror on her face if he farted.

And then something else struck him. "You're both the same

280

ages you were when you died. Why don't you make yourselves younger? Why be *old?*"

She looked at him wonderingly and for a moment her everlasting guard seemed to be down. "Why not be old?" she said.

It rushed upon him, overwhelmed him. There they sat, on his New York terrace, both in their physical sixties, with pale, sagging bodies, false teeth, bags under their eyes. And by choice. They could be whatever age they wanted to be in whatever Limbo they had their existence.

He stared at her. "Make yourself young for me, Mother," he said.

She seemed not to hear him. She had fallen into some kind of guarded reverie.

Throughout his adult life Barney had suffered a frustrating disparity between sexual desire and sexual performance. Years before, a psychiatrist had uncovered memories of Barney's mother undressing in front of him, when Barney himself had been three and four years old and had slept in a cot in Mother's room. "Now don't peek, Barney," she would say, and pull her dress over her head. He always did peek, at the peach-colored slips, the flared rayon panties, the dark triangle of hair between her legs.

When, in the psychiatrist's office, he tried to remember his mother's face at those times, tried to remember more than her hips and breasts and underwear, he was never able to. He could not remember his mother with a face other than the sagging old woman's face her ghost now wore.

"What was that, Barney?" Mother said, smiling faintly.

"Could you make yourself young for me?" He tried to keep his voice casual, but he could hear the strain in it.

Mother looked at him sharply. Then she smiled. "How young?"

He was flustered. "I don't know. Young."

"Well, it's sort of silly. But I'll try." Her face made a little pout of concentration. She put her knees together, sat up straight in the chair, squinted her eyes shut.

For a moment her body and clothes, in the still sunlight of the terrace, became murky and dark, shrinking. And then before him sat, in a middy blouse and pleated cotton skirt, a little girl of about twelve. She had a blue ribbon in her hair and her face was bright, pretty, well-scrubbed, pink-cheeked. She wore black shoes with buckles and little white socks.

The blue jay flew away. The cat, startled, turned back toward the kitchen.

"Jesus!" Barney said, and turned toward Daddy. Daddy remained unchanged, not even looking at his child-wife.

"Well," Mother said, "how do you like me?"

He stared at her. She was a very pretty little girl, very proper, but with a flirtiness in her eyes. She had the same pout that she would wear as an old woman with false teeth and sagging jowls—a woman who never exercised, never walked except to shop for dresses in drab department stores. The flirtiness in her now was frank and not hidden. And the astonishing thing about her was the look of health.

"Jesus, Mother," he said, "I've never seen you look better."

"Don't try to be funny, Barney," she said. And then, astonishingly, she winked at him. "Let me show you how I looked when I married your father."

She shut her eyes again and her form melted and darkened and grew. And she sat in front of him then, his mother, as a beautiful flapper of twenty-five. She wore a cream-colored cloche hat over dark, shiny bangs and a low-cut, scoop-neck jersey dress with a short skirt, also cream-colored. Her hose were pale beige silk and her shoes silken. She had a long rope of white beads. Her face shone with health, with sex. She was the most beautiful woman he had ever seen in his life.

He stared at her. She was clearly his mother, yet so different. So beautiful—more beautiful than Isabel—with her long white throat, her high breasts.

She leaned forward toward him, confidentially. "Barney," she said, in a youthful, trilling voice—a theatrical, coquettish voice, "I think I'd like a cigarette."

"Sure," he said weakly, and fumbled in his shirt pocket for a pack of Trues. He held the pack out to her and she reached out with scarlet fingernails and took one delicately. "These dumb filter tips," she said. "I always smoked Sobranies, or Cubebs." She laughed—a trilling, light, airy laugh.

Daddy was staring toward Central Park, his liver-spotted hands folded in his lap, his face set. Below his pants cuffs his clocked maroon socks were wrinkled over bony ankles.

Barney lit her True with his Cricket, then lit one himself. When she bent toward him he could see the edge of fine lace at the top of the beige chemise beneath her neckline and below that the hint of cleavage. He was becoming aroused. It did not frighten him. Somehow his spirit had moved imperceptibly to a place of no rules, here on this cedar deck in Manhattan with the spring sun heating the back of his neck.

Mother exhaled smoke open-mouthed; smoke curled in the sunlight around her face. She blinked her long lashes slowly. "I think I'd like a drink, Barney," she said. "Let's go in the kitchen."

Sometimes, as a child, he had heard that tone of voice; it had thrilled him then as it thrilled him now. It was a voice she could use on a picnic or when suddenly deciding that they should all forget about dinner at home and go to a movie and just eat candy and popcorn. Sometimes she would just drop the whole middle-class pretense, the whole anxious, fretful Motherhood role, and become for a while a lively, bouncy, sly person. And seeing it now, there with an erection pressing in his jeans, he knew that was the thing he had searched for in women, for years: the voice that said, "What the hell, Barney, anything goes."

He looked nervously for a moment toward his father, opened his mouth to speak.

And Mother said, "Why don't you just stay here and rest for a while, Allston? It'll do you good."

His father did not turn to face them. "Whatever you want, Anna," he said.

"Well then," she said and stood, smoothing her dress along her behind, checking her stocking seams. "Do you have any gin, Barney?" she said. "I'd like a Gibson."

"Sure," he said. Leaving the terrace, he reached for her arm, to help her across the threshold, to touch her.

She pulled away. "No touching, Barney," she said. "You mustn't touch the dead."

The reminder was a shock, knotting his stomach. The whole Oedipus fantasy dissolved: getting his young mother drunk, running his hand up under her dress, along those pale silk stockings, lolling his tongue gently into her crimson mouth . . .

As he closed the French doors to the terrace she said, "Your father was always a good man, Barney. But there were some things he never wanted to understand."

He looked through the glass at Daddy, sadly. There the man sat, alone as ever.

He fixed her a big, dry Gibson with trembling hands, and another for himself. She leaned against the refrigerator, cupped the drink in both hands, giggled. Then she drank greedily and he fixed her another.

"My father was rich, you know," she said.

"I know." Her father had been a banker in Cleveland. There had been pictures of him everywhere at home. He had died before Mother married, had left his money to a young mistress.

"This dress was made by Coco Chanel. Daddy would take me to New York in the summers, and we'd stay right there at the Pierre."

He was astonished at that. He did not remember her talking

about New York. But he had never imagined his mother, his anxious, cheaply dressed mother, as this gorgeous flapper.

Abruptly she took off her hat with one hand and set it on the dishwasher. Then she shook her head and the shiny black hair, short, beautifully cut, framed her face. His penis began to harden again, but hopelessly. She was dead, untouchable, now that the word "incest" was as meaningless to him, a virologist, as an obscure tribal taboo.

"It's warm in here," she said, smiling. "Fix me another drink and I'll take my clothes off for you."

His hands shook so much that he spilled gin in the sink, on the floor. But he mixed the drink somehow, not looking at her. He could hear the sound of silken clothes, of stockinged legs rubbing together. He looked up at the Kliban Cat Calendar over the stainless steel sink: "June, 1980" it read. In the morning he would have an appointment with his dentist. Isabel would be home from the museum in three hours. His penis ached. His whole body trembled.

When he turned, holding the drink out to her, he almost dropped it. She was still leaning back against the refrigerator but now her dress lay on the floor. She was wearing a beige silk chemise over her breasts—the breasts that had nursed him—and a matching silk half-slip, so short that the place where her garters stretched her stockings above her thighs was visible. She had kicked off her shoes and her legs and feet were beautiful.

She looped her thumbs under the waist of the slip as he stood there holding out the Gibson. Then she paused. "Set the drink on the counter, Barney," she said. She looked him over thoughtfully. "You know, Barney," she said. "My father was a tall man like you. And rich, like you are now."

"I know," he said, in almost a whisper.

"He always bought my clothes for me. Never Mother. Always Daddy."

"And you bought mine," he said.

She smiled. "That's right."

"Take your slip off, Mother," he said.

"Do you know, Barney?" she said. "You're old enough, right now, to be my father."

He thought about that a moment, here in this nice kitchen with its European fittings, its gray slate floor, its flawless white dishes. His trembling subsided, but not his penis. He began to take off his belt, unbuttoned the top button of his jeans. "Well, Mother," he said, as something in his chest seemed to open to the bright light in the kitchen, into the splendid vision of Eros in front of his gaze, "love always finds a way."

"Oh, yes," she said, her voice trembling, bending her young body to pull down her slip with slim fingers. "Oh, yes."

DADDY

Barney came back out on the terrace. After their half hour together, Mother was asleep on the living room couch, regressed to an infant.

"Daddy," Barney said. "Why didn't you come and see me in the hospital?"

Daddy shifted his weight uneasily in the deck chair. "Which hospital?" he said gruffly, not looking toward his son. He had never, when alive, looked toward his son while speaking to him.

"Oh, come on, Daddy," Barney said. There was bravado in this familiarity; Daddy's edge was not easily overcome.

Daddy said nothing. He was looking in the direction of Central Park.

"It was the Children's Hospital, Daddy. Where they gave me the heat treatment for rheumatic fever. Where they almost killed me."

"I remember," Daddy said.

"Well, why didn't you come and see me?" Barney said. "Why didn't you send me a postcard in that fine handwriting of yours? Or call me on the 'phone?"

There was silence for a while. Daddy's figure, for a moment, seemed to shimmer as Mother's had done when she had begun to change her form. But Daddy did not change. "Nothing to say," he said, finally.

Barney stared at him. To his surprise, he found himself crying. "Anything," he said. "You could have said *anything*."

Daddy shimmered again. "Silly," he said. "Childish."

"Daddy!" Barney cried. *"I needed you."*

Daddy shimmered more seriously. Then he turned and looked at Barney. He was younger than before, slightly less gray. "You were a Mama's boy," he said. "There was nothing for me to say to you."

It took an effort for Barney to speak. "You could have said 'Hi.' You could have mailed me a card that said 'Get Well Soon.'" Saying this, he felt a pain in his stomach, like a stitch. It grew and became a hot wire beneath his diaphragm. He began to sob, silently. He had been standing at the French doors; now, he seated himself in one of the director's chairs, arms around his middle, and squinted his eyes shut until the sobbing ended.

"You always were a crybaby, too," Daddy said, as if stating the weather report.

Barney opened his eyes but could not speak. He stared at his father, who was younger now—definitely younger. Daddy was no longer wearing his serge suit. He wore a white sport shirt with an open collar and white flannel pants. He looked like Don Budge, ready for a set. His hair had lost almost all its gray. His socks were white; his shoes, black and white.

It was early afternoon and hot; there was sweat at the back of Barney's neck. He was wearing Levi's; they were too heavy for this June afternoon. He began taking his shoes off to cool his feet. "I had a lot to cry about," he said.

Daddy looked at him a moment. "Who doesn't?" There was contempt in his voice. His eyes were pale blue. His face had lost twenty years while they were talking but the expression on the face had not changed: Daddy was angry, as he had always been. "My father beat me with his walking stick and I didn't cry."

"I'm sorry, Daddy," Barney said. "I'm sorry the son of a bitch beat you." He sighed. There had been no relief in saying it. Maybe he wasn't sorry at all.

"I never finished high school," Daddy was saying, looking toward Central Park again. There was a hint of suntan on his normally pale face, and the flesh of his jaw was tight, strong-looking. His hair was black and slick. "My first job was unloading sacks of Portland cement for eighty cents a day. I saved money and bought the Encyclopedia Americana so I could know where the Suez Canal was and what the names of the chemical elements were. I lived on cheap food and slept on the floor. After five years I bought my first car, a black Model A, and I was cheated on it; the differential was bent and when I drove it fast the axle broke and broke my left leg with it. When I married Anna—your mother—in nineteen twenty-four, I still walked with a limp and was still paying for that goddamned wrecked Ford." He grimaced. "I never even told anybody this before."

"I'm glad you're telling me," Barney said.

His father abruptly turned a hard, cruel face to him and looked directly at his eyes. "Are you?" he said. "Are you glad?"

Barney stared back at him, abashed. "I don't know."

"Good," Daddy said, with relief. "You can drop that psychotherapy horseshit. What you always wanted was to have Anna to yourself. Put your goddamned face against her tits."

Barney set his shoes on the deck, then took a cigarette out of his pocket. He had never, in his lifetime, heard his father say words like "tits." Daddy had never once discussed sex with him—not in any way at all. From the time he was five his father had hardly spoken to him. He lit a cigarette. This conversation was overdue. The pain in his stomach had changed to rawness. His hands had stopped shaking. "Daddy," he said levelly, "you didn't know how to keep her. I wanted her for myself."

"What do you mean I didn't know how?" Daddy said. "She never loved anybody."

"Maybe her father," Barney said.

Daddy looked at him a minute. "Maybe you aren't so stupid after all."

"I don't think she really wanted me either. I think she just liked teasing me. She never could let anything alone."

Daddy was more relaxed now. "I'll take one of your smokes," he said.

"Sure." Barney offered him the pack. There was an ease now in his stomach.

When Daddy lit up his whole body seemed to relax. It was wonderful to see—something Barney had waited to see for a long, long time.

"That goddamned woman could not make a sandwich without turning it into soap opera. She could not stop chattering and pissing and moaning. We would make love on Sunday mornings when you were at church with those crazy evangelists and she would have to get out of bed and put in her suppositories. Then when I got hard she had to get up and pull down the shades or take the phone off the hook. She said I was too animal for her spirit. I would tell her I loved her soul. It was all bullshit. Just bullshit."

"Were you scared?" Barney was watching him. He began to shimmer again. Now he looked to be twenty years old, was wearing a white sweater and navy blue pants.

"I never knew what I felt when we were in bed," Daddy said. "She kept everything so goddamned *confused . . .*"

"I know."

"The hell you know." Daddy stood up, springy on his young legs, looked around the terrace. "Get me a drink, you dumb son of a bitch," he said. "Get me a glass of gin."

"You stopped drinking when I was eleven. You wouldn't even eat Aunt Sallie's fruitcake, because of the little shot of whiskey she used."

"And I didn't cry about it, either. Get me that gin. It won't hurt now. I'm dead. God damn it to hell, I'm *dead.*"

When Barney gave him the gin, he asked, "Are you in Limbo?"

Daddy took a long swallow before answering. His throat trembled with the gin going down. "I suppose it is Limbo. There's nobody to tell you anything. You're free to come and go and to change around, but it doesn't mean anything anymore. Nothing means anything at all. It just goes on."

"That's how you *lived*," Barney said.

"Yes," Daddy said. "Maybe it's Hell. I don't know and I don't care."

Barney sat down and cried a moment. The tears came simply and easily; he mourned for his father's lost life and for his own, unable now to tell them apart. "You blew it, Daddy," he said. "Why did you have to blow it? Why didn't you shut her up? Why didn't you hit her in the face?"

"I wasn't a brute," Daddy said. "And she was too much for me." He finished off the glass and handed it back. "Barney," he said, "to tell the truth, *you* were too much for me. I'm no father. Nobody taught me to be a father. They talked about responsibility and I didn't know anything about a noisy kid with a diaper full of shit. They told me about the love of a man for a woman but I didn't know what to do with that neurotic bitch. *She talked all the time.* It was like she walked around rubbing herself. Twitching. And she aroused me so much. At the movies she would put her hand in my pocket and squeeze me and then we'd go home and she wouldn't let me touch her."

There were tears coming down his father's cheeks and his face was bright red. He seemed only fifteen years old now, and was wearing a frayed white shirt with no collar, and knickers. "I would go to the bathroom and . . . abuse myself."

Barney had never talked to anyone in his life this way. He was covered with goosebumps. "I jacked off in that bathroom, too," he said, with the words coming easily, relievingly. "Afterward I'd look in the bathroom mirror and I would hate myself. I was disgusted. I thought if you ever found out you would never speak to me again."

His father's voice was very youthful now. It was the voice of a boy at puberty, cracking into high pitch from time to time. "I could never get that part of myself *clean* enough." For a moment he looked as though he were going to vomit. He was about ten years old now, and smaller. "And I never wanted any of that . . . disturbance."

"I know," Barney said. "I know how that feels."

Daddy held out his short arms and looked at them. He was wearing a middy blouse and short pants. There was no hair on his arms and the hair on his head was neatly combed, jet black. Then he looked toward Barney shyly. "This is the way I like to be. This way or old. I don't want the things in between."

Daddy stood there in front of him as a child, scrubbed and slightly pretty. He looked up at Barney, shook his head. "I don't want to be a baby. Not yet."

He shimmered and then began to darken, to melt and flow in the bright afternoon light. After a moment he was an old man again in blue serge and with liver-spotted wrists. His face was deeply lined, weak, both hurt and angry. He seated himself cautiously. "Get me another drink. But mix it with something this time."

Barney got him gin and orange juice and stirred it with one of the silver spoons he had inherited from Mother. He went into the living room to check her out. She was still a three-month-old infant, chubby and scowling, with a wet thumb in her mouth and her body on its side in the fetal position. Both her small fists were clenched.

She slept on the black Chesterfield couch; he had pushed two dining chairs against it to keep her from falling off. Above her the huge living room windows looked out on two mansions with dark mansard roofs—older, most likely, than she. He reached down and felt her diaper; it was still dry.

On the terrace Daddy said, "My father was a state senator; he was an old man when I was born. My mother was his third wife and was far beneath him socially. She took in wash when she was a girl."

"I know." Barney had heard this before, but never from Daddy.

Daddy flashed a look at him—the same silent look he had always given Barney as a child. "What in hell do *you* know?" he said.

Barney sighed; his father had never *said* that before—had only burdened him with the silent weight of his contempt. "Right now," Barney said levelly, "I know more than you ever did know. More than you ever will. Your life was sheltered, and you hardly lived it."

His father's face darkened even more and he clenched a fist. "Don't threaten me," Barney said. "I can take her away from you."

Daddy turned his head away, forced a grim laugh. "Take her," he said. "You're what she wanted anyway. A mama's boy with poetry in his soul. An oversexed crybaby."

Barney looked at his set face, his lined face, and saw clearly the weakness in it. "You self-serving son of a bitch," he said.

"You're a weak sister and you know it, Barney," his father said. "You never had the guts to make your own way."

"You used to wet the *bed* when you took us on trips in the car. You'd get drunk on wine in tourist courts and sleep with your clothes on and wet your *pants*. You acted tough with me when I was eight but you cringed with every mailman or shoe clerk when you were in the real world . . ."

Daddy lurched forward and shouted, *"You* cringed when I came home from work and caught you sitting in the kitchen with her. You'd be drying the silver or telling her about your-

293

self—and she'd be smiling at you like a goddamned vamp. And you'd see me come in and you'd fidget because I caught you in your goddamned gigolo act." He paused, and then said, "You can *have* her."

Barney stared at him. "You don't mean that. You can't live in Limbo alone. And you never had anybody else but her. You could have had me . . ." His throat constricted without warning, and his eyes began to burn. ". . . But you didn't want me. You put me in that hospital and hoped you'd never see me again."

Daddy seemed now to be somehow subdued—nearly at peace. He said nothing to Barney's accusation. He finished his drink. When he handed him the empty glass there was a note of resignation in the gesture, but he said nothing.

Barney took the glass and stood up. "Do you want another?"

His father nodded. "The same."

"Daddy," Barney said. "I love you. I loved you more than I ever loved her . . ."

His father nodded silently.

Mother was awake now, her eyes staring upward, unfocused. She lay on her back, grasping; her small hands greedily opened and shut. He did not speak to her. She remained silent, wrapped up in her own thoughts, or plans . . .

He fixed gin and orange juice and made himself a cup of instant coffee. The pain was in his stomach. He had always loved that man out there. He had loved him when they flew kites together at the Embarcadero, had loved him when the man took him to see Eddie Cantor at the Fox Theatre on Market Street. He had ridden on Daddy's back in the living room, rejoicing at Daddy's warmth, Daddy's strength. And then, about the time of kindergarten, Daddy had started drinking every night. Once Barney had tried to climb on his back and Daddy had shoved him across the room. Barney had sat down and bawled and his father, huge and now terrifying, had thundred over to him and slapped his face twice and said, "Cry for your Mama; don't cry in front of me. Or I'll give you something to cry about." His breath stank. The rage in his voice was an earthquake.

Standing in the kitchen under the skylight, now, facing the Cat Calendar with 1980 written on it, Barney began crying again. He set the gin and orange juice down on the dishwasher and wept.

And then he heard a sound like the sound of his own crying and turned around, facing the pass-through into the living room. Mother, his greedy infant mother, her face red and twisted, was crying with him. She cried a baby's cry, furious at a world that did not continuously serve her wishes.

When he came out onto the terrace again it was a half hour later. He had decided to make himself a drink, and then another. His mother stopped crying, fell asleep again; her compact, narcissistic self was turned away from him, toward the black back of the couch. He carried two glasses with him: both were rich in gin.

The terrace was very hot. It was midafternoon and the sun was ferocious. Daddy had taken off his coat and sat in rolled-up white shirt-sleeves, still wearing his dark blue tie.

Barney did not feel drunk so much as he felt ready for anything. Anything at all. "Here's your drink." He held the glass out and Daddy took it with a curt nod. He seated himself and stared for a while at the green roof of the Hotel Pierre above the terrace fence. Isabel's black cat came through the French doors and began to explore some ivy leaves near the deck; he would look up hopefully from time to time as birds flew overhead and then would seem sad that none flew down to him.

He must feel, Barney thought, that the world owes him a bird now and then. And maybe it does, since the world made him a cat.

"Daddy," he said, "I want to tell you about the pyrotherapy they gave me when I was ten."

"Why bring that up now?" his father said wearily.

"Because you wouldn't let me tell you before. When you picked me up at the train station."

"You were chattering away like your mother. And I had to drive. It was rush hour."

"It always was."

"What good would it do to tell me?"

"I'll decide that."

His father scowled, began to shimmer. Quickly Barney got up, reached out, took the glass from Daddy's iridescent hand. "I'll pour your drink out if you don't stop that."

The shimmering stopped. Barney gave him back the drink.

"You need me to want you here in the world, don't you? Or back you go to Limbo where there aren't any drinks."

Daddy scowled and did not answer.

"They put me into a kind of homemade machine of brown-painted steel. It was half a cylinder and it covered my body from neck to ankles. I was flat on a hospital bed. They had already wrapped me tightly in a gray wool Army blanket and I was stifling with the heat of that before they even threw the switch on.

"There were about forty light bulbs screwed into sockets under the curved top of that brown thing, Daddy, and when they turned them on and the heat came pouring into that blanket it was unbearable. My hands were strapped to my sides under the blanket, so I wouldn't hurt myself when I had convulsions, or break the light bulbs . . ." He realized that he was sweating profusely. He set his drink on the deck and took off his shirt, wiped his wet chest with it, dabbed at his neck.

"Daddy," he said, "I've been afraid of heat all my adult life. They kept me in that thing fourteen hours a day for two weeks. Each day they brought my internal temperature up to a hundred seven. There was no clock in the room and when I'd ask the attendant what time it was she'd be cross with me. So I lay there and tried to count off the time in my head, a second at a time. Each minute was longer than I could imagine. I prayed to die, tried to will myself dead."

Daddy shifted his weight in the chair, sipped his drink. He rolled up his sleeves another notch, showing pale bony arms, with fine gray hairs on them and brown spots, like big freckles. The cat sniffed at an ivy leaf.

"The doctor had supervised my first day in the machine; the treatment was a project of hers—later abandoned, as too dangerous. She was like a Nazi, Daddy—a Nazi doctor who had me given to her. She said you had signed the authorization for the treatment." He looked at his father, sweat pouring down his forehead into his eyes. The afternoon sun was murderous.

His father did not look at him. He raised his drink slowly to his old, pale lips. Then Barney, moving very quickly, reached out and, with the edge of his right hand, knocked the drink from his father's weak grip. The glass flew across the terrace and smashed into the side of the fence. The cat spun around and fled into the house.

"The doctor said you'd come and see me on the weekend, Daddy. For the first five days I held in my mind a picture of you holding a glass of water for me while I lay under that torture box. But you didn't come."

His father turned, shocked by the lost drink, and looked at him open-mouthed. He looked hopelessly old, frail, vulnerable. "You worthless bastard," Barney said. "You didn't come. I want you to rot in hell for it."

"I was sick," his father said.

"You were not sick, Daddy. You were drunk. You were sitting in your moss-green overstuffed chair in the living room on that Saturday, drinking gin. That was June 17, 1938. It was the worst day I've ever lived, and it soiled my life."

"You're making a soap opera out of it, like your mother. Doctor Morton did charity work with poor children. She was no Nazi. You've built it up in your mind."

"That's horseshit, Daddy. The next kid they tried it on died, the poor bastard. After five days of it. I told you that in the car, in Dayton, when I got there on the train after the year in the hospital."

"I don't remember . . ."

"You remember moving out of the goddamned *state* after you and that flirt in there put me in the hospital, don't you? And you never . . ." Barney leaned forward, saying each word carefully. ". . . And you never wrote me a single word. When I tried to tell you about how I had gone through that treatment and *hadn't cried once,* the way you would have wanted me to, you told me to be quiet because you had to drive the fucking *car.* Daddy," he said, *"I didn't cry."*

"Those were tough times. It was the Depression . . ."

"The Jews in Auschwitz treated their children with more concern, Daddy. Most of them did." He turned his face away from his father's and looked toward the Pierre. "Some of them might have been looking, like you were, for somebody to blame."

"Blame for what?" Daddy's voice sounded weaker.

"For the way your life fell apart. For marrying that God-damned woman in there. For the way she stole your balls from you right in front of your eyes. So you could call me a Mama's boy . . ."

"You *were* a Mama's boy. Still are." There was a tremor now in the voice. "I know what the two of you were doing an hour ago in the kitchen."

Barney turned toward him. "That's right, Daddy. We climaxed together. It was wonderful."

"Bullshit," Daddy said. His voice shook. His face was gray.

Barney suddenly began to laugh. "Maybe you can't believe it."

"She was frigid. It was the way she was brought up . . ."

"Bullshit," Barney said, laughing. "She wasn't frigid for *me*, you cowardly son of a bitch."

Suddenly his father's face twisted in pain and his pale hand went to his chest, squeezing at the shirt pocket. His lips were blue.

Barney stared at him. "You can't have a heart attack when you're dead," he said.

Daddy choked and fell off the chair onto the deck. He lay there, silently writhing, for several minutes. His hands were white; they clenched into fists and unclenched rhythmically. After a while a kind of foam began to appear on Daddy's lips; his face was ghastly. His eyes stared upward toward the sky. He made no sound. Then, abruptly, he twitched over on one side, toward where Barney sat. Barney stared at him. His age had not changed but his position was now fetal. Barney remembered a time forty years before when as a small child he had seen his father lying like that in the bed of a cheap California motor court; his body had been pressed into a wet stain on the rumpled sheet. Barney remembered the smell.

"Oh, my God, Daddy," he said aloud, looking down at his father, *"you're just like she is. You're a goddamned infant. You always were."*

A blue jay was chattering somewhere beyond the terrace fence. The black cat came softly back outside into the sun and walked toward Daddy. There came a soft, hissing sound from Daddy's throat and then a hoarse, convulsive shuddering, and then silence. The cat nudged Daddy with his nose and then began to purr. Daddy was clearly dead.

Barney heard footsteps from the French doors and turned to look. Mother was there, as a middle-aged woman in a

299

cheap dress. She spoke through loose false teeth. "It looks as if Allston's died again," she said, matter-of-factly.

"How can that be . . . ?" Barney said.

Mother shook her head worriedly. "I don't know, Barney, but it happens to both of us all the time where we are. The same deaths."

Barney stared at her. "Then you have to go through lung cancer?"

Mother pursed her lips. "Often," she said.

"Jesus!" Barney said. "Then maybe it isn't Limbo at all. Maybe it's Hell."

"Best not to know," Mother said, briskly. "I've got to get him back now, and get back myself. Strict rules." She looked away from him toward the Hotel Pierre and began to shimmer. "My Daddy always stayed at the Pierre," she said, wistfully. "And there were always flowers in his room." As her body began to fade, Barney glanced down and saw that Daddy's dead body was fading too. There was shattered glass on the deck. He felt tears again, just beginning.

He looked back to Mother, who was now translucent. "I loved him, Mother," he said. "I still love him."

She smiled at him flirtatiously. "What we did in the kitchen was naughty," she said. She winked at him.

"*Damn you*," he said. "It's him I love. It's *Daddy*."

She was hardly visible now, and her voice was faint, far away. "It's not for you to have him, Barney," she said. "Daddy's *mine*." And they were both gone.

After twenty minutes, Barney stopped crying. Something had ended for him. He stayed in his chair for the rest of the afternoon, tremulously, testing his new life. Toward suppertime, when Isabel would be coming home from work, he began to whistle.

From time to time he looked up at the Hotel Pierre, which rose with great clarity into the New York sky.

THE APOTHEOSIS OF MYRA

Out beyond the French windows during the day's second sunset the grass began singing. It had begun as a hum and as it gained in strength quickly became song. Edward pushed the French windows farther open and stepped out onto the terrace. Lovely there now, with a sky dark blue like an Earth sky. And, frightening though it was, the singing too was lovely—melodic, slow-tempoed, a sort of insistent lullaby. In three years here he had heard about it; this was the first time he had ever heard it. He sipped from the glass of gin in his hand. He was half drunk and that made it easier to take than it might have been. An enormous plain of dark grass lay before him in twilight, motionless, singing. No one knew the language. But it was clearly a language.

After a few minutes Myra came out from the living room, moving stiffly and rubbing her eyes. She had been asleep on the couch. "Goodness!" she said. "Is that the *grass?*"

"What else?" he said, turning away from her. He finished his drink.

Myra's voice was excited. "You know, Edward, I heard a recording of this . . . this grass. Back in college, years ago. It was before anybody had even heard of Endolin." She was trying to make her voice sound lively, but she could not override the self-pity in it. Myra, Edward felt, swam in self-pity as a goldfish swam in water. It was her own transparent medium. "It was in a course called 'The Exploration of our Galaxy,' I think. Dull as dishwater. But the professor played some records of life forms, and I still remember Belsin grass." Belsin was the name of the planet. "There was a question about it on the midterm. What are you drinking there, Edward?"

He did not look at her. "Gin and tonic. I'll get you one."

He walked along the moonwood deck past her and into the house. The liquor was in the kitchen. During the last year he had taken to bringing a case at a time out of the storage room, where supplies from Earth were kept. There was the half-empty last case of Gordon's gin and a nearly empty one of Johnnie Walker side by side on the kitchen counter next to a stack of unwashed dishes. The dishwasher had broken down again and he hadn't felt like trying to fix it. He grinned wryly, looking at the pile of dirty Haviland that Myra had insisted on bringing with her out to this godforsaken part of the galaxy. If he could get her to do the dishwashing he might not kill her. Fat chance.

The idea of killing her was fairly recent. Originally he had thought the arthritis and the self-pity and the booze would do it for him. But Belsin had worked for her far better than he had expected, with the fresh Endolin that had made her demand to come here in the first place. Endolin was a scraggly little plant and the finest pain-killer and anti-inflammation drug ever known. It grew only on Belsin and did not travel well even in total vacuum. Myra was rich and her family was powerful; she had provided the money and her grandfather the power to get him the job here. She was thirty-four and had had violently painful arthritis since the age of six.

He made her drink, as usual, stronger than his own. There was no ice, since that wasn't working either.

She had seated herself on the moonwood bench when he got back out on the terrace and was looking at the stars, her head slightly inclined toward the singing of the grass. For a moment he paused; she was really very beautiful. And the look of self-pity had gone from her face. He had loved her, once, when she was like this. He hadn't married her only for her money. The singing had become softer. It would end soon, if what he had heard about it was true. It happened so rarely, though, that everything about it was uncertain and no one had the foggiest notion of how the grass did it in the first place, let alone why.

Myra smiled at him, not even reaching for the drink. "It sings so . . . *intelligently,*" she said, smiling. "And feelingfully." She took the drink finally and set it on the moonwood bench beside her. Moonwood was not really wood; it was sliced from quarries and outcroppings near Belsin's north pole. You could drive nails into it and even build houses from it. Their house, though, was a prefab, cut from steel and glass in a factory in Cleveland and shipped out here, for a king's ransom.

"And nobody knows why it sings?" she said.

"Correct," Edward said. "How are your hands?"

She smiled dreamily toward him. "Very good." She flexed them. "Hardly any pain at all. And my neck is easy tonight. Supple."

"Congratulations," he said, without feeling. He walked over to one of the deck chairs and seated himself. The problem with killing her was not the killing itself. That would be very easy out here, on a planet with only a few hundred settlers. The problem was in making it totally unambiguous, clear and simple and with himself blameless, so he could inherit. The laws concerning extraterrestrial death were a mess. One little snag could keep it in court for thirty years.

"You know what I'd like to do, Edward?" she said.

He took a swallow from his drink. "What's that?"

"I'd like to get out the EnJay and take a ride to the orchids."

"Christ!" he said. "Isn't it pretty late?" She had not ridden in the EnJay for a year or more. "And doesn't the bouncing hurt your legs? And back?"

"Edward," she said, "I'm better. Really."

"Okay," he said. "I'll get a bottle. And some Endolin."

"Forget the Endolin for now," she said brightly. "I'll be all right."

The Nuclear Jeep was in a moonwood shed at the back of the house, next to the dark-green Mercedes and the two never-used bicycles. He backed the jeep out, shifted gears, and scratched off around the house. In the low gravity of Belsin scratching off was difficult to do but he had learned the trick. He pulled up to the turnaround in front of the house where Myra's elevator normally let her out and was astonished to see her walking down the stairs, one hand on the banister, smiling toward him.

"Well!" he said as she got into the jeep.

"Pretty good, huh?" she said, smiling. She squeezed his arm.

He drove off with a jerk and across the obsidian surface of their front yard. Much of Belsin was obsidian; it was in fissures in that glasslike surface that the Endolin grew. At the end of the yard a winding path, barely wide enough for the jeep, went through the Belsin grass, which was still singing, but much more softly. He liked driving the path, with its glassy low traction and its narrow and often wrongly banked curves. There was hardly any way to build a real road on Belsin. You could not cut Belsin grass—which wasn't grass at all and seemed to grow out of the granitic rock beneath it like hair—and if you drove on it it screamed and bled. Bringing from Earth the equipment to grade and level the obsidian would have been almost enough to bankrupt even Myra's family. So when you drove on Belsin you used a car with a narrow axle, and you followed the natural, vein-like pathways on the planet's surface. There weren't many places to drive *to*, anyway.

The singing, now that they were driving with the grass on either side of them, was remarkable. It was like a great chorus of small voices, or a choir chanting at the edge of understanding, alto and soprano. It was vaguely spiritual, vaguely erotic, and the truly remarkable thing about it was that it touched the human feelings so genuinely. As with Endolin, which magically dovetailed so well with the products of terrestrial evolution, producing a molecule that fit a multichambered niche in the human nervous system as if made for it, the grass seemed to have been ready for humanity when humanity first landed on Belsin sixty years before. Captain Belsin himself had heard it during the first explorations. The grass had sung for that old marauding tycoon and he had written in his journal the now famous words, "This planet speaks my language." When Endolin had been found, years later, it had seemed fitting that the planet, able somehow to touch human feeling with its astonishing music, could also provide one of the great anodynes. Endolin was hard to come by, even in the richest obsidian fields, but it was nearly perfect when fresh. It could all but obliterate physical pain without affecting the reason or the perceptions. And there was no hangover from it. Myra's life on Earth had been hell. Here, it was passable.

"Boy, do I feel good!" Myra said. "I think I could dance till dawn."

He kept his eyes on the road, following it with the wheel. "In an hour you'd be screaming from the pain. You're forgetting how Endolin burns out." That was its great drawback, and he was glad to remind her of it. That, and the fact that you couldn't take it constantly. If you did it paralyzed you.

For a moment she sounded crushed. "Honey," she said, "I haven't forgotten." Then she brightened. "But lately my bad hours between pills have been easier."

"That's good," he said. He tried to put conviction in it.

After a while they were driving along a ridge from which they could see, far off to the right, the lights of the Endolin packing plant and the little spaceport beside it.

"I didn't know they worked at *night*," Myra said.

"For the last six months they have."

"Six months Earth time?" There was Belsin time, with its seventeen-hour day and short year, and there was Earth time. Edward had a way of shifting from one to the other without warning.

"Earth time," he said, as if talking to a child.

"You almost never tell me about your work, Edward," she said. "Have orders gone up?"

"Yes," he said. "Business is booming. We're sending out a shipload every month now." He hesitated and then said, "Earth time."

"That's terrific, Edward. It must make you feel . . . useful to be so successful."

He said nothing. It made no difference to him how well the business did, except that more shippings meant more supplies of gin and of television tapes and things like peanut butter and coffee and caviar from Earth. Nothing on Belsin could be eaten. And the only business—the only real reason for humanity to be there at all—was Endolin.

"Will you have to increase the number of workers?" Myra said. "To keep up with bigger harvests?"

He shook his head. "No. The equipment has been improved. Each man brings in two or three pounds a day now. Faster vehicles and better detectors."

"That's *fascinating!*" Myra said, sitting upright with a slight wince of pain. "I had no idea what was going on."

"You never asked," he said.

"No," she said, "I suppose I didn't."

They drove on northward in silence for a long time, listening to the grass. Edward himself, despite his hidden anger and his frustrations, became calmed by it. Finally Myra spoke. "Listening to that singing is . . . is amazing," she said softly. "It seems to go very deep. You know"—she turned abruptly in her seat to face him—"the more I take Endolin the more . . . mystical my feelings are. Or spiritual." She looked a little self-conscious saying it, probably because she knew how impatient he was with her interests in poetry and in music. And in reincarnation.

"It's bound to affect your mind . . ." he said.

"No," she said. "I know that's not it. It's something I've had since I was a child. Sometimes after the arthritic pain I'd have a . . . a burned-out feeling in my nerves and a certain clarity in my head. I would lie in my bed in the hospital or whatever and I felt I knew things just the other side of the edge of knowing."

He started to speak and glanced over at her. He saw that she had not finished the drink she was carrying. That was unusual, since Myra was close to being an alcoholic—something he encouraged in her. He decided to say nothing.

"I lost those feelings when I got older," she went on. "But lately I've been getting them back. Stronger. And the grass, singing like that, seems to encourage it." She stopped for a minute. "You know," she said, "the grass is giving me the same feeling. That something on the other side of knowledge can really be known. If we could only . . . only relax somehow and clear our minds and grasp it."

Edward's voice was cool. "You can get the same effect from two martinis on an empty stomach."

She was unperturbed. "No, you can't, Edward," she said. "You cannot."

They were silent again for several miles. Past the plant the road broadened for a while and became straighter. Edward speeded up. It was late and he was getting bored. The grass's singing had become quieter. He was focusing on the road when he heard a sharp intake of breath from Myra and then he saw that somehow there was more light on the road. And Myra said softly, "The *rings*, Edward," and he looked up and there they were: the lavender and pale blue rings of Belsin. Normally invisible but now glowing in a great arc from east to west above them. Fairy rings. Rings of heaven.

The grass seemed to crescendo for a moment, in some kind of coda, and then became silent. The rings brightened. The effect was stunning.

"Stop the jeep," Myra said. "Let's look."

"Haven't time," Edward said, and drove on.

And Myra did something she had never done before because of the pain her unlucky body could cause her: she pushed the lever on her seat and leaned in it all the way back and looked up at the beautiful rings in the sky. She did it with care and lay back and relaxed, still holding her unfinished drink, now in her lap. Her dark hair blew behind her in the jeep's wind. Edward could see by the light of the rings that her face was glowing. Her body looked light, supple, youthful in the light. Her smile was beatific.

He noticed the unfinished drink. "God," he thought, "she may be getting well."

The orchids grew down the sides of the only cliffs on Belsin. Belsin was a nearly flat planet with almost nothing to fall from. That, and the low gravity, made it a very safe place, as Edward had noted early in his life there.

The orchids were not orchids, were not even plants, but they looked somewhat like orchids. They were the outward flowerings of some obscure life form that, like the grass, seemed to go down to the center of the planet. You could not uproot an orchid any more than you could pull a blade of the grass loose from the surface; a thin but incredibly tenuous filament at the base of each of them went through solid obsidian down to a depth far below possible exploration or investigation. They were stunningly beautiful to see.

They glowed in shades of green and yellow with waving plumes and leaves shaped like enormous Japanese fans. They were both luminous and illuminated and they shifted as they moved from transparent to translucent to opaque.

When he stopped the jeep near the orchid cliffs, he heard a

small cry from Myra and looked over to see her features in the familiar grimace of pain; riding that way had almost certainly been too much for her, even with Endolin.

Yet she sat up easily enough, though very slowly, and got out of the jeep. He did not offer to help; she had told him years before that she preferred doing things by herself when she could. By the time she was standing she was smiling again. As he came around to her side of the jeep he saw her casually emptying her drink on the ground at her feet, where it made several pools in the obsidian. She set the glass in the jeep.

They walked forward slowly. Both wore gum-rubber soles on their shoes, but the surface could be treacherous. She appeared to have recovered from the pain in the jeep; her walking was as certain as his own. Possibly steadier. "Myra," he said, "I think you're getting better." His voice was flat.

"It would be really something, Edward, not to be just a sick rich girl. To be able to do something besides lie around and take pills and try to get around the pain. It would be great to *work*."

"Work?" he said. "At what?"

"I don't know," she said. "At anything. I could learn to be a pilot, or a librarian. You know, Edward, I'm not terribly smart. I think I could be very happy doing housework. Having children. Just being *busy* for the rest of my life, instead of living in my mind all the time."

"It's good to see you thinking about it," he said. But it wasn't. He hated the whole idea. A sick Myra was bad enough; he did not want this chipper, nearly well one around to clutter up his life.

And the more well she became the harder it would be to kill her and to blame her death on the arthritis.

He looked toward the orchid observation platform. There was another couple standing there, and as they came closer Edward could see that the man was an engineer named Strang

—one of the steadier, more reliable people from the plant. The girl was somebody from Accounting.

And it began to shape up for him then. The situation was really good. He had long suspected that the orchid cliffs were the best place for it. And here were the perfect witnesses. It was dark and everyone knew the orchid cliffs were dangerous at night. Myra had been drinking; the autopsy would show that.

It began to click off for him the way things did sometimes. He embellished it. As they approached the other couple enough to be overheard he said, "Myra, it's really strange of you to want to come out here like this. Maybe we shouldn't go to the cliffs. We can come back in daylight tomorrow . . ."

She laughed in a way that he hoped would sound drunken and said, "Oh, come on, Edward. I feel marvelous."

"Okay, darling. Anything you say." He spoke to her lovingly and then looked up to greet the other couple.

"Nice seeing you, Mr. MacDonnell," the engineer said. "The orchids are really fine by ringlight."

"I'd still rather be in bed," Edward said amiably. "But Mrs. MacDonnell wanted to come out here. She says she could dance till dawn."

Myra beamed at Strang and Strang and his girl nodded politely at her. Myra never saw people on Belsin. Arthritis had made her life sedentary, and even though Belsin had relieved the pain greatly she had never learned to be sociable. Most of her time was spent reading, listening to music, or puttering around the house.

"More power to you, Mrs. MacDonnell," Strang said. And then, as they went out on the ledge toward the staircase, "Careful out there, you two!"

There was a meandering walkway, partly carved from obsidian, partly constructed from moonwood, that ran along the cliff face toward a high waterfall. The steps were lighted by hidden electric lights and there was still ringlight from above. There was a safety rail, too, of heavy moonwood, waist high. But it was only a handrail and a person could slip under it. The thing could have been done better, but there was only so much human labor available on the planet for projects of that kind.

The two of them went slowly along the staircase, still in view of Strang and his girl. The light on the orchids was gorgeous. They could hear the sound of the waterfall. It was very cool. Myra was becoming excited. "My God," she said, "Belsin is really a lovely place. With the grass that sings, and the orchids." She looked up at the sky. "And those rings."

"Watch your step," he said. He looked back at Strang and waved. Then they went around the edge of a cliff, and along a wet obsidian wall where the light glared off the wetness and was for a moment almost blinding. For an instant he thought of pushing her off there, but they were too close to Strang: if there were a struggle it might be heard. They walked along a level place for a while. Myra would look across at the orchids on the other side, with their fans gently changing color in the night air and would gasp at the beauty of them. Sometimes she squeezed his arm strongly or hugged him in her excitement. He knew it was all beautiful, but it had never really touched him and it certainly wasn't touching him now. He was thinking coolly of the best way to kill Myra. And some part of him was second-guessing, thinking that it might not be bad to go on living with Myra if she got well, that it was cruel to think of killing her just when she was beginning to enjoy her life. But then he thought of her dumbness, of her innocence. He thought of her money.

Suddenly they came around a turn in the walkway and there was the waterfall. Part of it reflected the colors of the rings above. There was spray on his face. He looked down. Just ahead of them was a place where the obsidian was wet.

The moonwood railing had been doubled at that point but there was still a distance of at least two feet from the bottom where a person could easily slip under. He looked farther down—straight down. The chasm was half a mile—the highest drop on Belsin.

He looked behind him. They could not be seen. *Okay,* he thought. *Best to be quick about it.*

He took her firmly by the arm, put his free arm around her waist.

She turned and looked at his face. Hers was calm, open. "You're going to kill me. Aren't you, Edward?" she said.

"That's right," he said. "I didn't think you knew."

"Oh, I knew all right," she said.

For a moment he was frightened. "Have you told anyone? Written anyone?"

"No."

"That's stupid of you. To tell me that. You could have lied."

"Maybe," she said. "But Edward, a part of me has always wanted to die. My kind of life is hardly worth the effort. I'm not sure that getting well would change that either."

They stood there like that by the waterfall for a full several minutes. He had her gripped firmly. It would only be a matter of putting one of his feet behind hers, tripping her and pushing her under the railing. She looked very calm and yet not passive. His heart was beating furiously. His skin seemed extraordinarily sensitive; he felt each drop of spray as it hit. The waterfall sounded very loud.

He stared down at her. She looked pathetic. "Aren't you frightened?" he said.

She did not speak for a moment. Then she said, "Yes, I'm frightened, Edward. But I'm not terrified."

He had to admit that. She was taking it very well. "Would you rather jump?" he said. He could let go of her. There was no way she could outrun him. And he wanted no bruises from his hands on her arms, no shoe mark of his on her legs. Her body—what was left of her body—would be studied by the best criminologists from Earth; he could be sure her family would see to that. She'd be kept frozen in orbit until the experts got there.

Thinking of that, he looked up toward the sky. The rings had begun to fade. "No," Myra said. "I can't jump. It's too frightening. You'll have to push me."

"All right," he said, looking back to her.

"Edward," she said. "Please don't hurt me. I've always hated pain."

Those were her last words. She did not fight back. When he pushed her off she fell silently, in the low gravity, for a long, long time before smashing herself on the obsidian at the bottom of the chasm.

As he looked up the rings appeared again, but only for a moment.

Getting her out with a helicopter and then making the statement and getting Strang and his girl to make their statements took all night. There was no police force and no "law" as such on Belsin, but the factory manager was Acting Magistrate and took testimony. Everyone appeared to believe Edward's story —that Myra was drunk and slipped—and condolences were given. Her body was put in a plastic capsule from a supply that had sat idle for years; she was the first person ever to die on Belsin.

Edward drove back at daybreak. His fatigue was enormous but his mind was calm. He had almost begun to believe the story himself.

As he approached the now empty house across the broad plain a remarkable thing began to happen: the grass began to sing again. Belsin grass was only known to sing in the eve-

313

ning. Never at dawn. But there it was singing as the first of the planet's two suns was coming up. And somehow—perhaps because of the clarity in the fatigue he felt—it seemed to him that the grass's song was almost comprehensible. It seemed to be singing to him alone.

He spent half the next day sleeping and the other half of it sitting in various rooms of the house, drinking gin. He did not miss Myra, nor did he feel guilty, nor apprehensive. He thought for a while, half-drunkenly, about what he would do, back on Earth as a rich, single man. He was still under forty; if he was lucky he would begin to inherit some of Myra's millions within a year.

There were still a few things to decide upon now and as he drank he thought about them from time to time: should he continue running the Endolin plant while waiting for the inquest into Myra's death and for the ship that would take him back to Earth? If not, there was very little else to do on Belsin. He could spend some time exploring down south, where the obsidian was a light gray and where no Endolin had been found. He could sit around the house drinking, listen to some of Myra's records, watch TV from the tape library, work out in the basement gym. None of it really appealed to him and he began to fear the dullness of the wait. He wanted to be on Earth right now, at the heart of things, with bright lights, and variety and speed and money. He wanted his life to start moving fast. He wanted travel: loose and easy nights on gamier planets with well-dressed women, guitars playing. He wanted to buy new clothes on Earth, take an apartment in Venice, go to the races in the Bois de Boulogne. Then see the galaxy in style.

And then, as twilight came, he moved out onto the terrace to watch the setting of the second of Belsin's two small suns, and realized that the grass was singing again. Its sound was very faint; at first he thought it was only a ringing in his ears. He walked, drink in hand, to the railing at the end of the big moonwood terrace, walking softly in bare feet across the silvery surface, cool as always to the touch. Belsin, bare and nearly devoid of life as it was, could be—as Myra would say —lovely. He remembered Myra's falling, then, as in a dream. At one-half Earth gravity her body had fallen away from him slowly, slowly decreasing its size as it had lazily spun. She had not screamed. Her dress had fluttered upward in his direction as he stood there with his hands lightly on the wet railing of the Orchid Chasm.

Suddenly and surprisingly he began to see it from her falling-away point of view; looking up at himself standing there diminishing in size, seeing his own set features, his tan cotton shirt, blue jeans, his rumpled brown hair. His cold unblinking eyes looking down on himself, falling.

The grass was not really singing. It was talking. Whispering. For a shocked moment it seemed to him that it whispered, "Edward. Edward." And then, as he turned to go back into the house for another drink, "Myra is here. Edward, Myra is here."

Another very strong drink put him to sleep. He dreamed of himself in lines of people, waiting. Long, confusing lines at a cafeteria or a theater, with silent people and he among them also silent, impatient, trapped in an endless waiting. And he awoke sweating, wide awake in the middle of the Belsin night. Before his open eyes Myra fell, at a great distance from him now, slowly spinning. He could hear the sound of the waterfall. He sat up. He was still wearing his blue jeans.

It was not the waterfall; what he heard was the grass, whispering to him.

He pushed open the bedroom window. The grass was clearer now. Its voice was clearly speaking his name: "Edward," it said. "Edward. Edward."

Into his mind leaped the words from the old poem, studied in college:

> Why does your sword so drip wi' blood
> Edward, Edward?

The fuzziness of liquor had left him. His head was preternaturally clear. "What do you want?" he said.

"I want to talk," the grass said. Its voice was lazy, sleepy.

"Can't you be heard everywhere?"

"Do you fear overhearing?" The voice was fairly clear, although soft.

"Yes."

"I'm only speaking near the house." That was what he thought it said. The words were a bit blurred toward the end of the sentence.

"Near the house?" He pulled the window open wider. Moved closer. Then he sat on the edge of the bed by the window and leaned out into the night. Two small moons were up and he could see the grass. It seemed to be rippling, as though a slight, thin-aired wind were stroking it. The grass grew about two feet high and was normally a pale brown. The moonlight was like Earth moonlight; it made it look silver, the color of moonwood. He sat with his hands on his upper thighs, his bare feet on the floor carpeting, listening to the grass.

"Near the house, Edward," the grass said.

"And you're Myra?"

"Oh, yes, I'm Myra." There was a tone of gaiety in this, a hushed joyfulness in the whispering. "I'm Myra and I'm Belsin. I've become this planet, Edward."

"Jesus Christ!" he said. "I need a drink. And a cigarette."

"The cigarettes are in the kitchen cabinet," the grass said. "Come out on the terrace when you get them. I want to see you."

"See me?" he said.

"I can see with my rings," the voice said. Myra said.

He got up and padded into the kitchen. Strangely he did not feel agitated. He was on some ledge somewhere in the middle of the quiet night, hung over and a wife-murderer, yet his soul was calm. He found the cigarettes easily, opened them, took one out and lit it. He poured a small amount of gin into a glass, filled it the rest of the way with orange juice, thinking as he did so of how far a distance from California that juice had come, to be drunk by him here in this steel kitchen in the middle of the night on a planet where the grass had become his wife. The whole planet was his wife. His ex-wife. He drank a swallow from the glass, after swishing it around to mix the gin in. The glow from it in his stomach was warm and mystical. He walked slowly, carrying his glass and his cigarette, out to the terrace.

"Ooooh!" the grass said. "I can see you now."

He looked up to the sky. "I don't see the rings," he said. "Your rings."

And then they appeared. Glowing pink and lavender, clearly outlined against the dim-lit sky. They disappeared.

"I'm only learning to show my rings," Myra said. "I have to thicken the air in the right place, so the light bends downward toward you." There was silence for a while. The grass had become clearer when it last spoke. It spoke again finally and was clearer still, so that it almost seemed as if Myra were sitting on the terrace next to him, her soft voice perfectly audible in the silent night. "There's a lot to learn, Edward."

He drank again. "How did it happen?" And then, almost blurting it out, "Are you going to tell people about what I did?"

"Goodness, Edward, I hadn't thought about that." The voice paused. "Right now I don't know."

He felt relieved. Myra had always been good-hearted, despite the self-pity. She usually gave the benefit of the doubt.

He sat silent for a while, looking at the vast plain in front of his eyes, concentrating on his drink. Then he said, "You didn't answer me, Myra. About how it happened."

"I know," the grass said. "I know I didn't. Edward, I'm not only Myra, I'm Belsin too. I am this planet and I'm learning to be what I have become." There was no self-pity in that, no complaint. She was speaking to him clearly, trying to tell him something.

"What I know is that Belsin wanted an ego. Belsin wanted someone to die here. Before I died and was . . . was taken in, Belsin could not speak in English. My grass could only speak to the feelings of people but not to their minds."

"The singing?" he said.

"Yes. I learned singing when Captain Belsin first landed. He carried a little tape player with him as he explored and played music on it. The grass learned . . . I learned to sing. He had headaches and took aspirin for them and I learned to make Endolin for him. But he never used it. Never discovered it." The voice was wistful, remembering something unpleasant. "I couldn't talk then. I could only feel some of the things that people felt. I could feel what happened to Captain Belsin's headache when he took aspirin and I knew how to improve on it. But I couldn't tell him to use it. That was found out later." The grass rippled and was still. It was darker now; one of the moons had set while they were talking.

"Can you bring up some more moons? So I can see you better? See the grass?" There were four moons.

"I'll try," Myra said. There was silence. Nothing happened. Finally Myra said, "No, I can't. I can't change their orbits."

"Thanks for trying," he said dryly. "The first person to die here would become the planet? Or merge with its mind? Is that it?"

"I think so," Myra said. He thought he could see a faint ripple on the word "think." "I became reincarnated as Belsin. Remember the rings lighting after you pushed me over?"

"Yes."

"I was waking up then. It was really splendid for me. To wake into this body. Edward," she said, "I'm so alive now, and vigorous. *And nothing about me hurts.*"

He looked away, back toward the silent house. Then he finished his drink. Myra's voice had been strong, cheerful. He had been calm—or had been *acting* calm—but something in his deep self was disturbed. He was becoming uneasy about all this. Talking with the grass did not disturb him. He was a realist, and if grass could talk to him in the voice of his dead wife he would hold conversation with grass. And Myra, clearly, wasn't dead—although her old, arthritic body certainly was. He had seen it as they brought it in from the helicopter; even in low gravity, falling onto jagged obsidian could lacerate and spatter.

"Do you hate me for what I did?" he said, fishing.

"No, Edward. Not at all. I feel . . . removed from you. But then I really always did. I always knew that you only allowed a small part of yourself to touch my life. And now," she said, "my life is bigger and more exciting. And I only need a small part of you."

That troubled him, sent a little line of fear across a ridge somewhere in his stomach. It took him a moment to realize that it was her word "need" that had frightened him.

"Why do you need me, Myra?" he said, carefully.

"To read to me."

He stared. "To read to you?"

"Yes, Edward. I want you to read from our library." They had brought several thousand books on microfilm with them. "And I'll want you to play records for me."

"My God!" he said. "Doesn't a whole planet have better things to do?"

The grass seemed to laugh. "Of course. Of course I have things to do. Just getting to know this body of mine. And I can sense that I am in touch with others—others like the Belsin part of me. Now that I have an ego—Myra's ego—I can converse with them. Feel their feelings."

"Well then," he said, somewhat relieved.

"Yes," she said. "But I'm still Myra, too. And I want to read. And I want music—honest, old-fashioned Earth music. I have this wonderful new body, Edward, but I don't have hands. I can't turn pages or change records. And I'll need you to talk to, from time to time. As long as I remain human. Or half human."

Jesus Christ! he thought silently. But then he began to think that if she had no hands, even needed him to run microfilm, that she could not stop him from leaving. She was only a voice, and rings, and ripples in the grass. What could she do? She couldn't alter the orbits of her moons.

"What about the other people here on Belsin?" he said, still careful with his words. "One of them might want to read to you. A younger man, maybe . . ."

This time her laughter was clearly laughter. "Oh no, Edward," she said. "I don't want them. It's you I want." There was silence for several long moments. Then she continued, "They'll be going back to Earth in a few months anyway. I've stopped making Endolin."

"Stopped . . . ?"

"When you were asleep. I was planning things then. I realized that if I stopped Endolin they would all go away."

"What about all those people on Earth who need it?" he said, trying to play on her sympathies. He did not give a damn, himself, for the pains of other people. That was why living with Myra had not really been difficult for him.

"They'll be making it synthetically before the supplies run out," she said. "It's difficult, but they'll learn. It would make people rich to find out how. Money motivates some people strongly."

He said nothing to that except "Excuse me" and got up and went into the kitchen for another drink. The sky was lightening; the first little sun would be up soon. He had never known Myra to think as clearly as she could think now. He shuddered and poured himself a bigger drink. Then, through the terrace doors, he heard her voice. "Come on back out, Edward."

"Oh, shut up!" he said and went over and slammed the doors shut and locked them. It was triply thick glass and the room became silent. He walked into the living room, with its brown-enameled steel walls and brown carpet and the oil paintings and Shaker furniture. He could hear the grass from the windows in there, so he closed them and pulled the thick curtains over them. It was silent. "Christ!" he said aloud and sat down with his drink to think about it.

Myra kept several antique plates on little shelves over the television set. They were beginning to vibrate. And then, shockingly, he heard a deep bass rumbling and the plates fell to the floor and broke. The rumbling continued for a moment before he realized that it had been an earthquake. He was suddenly furious and he hung on to the fury, covering up the fear that had come with it. He got up and went through the kitchen to the terrace doors, flung them open into the still night. "For Christ's sake, Myra," he said, "what are you trying to do?"

"That was a selective tremor," the grass said. There was a hint of coyness in its tone. "I pushed magma toward the house and let a fissure fall. Just a tiny bit, Edward. Hardly any at all."

"It could have fallen farther?" he said, trying to keep the anger and the sternness in his voice.

"Lord, yes," Myra said. "That was only about a half on the Richter scale." He suddenly remembered that Myra had studied geology at Ohio State; she was well prepared to become a planet. "I'm pretty sure I could go past ten. With hardly any practice."

"Are you threatening to earthquake me into submission?"

She didn't answer for a minute. Then she said, pleasantly, "I want to keep you here with me, Edward. We're married. And I need you."

The earthquake had been frightening. But he thought of the supply ships and of the ship that would be bringing the people for the inquest. All he would have to do would be to lie to her, act submissive, and then somehow get on board the ship and away from Belsin before she earthquaked.

"And you want me to read aloud? Or run the microfilm for you?"

"Aloud, Edward," she said. "I'll let the others leave, but I want you to stay here. Here in the house."

"I'll have to get out every now and then."

"No, you won't," Myra said.

"I'll need food."

"I'm already growing it for you. The trees will be up in a few days. And the vegetables: carrots and potatoes and beans and lettuce. Even tobacco, Edward. But no liquor. You'll have to do without liquor once the supply is gone. But this place will be *lovely*. I'll have a lake for you and groves of fruit trees. I can grow anything—the way I grew Endolin before. This will be a beautiful place for you, Edward. A real Eden. And you'll have it all to yourself."

He thought crazily of Venice, of women, guitar music. Venice and Rome. Panicked suddenly, he said, "I can run away with the others. You can't earthquake us all to death. That would be cruel. . . ."

"That's true enough," Myra said. "But if you leave this house I'll open a fissure under you and down you'll go." She paused a long moment. "Just like I did, Edward. Down and down."

He began to talk faster, louder. "What if they come to take me away, to force me to go back to Earth?"

"Oh, come on, Edward. Quit it. I won't let them ever get to

the house. They'll go away eventually. And I'll never let anyone land again. Just swallow them up if they try it."

He felt terribly weary. He walked out onto the terrace and slumped onto the moonwood bench. Myra remained silent. He had nothing to say. He sipped his drink, letting his mind go blank. He sat there alone for a half hour. Or not really alone. It was beginning to dawn on him that he might never be alone again.

Then Myra spoke again, softly. "I know you're tired, Edward. But I don't sleep. Not anymore. I wonder if you would read to me a while. I was in the middle of *The King's Mistress*. If you'll switch the microfilm machine on you'll find my page."

"Christ!" he said, startled. "You can't *make* me read." There was something petulant in his voice. He could hear it and it disturbed him. Something of the sound of a small boy trying to defy his mother. "I want to have another drink and go back to bed."

"You know I don't like insisting," Myra said. "And you're perfectly right, Edward. I can't make you read. But I can shake the house and keep you awake." Abruptly the house shook from another tremor, probably a quarter of a point on the Richter scale. "And," Myra said, "I can grow food for you or not grow food for you. And I can give you what you want to eat or not give you what you want. I could feed you nothing but persimmons for a few months. And make the water taste terrible."

"Jesus Christ!" he said. "I'm *tired*."

"It'll only be a couple of chapters," Myra said. "And then maybe a couple of old songs on the player, and I'll go back to contemplating my interior and the other planets around here."

He didn't move.

"You'll be wanting me to grow tobacco for you. There are only a few cartons of cigarettes left." Edward smoked three packs a day. Three packs in a short Belsin day.

He still didn't move.

"Well," Myra said, conciliatory now. "I think I could synthesize a little ethyl alcohol. If I could do Endolin, I suppose I could do that too. Maybe a quart or so every now and then. A hundred ninety proof."

He stood up. He was terribly weary. *"The King's Mistress?"* he said.

"That's right!" the grass said, sweetly, joyfully. "I've always liked your voice, Edward. It'll be good to hear you read."

And then, before he turned to go into the house, to the big console that held thousands of books—thousands of dumb Gothic novels and books on gardening and cooking and self-improvement and a few technical books on geology—he saw everything get suddenly much lighter and looked up to see that the great rings of Belsin were now fully visible, bright as bands of sunlight in the abruptly brightened sky above his head. They glowed in full realization of themselves, illuminating the whole, nearly empty planet.

And Myra's voice came sighing joyfully in a great, horizon-wide ripple of grass. "Ooooooh!" it said happily. "Ooooooh!"

OUT OF LUCK

It was only three months after he had left his wife and children and moved in with Janet that Janet decided she had to go to Washington for a week. Harold was devastated. He tried not to let her see it. The fiction between them was that he had left Gwen so he could grow up, change his life and learn to paint again. But all he was certain of was that he had left Gwen to have Janet as his mistress. There were other reasons: his recovery from alcoholism, the years he had wasted his talent as an art professor, and Gwen's refusal to move to New York with him. But none of these would have been sufficient to uproot him and cause him to take a year's leave from his job if Janet had not worn peach-colored bikini panties that stretched tightly across her lovely ass.

He spent the morning after she left cleaning up the kitchen and washing the big pot with burned zucchini in it. Janet had made him three quarts of zucchini soup before leaving on the shuttle, along with two jars of chutney, veal stew in a blue casserole dish, and two loaves of Irish soda bread. It was very international. The mess in the tiny kitchen of her apartment took him two hours to clean up. Then he cooked himself a breakfast of scrambled eggs and last night's mashed potatoes, fried with onions. He drank two cups of coffee from Janet's Chémex. Drinking the coffee, he walked several times into the living room where his easel stood and looked at the quarterdone painting. Each time he looked at it his heart sank. He did not want to finish the painting—not that painting, that dumb, academic abstraction. But there was no other painting for him to paint right now. What he wanted was Janet.

Janet was a very successful folk art dealer. They had met at a museum party. She was in Washington now as a consultant to the National Gallery. She had said to him, "No, I don't think you should come to Washington with me. We need to be apart from each other for a while. I'm beginning to feel suffocated." He had nodded sagely while his heart sank.

One problem was that he distrusted folk art and Janet's interest in it, the way he distrusted Janet's fondness for her cats. Janet talked to her cats a lot. He was neutral about cats themselves, but he felt people who talked to them were trivial. And being interested in badly painted nineteenth-century portraits also seemed trivial to him now.

He looked at the two gold-framed American primitives above Janet's sofa, said, "Horseshit!" and drew back his mug in a fantasy of throwing coffee on them both.

Across from the apartment, on Sixty-third Street, workmen were renovating an old mansion; they had been at it three months before, when Harold had moved in. He watched them for a minute now, mixing cement in a wheelbarrow, and bringing sacks of it from a truck at the corner of Madison Avenue. Three workmen in white undershirts held sunlit discourse on the plywood ramp that had replaced the building's front steps. Behind windows devoid of glass he could see men moving back and forth. But nothing happened; nothing seemed to change in the building. It was the same mess it had been before, like his own spiritual growth: lots of noise and movement and no change.

He looked at his watch, relieved. It was ten-thirty. The morning was half over and he needed to go to the bank. He put on a light jacket and left.

As he was waiting in a crowd at the Third Avenue light he heard a voice shout "Taxi!" and a man pushed roughly past him, right arm high and waving, onto the avenue. The man was about thirty, in faded blue jeans and a sleeveless sweater. A taxi squealed to a stop at the corner and the man conferred with the driver for a moment before getting in. He seemed to be quietly arrogant, preoccupied with something. Harold could have kicked him in the ass. He did not like the man's look of confidence. He did not like his sandy, uncombed hair.

The light changed and the cab took off fast, up Third Avenue.

Harold crossed and went into the bank. He went to a table, quickly made out a check to cash for a hundred, then walked over toward the line. Halfway across the lobby, he stopped cold. The man in the sleeveless sweater was standing in line, holding a checkbook. His lips were pursed in silent whistling. He was wearing the same faded blue jeans and—Harold now noticed—Adidas.

He was looking idly in Harold's direction. Harold averted his eyes. There were at least ten other people waiting behind the man. He had to have been here awhile. An identical twin? A mild hallucination, making two similar people look exactly alike? Harold got in line. After a while the man did his business and left. Harold cashed his check and left, stuffing five twenties into his billfold. Another drain on the seven thousand he had left Michigan with. He had seven thousand to live on for a year in New York, with Janet, while he learned to paint again, to be the self-supporting artist his whiskey dreams had been filled with. Whiskey had left him unable to answer the telephone or open the door, in Michigan. That had been two years ago. Whiskey had left him sitting behind closed suburban blinds at two in the afternoon, reading the J. C. Penny catalog and waiting for Gwen to come home from work. Well. He had been free of whiskey for a year and a half now. First the hospital, then A.A.; now New York and Janet.

He walked back toward her apartment, thinking of how his entire bankroll of seven thousand could not pay Janet's rent for three months. And she had taken this big New York place

327

after two years of living in an even larger apartment in Paris. On a marble-topped lingerie chest in one of the bathrooms was a snapshot of her, astride a gleaming Honda, on the Boulevard des Capucines by the ironwork doorway of that apartment. When that photograph was taken Harold had been living in a ranch house in Michigan and was driving a Chevrolet.

He glanced down Park Avenue while crossing it and saw a sleeveless sweater and faded jeans, from the back, disappearing into one of the tall apartment buildings. He shuddered and quickened his pace. He shifted his billfold from a rear to a front pocket, picturing those pickpockets who bump you from behind and rob you while apologizing, on the streets of New York. His mother—his very protective mother—had told him about that twenty years before. Part of him loved New York, loved its action and its anonymity, along with the food and clothes and bookstores. Another part of him feared it. The sight of triple locks on apartment doors could frighten him, or of surly Puerto Ricans with well-muscled arms, carrying their big, noisy, arrogant radios. Their kill-the-Anglo radios. The slim-hipped black men frightened him, with long, tight-assed trousers in pale colors, half covering expensive shoes—Italian killer shoes. And there were drunks everywhere. In doorways. Poking studiously through garbage bins for the odd half-eaten pizza slice, the usable worn shirt. Possibly for emeralds and diamonds. Part of him wanted to scrub up a drunk or two, with a Brillo pad, like the zucchini pan. Something satisfying in that.

The man in the sweater had been white, clean, non-menacing. Possibly European. Yet Harold now, crossing Madison, felt chilled by the thought of him. Under the chill was anger. That spoiled, arrogant face, that sandy hair! He hurried back to Janet's apartment building, walked briskly up the stairs to the third floor, let himself in. There in the living room stood the painting. He suddenly saw that it could use a sort of rectangle of pale green, like a distant field of grass, right there. He picked up a brush, very happy to do so. Outside the window, the sun was shining brightly. The workmen on the building were busy. Harold was busy.

He worked for three solid hours and felt wonderful. It was good work too, and the painting was coming along. At last.

For lunch he made himself a bacon and tomato sandwich on toast. It was simple midwestern fare and he loved it.

When he had finished eating, he went back into the living room, sat in the black director's chair in front of the window and looked at the painting by afternoon light. It looked good —just a tad spooky, the way he wanted it to be. It would be a good painting after all. It was really working. He decided to go to a movie.

The movie he wanted to see was called *Out of Luck*. It was a comedy from France, advertised as "an hilarious sex farce," with subtitles. It sounded fine for a sunny fall afternoon. He walked down Madison toward the theater.

There were an awful lot of youthful, well-dressed people on Madison Avenue. They probably all spoke French. He looked in the windows of places with names like Le Relais, La Bagagerie, Le Bijou. He would have given ten dollars to see a J. C. Penney's or a plain barber shop with a red and white barber's pole.

As he was crossing Fifty-seventh Street, traffic-snarled as usual, there was suddenly the loud *harrumphing* of a pair of outrageously noisy motorcycles and with a rush of hot air two black Hondas zoomed past him. From the back the riders appeared to be a man and a woman, although the sexual difference was hard to detect. Each wore a spherical helmet that reflected the sun; the man's helmet was red, the other green. Science fiction helmets, they hurt the eyes with reflected and dazzling sunlight. There was a smell of exhaust.

Each of the riders, man and woman, was wearing a brown sleeveless sweater and blue jeans. Each wore Adidas over white socks. Their shirts were short-sleeved, blue. So had been the shirts of the man in the taxi and the man in line at Chemical Bank. Harold's stomach twisted. He wanted to scream.

The cyclists disappeared in traffic, darting into it with insouciance, tilting their black bikes first this way and then that, as though merely leaning their way through the congestion of taxis and limousines and sanitation trucks.

Maybe it was a fad in dress. Maybe coincidence. He had never noticed before how many people wore brown sleeveless sweaters. Who counted such things? And everyone wore jeans. He was wearing jeans himself.

The movie was at Fifty-seventh and Third. The theater had only a scattering of people in it, since it was the middle of the afternoon. The story was about a woman who was haunted by the gravelly voice of her dead lover—a younger man who had been killed in a motorcycle accident. She was a gorgeous woman and went through a sequence of affairs, breaking up with each new lover after the voice of her old, dead one pointed out their flaws to her, or distracted her while making love. It really was funny. Sometimes, though, it made Harold edgy, when he thought of the young lover Janet had had before him, who had disappeared from her life in some way he, Harold, did not know about. But several times he laughed loudly.

And then, toward the end of the movie, her lover reappeared, apparently not dead at all. It was on a quiet Paris street. She was out walking with an older man she had just slept with, going to buy some coffee, when a black Honda pulled up to the curb beside her. She stopped. The driver pulled off his helmet. Harold's heart almost stopped beating and he stared crazily. There in front of him, on the Cinemascope movie screen, was the huge image of a youngish man with sandy hair, a brown sleeveless sweater, blue shirt,

Adidas. The man smiled at the woman. She collapsed in a faint.

When the man on the motorcycle spoke, his voice was as it had been when it was haunting her: gravelly and bland. Harold wanted to throw something at the screen, wanted to scream at the image, "Get out of here, you arrogant fucker!" But he did nothing and said nothing. He stayed in his seat, waiting for the movie to end. It ended with the woman getting on the dead lover's motorcycle and riding off with him. He wouldn't tell her where he lived now. He was going to show her.

Harold watched the credits closely, wanting to find the actor who had played the old lover. His name in the film had been Paul. But no actor was listed for the name of Paul. The others were there, but not Paul. *What in God's name is happening?* Harold thought. He left the theater and, hardly daring to look around himself on the bright street, flagged down a cab and went home. Could a person hallucinate a character into a movie? Was the man at the bank in fact a French movie actor? Twelve years of drinking could fuck up your brain chemistry pretty badly. But he hadn't even had the D.T.s. His New York psychiatrist had told him he was badly regressed at times, but his sanity had never been in question.

In the apartment he was able, astonishingly, to get back into the painting for a few hours. He made a few changes, making it spookier. *He* felt spookier now and it came out onto the canvas. The painting was nearly done. When he stopped, it was eight o'clock in the evening. The workmen across the street had finished their day hours before. They had packed up their tools and had gone home to Queens or wherever. The building, as always, was unchanged; its doorways and windows gaped blankly. There was a pile of rubble by the plywood entry platform where there had always been a pile of rubble.

He went into the kitchen, ignored the veal stew Janet had

made for him and lit the oven. Then he took a Hungry Man chicken pie out of the freezer, ripped off the cardboard box, stabbed the frozen top crust a few times with her Sabatier, slipped it into the oven and set the timer for forty-five minutes.

He went back into the living room, looked again at the painting. "Maybe I needed the shit scared out of me," he said aloud. But the thought of the man in the sweater chilled him. He went over to the hutch in the corner, opened its left door, flipped on the little Sony TV inside. Then he crossed the big room to the dry sink and began rummaging for candy. He kept candy in various places.

He found a couple of pieces of butterscotch and began sucking on one of them. Back in the kitchen he opened the oven door a moment, enjoying the feel of the hot air. His little Hungry Man pie sat inside, waiting for him.

There had been a man's voice on television for a minute or so, reciting some kind of disaster news. A California brush fire or something. There in the kitchen Harold began to realize that the voice was familiar, gravelly. It had a slight French accent. He rushed into the living room, still holding a potholder. On the TV screen was the sandy-haired man in the sweater, saying ". . . from Pasadena, California, for NBC news." Then John Chancellor came on.

Harold threw the potholder at the TV screen. "You son of a bitch!" he shouted. "You ubiquitous son of a bitch!" Then he sank into the director's chair, on the edge of tears. His eyes burned.

It was dark outside when his pie was ready. He ate it as if it were cardboard, forcing himself to eat every bite. To keep his strength up, as his mother would have said, for the oncoming storm. For the oncoming storm.

He kept the TV off that evening and did not go out. He finished the painting by artificial light at three in the morning, took two Sominex tablets and went to bed, frightened. He had wanted to call Janet but hadn't. That would have been chicken. He slept without dreaming for nine hours.

It was noon when he got up from the big platform bed and stumbled into the kitchen for breakfast. He drank a cup of cold zucchini soup while waiting for the coffee from yesterday to heat up. He felt okay, ready for the man in the sweater whenever he might strike. The coffee boiled over, spattering the white wall with brown tears. He reached to pull the big Chemex off the burner and scalded himself. "Shit!" he said, and held his burned hand under cold tapwater for a half minute. He walked into the living room and began looking at the painting in daylight. It was really very good. Just the right feeling, the right arrangement. Scary, too. He took it from the easel, set it against a wall. Then he thought better of that. The cats might get at it. He hadn't seen the cats for a while. He looked around him. No cats. He put the painting on top of the dry sink, out of harm's way. He would put out some cat food.

From outside came the sound of a motorcycle. Or of two motorcycles. He turned, looked out the window. There was dust where the motorcycles had just been, a light cloud of it settling. On the plywood platform at the entryway to the building being renovated stood two men in brown sleeveless sweaters, blue shirts, jeans. One was holding a clipboard, and they were talking. He could not hear their voices even though the window was open. He walked slowly to the window, placed his hands on the ledge, stared down at them. He stared at the same sandy hair, the same face. Two schoolgirls in plaid skirts walked by, on their way to lunch. Behind them was a woman in a brown sleeveless sweater and blue jeans, with sandy hair. She had the same face as the man, only slightly feminized in the way the head set on the shoulders. And she walked like a woman. She walked by the two men, her twins, ignoring them.

Harold looked at his watch. Twelve-fifteen. His heart was

pounding painfully. He went to the telephone and called his psychiatrist. It was lunch hour and he might be able to reach him. He did, for a minute or two. Quickly he told him that he was beginning to see the same person everywhere. Even in the movies and on TV. Sometimes two or three at a time.

"What do you think, Harold?" he said to the doctor. The psychiatrist's name was Harold, too.

"It would have to be hallucination. Maybe coincidence."

"It's not coincidence. There've been seven of them and they are identical, doctor. *Identical*." His voice, he realized, was not hysterical. It might become that way, he thought, if the doctor should say "Interesting," as they do in the movies.

"I'm sorry that you have an hallucination," Harold the psychiatrist said. "I wish I could see you this afternoon, but I can't. In fact, I have to go now. I have a patient."

"Harold!" Harold said. "I've had a dozen sessions with you. Am I the type who hallucinates?"

"No, you aren't, Harold," the psychiatrist said. "You really don't seem to me to be like that at all. It's puzzling. Just don't drink."

"I won't, Harold," he said, and hung up.

What to do? he thought. *I can stay inside until Janet comes back. I don't have to go out for anything. Maybe it will stop on its own.*

And then he thought, *But so what? They can't hurt me. What if I see a whole bunch of them today? So what? I can ignore them.* He would get dressed and go out. What the hell. Confront the thing.

When he got outdoors, the two of them were gone from in front of the building. He looked to his right, over toward Madison. One of them was just crossing the street, walking lightly on the Adidas. There were ordinary men and women around him. Hell, *he* was ordinary enough. There were just too many of him. Like a clone. Two more crossed, a man and a woman. They were holding hands. Harold decided to walk over to Fifth Avenue.

Just before the corner of Fifth was a wastebasket with a bum poking around in it. Harold had seen this bum before, had given him a quarter once. Fellow alcoholic. There but for the grace of God, et cetera. He fished a quarter from his pocket and gave it to the bum without solicitation. "Say," Harold said, on a wild impulse, "have you noticed something funny? People in brown sweaters and jeans?" He felt foolish, asking. The bum was fragrant in the afternoon sun.

"Hell, yes, buddy," the bum said. "Kind of light brown hair? And tennis shoes? Hell yes, they're all over the place." He shook his head dazedly. "Can't get no money out of 'em. Tried 'em six, eight times. You got another one of those quarters?"

Harold gave him a dollar. "Get yourself a drink," he said.

The bum widened his eyes and took the money silently. He turned to go.

"Hey!" Harold said, calling him back. "Have a drink for me, will you? I don't drink, myself." He held out another dollar.

"That's the ticket," the bum said, carefully, as if addressing a madman. He took the bill quickly, then turned toward Fifth Avenue. "Hey!" he said. "There's one of 'em," and pointed. The man in the brown sleeveless sweater went by, jogging slowly on his Adidas. The bum jammed his two dollars into a pocket and moved on.

Well, the bum had been right. Don't let them interfere with business. But it wasn't hallucination—not unless he had hallucinated the bum and the conversation with the bum. He checked his billfold and found the two dollars were indeed gone. Where would they have gone if he had made up the bum in his unconscious? He hadn't eaten them. If he had, the whole game was over anyway and he was really in a straitjacket somewhere, being fed intravenously, while somebody took notes. Well.

He turned at Fifth Avenue, toward the spire of the Empire State Building, and stopped cold. Most of the foot traffic on the avenue was moving uptown toward him, and every third or fourth one of them was the person in the brown sweater and the blue short-sleeved shirt. It was like an invasion from Mars. And he saw that some of the normal people—the people like himself—were staring at them from time to time. The brown-sweatered person was always calm, whistling softly sometimes, cool. The others looked flustered. Harold jammed his hands into his pockets. He felt suddenly cold.

He began walking down Fifth Avenue. He kept going for several blocks, then on an impulse ran across the street to the Central Park side and climbed up on a park bench that faced the avenue and then from the bench onto the stone railing near the Sixtieth Street subway station. He looked downtown, up high now so that he could see. And the farther downtown he looked, the more he saw of an array of brown sweaters, light brown in the afternoon sunlight, with pale, sandy-haired heads above them. On a crazy impulse, he looked down at his own clothes and was relieved to see that he was not himself wearing a brown sleeveless sweater and that his jeans were not the pale and faded kind that the person—that the multitude—was wearing.

He got down from the bench and headed across Grand Army Plaza, past people who were now about one-half sandy-haired and sweatered and the other half just random people. He realized that the repeated person hadn't seemed to crowd the city any more than usual. They weren't *new*, then. If anything, they were replacing the others.

Abruptly, he decided to go into the Plaza Hotel. There were two of them in the lobby, talking quietly with one another, in French. He walked past them toward the Oak Bar; he would get a Perrier in there.

In the bar, three of them sat at the bar itself and two of them were at a table near the front. He seated himself at the bar. A man in a brown sweater turned from where he was washing glasses, wiped his hands on his jeans, came over and said, "Yes, sir?" The voice was gravelly with a slight French accent, the face blank.

"Perrier with lime," Harold said. When the man brought it, Harold said, "How long have you been tending bar here?"

"About twenty minutes," the man said and smiled.

"Where were you before?"

"Oh, here and there," the man said. "You know how it is."

Harold stared at him, feeling his own face getting red. *"No, I don't know how it is!"* he said.

The man started to whistle softly. He turned away.

Harold leaned over the bar and took him by the shoulder. The sweater was soft—probably cashmere. "Where do you come from? What are you doing?"

The man smiled coldly at him. "I come from the street. I'm tending bar here." He stood completely still, waiting for Harold to let go of him.

"Why are there so many of you?" Harold said.

"There's only one of me," the man said.

"Only one?"

"Just one." He waited a moment. "I have to wait on that couple." He nodded his head slightly toward the end of the bar. A couple of them had come in, a male and a female as far as Harold could see in the somewhat dim light.

Harold let go of the man, got up and went to a pay telephone on the wall. He dialed his psychiatrist. The phone rang twice and then a male voice said, "Doctor Morse is not in this afternoon. May I take a message?" The voice was the gravelly voice. Harold hung up. He spun around and faced the bar. The man had just returned from serving drinks to the identical couple at the far end. "What in hell is your name?" he said, wildly.

337

The man smiled. "That's for me to know and you to find out," he said.

Harold began to cry. "What's your goddamned *name?*" he said, sobbing. "My name's Harold. For Christ's sake, what's yours?"

Now that he was crying, the man looked sympathetic. He turned for a moment to the mirrored shelves behind him, took two unopened bottles of whiskey and then set them on the bar in front of Harold. "Why don't you just take these, Harold?" he said pleasantly. "Take them home with you. It's only a few blocks from here."

"I'm an alcoholic," Harold said, shocked.

"Who cares?" the man said. He got a bright orange shopping bag from somewhere under the bar and put the bottles in it. "On the house," he said. Harold stared at him. "What is your goddamned, fucking *name?*"

"For me to know," the man said softly. "For you to find out."

Harold took the shopping bag, pushed open the door and went into the lobby. There was no doorman at the big doorway of the hotel, but the man in the sleeveless sweater stood there like a doorman. "Have a good day now, Harold," the man said as Harold left.

Now there was no one else on the street but the man. Everywhere. And now they all looked at him in recognition, since he had given his name. Their smiles were cool, distant, patronizing. Some nodded at him slightly as he made his way slowly up the avenue toward Sixty-third, some ignored him. Several passed on motorcycles, wearing red helmets. A few waved coolly to him. One slowed his motorcycle down near the curb and said, "Hi, Harold," and then sped off. Harold closed his eyes.

He got home all right, and up the stairs. When he walked into the living room he saw that the cats had knocked his new painting to the floor and had badly smeared a corner of it. Apparently one of them had rolled on it. The cats were nowhere in sight. He had not seen them since Janet had gone.

He did not care about the painting now. Not really. He knew what he was going to do. He could see in his mind the French movie, the man on the motorcycle.

In the closet where she kept her vacuum cleaner, Janet also kept a motorcycle helmet. A red one, way up on the top shelf, behind some boxes of candles and light bulbs. She had never spoken to him of motorcycles; he had never asked her about the helmet. He had forgotten it, having noticed it when he was unpacking months before and looking for a place to put his Samsonite suitcase. He set the bag of bottles on the ledge by the window overlooking the building where men in brown sleeveless sweaters were now working. He opened one bottle with a practiced fingernail, steadily. The cork came out with a *pop*. He took a glass from the sideboard and poured it half full of whiskey. For a moment he stood there motionless, looking down at the building. The work, he saw without surprise, was getting done. There was glass in the window frames now; there had been none that morning. The plywood ramp had been replaced with marble steps. Abruptly he turned and called, "Kitty! Kitty!" toward the bedroom. There was silence. "Kitty! Kitty!" he called again. No cat appeared.

In the kitchen there was a red-legged stool by the telephone. Carrying his untasted glass of whiskey in one hand, he picked up the stool with the other and headed toward the closet at the back of the apartment. He set the whiskey on a shelf, set the stool in the closet doorway. He climbed up carefully. There was the motorcycle helmet, red, with a layer of dust on top. He pulled it down. There was something inside it. He reached in, still standing on the stool, and pulled out a brown sleeveless sweater. There were stains on the sweater. They looked like bloodstains. He looked inside the helmet.

There were stains there, too. And there was a little blue plastic band with letters on it. It read Paul Bendel—Paris. Once, in bed, Janet had called him Paul. *Oh, you son of a bitch!* he said.

Getting down from the stool he thought, *For him to know. For me to find out.* He stopped only to pick up the drink and take it to the bathroom, where he poured it down the toilet. Then he went into the living room and looked out the window. The light was dimming; there was no one on Sixty-third Street. He pushed the window higher, leaned out. Looking to his right he could see the intersection with Madison. He saw several of them crossing it. One looked his way and waved. He did not wave back. What he did was take the two bottles and drop them down to the street where they shattered. He thought of a man's body, shattering, in a motorcycle wreck. In France? Certainly in France.

A group of four of them had turned the corner at Madison and were walking toward him. All of them had their hands in their pockets. Their heads were all inclined together and they appeared to be having an intimate, whispered conversation. *Why whisper?* Harold thought. *I can't hear you anyway.*

He pulled himself up and sat on the window ledge, letting his legs hang over. He stared down at them and forced himself to say aloud, "Paul." They were directly below him now, huddled and whispering. They seemed not to have heard him.

He took a breath and said it louder: *"Paul."* And then he found somewhere the strength to shout it, in a loud, clear, steady voice. "Paul," he shouted. *"Paul Bendel."*

Then the four faces looked up, shocked. "You're Paul Bendel," he said. "Go back to your grave in France, Paul."

They stood transfixed. Harold looked over toward Madison. Two of them there had stopped in their tracks in the middle of the intersection.

The four faces below were now staring up at him in mute appeal, begging for his silence. His voice spoke to this appeal with strength and clarity: "Paul Bendel," he said, *"you must go back to France."*

Abruptly all four of them averted their eyes from his and from one another's. Their bodies seemed to become slack. Then they began drifting apart, walking dispiritedly away from one another and from him.

He was redoing a smeared place on the painting when the telephone rang. It was Janet. She was clearly in a good mood and she asked if the zucchini soup had been all right.

"Fine," he said. "I had it cold."

She laughed. "I'm glad it wasn't too burned. How was the *jarret de veau?*"

Immediately, at the French, his stomach tightened. Despite the present clarity of his mind, he felt the familiar pain of the old petulance and jealousy. For a moment, he hugged the pain to himself, then dismissed it with a sigh.

"It's in the oven right now," he said. "I'm having it for dinner."

ECHO

"How many electrodes are there in that thing?" Arthur said.

Mel gave him an irritated look. "More than anyone could count, old buddy." He was checking some of the connections of the coils that went from the big tape recorder to the helmet; they were as profuse on the helmet as Medusa's snakes. Arthur and Mel had left the party upstairs to come down to Mel's basement laboratory. Mel taught paraphysics at the University.

"You mean you don't *know* how many there are? You put the fucker together and you don't know yourself?"

"*I* didn't put the fucker together, old buddy." Mel gave a jerk to the coil between his hands and somewhere deep in the recording device there was a *click*. "A Hewlett-Packard computer did. I only told it what to make, and it made it."

Arthur just stared at him. Then he took an annoyed swallow from the glass of whiskey in his hand. *These Goddamn paraphysicists. It would be just like the sons of bitches not to want to know how many connections you had to make to record an entire human mind.* But he said nothing. When Denise had talked him into doing this thing he had made enough objections. Such as, "Why me? Why should I be the guinea pig for some crazy attempt to make a recording of a whole personality?" Denise's answer had merely been, "Because Mel is your *friend*." And so on.

So he sat and drank his drink and watched Mel finish checking out the helmet and submitted quietly when Mel

343

placed the heavy thing on his head. He could just barely see beneath and around dangling wires and he was wondering how long he would have to put up with it to please his wife and Mel when he heard and slightly saw Mel walk over to the recorder and heard him say, "Here we go, old buddy." Then he threw a switch. . . .

And Arthur awoke to a world askew and furred. Something was madly wrong with his vision, even though the wires were gone. His eyes could not encapsulate the scene for him; all he really saw were pale colors, pale lights, some slight movements. There were smells somewhere, too, but they made no sense: roses, maybe, and vinegar. Somebody somewhere was singing in Chinese, or Anglo-Saxon. He closed his eyes. Only one thing was certain. He had an erection. He went to sleep.

Even the dreams were not right. They seemed to be someone else's dreams.

Days passed. He woke from time to time, and was fed. Sometimes there were tall, slim people in the room with him. They spoke Chinese. Or Anglo-Saxon. Once a long-haired person spoke to him in strange English, "How are *you*, sir or madam?" He had no answer for that.

Finally he woke up and was able to focus his eyes and brain well enough to see that he was not in his own body. He learned that from his arms, which were hairless and chocolate. Was he a Black? A Polynesian? He did not feel as shocked as it seemed he should have felt. *Drugged? Very likely. Whom by? God knows*. He felt of his face. It was all wrong: the nose was too broad, the chin too soft, the ears were too big. *Why is it I'm not upset at this? Drugs?* But then he had been wanting to be dead for over a year, had been thinking of suicide with the intensity that some of his colleagues had when they thought of a promotion. So maybe whatever had happened to him didn't make any difference. If he didn't like it he could always kill himself. And there was no pain in whatever was going on. He felt all right.

A person in a sort of well-tailored red bathrobe came into the room. He was tall and thin and pale, and his face was smiling shyly. His hair was blond and straight and came down nearly to his waist. Or maybe it was a she. But then the person spoke and the voice was male. "How are *you* nowadays?" The man was smiling at him more broadly now.

"I'm okay," Arthur said. "But where am I? And who?" He held up his dark brown arm. "In this . . . body?"

The other man looked pleased. "It's artful," he said.

Arthur stared at him. *"Artful?"*

The man looked embarrassed. Then he said, "Artificial."

"Artificial?"

"Your body," the man said, with more confidence. "It is artificial now."

"For Christ's sake," Arthur said. And then, "I liked the other one well enough."

The man smiled sweetly. "Long dead," he said. "And rotten."

"Jesus Christ," Arthur said. "Jesus Christ."

He slept after that and the next day the long-haired man was there when he awoke. Arthur assumed that a day had passed because the man's bathrobe was yellow this time. Arthur had a question ready. "Where did this body come from?"

The man smiled at him with encouragement. "Cleveland."

He hadn't been ready for that. He felt he might never be ready for whatever this childlike and epicene person might tell him. "Did you grow this body in Cleveland, or something?"

"Or something is correct. We made you first in Cleveland in bodily form before we grew you big in here. The mind was poured into you. Poured into your pretty and always body." The man looked at him quizzically. "Bodies not made in Cleveland in your time?"

"In my time?"

"In your time of the world. When you was alive and well and running around."

Arthur continued to stare. "Is this the *future?*" he said.

The man shook his head. "It's only nowadays," he said. "Like always." Then he smiled. "And you was born in the twenty-second century anno domini, in crowded times and places?"

Arthur let out a heavy sigh. Then he said, "Can you get me a drink? With whiskey or gin? Ethyl alcohol?"

The man did not seem to understand.

"An intoxicating drink."

The man smiled again. "I understand that thing. And yes, I will." He turned to leave the room. "Not the twenty-second century anno domini?"

"The twentieth," Arthur said in a voice near a whisper. Finally it was all coming down on him. "What century is this?"

The man turned and smiled at him before he left the room. "The forty-seventh," he said. "Anno domini."

The drink turned out to be a sort of screwdriver—spiked orange juice. It was in a simple glass that did not look at all futuristic. After Arthur drank it, he said, "How did I get here? In this body from . . . from Cleveland?"

"Refrigerator," the man said. "We found a refrigerator, all wrapped and sealed underground where a city was. With a tape of you inside. Under rubble. From time so far and distant long agone so hard to tell."

From time so far and distant long agone. . . . "Have you a name?" Arthur asked.

"Yes. I am always Ben."

"Ben?"

"Yes. Always Ben."

Arthur began to sit up for the first time. It was not as

346

difficult as he had feared it might be. He felt fairly strong. "What kind of tape, Ben?"

"Oh, machine tape. Ancient computer tape," Ben said. "They had all of you all over on the tape. Except a body."

Arthur had already figured that one out. Some time or other, even years after that night with the thing on his head, Mel had stuck that tape in a refrigerator for some reason. And twenty-seven centuries later somebody had dug it out, freakishly preserved, and figured out what it was: a record of the memory, mind, imagination, personality, lusts, ambitions, neuroses and everything else of Arthur Franks. Then somebody had gotten some kind of artificial body from a factory in Cleveland and had played the tape into it. And here he was, reconstructed from some point before his life's end. Somewhere out in this strange world the dust of his first life lay; he was now being given a chance to live out the last part of that life again. If he wanted to.

How long had he lived, a near-suicide, back in the twentieth century? Had he killed himself?

"You found me as a recording," he said. "Without a body."

"Yes," Ben said. "And as a student of the ancient tongue of English and of old times long agone I had you made especially a body. To have a thing to put the tape into so then to talk with me. As we indeed are doing now."

"Do you know anything more about me? Like when I . . . died? Or about my wife?"

Ben looked sad, his normally smooth forehead wrinkling. "Sorry always." Then he smiled. "All I know for sure and always is America was home for you."

"Okay," Arthur said. Maybe it was better not to know what had become of himself—of that other himself. "Is there still an America?"

Ben continued smiling. "Two. One north and one is always south."

347

"That's good to know," Arthur said. "Could I have another drink?"

The bathroom was much like a twentieth-century one except that the water from the taps was scented and the light coming from the ceiling was like daylight—yellowish and very pleasant to his eyes. Over the sink was a mirror.

He stood and stared at himself for several minutes, shocked.

He was very Negroid and very handsome, with a short Afro of glossy black hair, a broad nose, generous ears, thick lips and clear eyes. His shoulders were broad and the chest beneath them was smooth, hairless, and powerful. His stomach was flat, his arms well muscled but soft-looking, like a woman's.

He stood back to see himself full length. His body was perfect; there wasn't a blemish on it. He looked at his face again—his new face—and smiled. *What the hell,* he thought, *this beats suicide.*

Later, when Arthur was able to walk a little each day, Ben brought others. Some were apparently women—very calm, straightforward types, like Ben. But none of them spoke English. They smiled a lot. They were all nice-looking, but a bit forceless, passive; and they all seemed young. He wondered if they had some way of staying young-looking whatever their ages. Probably so. Or maybe their bodies came from another factory in Cleveland.

He liked the sounds of the women's voices, more like Chinese than Anglo-Saxon, soft and slurred in speech and with musical pitch. Sometimes they sang. He liked the way they moved around and looked over at him, in his bed, from time to time, with curiosity but with no hint of flirtatiousness.

Outside the room's only window, where the view was of an empty field and, beyond that, a dark row of trees, it was rain-ing heavily under an iron-colored sky. There was no work of human building to be seen from that window, only grass and sky and the line of trees.

Ben left the room for a while and returned with another woman, different from the others, and stood with her near the door and talked for a moment. Arthur looked at her. She was dressed like the others in some kind of a tan robe. But her hair was cut short and her face had a puzzled animation about it and a sense of some quality—urgency maybe—that was missing in the others. She had very pale skin and auburn hair; she was tall and her figure was splendid.

Ben brought her over and introduced her to him as Annabel. Surprisingly, she spoke English. He was astonished at this at first, until she smiled and said, "Ben tells me I'm from the same century you're from. We thought it was the twenty-second at first."

"Don't you remember?" Arthur said.

"No," she said, "I don't remember. Something about the way the tapes were played into this body, Ben says. I know how to speak, but I don't remember a thing . . ." She looked toward Ben.

"It is always amnesia," Ben said. "She was the first to be made from ancient tapes a year ago. But the tapes were not right for her brain so she forgot it all. She forgot all the time long agone when she lived before. Then we made you and did always better with your tape."

"Maybe it's best not to remember," Arthur said.

She smiled at him wistfully. "Still I'd like to know. I don't even know what my name was. I'd like you to tell me about our time—the twentieth century—and maybe it'll help me remember."

"Sure," Arthur said. "What do you want to know?"

For several weeks she came to his room at breakfast and asked questions. He told her about cities and government and clothing and animals and the way things looked and how people lived. But none of it touched her memory. Arthur liked her, and there seemed at times something familiar about her. It made sense that there would be, since she had probably been taped by Mel—possibly after the same dinner party, after he himself had been "copied" onto the tapes. She could be Denise. Except she wasn't, and he knew that. Maybe she was the wife of someone he knew, some woman he had talked to briefly once and then forgot about. She was clearly as intelligent as he, and as quick; her vocabulary was excellent. And her personality—something about her personality sometimes haunted him. He would be drinking coffee with her and would happen to look at her hand holding the cup or at the way she brought the cup to her lips and there would be something terribly familiar about it. But he could not place it. It was like *déjà vu*.

On his first day outside, with Ben gently helping him walk on wobbly legs, the thing he felt most was the clarity and cleanness of the outside air. It was a spring morning, with small leaves on the trees by the door of the building; on the grass near the door a thick robin stood attentive, its ear cocked toward the ground. A small white dog scampered as such dogs always had toward a hill and then disappeared from view. There was a warm breeze, riffling his kinky hair.

Arthur walked a few yards, then turned to look at the building he had just left for the first time. It seemed to be made of green stone, with a slightly peaked green roof, and large windows. Except for the green color it could have been a large bank from downtown St. Louis or Denver. There were five other buildings, more or less like it, making a complex, with gray rubbery walkways between them. At a distance two long-haired men walked hand in hand in quiet conversation from one building to another, one of them smoking a cigarette. Arthur's heart was light, his stomach fluttery with the warmth of the day and the sense of the new. They walked around the building and Arthur stood and looked toward the dark green line of woods in the distance and then they went back inside; he was still too weak to walk anymore. But he could tell that the body he inhabited was healthy and youthful and would soon be strong. There were firm muscles under the brown skin; his arms and legs were straight, well formed; and there were good, springy arches in his feet. His hands were capacious and wise; he could sense the power, the aptitude and heft, of them.

The next day he and Annabel went for a walk, going about a third of the way down the gray path toward the woods before he became too tired to go further.

They said little. For a few moments he took her hand, but he sensed something in her that stiffened when he did so. Somehow, he felt no desire for her, even though she was clearly a lovely woman, and he could not understand why. There was nothing wrong with his sexuality in this new and young body; even in his old, haggard and soft one there had been no problems there. He had always been a strong lover; that alone had kept him going for years against the tide of his old life that had pulled so strongly in other ways toward death. Toward drink, and guilt, and alienation and despair.

But Annabel with her fine breasts and firm round ass did not turn him on. He could not understand it.

Later, in his room, when she was in a chrome-and-leather chair and he was lying against the pillows in bed, he tried talking about it. "If this were a movie," he said, "we would be falling in love by now."

She looked toward him thoughtfully. "I suppose so. I think I may be homosexual. A lesbian."

He looked at her. What she said seemed true. Maybe that explained his lack of feeling toward her. "Do you find the women here attractive?"

351

"No," she said, and then smiled at him. "I bet you don't either."

He smiled back. "No, I don't," he said. And then, "Why don't you come over here and kiss me on the mouth? It couldn't hurt anything."

"Okay," she said and got up. She walked over toward him, seated herself on the edge of the bed, bent over slowly, and kissed him, with her mouth open and soft. At first he felt almost nothing, as though he were kissing the smooth palm of his own hand. But they held the kiss and, gradually, he felt an excitement begin in his stomach. It was a different feeling from what he was used to; there was some kind of very strong and frightening power to it. He continued kissing her, working his lips a bit now but not using his tongue and not reaching his hands toward her breasts that hung down over his chest. There *was* some great power there; but something in him would not let him yield to it. There was something he was afraid of. He pulled away from her, and looked up. Her face was very serious and just a bit frightened.

"Something is scaring me," he said quietly.

"Me too," she said. "I think I'd better go."

She got up from the bed and left the room without saying good-bye. He lay there silently for a long while, thinking of her. Somewhere in his stomach there was still a ribbon of unpleasantness—of fear. But the fear was being buried by the excitement of desire, becoming indistinguishable from it.

In the middle of that night he was awakened by her wet mouth kissing his breasts, under the sheet. He could smell the faint smell of sweat from her warm body—had been smelling it even while asleep. It aroused him immediately. Then without saying a word she moved her head down to him and took him in her mouth. Still in his stomach was the ribbon of fear, but the excitement, the movement toward ecstasy, buried it. And he exploded into her mouth, beneath the sheet. She stayed with him, holding his hips, for only a minute afterward and then left, padding slowly—somehow, it seemed, thoughtfully—out of the room in bare feet, leaving him alone in bed. Neither of them had said a word.

He did not see her the next morning at breakfast; for several days she had been joining him for the farrago of oats and wheat and honey that a silent male nurse brought him every morning together with a yellow cup full of powerful, astringent coffee. Nor did she join him for his lunch of odd-looking vegetables and what he thought of as "Mystery Soup."

Ben dropped in on him after lunch for a conversation about twentieth-century America; Arthur told him about movies and cars. His heart wasn't in it; he could not get Annabel off his mind.

"Are there still cars?" he asked Ben.

"Oh, no. Very little mechanical nowadays."

"How do you travel?"

"Walking. Always walking," Ben said. "Sometimes we use a flyer, for traveling long."

"Is a flyer an airplane?"

"Somewhat," Ben said. "But no motor and no jets."

"How does it work?"

"Nobody knows," Ben said. "No need to know."

"Who does the cooking around here?"

"Cooking?" Ben said.

"Yes. Preparing food to eat." He almost said "always" before "eat."

"Food is always assembled," Ben said. "Assembled from little atoms by the cooker. Like clothes and buildings."

"Oh," Arthur said, and thought *Jesus.* "Then nobody does any work?"

"I study things. Always ancient America. Others study things. And we talk a lot."

"And that's all you do?"

Ben smiled at him benignly. "Always."

"I've never seen any children around, Ben. Do you have children in other places?"

"No. No children. And there are only very few and small other places and no children there. Only big ones like you and me."

"Then what . . . ? Then how do you reproduce?"

Ben smiled and shook his head. "Oh, we never reproduce. We always live ourselves. Always."

"You're *immortal?*"

"Oh, of course," Ben said. "We live forever. And you indeed will live forever too in that strong body."

"*Jesus,*" he said aloud and lay back against the pillows. And then, "Don't you get *bored?*"

"Oh, sure," Ben said. "But it goes away. And we forget a lot and always learn things over."

"How old are you, Ben?"

Ben shook his head. "I never know at all how old. Centuries. Someday I'll die myself by fire as others do and that will be an end."

"Then someday you'll tire of it and kill yourself. And that's been happening for some time now and there aren't many left."

Ben smiled dolefully, his youthful and bland face registering a kind of pleasant painfulness. "That's all there is to know," he said.

Ben turned to leave, walking out of the room with his loose-jointed gait, his long hair covering his narrow shoulders and back. At the door he stopped and turned back toward Arthur. "Long life is good enough for most," he said, "and death is not so bad."

Arthur said nothing. When Ben was gone he began working at the room's little table on the chess set he was making from a soft material like Styrofoam. He was using a knife that Ben had gotten him, and he began working on the most difficult pieces, the knights, carving them with a great deal of care.

When he had finished the first one and had begun to copy it for the second, Annabel came in. She was wearing a green robe and she looked beautiful to him.

At first he did not know what to say. Then he looked at her and said, "Thanks. Thanks for last night."

"Sure," she said. "It was strange. But I liked it."

"Then you aren't a lesbian," he said, trying to make his voice light but feeling some kind of embarrassment in it. He set the unfinished piece and the knife on the desk in front of him and swiveled in the chair to see her better. She was tall and fair-skinned—a beautiful woman. "Would you like to take a walk?" he said. "I think I could make it to the woods."

She was silent for a minute. Then she said, "Sure." She walked over to the table and carefully, thoughtfully, picked up the finished piece and held it between thumb and forefinger. "This is a knight," she said.

He stared at her. "How did you know that?" Chess did not exist, as far as he had been able to find out, in this world. Ben's people did not play games. "It's a twentieth-century thing."

"I don't know," she said. "I really don't. I just know it's called a knight."

"Do you know what 'chess' means?" he said.

"'Chess'?" She said the word carefully. "No. No, I don't."

He shook his head and then took the piece from her and set it down by the finished pawns. "Let's take that walk."

While they were walking and he had his hands in the pockets of his robe and his eyes down on the strange plastic shoes he had been given, he said, "Ben tells me I'll be very strong when my body has a chance to . . . to ripen or whatever it is."

"Do you look the way you looked before? In your other life?" she said.

"No," he said. "God, no. I was white, and middle-aged. A professor of chemistry and getting pot-bellied."

"Yes," she said. "I have no idea what I looked like, but I know it wasn't like this." She extended her long and pale arms from her sides, palms upward, and looked earnestly at him. "I know I'm entirely different now from what I once was."

"It's a strange feeling," he said. "Still, the way you look now is fine by me." But that wasn't exactly true; there was a touch of idle and self-assuring flattery in it. She was beautiful enough, but he still was not at ease with her beauty. Something about it haunted him as though at times there were superimposed upon her face and body another face and body, from his past, very faint but disquieting.

He did make it to the woods, although he was tired when he got there. Ben had told him it would take months to get the full strength of his new body. The body had been cloned from synthetic, composite genes, but it had never been exercised and its muscles were soft and new.

In the woods they sat on a fallen log and smoked the odd-tasting cigarettes that Ben supplied them with. Then they began to make love, slowly and cautiously, first with their hands and then with their mouths. He brought her to a light orgasm in the spotted daylight that filtered through old trees, while she sat on the log dreamily and he kneeled in front of her. After that they found a grassy clearing with dry ground and lay together. Somehow they were perfectly matched, and knew exactly what to do for each other.

But then, as he was beginning to feel the oncoming orgasm, she looked down on him from her position above him and said, "Jesus, do I love this." The words fell somehow like lead on his spirit and he became suddenly afraid, frozen in his movements. The same fear came in her face. They stared at each other while his soul shrank from her. He did not know what had happened; he only knew that her words—words that were somehow terribly familiar to him—had frightened him. Forest light flecked her beautiful and glowing skin; her fine breasts were warm in his upward-reaching hands; somewhere a bird was singing jubilantly, and wind rustled the leaves of the trees. Inside himself he was cold, trembling. He rolled out from under her and lay on the grass in turmoil—frightened and angry. "What happened?" he said.

"I don't know. I said that, and something went wrong. I don't know."

He shook his head. "Maybe it's these new bodies," he said. "Maybe we'll have to just get used to them."

She shook her head and said nothing.

He did not see her for several days and was relieved not to. He spent the time easily enough—when he was not troubled by thinking about her—finishing his chess set, exercising lightly, and wandering through the building where he lived.

On the third day Ben and another man whose only English was the word "Hello" took him to the far end of the building to a laboratory. There were four large tanks, coffin-like and bright green, lined up along one wall. Ben walked over to the second of these from the left, set his long-fingered hand on its lid, and said, "This is where we grew your self for years."

Arthur walked over to it and Ben lifted the hinged lid for him. Inside it was like a large, green bathtub, with about half a dozen little metal pipes entering it on one side. "How long was I in this thing?" he asked.

"Three years," Ben said. "No way to go faster."

"Was it difficult to play the tape into . . . into me?"

Ben smiled and shook his head. "Oh, yes," he said. "We did it wrong two times. First we had the body wrong and next the tape. But then we got you always right and here you stand." Then he looked at the other man with him, who was apparently some kind of technician, and the other nodded toward Ben with a faint smile.

Arthur started to pursue this but Ben, abruptly for him, turned and walked over to one of the consoles and took from an otherwise empty shelf a box about the size of a candy box, walked back to Arthur and handed it to him. "Here is your soul," he said, softly.

Arthur took the box in both hands. "My tape?" he said.

"Of course," Ben said. "Your ancient tape. Your soul."

Arthur opened the box with care. Inside was a full plastic reel with a label that read "Advent Corporation. Boston, Mass." And under that someone had written with a ballpoint pen, "Arthur Franks."

That evening he finished his chess set and then made a board by ruling the sixty-four squares on a sheet of white, flexible plastic and darkening half of them with what seemed to be a Magic Marker. It was late and he was tired, but he set the pieces up, the white ones on his side of the board, and began to play King's Gambit against the black, using Morphy's way of sacrificing the king's knight for a heavy attack on black's kingside. It was strange to see his brown arm and hand moving chess pieces around on a board; he thought he had become used to his new color—even liked it—but it was a shock to see himself in this old context; he had been captain of his chess club in high school and when other kids had been out shooting basketball or stealing hubcaps or whatever, he had sat in his room at home working out variations of chess attacks. But with a thin white arm, a pale hand on the pieces—not this smooth and chocolate arm with the big and nimble hand at the end of it.

Outside the window was a nearly full moon in a jet-black sky. The window was open, and warm air, hinting of summer nights, filled the room. He could hear the shrill sounds of tree frogs and somewhere a cricket.

Then the door opened quietly and Annabel walked in. He

turned to look at her. She was barefoot, dressed in a white robe. Her hair had been pulled back and was tied behind her head, framing her face. She was lovely. He felt tense, frightened. "What do you want?" he said.

"I wanted to make love the way I did before. I thought you would be asleep." Each word came to him as if it had been spoken for him before, as if he had thought it just before she said it. *Déjà vu.* He shook his head, trying to shake it off.

"No," he said, "I don't want that right now."

"I know," she said. She took off her robe and sat on the edge of the bed. "I think we ought to start where we left off yesterday."

He stared at her as she lay back, naked, against a pillow. "I don't know if I can . . ."

"Yes, you can," she said. "That was only a barrier for us. We've crossed it now."

"I was thinking something like that myself," he said. He came over and sat beside her on the bed.

"Sure you were," she said. "We're really very much alike. We think the same things."

He slipped off his sandals. "You're really something," he said.

"So are you," she said.

She was right. The barrier or whatever it was had fallen. The fear had subsided. The pleasure of lovemaking was different from what it had been before for him, with other women he had had. It was very inward, very intense. He hardly looked at her.

When he climaxed something seemed to open up inside him. There was a sense of release in a secret part of himself, at the center of his aching and suicidal life. His eyes were shut and he heard himself laughing, immersing himself in himself.

He lay back afterward, spent and blissful. They did not

speak, nor did they look at one another. He stared at the moon outside the window, the early summer moon, as cold and luminous and clear in the black sky as was his soul within himself.

They slept together that night for the first time. Not touching, but naked together in the same bed, each turned to the right in a nearly fetal position, like a pair of twins.

In the morning they awoke silently together and silently drank coffee, sitting side by side in bed. There seemed to be no need to speak.

And then, as they were drinking their second cup of coffee, she began looking at something on the other side of him and he saw that it was the chessboard, still set up from the night before. She was looking at it intently and her eyes began to widen.

"What is it?" he said. "Is something wrong?"

"That's the King's Gambit," she said. "Morphy's Attack."

Something prickled at the back of his neck and he heard a tremor in his own voice. *"Yes, it is,"* he said.

"And the next move is bishop takes bishop's pawn." She turned and stared at him, her eyes wide and her lips trembling.

"Yes," he said. "Bishop takes bishop's pawn. . . . Not many people know that."

"I've known it since high school," she said. "Grover Cleveland High School. Where I was . . ."

"Captain of the chess team." His voice was like gravel in his throat. His heart was pounding and his mouth was dry. "Ben's mistake," he said, whispering because his dry mouth made him whisper it. "You're Ben's wrong body."

And she whispered too. "I'm Arthur Franks," she said.

"Oh Jesus," he said. "Oh sweet Jesus." He lay back in bed and stared at the ceiling for a long while. And then, later, when a calmness had come into him and he let his hand reach out slowly and gently and let it fall sensuously upon her smooth and cool thigh he felt, at exactly the same instant, her hand soft and sexual upon his own thigh. "Oh, yes," he said aloud, softly. "Oh, yes."

And he heard her say it too. "Oh, yes. Oh, yes."

SITTING IN LIMBO

Sitting here in Limbo, I have found I can return to and make corrections in the life I once lived. I calculate that seventeen years have passed since I died in Columbus, Ohio; it was about two years ago that I learned to return to various parts of my life and change them for the better. The work is difficult but rewarding. And what else has a dead person to do with his time?

There are no physical discomforts here under this pale and sunless sky; the boredom and emptiness that make up my existence are not intolerable. In many ways it is not as bad as being alive was. There is no one to talk to here and nothing, really, to think about except that life of fifty-one years that I was permitted to have. From my present perspective I see it as a unity, like a complex circuit diagram or an abstract-expressionist painting. I see that a part here or there may be altered —a diode or a blob of color—and the pattern will be forever changed. From my birth in the Good Samaritan Hospital in Lexington, Kentucky, to my death from a coronary in Columbus, it is all a single, sometimes baffling, entity. And I can change it now, a small part at a time. I have the distance.

It was quite by accident that I discovered I could go back there. I have seven chairs here on which I can sit; they have been here since I arrived. Each is different from the others. One of them is a hard wooden chair of varnished oak. I sit in it when I wish to be wakeful. Sometimes I let myself drowse in a reverie for days; at other times I sit upright, my body expectant, waiting. There is, of course, nothing to wait *for* here, but I take comfort in adopting the posture. The wooden chair is exactly right for this. It is high-backed and sturdy; it squeaks when I shift my weight from one buttock to the other. There are very few noises here in Limbo and I appreciate the contribution this chair makes.

I was sitting in it some time ago when I became reminded of a desk at Morton Junior High School, in Lexington. It, too, was made of varnished oak and it, too, squeaked. It had an arm on it for writing and my Limbo chair does not, but otherwise they are much alike. I was sitting in the chair and staring at the fuzzy horizon of Limbo and squeaking every minute or so in a kind of slow dirge. And suddenly my memory came alive with myself in the eighth grade, in Miss Ralston's Social Science class. That class met for an hour every day after lunch, and it was one of the most tedious things in my life. Remembering it here was like *déjà vu;* perhaps I had been in a kind of Limbo then and had not known it. I remembered the gravelly sound of Miss Ralston's voice. I remembered the way she would adjust her teeth in her mouth with a kind of sucking between paragraphs. I remembered her dark flowered dresses, her grayish hair in a bun, her heavy brown shoes. I remembered the fight to stay awake.

And then I remembered a whimsical promise I had made myself as a teen-aged boy in that classroom: I promised I would return to that room at that time if I ever learned the secret of time travel when I grew up. I imagined myself astonishing everyone by my sudden appearance. I would be a grown and vigorous time-traveler stepping with confidence from a glass-and-chromium machine that would materialize just to the right of Miss Ralston's desk. She would stop in midsentence and her jaw would drop. Everyone would stare. In that fantasy I was both observer and observed, both adult and boy, and the imagined pleasure was exquisite.

Then, in Limbo, I remembered the date I had made myself

that promise: September 23, 1942. I was born in 1928, so I must have been fourteen. I had repeated the date over and over in that classroom so I would remember it years later. And clearly it had worked. I was joyful, pleased with the continuity.

Then something inside me told me to cross my ankles in a certain way and to slump in my oak chair in a certain way and to breathe in slowly and I did all this without really thinking about it and there I was. I was in Miss Ralston's classroom in September of 1942. But I did not materialize as a grown man to see myself sitting as a young student. I found myself as that student again—ankles crossed, slumped in my chair, breathing in slowly. I heard Miss Ralston's voice droning about the primary exports of Latin America. Fawn Harrington was on my left in a green tartan skirt and green sweater; Toby Kavanaugh sat on my right. I was wearing my Thom McAn shoes, the brown ones. They were too tight and my feet hurt. I had a headache; Mother and Daddy had been fighting in the kitchen the night before and I had barely slept. I hadn't done my homework. Fawn had tried flirting with me before class but I had ignored her. I did not like flirts; I always felt they were up to something.

It was all completely familiar and all clear and real. It was no dream. I tried to stand, to get up and leave that awful room; but I could not. I found that I had no control over my body. It was doing whatever it had done on that day the first time I had lived it. I was only there, it seemed, as an observer. I felt that I could return to Limbo whenever I willed it. I calmed myself and watched.

Miss Ralston finished her reading and then called on Jack Mowbray to read. He stood—a sly, freckled boy whom I distrusted—and read a paragraph about Simon Bolivar. Miss Ralston corrected his pronunciation of Bolivar, pronouncing it poorly herself. She called on Marylinne Saunders to read. And on it went. I watched and listened, fascinated, waiting for it to come to me. I had no awareness of what I was thinking—that other, fourteen-year-old I—but I began to be aware that this was a time when something bad had happened. It was about to happen again. It was going to happen when I was called on to read. I sat in the second row; it would be soon.

When it came to me I found myself standing up awkwardly and looking down at the text. I knew that a humiliation was coming but I could not remember what it was. I heard myself begin to read. My voice was tired and a bit resentful.

Suddenly I was shocked by Miss Ralston's voice, harshly interrupting me. "Billy!" she said. "Billy Whaley. Will you please consider your appearance?"

I looked at her stupidly.

She stared at me with an ironic, prissy frown. "Please go to the boy's room and button yourself." There was something triumphantly cruel in her voice, and it withered me. I looked down. My corduroys were open at the fly, unbuttoned. I heard a snicker from somewhere behind me, the snicker of a female voice . . .

Immediately I was back in Limbo. I was alone, standing in front of my oak chair, looking down. I am always in faded jeans here. They never wear out, never become dirty. Their fly was properly zipped, as always. I sighed aloud with relief and sat down. I was still shaking. I felt, in some obscure way, a victim.

There is a progression of time here. There are nights and days even though there is no visible sun, and I count them and remember the count. That is how I know it is seventeen years since I died. I do not know if I will be here for eternity or not. There has been no judgment of me, no communication from any god, devil or angel. Nothing has been promised, nothing explained, and I do not care. Yet I have come to believe that there may be a way out of Limbo. I have begun to feel that if I properly edit and rectify my former life that I will be able to pass on from here and be reborn. I sense that I await reincarnation and another life. I feel hopeful. Change is frightening to me and yet I feel hopeful of change.

After my first experience of return I marked off ten days while I thought of various things in my former life, as I often do, or merely counted numbers in my mind as I also often do here, and then I decided to try going back to Miss Ralston's class on that same day. It would be interesting to find myself alive again, even in that dreary schoolroom, and to be among people again. Yet I am not really bored with being dead. I could stay in Limbo for eternity. There is no pain here, no fatigue; there are no appetites. There is no danger. There are no misunderstandings.

I seated myself in the wooden chair and thought of the classroom. I visualized Miss Ralston and her false teeth and the blackboard behind her that was gray with chalk dust. I found myself crossing my ankles again and there I was again at precisely the moment I had reentered the first time. Miss Ralston was reading the same things about Latin America. She called on Jack Mowbray to read, corrected his pronunciation of Bolivar. Knowing now what was going to happen to me and knowing, too, how trivial it really was, I felt calmer this time. I decided to try something. I tried to move my hand down to my lap and button my fly. Nothing happened. My hand remained gently resting on my desk. Jack went on reading. I concentrated on moving the hand. It moved about an inch and then lay still again. Jack finished reading and Miss Ralston called on Fawn Harrington to read. Fawn stood up— a beautiful, soft-voiced girl with long lashes—and read quietly. Concentrating, I made my mind picture my right hand lifting from the desk and settling into my lap and after a moment I realized with surprise that it now *was* in my lap. I began picturing my fingers fastening the buttons. It was slow and difficult, but I could feel it happening. I got them buttoned.

When the reading came to me I stood up and read a passage about the principal fuels of Latin America and then sat down. Miss Ralston had not spoken to me! She called on Toby Kavanaugh. Toby stood up, his open book close to his weak eyes, and began to read. And then I found myself back here in Limbo, sitting in my wooden chair. I was exultant, almost awed. I had changed the past!

Immediately I wondered if that change would provoke others further along. Would I be less shy and difficult with girls when I began to date them at seventeen? Would I make a better grade in Social Science, do better in college, get a better job when I graduated, and so on? Such changes might well prevent my death at fifty-one. Yet clearly I was still dead and nothing in Limbo had changed. It was the same as ever, such as it was.

I remembered my first job interview, in my twenties, when I had become frightened and couldn't even remember my telephone number when the interviewer asked for it. Would erasing the incident of the unbuttoned fly have made me more confident in my twenties? I had invented a phone number for that man and he had ended the interview later, saying, "I'll call you."

I had sat in an armchair in that office, somewhat like the one I have in Limbo. I got up from the oak chair and seated myself in the armchair. I gripped its arms with my hands as I remembered doing. My body fell into that old tense position as though I were an actor who had played the scene a thousand times.

And there I was living it again in a small room with Currier and Ives prints on the wall and the interviewer, a florid man in a brown suit, smiling blandly at me. I knew instantly that it was all as it had been and that it would not end differently. Buttoning my fly in the classroom had changed nothing.

I remained through the inventing of the phone number and then I returned to Limbo. It was clear that I could only change things one at a time; I could not start new chains of circumstance.

Eventually I was to find out that my intuition was correct. I could change particular scenes in my life, erasing mistakes as it were and adding corrections, but I could not seriously change the substantive details. I was a high school teacher for my adult life and I could not change that. I was married twice and divorced twice; I could not alter that either, although I could edit my more unfortunate scenes with my wives. Honesty compels me to say there were many of these scenes. By judicious editing over a period of Limbo-years and hundreds of trips back I was able to improve my behavior in arguments, make myself kinder and more understanding, and the like. But I still divorced them and I could not change that. And truly I did not want to.

I could only make the transition to the past while sitting in the appropriate chair. I found that with some effort it was always possible to associate a chair with every part of my past I wished to explore and then, when needed, change. I have come to believe that the chairs were put here as vehicles for me to render my former life less painful to remember—less embarrassing and wrong. Perhaps other inhabitants of Limbo have more or fewer chairs. Perhaps not. I have never seen another inhabitant.

My first wife was Jane; I was married to her five years. It took me all of two years in Limbo to edit the relationship, yet with all the changes the divorce took place on the same date it had the first time around.

After three years of marriage to Jane I had lost interest in her and had stopped having sex with her. I had found—and I shudder to mention this—ways to blame her for my lack of interest. I told her that her clothes were all wrong—especially her underwear. I told her her education was lacking, that I felt she was afraid of sex. I had married her in the first place because she was a kind of boyish, no-nonsense woman, and now I blamed her for being that way, told her I wanted her to be more feminine. Yet the truth was that I mistrusted women who were very feminine. I told Jane in anger that I thought she was a repressed lesbian because of the way she wore blue jeans all the time. It was horrible of me to say such things. I had winced over them more than once, here in Limbo, before I discovered that I could change them. I am not a cruel person; I really wanted to erase those cruelties.

And I did. I went through the five years with Jane, making myself into a pleasant and honest person. I told her of the tapering off of my desire for her. I was kind to her in every way. She was understanding, and grateful for my straightforwardness. There were no fights.

I did not have sex with her any more than I had had originally. Living in Limbo all these years had obliterated any interest in sex for me. I made no changes in that department.

My second wife was named Millie. She was a librarian for a chemical company and very serious. Millie was a *very* serious person. It was eventually that seriousness that I learned to hate. Whenever I spoke to her, even about unimportant matters like the grade of hamburger we were using or the best kinds of plant food, she was always incredibly attentive. Millie had a good figure and an earnest sexual style, but she wore drab clothes. She looked like the librarian she was to the core.

Within a year of our marriage I had stopped making love with her. I was drinking a good deal by then and I would sometimes find a seductive woman at one of the bars I went to and take her to a motel for the night. Millie would look even more serious the next day but she would never ask where I had been. I knew she felt lucky to have gotten me in the first place. I was a respected biology teacher at a large high school and my salary was far above the average. I had clean habits and was generally polite. My indiscretions were always careful. I had no interest in provoking scandal. Besides I had no real liking for any of the women I took to bed in motels. It was just something I did. Sometimes, in fact, there would be no real sex involved. I would just watch the woman undress herself, feel satisfied enough, and fall drunkenly asleep.

Yet I felt guilty. And from Limbo I was greatly relieved to make the necessary changes, to spend those motel nights at home with Millie, reading or watching television.

In something like four and a half years of Limbo-time I have managed to edit my relationships with my wives in such a way that I now feel guiltless and at ease about what happened. I have altered some other aspects of my life—as a student, a teacher and a church member. I am satisfied. I hope to be reborn, to have another life. So far it has not happened, but it may not take place immediately. Limbo is slow, and I understand that. I would like to be reborn as a woman—as a vivacious and sexy woman. Why not?

Days pass and nothing happens. I sit and wait, moving from chair to chair. Must I go back and reedit? Was I wrong in expecting a second life after rectifying the first? I think not. I feel certain that good editing will propel me toward a new existence. I no longer feel content with Limbo. I am ready to move on. I want to be a girl. I want my name to be Beth. I want to be white, middle-class, pretty, and I want to be given a good education and be well dressed.

One of my chairs is smaller than the others. It is clear to me now that it is a child's chair. I have never sat on it. I am beginning to feel that I must, however uncomfortable it may be, if I am to finish my first life properly. I must sit in the child's chair. I am afraid to.

Eventually I sat in the small chair. I folded my hands in my lap, because that seemed the thing to do, and inclined my head. The chair was not uncomfortable at all. I felt quite natural and comfortable in it. I closed my eyes.

When I opened them after a bit I found that I was looking at my own small knees. They were bare below short pants and were scraped and rough-looking the way boys' knees sometimes are. I looked up. I was sitting facing the corner of a small bedroom papered in pink wallpaper. To my right was an open closet and to my left a bed. It was Mother's bedroom. I had been sent there to sit in the corner for an hour because of something bad I had done. I was not to speak or squirm or wriggle. I felt terribly uncomfortable and for a moment I panicked and almost willed myself back here to Limbo, but I decided to hold off for a while to see what would happen. My heart was beating fast. I was about six years old and I knew I had been here in this chair in the corner many times and I knew that something important was going to take place. Something would happen that always happened when I was sent to sit in the corner. I began to have a dim sense that I had *wanted* to be sent there, had done something deliberately bad so that it would happen.

Time passed. I sat and tried to remember how my mother had looked when I was a small child, but I could not. My father—that weak, almost absent man—had told me that she was an "extraordinarily beautiful" woman when he had married her. All I could remember was the way she had looked in the few years before she had died, when I was in my late thirties. Both of my wives had hated her and said I was too good to her, had resented the closeness of the two of us. Well. That had been their problem, not mine. I only saw my mother when she came to visit. She was thick-waisted and had gray

372

hair then and she wore cheap print dresses. But she was fun to talk to and she laughed a lot when we would sit and drink sherry together in the living room. Mother could be really funny when she was a little tipsy, and she was devastating in the way she could point out the pretensions of others. I have always admired her mind.

I sat there for about twenty minutes and thought of Mother and her false teeth and her wit and the big gestures she would use when talking and how she would say things like "to my utter astonishment" and "That, my dear, will be the day." Whatever my wives had said, she was a pleasure to be with.

And then in my chair there in the past I heard footsteps behind me and heard a voice saying, "Billy, it's getting too warm in the living room. I'm going to change into something cooler. You mustn't look."

She had stopped talking before I recognized with a distinct shock that it had been Mother's voice. It was the same cadence that I had remembered, but so much more youthful, so much . . . so much *richer,* than when I was grown up. I heard more footsteps. I heard her opening a drawer somewhere in back of me.

On the inside of the closet door to my right was a full-length, framed mirror. The frame was enameled in a creamy yellowish-white. A few men's jackets hung in the closet—gray and brown ones—and I knew they were Daddy's and that Daddy was away. Daddy was almost always away. Somehow I was glad he was.

I could see the mirror without moving my head. All I had to do was open my eyes slightly and look to the right. The mirror reflected the bed and part of a white-painted dresser, with silver-backed brushes on it and two photographs. One photograph was of me as a baby, the other was of Mother herself; they were both in yellowed ivory frames.

And then someone came into view in the mirror and something deep in me thrilled to see. It was Mother; I could tell even though her back was toward the mirror because she was walking toward the bed. Her waist was slim and her step was light and youthful. She turned and looked past me toward the mirror and smiled. She must have been smiling at her reflection, seen across the room. She was so beautiful, so shockingly, overwhelmingly beautiful, that my heart almost stopped. Her hair was jet black and bobbed; her skin was creamy white. Her lips were scarlet, her eyelashes long, her neck and jaw smooth and perfect and the scarlet of her fingernails matched the scarlet of her lips. Her eyes were big, dark and mischievous. She was wearing a blue dress with a short pleated skirt and shiny silk stockings with no shoes. She sat on the bed, still smiling.

I saw her with the eyes of a grown man who knows a beautiful woman when he sees one, and I saw her also with the eyes of a six-year-old child—an only child to whom his mother is the most wonderful thing in the world. The combined effect was devastating. I was hypnotized. I did not move a muscle.

Then she pulled up her dress lazily and began to unfasten her garters. When I saw the cream white of the insides of her thighs I felt for a moment as though I would faint. I had never seen anything so exciting in my life. I remained frozen in my little chair. She took her silk stockings off, laid them beside her on the bed's pink coverlet. The room was silent; from somewhere outside I could hear the chattering of a squirrel. For a moment I tried to turn my eyes away from the mirror, but I could not do it.

She stood up and, facing the window now so that she was reflected in profile, she began taking the dress off, pulling it over her head. She was wearing a short pink slip underneath.

Sometimes in my life I have wondered how it must feel to inject pure heroin into a vein. I think the pleasure would be electric in its intensity. I felt that now, looking at Mother through the eyes of both youth and age. There was, too, the sense of danger and of power that comes with seeing another intimately without being seen. There was the erotic joy of seeing a woman so beautiful, so self-absorbed, take off her clothes. And it was such a *forbidden* thing to see my mother expose her body. I could not take my eyes away—not while this heroin was in my blood.

She continued, as I knew by now she would. She pulled the slip slowly over her head, shook her lovely black hair back into order, and laid the slip on the bed by her hose. She was wearing pink silk step-ins and a lacy pink brassiere. Her figure was perfect and her skin perfectly white. I sat transfixed. The feelings in me were like a hurricane, and my soul was in the eye of it. I felt frozen in the moment. I wanted to stay in it forever.

And then I heard her voice again as from a distance. It was softer now and a bit throaty. What she said was, "Now be sure you don't peek, dear." Then as I watched she bent and took off her panties. I saw the jet black of her pubic hair, so flawlessly seated in that charismatic V. I could see the tiny lips of her vagina, as pink as the coverlet on the bed, as pink as the wallpaper, as her slip, her panties. My heart pounded like a mallet in my chest and then as she removed her brassiere and stood there naked by the bed, still smiling, smiling now toward where I sat upright in my little chair, I felt a swooning inside myself. The heroin had me. My vision blurred and I was back in Limbo.

I sat stunned for several moments. And then I felt a brief flash of anger shake my body. I felt *had,* in some fundamental way, felt pinned down and tormented by the tableau I had just lived through.

But the anger left me soon. I was washed out, vaguely guilty, empty. I slept. I dreamed of Mother in her black wool coat in autumn when I was in the first grade. She would walk me carefully to school, helping me with the intersections. I dreamed of the way she would hold my right hand tightly in her left and I could feel the firm, metallic pressure of her engagement ring and her wedding ring. She would talk to me aimlessly of this and that—the weather, the new dresses she was going to buy—and I would hang on every word. I loved her terribly.

That was a long time ago in Limbo-time since I first went back to Mother's pink bedroom. I have stopped counting days and years here but I know that a great deal of time has passed.

Sometimes I feel restless and I yearn to finish the editing of my past so that I can be reborn to continue in whatever plan whatever god there is has made, and I feel that I know what needs to be done. I need to go back to Mother's bedroom and merely close my eyes and keep them closed. *I must not look in that mirror.*

And God knows I have tried. I have gone back there a hundred times and more, have sat in that chair and heard that soft and throaty voice saying, "Now be sure you don't peek, dear," and have stared at that face, those hips, those breasts, that lovely flesh. I have swooned, over and over. Her movements exist now in frozen choreography in my brain; they seem to have erased everything afterward in my one life so that the ten minutes in the bedroom when I was six years old are what that life was *for.* My swoon is like the hub around which the rest of my life revolves; should I change it the rest of my life might scatter into empty and frightening disorder.

Yet it would seem simple to close my eyes or turn them downward, only once, to render those ten minutes of my past null and void, so that I may move on to whatever other destiny waits for me—to that pleasant Beth I have wanted to be, in my warm home with dolls and a pet cat and children's books. I can feel at times the yearning of Beth within me wanting to become real and alive in the world. And so I go back to the pink bedroom from time to time, but I cannot change a thing.

It is always the same: Mother, the bed, the small chair, the long mirror on the closet door. And I never close my eyes.

I pray sometimes to God that Beth, who will never live, will forgive me, for I cannot erase those ten minutes from my life no matter how many times I try. I truly cannot.

Part Two

Far From Home

THE OTHER END OF THE LINE

Hungover from cheap whiskey, George Bledsoe made a simple error that many people make: he mistakenly dialed his own number on the telephone. He was attempting to call a girl he knew—a homely girl, but one with the virtues of being quick and easy—and, through his customary impatience and general fogginess, let the wrong pattern of digits govern his pudgy index finger: BE-8-5883.

He did not get the busy signal. He should have; but he did not. Instead, the phone began clicking and an operator's voice announced dimly, as if from a great distance, "That's a ship-to-shore connection, sir." George Bledsoe, just then realizing that he *had,* in fact, dialed his own number, said, "What the hell?" There was a great deal of static and then a man's voice said, "All right. Who is it?"

George blinked. The voice was loud and arrogant. It sounded somehow familiar, but he could not place it.

But George was not by nature a deferential person. "Who in hell are *you*, friend?" he said.

The voice paused a moment and then it said, "This is George Bledsoe."

"Look, friend," George Bledsoe said, "You can take that and . . ." He started to hang up and then stopped. *How could . . . ?*

"That's right," the voice said. "How could I *know?*" And then, "You let it sink in a minute, George, and then you get that tablet of paper out of the top dresser drawer and get yourself a pencil out of the box on the refrigerator and you get ready to write some things down. We don't have all day."

George was staring at the phone in disbelief. It *was* his voice, as if on a tape recorder. He blinked, and found himself sweating. But, unused to taking orders, he said, "Why should I?"

"Don't argue, dammit. I'm talking to you from October ninth. I'm sitting in a boat, twenty-eight miles and two months from where you are and I've got a pile of newspapers, Georgie, that haven't even been printed yet, back there in August where you're talking from. I'm going to make you rich."

It sounded like a con game. George's eyes narrowed. "Why should you?"

"Because I'm you, you stupid bastard. Get that paper and start writing. I'm going to give you the names of some racehorses and of three issues of stocks. And a baseball team. You'd better get them right the first time. There won't be another."

George was staring around the room dizzily; the hand that held the phone was sticky with sweat. "How can . . . ?"

"Dammit, shut up. *I* don't know how. It just is."

He got the notepad, and got them all down. Twenty-six racehorses and three stocks and the ball team that was going to win the World Series. Then the phone clicked and the line went dead. Thoroughly dead; he could not even get the dial tone.

There were three horses on his list for the next day. They were all medium-long shots, and they all won. He had started with fifty dollars; he left the track in a kind of cold, glassy-eyed frenzy, with over seven thousand dollars in cash in his pockets. In his shirt pocket, over his heart, was the sheet of notepaper, his greatest gift in the world—a gift from himself.

During the next two months the horses all won at their different tracks and the stocks all split, shot up, declared unexpected dividends. By nosing out the wealthiest bookies at home, in Miami, and in four other cities, and by careful spreading of his bets, George was able to make himself a millionaire after the first five weeks. He won a quarter million on the World Series alone. It was on this last that a bookie who hadn't hedged his bets adequately against George's hundred-thousand-dollar lay-out was forced to offer him his own luxury fishing boat, anchored off Key West, as part payment. George, seeing the handwriting on the wall plainly enough, accepted with what was for him considerable graciousness. That is, he merely called the bookie a chiseling bastard, trimmed five thousand off the boat's evaluation, and took it.

He knew that it was somehow in the nature of things that he must be aboard a boat with a telephone on October ninth. He would be getting a phone call.

The ordaining of it all took no effort on his part. He was called a week later by the telephone company, who wished to know if he planned to continue the ship-to-shore service on the boat. He told them yes, and then, as if it were an afterthought, mentioned that he would like his old Miami number transferred to the boat—important friends would be calling. The number? BE-8-5883. Then, when he had bet the final horse on his list, betting the track odds down to the point of diminishing returns, phoning and nagging the nine remaining New York and Chicago bookies who would still take his bets, he hired a chauffeured limousine to take him to Key West. He did not go alone; with him were two attractive young ladies, a gambling friend, a large box of frozen prime steaks, and two cases of twenty-dollar-a-bottle whiskey. And a pile of newspapers.

It was during the ebullient stage of his drunkenness on this automobile ride, after he had tired of needling his friends, that a striking thought occurred to him: what if he decided not to go to the boat at all? His mind fogged at the thought. But how could he *not* be on that boat October ninth? He had, in a sense, already been there. That part of his future was a part of his past, and you couldn't change the past. But you could change the future, couldn't you? He could not understand it. He drank more whiskey and tried to forget about it; it wasn't important anyway. What was important was his twelve-hundred-dollar platinum wristwatch, his two-hundred-dollar shoes, his cashmere jacket, his bank accounts. He had come a long way in those two months. One of the girls, whose name was supposed to be Lili, snuggled up to him. He began playing with her and tried to forget about time paradoxes.

The boat looked to George like something out of a Man of Distinction ad; it was big, sleek, polished, and beautifully equipped. His heart swelled with something resembling pride when he surveyed its lines, standing drunkenly on the dock, with a disheveled Lili hanging on his arm. They went aboard, and Lili giggled, and whistled at the mahogany bar, the innerspring mattresses, the hi-fi, the impeccable little stainless steel galley. George, suddenly pensive, left Lili fixing drinks at the bar for the party and went into the boat's little air-conditioned cabin, to look around.

Somehow the sight of it shook him: sitting on a small table, next to a tan leather armchair, was a bright, glossy red telephone. He walked over to it slowly and read the number on the dial. The man from the company had been there, for it read MIAMI: BE-8-5883. Outside on the deck the girls were laughing now, and there was the sound of ice clinking in glasses. Someone called out drunkenly, "Come on out, Georgie, and have a *bon voyage.*" He didn't answer, still looking at the phone.

A pilot had been hired and he took them out that afternoon. They fished in a desultory way, too drunk and noisy to care. George drank continuously, bullied everyone loudly, made no attempt to fish. A restlessness, an impatience, was eating at him; in his mind telephones were ringing faintly all day. By sundown of the first day they were spent with liquor, sex, sunshine and quarreling. George passed out across the deck, near the one fish that Lili had, miraculously, caught: a small, wide-eyed bonito with a white, flabby belly. The last fleeting thought to enter his mind before he fell into smirking unconsciousness was *Why can't that lousy son of a bitch call me early? Why should I wait?* . . .

The ninth of October was overcast—cold and muggy—as was George's disposition. No one was any longer interested in fishing. The gambler slept; the girls kept to themselves on deck; and George shut himself up in the cabin, waiting for the phone to ring. He swore under his breath occasionally, but otherwise passed the morning in silence. He contemplated the luxury of his silk dressing gown, the brass and mahogany furnishings around him, the good, solid teakwood deck beneath his feet; and the thought of the virtually penniless and belligerent drunkard who was about to call him from a crumby little beach house in Miami. At his feet sat the pile of newspapers, opened to the sporting pages. He looked down at them now and swore. He was beginning to sweat.

Outside the cabin window the sky was dead white, hanging thickly over the cold green Atlantic horizon. They were ninety miles out from shore, the pilot had said. George continued drinking, angry now at himself—the other himself—for not having bothered to mention the time of day his call had been received. He had dialed the number at about two in the afternoon; but of course that didn't mean that two o'clock was the time it was received, two months later. He continued looking at his watch and at the telephone and at his watch again, drinking. Occasionally he would look out the window at the serenely violent ocean, ice green beneath the fishbelly sky, and curse.

And then, just before two o'clock, an idea struck him, a very simple idea: Why should *he* wait? He would make the call himself. He had never, in the two months since it had happened, tried dialing his own number again—why had he never thought of it? Why should he wait for that poor slob of a hungover George Bledsoe to call *him*—him with his private fishing boat and his twenty-dollar whiskey?

He picked up the phone angrily, with thick fingers, and began dialing: BE-8-5883. He was breathing heavily. After the last digit the phone began to buzz, ringing. He smiled sweatily and leaned back in his chair. Then there was a *click* and a voice answered. "Hello?"

He sat bolt upright in his chair. It was a woman's voice.

He hesitated and then said, "Hello." *Could he have dialed the wrong number?* "What number is this?"

The voice was that of an old woman, quavery but matter-of-fact. "This is BE-8-5883. Mrs. Arthur Cavanaugh talking."

"Oh." He took a quick sip from his drink. "Is . . . is George Bledsoe there?"

"No. No, he isn't." There seemed to be some hesitation in her voice. "Mr. Bledsoe hasn't lived in this house for some time."

Abruptly he felt relieved—he had probably only moved to a bigger home. About time, anyway. But why had he been frightened of this old bat on the phone?

The woman was saying querulously, "Are you a friend . . . of Mr. Bledsoe's?"

He laughed suddenly, coarsely. "That's right, lady. I'm a friend of Mr. Bledsoe's."

"Well, I don't know just how to tell you this," the woman said, "but a person would have thought you'd read about it in the papers. It was in all the papers. They found Mr. Bledsoe's body, stark naked, a hundred miles out in the Gulf. It was about two months ago they found him, and the thing is there's nobody yet knows how he got out there."

He sat silent for what seemed a very long time. There was a faint clicking in the phone, but he ignored this. The woman must be mistaken. An old fool. A bitch. Although the cabin was tightly closed, he felt the distinct sensation of a cold wind blowing on the back of his neck. Shaking himself, he gathered his voice together. The woman was a lying bitch. "How George Bledsoe got out there, lady, was in his private boat," he said, more to himself than to her. "The same way he's gonna get back to shore. In his private boat."

The wind on the back of his neck was stronger now, and he was shivering. The wind seemed to be penetrating his clothes, even, blowing through his dressing gown, through the tailored silk shirt beneath it. Dimly, as if from a great and dreadful distance, he heard the old woman's voice saying, "Why, Mr. Bledsoe never had a boat, Lord forbid. Mr. Bledsoe was a poor man . . ."

Abruptly he leaned forward, shouting, *"No.* No, you rotten bitch!" and he slammed the phone back in its cradle. It was cold in the room. He was shivering. There was a bright, grayish light in the cabin, getting brighter. He grabbed the phone again, shaking, and dialed *O,* for the operator. The dial felt soft to his finger, squashy.

The operator's voice came, faint. "Ship-to-shore service."

His voice was hoarse, strange in his ears. "This is Bledsoe. BE-8-5883. Is there a call for me?"

"No, sir. Or, yes, there was a call."

"From who?" It took an effort to keep from shouting—or screaming.

"Just a moment." And then, "That's odd, sir; it must be an error. I have the number calling listed as BE-8-5883. And that's your number, sir."

"My God, I know. Put the call through."

Her voice was fainter, fading away from him. "I'm sorry, you'll have to wait until the party calls again. When he called, a few moments ago, the line was busy . . ." The last words were so faint that he could hardly hear them. He was screaming when she finished, *"Put the call through, God damn it, put the call through."*

From the receiver her voice was the minute thread of a

whisper, but he heard it plainly. "I'm sorry sir, the line was busy."

And then the phone went altogether dead.

Then, after sitting for a moment with his eyes shut against the impossible white daylight in the closed cabin, his body huddled against the cold wind that was blowing through the bulkheads of the rich man's boat that he could not possibly have been in, blowing coldly against his body through the rich man's clothes that he, George Bledsoe, could not possibly have afforded, he took a deep breath and opened his eyes, looking down.

Below him, through the fading, now translucent teakwood deck, he could see the flat, ice-green water of the Atlantic Ocean, ninety miles from shore.

THE BIG BOUNCE

"Let me show you something," Farnsworth said. He set his near-empty drink—a Bacardi martini—on the mantel and waddled out of the room toward the basement.

I sat in my big leather chair, feeling very peaceful with the world, watching the fire. Whatever Farnsworth would have to show tonight would be far more entertaining than watching TV—my custom on other evenings. Farnsworth, with his four labs in the house and his very tricky mind, never failed to provide my best night of the week.

When he returned, after a moment, he had with him a small box, about three inches square. He held this carefully in one hand and stood by the fireplace dramatically—or as dramatically as a very small, very fat man with pink cheeks can stand by a fireplace of the sort that seems to demand a big man with tweeds, pipe and, perhaps, a saber wound.

Anyway, he held the box dramatically and he said, "Last week, I was playing around in the chem lab, trying to make a new kind of rubber eraser. Did quite well with the other drafting equipment, you know, especially the dimensional curve and the photosensitive ink. Well, I approached the job by trying for a material that would absorb graphite without abrading paper."

I was a little disappointed with this; it sounded pretty tame. But I said, "How did it come out?"

He screwed his pudgy face up thoughtfully. "Synthesized the material, all right, and it seems to work, but the interesting thing is that it has a certain—ah—secondary property that would make it quite awkward to use. Interesting property, though. Unique, I am inclined to believe."

This began to sound more like it. "And what property is that?" I poured myself a shot of straight rum from the bottle sitting on the table beside me. I did not like straight rum, but I preferred it to Farnsworth's imaginative cocktails.

"I'll show you, John," he said. He opened the box and I could see that it was packed with some kind of batting. He fished in this and withdrew a gray ball about the size of a golf ball and set the box on the mantel.

"And that's the—eraser?" I asked.

"Yes," he said. Then he squatted down, held the ball about a half-inch from the floor, and dropped it.

It bounced, naturally enough. Then it bounced again. And again. Only this was not natural, for on the second bounce the ball went higher in the air than on the first, and on the third bounce higher still. After a half minute, my eyes were bugging out and the little ball was bouncing four feet in the air and going higher each time.

I grabbed my glass. "What the hell!" I said.

Farnsworth caught the ball in a pudgy hand and held it. He was smiling a little sheepishly. "Interesting effect, isn't it?"

"Now wait a minute," I said, beginning to think about it. "What's the gimmick? What kind of motor do you have in that thing?"

His eyes were wide and a little hurt. "No gimmick, John. None at all. Just a very peculiar molecular structure."

"Structure!" I said. "Bouncing balls just don't pick up energy out of nowhere, I don't care how their molecules are put together. And you don't get energy out without putting energy in."

"Oh," he said, "that's the really interesting thing. Of course you're right; energy *does* go into the ball. Here, I'll show you."

He let the ball drop again and it began bouncing, higher and higher, until it was hitting the ceiling. Farnsworth reached out to catch it, but he fumbled and the thing glanced off his hand, hit the mantelpiece and zipped across the room. It banged into the far wall, ricocheted, banked off three other walls, picking up speed all the time.

When it whizzed by me like a rifle bullet, I began to get worried, but it hit against one of the heavy draperies by the window and this damped its motion enough so that it fell to the floor.

It started bouncing again immediately, but Farnsworth scrambled across the room and grabbed it. He was perspiring a little and he began instantly to transfer the ball from one hand to another and back again as if it were hot.

"Here," he said, and handed it to me.

I almost dropped it.

"It's like a ball of ice!" I said. "Have you been keeping it in the refrigerator?"

"No. As a matter of fact, it was at room temperature a few minutes ago."

"Now wait a minute," I said. "I only teach physics in high school, but I know better than that. Moving around in warm air doesn't make anything cold except by evaporation."

"Well, there's your input and output, John," he said. "The ball lost heat and took on motion. Simple conversion."

My jaw must have dropped to my waist. "Do mean that that little thing is converting heat to kinetic energy?"

"Apparently."

"But that's impossible!"

He was beginning to smile thoughtfully. The ball was not as cold now as it had been and I was holding it in my lap.

"A steam engine does it," he said, "and a steam turbine. Of course, they're not very efficient."

"They work mechanically, too, and only because water expands when it turns to steam."

"This seems to do it differently," he said, sipping thoughtfully at his dark-brown martini. "I don't know exactly how—maybe something piezo-electric about the way its molecules slide about. I ran some tests—measured its impact energy in foot pounds and compared that with the heat loss in BTUs. Seemed to be about 98 percent efficient, as close as I could tell. Apparently it converts heat into bounce very well. Interesting, isn't it?"

"*Interesting?*" I almost came flying out of my chair. My mind was beginning to spin like crazy. "If you're not pulling my leg with this thing, Farnsworth, you've got something by the tail there that's just a little bit bigger than the discovery of fire."

He blushed modestly. "I'd rather thought that myself," he admitted.

"Good Lord, look at the heat that's available!" I said, getting really excited now.

Farnsworth was still smiling, very pleased with himself. "I suppose you could put this thing in a box, with convection fins, and let it bounce around inside—"

"I'm way ahead of you," I said. "But that wouldn't work. All your kinetic energy would go right back to heat, on impact—and eventually that little ball would build up enough speed to blast its way through any box you could build."

"Then how would you work it?"

"Well," I said, choking down the rest of my rum, "you'd seal the ball in a big steel cylinder, attach the cylinder to a crankshaft and flywheel, give the thing a shake to start the ball bouncing back and forth, and let it run like a gasoline engine or something. It would get all the heat it needed from the air in a normal room. Mount the apparatus in your house and it would pump your water, operate a generator and keep you cool at the same time!"

I sat down again, shakily, and began pouring myself another drink.

Farnsworth had taken the ball from me and was carefully putting it back in its padded box. He was visibly showing excitement, too; I could see that his cheeks were ruddier and his eyes even brighter than normal. "But what if you want the cooling and don't have any work to be done?"

"Simple," I said. "You just let the machine turn a flywheel or lift weights and drop them, or something like that, outside your house. You have an air intake inside. And if, in the winter, you don't want to lose heat, you just mount the thing in an outside building, attach it to your generator and use the power to do whatever you want—heat your house, say. There's plenty of heat in the outside air even in December."

"John," said Farnsworth, "you are very ingenious. It might work."

"Of course it'll work." Pictures were beginning to light up in my head. "And don't you realize that this is the answer to the solar power problem? Why, mirrors and selenium are, at best, ten percent efficient! Think of big pumping stations on the Sahara! All that heat, all that need for power, for irrigation!" I paused a moment for effect. "Farnsworth, this can change the very shape of the earth!"

Farnsworth seemed to be lost in thought. Finally he looked at me strangely and said, "Perhaps we had better try to build a model."

I was so excited by the thing that I couldn't sleep that night. I kept dreaming of power stations, ocean liners, even automobiles, being operated by balls bouncing back and forth in cylinders.

I even worked out a spaceship in my mind, a bullet-shaped

affair with a huge rubber ball on its end, gyroscopes to keep it oriented properly, the ball serving as solution to that biggest of missile-engineering problems, excess heat. You'd build a huge concrete launching field, supported all the way down to bedrock, hop in the ship and start bouncing. Of course it would be kind of a rough ride . . .

In the morning, I called my superintendent and told him to get a substitute for the rest of the week; I was going to be busy.

Then I started working in the machine shop in Farnsworth's basement, trying to turn out a working model of a device that, by means of a crankshaft, oleo dampers and a reciprocating cylinder, would pick up some of that random kinetic energy from the bouncing ball and do something useful with it, like turning a drive shaft. I was just working out a convection-and-air-pump system for circulating hot air around the ball when Farnsworth came in.

He had a sphere of about the size of a basketball and, if he had made it to my specifications, weighing thirty-five pounds. He had a worried frown on his forehead.

"It looks good," I said. "What's the trouble?"

"There seems to be a slight hitch," he said. "I've been testing for conductivity. It seems to be quite low."

"That's what I'm working on now. It's just a mechanical problem of pumping enough warm air back to the ball. We can do it with no more than a twenty percent efficiency loss. In an engine, that's nothing."

"Maybe you're right. But this material conducts heat even less than rubber does."

"The little ball yesterday didn't seem to have any trouble," I said.

"Naturally not. It had had plenty of time to warm up before I started it. And its mass-surface area relationship was pretty low—the larger you make a sphere, of course, the more mass inside in proportion to the outside area."

"You're right, but I think we can whip it. We may have to honeycomb the ball and have the machine operate a hot-air pump; but we can work it out."

All that day, I worked with lathe, milling machine and hacksaw. After clamping the new big ball securely to a workbench, Farnsworth pitched in to help me. But we weren't able to finish by nightfall and Farnsworth turned his spare bedroom over to me for the night. I was too tired to go home.

And too tired to sleep soundly, too. Farnsworth lived on the edge of San Francisco, by a big truck bypass, and almost all night I wrestled with the pillow and sheets, listening half-consciously to those heavy trucks rumbling by, and in my mind, always, that little gray ball, bouncing and bouncing and bouncing . . .

At daybreak, I abruptly came fully awake with the sound of crashing echoing in my ears, a battering sound that seemed to come from the basement. I grabbed my shirt and pants, rushed out of the room, almost knocked over Farnsworth, who was struggling to get his shoes on out in the hall, and we scrambled down the two flights of stairs together.

The place was a chaos, battered and bashed equipment everywhere, and on the floor, overturned against the far wall, the table that the ball had been clamped to. The ball itself was gone.

I had not been fully asleep all night, and the sight of that mess, and what it meant, jolted me immediately awake. Something, probably a heavy truck, had started a tiny oscillation in that ball. And the ball had been heavy enough to start the table bouncing with it until, by dancing that table around the room, it had literally torn the clamp off and shaken itself free. What had happened afterward was obvious, with the ball building up velocity with every successive bounce.

But where was the ball now?

Suddenly Farnsworth cried out hoarsely, "Look!" and I followed his outstretched, pudgy finger to where, at one side of the basement, a window had been broken open—a small window, but plenty big enough for something the size of a basketball to crash through it.

There was a little weak light coming from outdoors. And then I saw the ball. It was in Farnsworth's backyard, bouncing a little sluggishly on the grass. The grass would damp it, hold it back, until we could get to it. Unless . . .

I took off up the basement steps like a streak. Just beyond the backyard, I had caught a glimpse of something that frightened me. A few yards from where I had seen the ball was the edge of the big six-lane highway, a broad ribbon of smooth, hard concrete.

I got through the house to the back porch, rushed out and was in the backyard just in time to see the ball take its first bounce onto the concrete. I watched it, fascinated, when it hit —after the soft, energy-absorbing turf, the concrete was like a springboard. Immediately the ball flew high in the air. I was running across the yard toward it, praying under my breath, *Fall on that grass next time.*

It hit before I got to it, and right on the concrete again, and this time I saw it go straight up at least fifty feet.

My mind was suddenly full of thoughts of dragging mattresses from the house, or making a net or something to stop that hurtling thirty-five pounds; but I stood where I was, unable to move, and saw it come down again on the highway. It went up a hundred feet. And down again on the concrete, about fifteen feet further down the road. In the direction of the city.

That time it was two hundred feet, and when it hit again, it made a thud that you could have heard for a quarter of a mile. I could practically see it flatten out on the road before it took off upward again, at twice the speed it had hit at.

Suddenly generating an idea, I whirled and ran back to Farnsworth's house. He was standing in the yard now, shivering from the morning air, looking at me like a little lost and badly scared child.

"Where are your car keys?" I shouted at him.

"In my pocket."

"Come on!"

I took him by the arm and half dragged him to the carport. I got the keys from him, started the car, and by mangling about seven traffic laws and three rosebushes, managed to get on the highway, facing in the direction that the ball was heading.

"Look," I said, trying to drive down the road and search for the ball at the same time. "It's risky, but if I can get the car under it and we can hop out in time, it should crash through the roof. That ought to slow it down enough for us to nab it."

"But—what about my car?" Farnsworth bleated.

"What about that first building—or first person—it hits in San Francisco?"

"Oh," he said. "Hadn't thought of that."

I slowed the car and stuck my head out the window. It was ligher now, but no sign of the ball. "If it happens to get to town—any town, for that matter—it'll be falling from about ten or twenty miles. Or forty."

"Maybe it'll go high enough first so that it'll burn. Like a meteor."

"No chance," I said. "Built-in cooling system, remember?"

Farnsworth formed his mouth into an "Oh" and exactly at that moment there was a resounding *thump* and I saw the ball hit in a field, maybe twenty yards from the edge of the road, and take off again. This time it didn't seem to double its velocity, and I figured the ground was soft enough to hold it back—but it wasn't slowing down either, not with a bounce factor of better than two to one.

Without watching for it to go up, I drove as quickly as I could off the road and over—carrying part of a wire fence with me

—to where it had hit. There was no mistaking it; there was a depression about three feet deep, like a small crater.

I jumped out of the car and stared up. It took me a few seconds to spot it, over my head. One side caught by the pale and slanting morning sunlight, it was only a bright diminishing speck.

The car motor was running and I waited until the ball disappeared for a moment and then reappeared. I watched for another couple of seconds until I felt I could make a decent guess on its direction, shouted at Farnsworth to get out of the car—it had just occurred to me that there was no use risking his life, too—dove in and drove a hundred yards or so to the spot I had anticipated.

I stuck my head out the window and up. The ball was the size of an egg now. I adjusted the car's position, jumped out and ran for my life.

It hit instantly after—about sixty feet from the car. And at the same time, it occurred to me that what I was trying to do was completely impossible. Better to hope that the ball hit a pond, or bounced out to sea, or landed in a sand dune. All we could do would be to follow, and if it ever was damped down enough, grab it.

It had hit soft ground and didn't double its height that time, but it had still gone higher. It was out of sight for almost a lifelong minute.

And then—incredibly rotten luck—it came down, with an ear-shattering thwack, on the concrete highway again. I had seen it hit, and instantly afterward I saw a crack as wide as a finger open along the entire width of the road. And the ball had flown back up like a rocket.

My God, I was thinking, *now it means business. And on the next bounce* . . .

It seemed like an incredibly long time that we craned our necks, Farnsworth and I, watching for it to reappear in the sky. And when it finally did, we could hardly follow it. It whistled like a bomb and we saw the gray streak come plummeting to earth almost a quarter of a mile away from where we were standing.

But we didn't see it go back up again.

For a moment, we stared at each other silently. Then Farnsworth almost whispered, "Perhaps it's landed in a pond."

"Or in the world's biggest cowpile," I said. "Come on!"

We could have met our deaths by rock salt and buckshot that night, if the farmer who owned that field had been home. We tore up everything we came to getting across it—including cabbages and rhubarb. But we had to search for ten minutes, and even then we didn't find the ball.

What we found was a hole in the ground that could have been a small-scale meteor crater. It was a good twenty feet deep. But at the bottom, no ball.

I stared wildly at it for a full minute before I focused my eyes enough to see, at the bottom, a thousand little gray fragments.

And immediately it came to both of us at the same time. A poor conductor, the ball had used up all its available heat on that final impact. Like a golf ball that has been dipped in liquid air and dropped, it had smashed into thin splinters.

The hole had sloping sides and I scrambled down in it and picked up one of the pieces, using my handkerchief, folded— there was no telling just how cold it would be.

It was the stuff, all right. And colder than an icicle.

I climbed out. "Let's go home," I said.

Farnsworth looked at me thoughtfully. Then he sort of cocked his head to one side and asked, "What do you suppose will happen when those pieces thaw?"

I stared at him. I began to think of a thousand tiny slivers whizzing around erratically, ricocheting off buildings, in downtown San Francisco and in twenty counties, and no matter what they hit, moving and accelerating as long as there was any heat in the air to give them energy.

And then I saw a tool shed, on the other side of the pasture from us.

But Farnsworth was ahead of me, waddling along, puffing. He got the shovels out and handed one to me.

We didn't say a word, neither of us, for hours. It takes a long time to fill a hole twenty feet deep—especially when you're shoveling very, very carefully and packing down the dirt very, very hard.

THE GOLDBRICK

Two army engineers found it while drilling a hole through one of the Appalachian Mountains, in the Primitive Reservation, on a lovely spring day in 1993. The hole was to be used for a monorail track; and although in 1993 it was very simple to run monorail lines *over* mountains, it was also quite easy to drill large, straight holes through almost anything; and the U. S. Army liked to effect the neatness of straight lines. So the engineers had set up a little converter machine on a tripod, pointed it, and proceeded to convert a singularly neat hole, twenty-two feet in diameter, in the side of the mountain. At first the mountain converted nicely, the hole tunneling along at an efficient thirteen feet per hour; and the engineers, whose names were George and Sam, were quite pleased with themselves and rubbed their hands together with pleasure; while the little machine on the tripod hummed merrily, birds sang, and wisps of brown smoke floated off from the mountain into an otherwise clear blue sky.

And then they found it. Or, rather, the converter did, by abruptly ceasing to convert. The machine continued to hum; but the little feedback-controlled counter, which normally clicked off the number of tons of material substance that had been converted into immaterial substance, stopped. The last wisps of smoke disappeared from the mountainside. The two engineers looked at one another. After a minute George picked a rock up from the ground, a large one, and threw it out in front of the lens of the machine. The rock vanished instantly. The one-tenth ton counter wheel trembled, and was still.

"Well," Sam said, after a minute. "It's still working."

George thought about this for a minute. Then he said, "I guess we'd better look at the tunnel."

So they shut the machine off, walked over to the hole in the mountainside and went in. Fortunately the sun was behind them and they had no difficulty seeing as they made their way down the glassy-smooth shaft—which needed no shoring since the converter had been set to convert part of the materials removed into a quite sturdy lining of neo-adamant. The shaft ended in a forbidding, twenty-two foot, black disk of unconverted mountain bowels. The two of them peered uneasily at this for a few minutes and then Sam said, "What's this?" and kneeled down to inspect a rectangle, gold in color, about ten inches long and four high, which appeared to be engraved in the rock at the dead end of the tunnel.

"Let me see," George said, stooping beside his co-scientist and pulling from his pocket a pocketknife, with which he proceeded to scrape around the edges of the rectangle. Some of the loose rock crumbled away, revealing that the rectangle was, actually, one surface of a solid bar of some sort.

He continued to scrape for a few minutes, removing enough rock to get a grip on the sides of the bar with his fingers, took a good hold and began to try to work the bar loose. The other engineer helped him, and they pulled, strained, wedged and pushed for about ten minutes, until finally George said, "It won't move," and they stopped, perspiring. And it hadn't moved, not a millimeter.

The two of them glared, for a moment, at the smooth surface of the golden bar, which shone, lustrous, back at them. Then Sam said, "Let's get a pick."

"A pick?"

Sam, who knew something of Army history, was patronizing. "Yes. A kind of manual-powered converter."

George was impressed. "But where?" he said.

"At U-10 Supply."

They left the uncompleted tunnel, stepped into their Minnijet, field model, officer-type helicopter and flew at a leisurely five hundred miles per hour to U-10. U-10 had been, before the 1980s Decade of Enlightenment, the University of Tennessee—the 1980s had held no illusions about what was important to the American Way of Life—and they landed their little olive-drab plastic craft in front of the library. Inside, the librarian, a young sergeant, was put into something of a tizzy at their request for a pick, and explained to them that the library shelves held only *weapons* of the past, and, as far as he knew, there was no such weapon as a *pick*. He sent them to the captain.

The captain knew what a pick was, all right; but when the two engineers told him what it was for he called the major. The major was a tall, athletic officer with wavy hair, a very neat mustache, a firm, undaunted jaw, and clear eyes that looked squarely into the future. He smoked a pipe, of course, and was wearing a natty black field uniform with regulation crimson cummerbund and beret. His voice was friendly but there was a "no-nonsense" tone in it. "What's the deal, men?" he said out of the side of his mouth, the other side being engaged in biting, squarely, on his pipestem.

They told him about the gold bar.

"Interesting," he said. "Let's have a look-see." And he sent for a pick, a heavy-duty converter, a portable lighting system, two quarts of synthetic scotch and three privates. All of these were stowed away in a staff helicopter and then the three officers—the two engineers and the major—flew to the mountains. This being a staff helicopter, the trip took three and one-half minutes.

At the mountain, two of the privates set up the portable lighting system in the tunnel while the other studied the manual that had come with the pick. The major was first charmed, and then somewhat piqued, by the bar, after trying to prod it loose with his pipestem. The private with the pick was called, and after some difficulty with determining the proper stance and grip for swinging that instrument—the private was a recent recruit of only fourteen and naturally knew nothing whatever about manual converters of any sort—a few desultory swings were taken at the granite surrounding the bar. After a while the other two privates joined in, alternating in swinging the pick, until, finally, a rough area of about two or three square feet had been hollowed out around the bar, which was found at that time to extend only about four inches back into the mountain. Above the bar they noticed a sort of fissure, like a cicatrice, in the granite; and one of the privates remarked that it looked like the mountain either had been split open to admit the bar from the top, or that, maybe, the bar had just been there and the mountain had grown up around it.

It was impossible to cut away the rock on the other side, so the three privates got a strong grip on the bar and began to pull. Then the officers began to pull on the privates. The bar stayed where it was. They pulled harder. The bar stayed. The major took off his cummerbund and beret and began to sweat. The bar didn't move. The major began to curse, pushed the others aside, grabbed the pick handle, gave a mighty heave, and hit the bar solidly with the point. There was no sound from the impact, and the pick did not rebound, nor did the bar move. The major tried again. And again. Then they knelt and looked at the bar. It still gleamed. No scars.

The major swore for five minutes. Then he said, "Who owns this mountain?"

George spoke up, "The Army, sir. Of course."

"Good," said the major, beginning to look undaunted again. "We'll get at that son of a bitch."

"How, sir?"

"We'll convert this goddamn mountain, that's how." The major began wrapping his cummerbund back around his waist.

"The whole *mountain?*" Sam said, aghast.

"Level it." The major dusted off his beret and replaced it.

Sam spoke up querulously, "But wouldn't that be . . . ah . . . misusing our natural resources, sir?"

"Nonsense." This mountain belongs to the Army. It's not a natural resource. As a matter of fact, it's an eyesore. I order you to vaporize it."

So they vaporized the mountain. Since the converter could not cut through the bar they set it up—the heavy-duty one—to shear off the top of the mountain. Then they moved the machine around to each of the four sides and sliced them off. Their instruments were very accurate, and when the last wisp of smoke had drifted away there stood in the middle of a plain so smooth billiards could have been played on it, sitting on a neat, rectangular column of granite, four feet high, what was now plainly seen as a shiny, gold colored brick, its sides glittering in the evening sun.

The major picked up the pick and walked slowly over to the column. There was a slight, almost unnoticeable swagger in his walk. He hefted the pick slowly, carefully, braced himself, and took aim. "All right, you son of a bitch," he said, and then gave the pick a magnificent swing.

The brick didn't move.

The major stood where he was, looking at the brick, for about three minutes. Then he said, softly, "All right. *All right!*"

He walked back to the converter—which was sitting on its tripod nearby—and began to adjust its aim and elevation and set its dials, all very carefully. When he was ready he stood behind it, his feet planted firmly, his fists clenched, his lower jaw firm and jutting, his eyes squarely ahead, focused on the brick.

"*Now!*" he said, and pressed the switch. There was a small hum and a tiny puff of smoke and the little column of granite disappeared. The brick was now unsupported and the major watched it, his eyes now betraying an intense gleam, waiting for it to fall to the earth. The major waited.

The brick stayed exactly where it was, four feet above the ground, completely unsupported.

It took the major a few minutes to realize that there was no use in waiting. He said nothing, however; but stepped over to the brick, looked at it a minute, and then reached casually over to it and pushed it, with his index finger. It didn't move. Then the major sat down on the ground and began to cry, very softly, as the sun sank in the west.

That, of course, was only the beginning of it. Within two weeks the little plain that had once been a mountain was covered with multicolored plastic Quonset huts through which moved so many people of such world-shaking importance that four gossip columnists had to be flown in from New York and Los Angeles to handle the overflow. Generals and admirals abounded, offering careful and profound opinions freely; slim, dark, intense young men with impeccable dark civilian suits and carrying dark attaché cases held hurried, *sotto voce* conferences; reporters did Profiles of everybody. The weather held fair, the neighborhood abounded in divers kinds of nature: birdsong and waterfall, poplar and mountain daisy, which most of the visitors found quaint and novel, and a good time was being had by all.

In the midst of this activity floated the still shiny golden brick, unperturbed, apparently as oblivious of the melee it had attracted as it was of the immutable laws governing the motion of masses: the laws of inertia and reaction, and the law of universal gravitation.

Some interesting things had been discovered about the brick. It was, for instance, completely impervious to any known form of radiant energy; it neither absorbed nor radiated heat; electron microscopes found its surface, on the atomic level, still smooth, metallic and shiny, without gaps; it apparently had no molecular—or, even, atomic—structure to speak of; it would conduct neither electricity, heat, nor anything else; and it obeyed no physical laws whatever. Thus far nine neo-adamant points, sharpened to submicroscopic pointedness and under pressures ranging up to three hundred fifty thousand tons, had failed to make any scratches in its surface; and all had eventually cracked.

The major had recovered most of his old poise and undauntedness, although his eyes now seemed to face the future with some hint of trepidation, and he was assigned to Operation Gold Brick—as the Army had cleverly named it—in an advisory capacity. In fact it was he who gave voice to a notion that had been whispered about for several days. After the ninth neo-adamant point had split against the surface of the brick it was he who marched to the orange Quonset of General Pomeroy and said, "Sir, let's try an H-bomb."

So they H-bombed it.

There was some confusion during the four days while the crater was being filled in; but after that was done and new Quonsets were built the Operation was even more pleasant and roomy, since nine more mountains had been leveled by the bomb, and about twenty others had been fused into interesting colors and shapes. The birds and trees and suchlike had, of course, been obliterated; but they had been beginning to pall on the visitors anyway; and now the area had something of the look of a neo-Surrealist landscape, or a Japanese garden. The radiation had, of course, been absorbed by the usual means.

The brick stayed right where it was, its surface parallel to the horizon, poised, immediately after the blast, over a crater two hundred and ninety-four feet deep.

After the failure of the H-bomb the generals' pique and frustration began to turn to anger and, in some cases, fear. One pacifistic lieutenant general did in fact suggest that the brick be left alone and the monorail rerouted; but it was to the credit of the Army that his superiors rallied together and denounced his defeatism for what it was. But the generals did agree at this conference to call in a theoretical physicist, provided one could be found, in a desperate hope that some light might be thrown on the nature of their adversary.

A call was sent out to headquarters at Big-H (once Harvard University) and a two-day scramble ensued while a theory man—or "egghead" as such men were cleverly called —was sought. One was eventually found, working in a weather observatory in the Kentucky Reservation, and he was brought—a gray-haired old fellow who freely admitted that he read books and refused to drink synthetic whiskey—to the site of the brick, which he surveyed with some attention.

"Well?" said one of the generals.

"Very interesting," said the theoretical physicist, whose name was Albert, and he produced from a trunk he had brought with him a collection of peculiar-looking instruments, which he began to set up on the ground. After peering down various tripod-mounted tubes, first at the brick and then at the sun, he then said, "Amazing!"

"Yes," said one of the generals. "We know that." There was a ring of generals in brilliant tunics and of security men in black flannel suits around the physicist.

"Amazing," he said again. "This seems to be the exact set point of Propkofski's principle!" He gazed at the brick reverently.

"*Whose* principle?" said one of the security men, raising his eyebrows and fetching a little black book from his breast pocket.

"Propkofski." The physicist's eyes were aglow. The security men were raising eyebrows at one another. "The principle of terrestrial orbital space-time suspension, formulated in 1987, I believe. This is the place, gentlemen, the *exact* point, where Propkofski maintained that the mass-influx lines of the Earth's field intersected. This is the very hub, provided that Propkofski was right," and he pointed to the brick. "Yet I believe that Propkofski said something about a mountain hindering his observations."

"Yes?" said the general. "We removed the mountain."

"My!" said the old physicist, looking up from the brick for the first time, "How did you do that? With faith?"

"With a converter," the general said. "But what about that brick? How do we move it?"

"The brick? Oh." The scientist went to the floating piece of golden metal, still unmarred by the H-bomb, and examined it carefully. When he had finished checking it with a good many instruments, mechanical and electronic, he said, "I wish Newton could see this."

The security man's eyebrows went up again. "Newton?"

The old man smiled at him, "Another physicist," he said. "Dead."

"Oh," said the security man. "Sorry."

"So," said the general, impatiently. "How do we move it?"

The old man looked at him a moment. "I suggest you don't."

"Thank you," said the general, crisply. "Then how would you say it *might* be moved?"

The physicist scratched his head, "Well," he said, "I suppose the Earth might be pushed away from it, since it seems to be a kind of Archimedes' fulcrum. A pressure of about seventeen trillion tons per square centimeter might accomplish that. Of course, moving the Earth might alter the length of the year considerably. And then, again, if Propkofski's principle, which states . . ."

"Thank you," said the general. "That will be all."

After the security men had taken the physicist away for investigation the general who had interviewed him looked at another general and then at the others. He could tell they were all having the same wild surmise. Finally, he said, "Well, why not?"

"Ah . . ." said one of the others.

"The cold war's been going on for fifty years. We may never get a chance to try it out."

"Ah . . . well . . ."

One of the other, younger generals could not contain himself and abruptly spoke up. "Let's use it!" he said, his voice quivering with emotion.

And all the rest of them began to chime in, their eagerness, now that one of their number had committed himself, unrepressed. "Let's use it!" they said. "Let's use the R-bomb!"

First a pit was dug—or converted—a mile and a half deep and three miles in diameter. This was then filled with neoadamant except for a hole in the center four by ten inches rectangular, directly under the brick. Then the R-bomb and its electronic detonator, the whole thing about the size and color of an avocado, was lowered into the hole, and then the neoadamant walls were built up six feet above the ground to enclose the brick in what amounted to the barrel of a monstrous cannon. The states of Virginia, West Virginia, Ohio and half of Kentucky were then evacuated, and a final check was made of the figures. It was determined that the kickback from the blast would throw the Earth approximately four hundred and ten miles out of her orbit, and shorten the length of the year to three hundred and sixty-three days, a number which all of the generals found to be eminently satisfactory, in fact, a decided improvement.

The generals decided to use the old physicist's weather station, in the Kentucky Reservation, as their observation point, its elevation and its distance from the brick being quite desirable.

The station was raised on a tripod to a height of one thousand feet, and the Army had the whole structure properly reinforced and shielded. Then the equipment for observation, the TV monitoring screens and the electron telescopes, was set up and the generals moved in. The old physicist had by this time taken a loyalty oath and he was allowed to remain in the observation dome for the event since, after all, he worked there.

At zero hour minus sixty seconds the senior general carefully pressed a small red button and unwittingly echoed the words of a forgotten subordinate. "We'll blast the son of a bitch sky high," he said. Flashbulbs popped. A counter began ticking off the seconds, loudly, efficiently. All eyes were on the large TV screen, which showed the huge circle of white neo-adamant four hundred miles away. The TV picture was being beamed from a satellite eighty miles above the location of the brick; they would be able to see the actual blast before the camera was destroyed. The physicist busied himself with his own instruments, making readings of the sun's position. The seconds ticked off.

At the sixtieth tick the counter became silent. There was no sound in the little observation tower. The white circle on the screen was unchanged. Then, suddenly, the screen erupted. In a burst of flame and steam the neo-adamant circle began to crumble. Flames shot up everywhere. Mountains seen at the edge of the screen began to sizzle and ooze out of shape. It was at this moment that the states of Virginia, West Virginia and Ohio were obliterated. Then, abruptly, the picture changed. A specially controlled monitoring camera had picked up a flash of gold. The brick. It appeared to be flying through the air.

"By God," said the senior general. "We did it!"

At this moment the screen went black. There was a roar, a rumble, starting from what seemed to be the very bowels of the Earth, building to a dynamic, deep-buried scream, a screeching of wrenched rock and of the tearing of the Earth's crust; and then a sickening lurch, a nauseous dip and lunge of sideward motion, a sense of acceleration; and then a howling sound, the howling of a sudden, tremendous wind. The generals were all thrown to the floor, trembling.

Somehow the physicist had remained standing, holding the sides of the table on which his instruments were mounted. His old hands were white with the strain and were trembling, but his face was ecstatic. "Amazing!" he said. "Amazing!" His eyes were shining.

"What happened?" one of the generals said weakly, from the floor.

"Propkofski! Propkofski was right!" said the other, his voice jubilant, shaking with emotion. "That *was* the intersection of the mass-influx lines. The brick, the gold brick, was the keystone, the hub! It held the Earth up."

"What," said the general, shouting above the roar of the wind that was now like a cyclone, above the screeching of twisted rock and the wrenching of the very bowels of the Earth. "What does that *mean?*"

"It means that Propkofski must have been right!" said the other, his voice quivering. "The Earth, it seems, is falling into the sun!"

THE IFTH OF OOFTH

Farnsworth had invented a new drink that night. He called it a mulled sloe gin toddy. Exactly as fantastic as it sounds—ramming a red-hot poker into a mugful of warm red gin, cinnamon, cloves and sugar, and then *drinking* the fool thing—but like many of Farnsworth's ideas, it managed somehow to work out. In fact, its flavor had become completely acceptable to me after the third one.

When he finally set the end of his steaming poker back on the coals for regeneration, I leaned back in my big leather chair—the one he had rigged up so that it would gently rock you to sleep if you pressed the right button—and said, "Oliver, your ingenuity is matched only by your hospitality."

Farnsworth blushed and smiled. He is a small, chubby man and blushes easily. "Thank you," he said. "I have another new one. I call it a jelled vodka fizz—you eat it with a spoon. You may want to try it later. It's—well—exceptional."

I suppressed a shudder at the thought of eating jelled vodka and said, "Interesting, very interesting," and since he didn't reply, we both stared at the fire for a while, letting the gin continue its pleasant work. Farnsworth's bachelor home was very comfortable and relaxing, and I always enjoyed my Wednesday night visits there thoroughly. I suppose most men have a deep-seated love for open fires and liquor—however fantastically prepared—and leather armchairs.

Then, after several minutes, Farnsworth bounced to his feet

and said, "There's a thing I wanted to show you. Made it last week. Didn't pull it off too well, though."

"Really?" I said. I'd thought the drinks had been his weekly brainchild. They seemed quite enough.

"Yes," he said, trotting over to the door of the study. "It's downstairs in the shop. I'll get it." And he bounced out of the room, the paneled door closing as it had opened, automatically, behind him.

I turned back to the fire again, pleased that he had made something in the machine shop—the carpentry shop was in a shed in the backyard; the chemistry and optical labs in the attic—for he was at his best with his lathe and milling machines. His self-setting, variable-twist thumb bolt had been a beautiful piece of work and its patent had made him a lot of money.

He returned in a minute, carrying a very odd-looking thing with him, and set it on the table beside my chair. I examined it for a minute while Farnsworth stood over me, half smiling, his little green eyes wide, sparkling in the flickering light from the fire. I knew he was suppressing his eagerness for my comment, but I was unsure what to say.

The thing appeared simple: a cross-shaped construction of several dozen one-inch cubes, half of them of thin, transparent plastic, the other half made of thin little sheets of aluminum. Each cube was hinged to two others very cunningly and the arrangement of them all was confusing.

Finally, I said, "How many cubes?" I had tried to count them, but kept getting lost.

"Sixty-four," he said. "I think."

"You *think?*"

"Well—" He seemed embarrassed. "At least I *made* sixty-four cubes, thirty-two of each kind; but somehow I haven't been able to count them since. They seem to . . . get lost, or shift around, or something."

"Oh?" I was becoming interested. "May I pick it up?"

"Certainly," he said, and I took the affair, which was surprisingly lightweight, in my hands and began folding the cubes around on their hinges. I noticed then that some were open on one side and that certain others would fit into these if their hinging arrangements would allow them to.

I began folding them absently and said, "You could count them by marking them one at a time. With a crayon, for instance."

"As a matter of fact," he admitted, blushing again, "I tried that. Didn't seem to work out. When I finished, I found I had marked six cubes with the number one and on none of them could I find a two or three, although there were two fours, one of them written in reverse and in green." He hesitated. "I had used a red marking pencil." I saw him shudder slightly as he said it, although his voice had been casual-sounding enough. "I rubbed the numbers off with a damp cloth and didn't . . . try it again."

"Well," I said. And then, "What do you call it?"

"A pentaract."

He sat back down again in his armchair. "Of course, that name really isn't accurate. I suppose a pentaract should really be a four-dimensional pentagon, and this is meant to be a picture of a five-dimensional cube."

"A *picture?*" It didn't look like a picture to me.

"Well, it couldn't *really* have five-dimensionality—length, width, breadth, ifth and ooth—or I don't think it could." His voice faltered a little at that. "But it's supposed to illustrate the layout of an object that did have those."

"What kind of object would that be?" I looked back at the thing in my lap and was surprised to see that I had folded a good many of the cubes together.

"Suppose," he said, "you put a lot of points in a row, touching; you have a line—a one-dimensional figure. Put four lines together at right angles and on a plane; a square—two-dimensional. Six squares at right angles and extended into real space give you a cube—three dimensions. And eight cubes extended into four physical dimensions give you a tesseract, as it's called—"

"And eight tesseracts make a pentaract," I said. "Five dimensions."

"Exactly. But naturally this is just a *picture* of a pentaract, in that sense. There probably isn't any ifth and oofth at all."

"I still don't know what you mean by a *picture*," I said, pushing the cubes around interestedly.

"You don't?" he asked, pursing his lips. "It's rather awkward to explain, but . . . well, on the surface of a piece of paper, you can make a very realistic picture of a cube—you know, with perspective and shading and all that kind of thing —and what you'd actually be doing would be illustrating a three-dimensional object, the cube, by using only two dimensions to do it with."

"And of course," I said, "you could *fold* the paper into a cube. Then you'd have a real cube."

He nodded. "But you'd have to *use* the third dimension— by folding the flat paper *up*—to do it. So, unless I could fold my cubes up through ifth or oofth, my pentaract will have to be just a poor picture."

"Well!" I said, a bit lost. "And what do you plan to use it for?"

"Just curiosity." And then, abruptly, looking at me now, his eyes grew wide and he bumped up out of his chair. He said breathlessly, "What have you done to it?"

I looked down at my hands. I was holding a little structure of eight cubes, joined together in a small cross. "Why, nothing," I said, feeling a little foolish. "I only folded most of them together."

"That's impossible! There were only twelve open ones to begin with! All of the others were six-sided!"

Farnsworth made a grab for it, apparently beside himself;

the gesture was so sudden that I drew back. It made Farnsworth miss his grab and the little object flew from my hands and hit the floor, solidly, on one of its corners. There was a slight bump as it hit, and a faint clicking noise, and the thing seemed to crumple in a peculiar way. Sitting in front of us on the floor was a little one-inch cube, and nothing else.

For at least a full minute, we stared at it. Then I stood up and looked in my chair seat, looked around the floor of the room, even got down on my knees and peered under the chair. Farnsworth was watching me, and when I finished and sat down again, he asked, "No others?"

"No other cubes," I said, "anywhere."

"I was afraid of that." He pointed an unsteady finger at the one cube in front of us. "I suppose they're all in there." Some of his agitation had begun to wear off and after a moment he said, "What was that you said about folding the paper to make a cube?"

I looked at him and managed an apologetic smile.

He didn't smile back, but he got up and said, "Well, I doubt if it can bite," and bent over and picked the cube up, hefting its weight carefully in his hand. "It seems to weigh the same as the—sixty-four did," he said, quite calmly now. Then he looked at it closely and suddenly became agitated again. "Good heavens! Look at this!" He held it up. On one side, exactly in the center, was a neat little hole, about a half-inch across.

I moved my head closer to the cube and saw that the hole was not really circular. It was like the iris diaphragm of a camera, a polygon made of many overlapping, straight pieces of metal, allowing an opening for light to enter. Nothing was visible through the hole; I could see only an undefined blackness.

"I don't understand how . . ." I began, and stopped.

"Nor I," he said. "Let's see if there's anything in here."

He put the cube up to his eye and squinted and peered for a minute. Then he carefully set it on the table, walked to his chair, sat down and folded his hands over his fat little lap.

"George," he said, "there *is* something in there." His voice now was very steady and yet strange.

"What?" I asked. What else do you say?

"A little ball," he said. "A little round ball. Quite misted over, but nonetheless a ball."

"Well!" I said.

"George, I'll get the gin."

He was back from the sideboard in what seemed an incredibly short time. He had the sloe gin in highball glasses, with ice and water. It tasted horrible.

When I finished mine, I said, "Delicious. Let's have another," and we did. After I drank that one, I felt a good deal more rational.

I set my glass down. "Farnsworth, it just occurred to me. Isn't the fourth dimension supposed to be *time,* according to Einstein?"

He had finished his second sloe gin highball, unmulled, by then. "Supposed to be, yes, according to Einstein. I call it ifth —or oofth—take your pick." He held up the cube again, much more confidently now, I noticed. "And what about the *fifth* dimension?"

"Beats me," I said, looking at the cube, which was beginning to seem vaguely sinister to me. "Beats the hell out of me."

"Beats me, too, George," he said almost gaily—an astonishing mood for old Farnsworth. He turned the cube around with his small, fat fingers. "This is probably all wrapped up in time in some strange way. Not to mention the very peculiar kind of space it appears to be involved with. Extraordinary, don't you think?"

"Extraordinary," I nodded.

"George, I think I'll take another look." And he put the

cube back to his eye again. "Well," he said, after a moment of squinting, "same little ball."

"What's it doing?" I wanted to know.

"Nothing. Or perhaps spinning a bit. I'm not sure. It's quite fuzzy, you see, and misty. Dark in there, too."

"Let me see," I said, realizing that, after all, if Farnsworth could see the thing in there, so could I.

"In a minute. I wonder what sort of time I'm looking into—past or future, or what?"

"And what sort of space . . ." I was saying when, suddenly, little Farnsworth let out a shriek, dropped the cube as if it had suddenly turned into a snake, and threw his hands over his eyes.

He sank back into his chair and cried, "My God! My God!"

"What happened?" I asked, rushing over to Farnsworth, who was squirming in his armchair, his face still hidden by his hands.

"My eye!" he moaned, almost sobbing. "It stabbed my eye! Quick, George, call me an ambulance!"

I hurried to the telephone and fumbled with the book, looking for the right number, until Farnsworth said, "Quick, George!" again and, in desperation, I dialed the operator and told her to send us an ambulance.

When I got back to Farnsworth, he had taken his hand from the unhurt eye and I could see that a trickle of blood was beginning to run down the other wrist. He had almost stopped squirming, but from his face it was obvious that the pain was still intense.

He stood up. "I need another drink," he said, and was heading unsteadily for the sideboard when he stepped on the cube, which was still lying in front of his chair, and was barely able to keep himself from falling headlong, tripping on it. The cube skidded a few feet, stopping, hole-side up, near the fire.

He said to the cube, enraged, "Damn you, I'll show you

. . . !" and he reached down and swooped up the poker from the hearth. It had been lying there for mulling drinks, its end resting on the coals, and by now it was a brilliant cherry red. He took the handle with both hands and plunged the red-hot tip into the hole of the cube, pushing it down against the floor.

"I'll show you!" he yelled again, and I watched understandingly as he shoved with all his weight, pushing and twisting, forcing the poker down with angry energy. There was a faint hissing sound and little wisps of dark smoke came from the hole, around the edges of the poker.

Then there was a strange, sucking noise and the poker began to sink into the cube. It must have gone in at least eight or ten inches—impossible, of course, since it was a one-inch cube—and even Farnsworth became so alarmed at this that he yanked the poker out of the hole.

As he did, black smoke arose in a little column for a moment and then there was a popping sound and the cube fell apart, scattering itself into hundreds of squares of plastic and aluminum.

Oddly enough, there were no burn marks on the aluminum and none of the plastic seemed to have melted. There was no sign of a little, misty ball.

Farnsworth returned his right hand to his now puffy and bloody eye. He stood staring at the profusion of little squares with his good eye. His free hand was trembling.

Then there was the sound of a siren, becoming louder. He turned and looked at me balefully. "That must be the ambulance. I suppose I'd better get my toothbrush."

Farnsworth lost the eye. Within a week, though, he was pretty much his old chipper self again, looking quite dapper with a black leather patch. One interesting thing—the doctor remarked that there were powder burns of some sort on the eyelid, and that the eye itself appeared to have been destroyed by a small explosion. He assumed that it had been a case of a

420

gun misfiring, the cartridge exploding in an open breech somehow. Farnsworth let him think that; it was as good an explanation as any.

I suggested to Farnsworth that he ought to get a green patch, to match his other eye. He laughed at the idea and said he thought it might be a bit showy. He was already starting work on another pentaract; he was going to find out just what . . .

But he never finished. Nine days after the accident, there was a sudden flurry of news reports from the other side of the world, fantastic stories that made the tabloids go wild, and we began to guess what had happened. There wouldn't be any need to build the sixty-four-cube cross and try to find a way of folding it up. We knew now.

It *had* been a five-dimensional cube, all right. And one extension of it had been in time—into the future; nine days into the future—and the other extension had been into a peculiar kind of space, one that distorted sizes quite strangely.

All of this became obvious when, three days later, it happened on our side of the world and the tabloids were scooped by the phenomenon itself, which, by its nature, required no newspaper reporting.

Across the entire sky of the Western Hemisphere there appeared—so vast that it eclipsed the direct light of the sun from Fairbanks, Alaska, to Cape Horn—a tremendous human eye, with a vast, glistening, green iris. Part of the lid was there, too, and all of it was as if framed in a gigantic circle. Or not exactly a circle, but a polygon of many sides, like the iris diaphragm of a camera shutter.

Toward nightfall, the eye blinked once and probably five hundred million people screamed simultaneously. It remained there all of the night, glowing balefully in the reflected sunlight, obliterating the stars.

Probably more than half the people on Earth thought it was God. Only two knew that it was Oliver Farnsworth, peering at a misty little spinning ball in a five-dimensional box, nine days before, totally unaware that the little ball was the Earth itself, contained in a little one-inch cube that was an enclave of swollen time and shrunken space.

When I had dropped the pentaract and had somehow caused it to fold itself into two new dimensions, it had reached out through fifth-dimensional space and folded the world into itself, and had begun accelerating the time within it, in rough proportion to size, so that as each minute passed in Farnsworth's study, about one day was passing on the world within the cube.

We knew this because about a minute had passed while Farnsworth had held his eye against the cube the second time —the first time had, of course, been the appearance over Asia —and nine days later, when we saw the same event from our position on the Earth in the cube, it was twenty-six hours before the eye was "stabbed" and withdrew.

It happened early in the morning, just after the sun had left the horizon and was passing into eclipse behind the great circle that contained the eye. Someone stationed along a defense-perimeter station panicked—someone highly placed. Fifty guided missiles were launched, straight up, the most powerful on Earth. Each carried a hydrogen warhead. Even before the great shock wave from their explosion came crashing down to earth, the eye had disappeared.

Somewhere, I knew, an unimaginably vast Oliver Farnsworth was squirming and yelping, carrying out the identical chain of events that I had seen happening in the past and that yet must be happening now, along the immutable space-time continuum that Farnsworth's little cube had somehow bypassed.

The doctor had talked of powder burns. I wondered what he would think if he knew that Farnsworth had been hit in the eye with fifty infinitesimal hydrogen bombs.

For a week, there was nothing else to talk about in the

world. Three billion people probably discussed, thought about and dreamed of nothing else. There had been no more dramatic happening since the creation of the earth and sun than the appearance of Farnsworth's eye.

But two people, out of those three billion, thought of something else. They thought of the unchangeable, preset space-time continuum, moving at the rate of one minute for every day that passed here on our side of the pentaract, while that vast Oliver Farnsworth and I, in the other-space, other-time, were staring at the cube that contained our world, lying on their floor.

On Wednesday, we could say, *Now he's gone to the telephone*. On Thursday, *Now he's looking through the book*. On Saturday, *By now he must be dialing the operator . . .*

And on Tuesday morning, when the sun came up, we were together and saw it rise, for we spent our nights together by then, because we did not want to be alone; and when the day had begun, we didn't say it, because we couldn't. But we thought it.

We thought of a colossal, cosmic Farnsworth saying, "I'll show you!" and shoving, pushing and twisting, forcing with all of his might, into the little round hole, a brilliantly glowing, hissing, smoking, red-hot poker.

THE SCHOLAR'S DISCIPLE

He appeared to be no more than twenty-five, and his eyes were bright orange. Except for these he would have looked like an ordinary, somewhat handsome young man. He stood in the center of the chalked diagram on Webley's kitchen linoleum and shifted his weight from one small foot to the other. He was dressed impeccably in an Oxford gray suit and he wore a "peace" button in his lapel.

Webley sat motionless on the kitchen stool for a moment, not knowing exactly what to say. This sort of . . . person was not at all what he had expected. His guest glanced uneasily at the two plastic mixing bowls that sat just inside the chalked lines. Finally he blinked his orange eyes and looked at Webley.

"Well?" Webley said.

"Yes, sir?" The fellow's voice was polite; it had the controlled tone of a proper young graduate student's.

Webley cleared his throat. "Aren't you going to drink the blood?" he said, "or do something with the entrails?"

The other shuddered. "No, sir."

Webley began to feel irritated; it had taken a great deal of work to gather the things. "Then why in Heaven's name are they in the . . . invocation?"

"In whose name, sir?" The young fellow blushed, averting his eyes.

"Sorry. In the name of Hell, then."

"Yes." The fellow smiled engagingly and, more at ease, withdrew a bright red cigarette case from his pocket, offering one to his host, who declined it. The cigarettes were long, and coal black. "I don't really know, sir, why some versions of the procedure call for such things as . . ." he glanced hesitatingly toward the bowls again, "those. Impure texts, possibly. It's all in the words. One has to say them right. Apparently you mastered the feat well." He pressed the end of a well-manicured forefinger against the tip of his cigarette and it lit in a tiny burst of flame. When he exhaled, the smoke had a perfumed odor.

Webley was somewhat placated by the compliment, although it had taken a year of searching to dig up those "impure texts." "Well," he said, "you *are* a demon, anyway, aren't you?"

"Oh, hell yes," the fellow said, with feeling. "By all means."

"And your name?"

"Makuka . . . It's hard to pronounce, sir . . . Makukabuzzeeliam. In Hell our clients generally call me Robert."

"And you can serve me?"

"After a fashion, yes. Of course, I have a good many other duties."

Webley poured himself a drink, offering one to the demon, who refused. "I don't think I would overwork you, Robert. What I want you to do, primarily, is to write a dissertation for me. And, perhaps, a few scholarly articles."

The demon seemed to think this over a moment. Then he said, "What field, sir?"

"English. English literature."

The demon smiled abruptly, revealing even, white teeth. "That might be interesting, sir," he said. "We have a good many of your English writers . . . available, so to speak." His orange eyes seemed to twinkle. "And a fine bunch too, sir, I might add. But why," he said, "would you ever call up a demon to write your dissertation for you?"

"Well," Webley said, "I am one of the few people who know how; that's one consideration. I have my first Ph.D. in Folklore, you see. Done a lot of research in Folklore. After twelve years of it I began to realize that most of the lore worked out very well. I cure a little asthma here and there, with black-eyed peas, practice a little Voodoo—nothing important, just to amuse my friends."

"Voodoo never has been very effective," Robert said understandingly. "Overrated."

"I fear so. Anyway, I began to realize that I'd never get anywhere in the academic world with a Folklore degree—just isn't recognized by enough schools. The logical thing was to get into a parallel but more respected field. And, with a few good articles, I might be able to swing a professorship." Webley finished his drink and shuffled, ponderously, over to the sink, where he began fixing another. "Trouble is, Robert, I hate writing—especially scholarly writing. Consequently, I thought I'd try invoking a demon to do it for me." He settled back in his chair, smiling, and began sipping the drink. "I think it's going to work out very well."

The demon smiled engagingly. "I hope so," he said. "I'll go check with the legal department—about a contract." He blinked his eyes and vanished. . . .

When Robert returned, after more than an hour, he had with him an estimate on the value of Webley's immortal soul. They haggled for a good while before agreeing on the terms, but Webley was quite pleased with them; he had done better than he had expected to. The young demon seemed to bluff very easily.

Webley would, of course, go to Hell upon his death; but he would have a suite there, a mistress—to be changed yearly—air conditioning—Robert tried to explain to him that Hell was not in the least bit hot; but Webley stuck to his guns on this point—weekly valet service, and ready access to his landlord should any inconvenience develop. He would be roasted over the coals for one day out of every month; but he was guaranteed that there would be no harmful aftereffects from this. "In fact," Robert said, "some of our clients look forward to that part of the life in Hell, since the possibilities for pain among the dead are so few, and the senses are so dulled by the extraordinary amount of pleasure we have to offer."

"Then why do you have this roasting business at all, if Hell is such a pleasant place?" Webley asked, pouring himself a drink.

"Well, we are under orders from the opposition. We can't make Him out to be a liar, you know. And then those coals *are* rather unpleasant."

"I see. But what, then, do they do in Heaven?"

Robert thought a moment. "It's been a long time since I was there, of course. They sing, mostly, I think. And do exercises or something."

In return for his agreeing to the damnation Webley would receive the services of Robert for one year, in which time an acceptable dissertation must be written, as well as at least ten publishable scholarly articles. Webley had with him a razor blade to open a vein for signing the contract; he was mildly piqued when the demon brought out a ball point pen, even though the ink was bright red. It dried brown, however.

Immediately after he finished signing there came the sound of a small and dry little voice, from somewhere, it seemed, in the basement. The voice said one word, which it enunciated with precision. "*Agreed.*"

"Who the devil is *that?*" Webley said.

Robert blushed again, momentarily. "Our . . . legal department, sir," he said. He folded the contract and then vanished gently. . . .

He appeared for work the next morning. Webley had already prepared an office for him in a disused upstairs bedroom, complete with typewriter, *The MLA Style Sheet,* and a small library of learned journals. He worked methodically and well, seemed to take a certain pleasure in his writing, and within three months had produced a monumental, definitive work, titled "The Lyric Cry in Colley Cibber: A Reappraisal." When this was finished, Robert suggested that he show it to Mr. Cibber, who, he said, had a small walk-up apartment in suburban Hell; but Webley would not hear of it. "Just stick to the scholarship, young man."

The dissertation, upon acceptance and publication by the University press, created a stir among a great many academic people, few of whom read it. Webley soon found himself in possession of a very congenial job, with a low salary and few duties. A month later he received a large fellowship from a foundation; and upon his first *PMLA* publication, the controversy-stirring article "Threads of Francophilism in John Webster's *The White Devil,*" found himself with an associate professorship and even fewer duties.

The demon's work was inspired. His style managed to be ornate and terse at one and the same time; he was greatly sardonic about everyone and everything except a handful of third-rate poets; he displayed an astonishing prowess at ignoring the obvious and seizing upon the manifestly impossible; and his footnotes were awe-inspiring. Within a year Webley's name had become an unshakeable star in the academic firmament.

When Robert handed the tenth paper to his employer he seemed actually sad that this would be the last of his scholarly work. He had grown to love his job.

Webley, interpreting Robert's hesitancy rightly, was immediately struck by an idea. He explained it to the demon. He, Webley, would appy for a year's leave of absence with pay, so that he might write a book. He had been feeling oppressed, of late, by the restrictions of his teaching schedule, however light; and, besides, there was a graduate assistant, a certain Miss Hopkins, with whom he was much taken. Miss Hopkins had already expressed a deep-seated wish to visit Acapulco. As for himself, he enjoyed spear fishing as well as the next fellow. Now, as for the book. . . . He would be glad to sign a new contract.

Robert's face showed doubt, although Webley could tell that he was pleased with the idea. "I don't know, sir," he said, "I do have my other duties; and my supervisor doesn't generally like to alter a contract. People are always accusing him of coercion when he does something like that. He's very scrupulous, you know."

"Well, see what you can do," Webley said. "And remember, you can write the book any way you want to."

"Well . . ."

"You can name your own subject."

The demon smiled sheepishly, "I'll see what I can do," he said, and vanished in a puff of perfumed smoke.

It was three days later that Robert returned with the new contract. The terms were fairly hard, but this time Webley was unable to talk them down. Robert said that this was the least his legal department would allow. There would now be three days per month on the coals, together with one day of boils, from sole to crown. Also he would have to share the bath in his suite, and his choice of mistresses would be limited to brunettes. But, in return, Robert promised to produce the finest, most significant and monumental work of English literary criticism ever written.

After four hours of bickering, Webley finally threw his hands in the air, "All right," he said, "I'll sign. After all, a man ought to produce one good book in a lifetime. And Miss Hopkins is growing impatient."

Robert smiled. "I'm certain you won't be disappointed in the book, sir." He blushed slightly. "Nor in Miss Hopkins ei-

ther. I took the liberty of checking on her file, and found her
. . . promising."

"That's interesting . . ." Webley said, smiling thoughtfully
and taking the ball point pen from the demon's outstretched
hand.

As before, there came the little voice, saying,
"Agreed. . . ."

Miss Hopkins was not disappointing, not in the least. Nor was
Acapulco, nor spear fishing, nor tequila. But especially not
Miss Hopkins. When the year ended and Robert appeared,
Webley was lying in bed in a small adobe hut, with a mild
headache and with Miss Hopkins, who was fortunately sound
asleep. The demon, appearing from Hell with a very thick
book under his arm, found him there.

During the past year Webley's face had taken on a certain
bloated haughtiness; and his tone now with Robert was patronizing. "What's the title, Robert?" he said, making no
move to get up from the bed.

The English Literary Tradition: A Re-evaluation." There
was a tiny hint of pride in Robert's voice.

Webley frowned. "That's a little general, Robert," he said.
"But I suppose it'll do. How long is it?"

"Seventeen hundred pages, sir."

"Yes. Well, that ought to impress them well enough." He
leaned over on one elbow. "Tell you what you do, Robert.
You pack that manuscript off to my editor for me; and then I
want you to take a message to the University. Tell them I'm
delayed and won't be back for about three or four weeks. Tell
them I'm working on the index or something." He reached a
chubby hand over and gave Miss Hopkins a gentle pat on the
rump. She stirred and giggled softly in her sleep. "Now do
that for me, Robert, and it'll be all wrapped up between us."

There seemed to be a hurt look in the demon's eyes.
"You're not going to read the book, sir?"

431

Webley waved a hand royally. "When it comes out in print, man," he said. "Right now I'm busy."

"Yes, sir," Robert said, vanishing.

It was six weeks later that Webley was mailed a copy of the book by his publisher. Since he was well absorbed at the time with other pursuits, it was another two weeks before he read it. Or he did not read it exactly—not entirely. He was two-thirds of the way through when, red in the face and eyes glaring, he shrieked the proper incantation and Robert appeared.

"What in the name of Hell do you mean by this—this asininity, this patent absurdity?" Webley said. "Any half-baked scholar with a quarter of a brain could demolish this, rip it to shreds! This is tripe, Robert. Fraudulent, unscholarly, unforgivable tripe. You've made an ass of yourself and of me."

Robert seemed dumbfounded; his entire face was an enormous blush. "But, Professor Webley," he said, "I . . . I thought you would like it, sir. Thought it would be . . . just the thing."

Webley seemed to explode. "Just the thing!" He slammed the book on his desk. "Good lord, Robert, if I couldn't write a more accurate work of literary criticism in six months' time I'd . . . I'd let you roast me in Hell. Seven days a week."

From somewhere beneath the floor came a little voice, saying *"Agreed."*

Webley stopped in the middle of a breath. Then he said, "Now wait a minute, Robert. You can't . . . surely you. . . ."

The demon's face showed embarrassment, and his tone was extremely polite, apologetic. "I'm afraid we can, sir," he said. "Verbal contract, you know. Hold up in any court."

For a moment Webley's eyes searched frantically around the room. Finally they landed on the book, which lay now on the table, and immediately the glance of uncertainty was replaced with a look of triumph. "All right," he said. "All right. You think you've got me, don't you? Think you've trapped me into a bad contract. The only thing you've neglected is that I *can* write a better book than this one." He picked up the book, flipping through it again, "Look at this. More than two hundred pages of Shakespeare analysis—not to mention the rest, from The Pearl Poet to Oscar Wilde—and not one genuine, scholarly idea in the lot. Well written, possibly. But any graduate student knows that Shakespeare didn't model Cleopatra on his *mother*—the idea's absurd. And an idiot would know that the textual problem is the only clue to *Hamlet*."

"But . . ." Robert said.

"But nothing!" Webley slammed the book back on his desk. "It's not merely your insidious way of trying to steal my soul that infuriates me—it's this fool book you're trying to do it with. Who in Hell ever gave you these stupid notions about literature?"

Robert seemed uneasy. "That's what I've been trying to tell you, Mr. Webley," he said. "It was a great many people in Hell. You see, I didn't exactly write the book myself, sir."

"Then who . . . who wrote this nonsense about Shakespeare?"

"Shakespeare, sir. I sobered him up and. . . ."

Abruptly, Webley's voice took on the tone of a small man speaking from the bottom of a well. "And Milton. Who . . . ?"

The demon managed a weak smile. "John had some revealing things to say about *Comus,* didn't he, sir?"

Webley's eyes were taking on a strange, hunted look. "And *Beowulf* . . . Surely you didn't . . ."

"I'm afraid I did, Mr. Webley. We have the author of that one too—he slipped up once on the Fourth Commandment. Fellow named Seothang the Imbiber. Drinks mead."

Webley stood in stony silence for several minutes, holding the heavy book in a limp hand. His eyes were closed.

After a few minutes he opened them. Robert had, tastefully, vanished. In his place was a small, black table. On this were arranged neatly a typewriter, a stack of white paper, and a calendar.

FAR FROM HOME

The first inkling the janitor had of the miracle was the smell of it. This was a small miracle in itself: the salt smell of kelp and seawater in the Arizona morning air. He had just unlocked the front entrance and walked into the building when the smell hit him. Now this man was old and normally did not trust his senses very well; but there was no mistaking this, not even in this most inland of inland towns: it was the smell of ocean—deep ocean, far out, the ocean of green water, kelp and brine.

And strangely, because the janitor was old and tired and because this was the part of early morning that seems unreal to many old men, the first thing the smell made him feel was a small, almost undetectable thrilling in his old nerves, a memory deeper than blood of a time fifty years before when he had gone once, as a boy, to San Francisco and had watched the ships in the bay and had discovered the fine old dirty smell of seawater. But this feeling lasted only an instant. It was replaced immediately with amazement—and then anger, although it would have been impossible to say with what he was angry, here in this desert town, in the dressing rooms of the large public swimming pool at morning, being reminded of his youth and of the ocean.

"What the hell's going on here . . . ?" the janitor said.

There was no one to hear this, except perhaps the small boy who had been standing outside, staring through the wire fence

435

into the pool and clutching a brown paper sack in one grubby hand, when the janitor had come up to the building. The man had paid no attention to the boy; small boys were always around the swimming pool in summer—a nuisance. The boy, if he had heard the man, did not reply.

The janitor walked on through the concrete-floored dressing rooms, not even stopping to read the morning's crop of obscenities scribbled on the walls of the little wooden booths. He walked into the tiled anteroom, stepped across the disinfectant foot bath, and out onto the wide concrete edge of the swimming pool itself.

Some things are unmistakable. There was a whale in the pool.

And no ordinary, everyday whale. This was a monumental creature, a whale's whale, a great, blue-gray leviathan, ninety feet long and thirty feet across the back, with a tail the size of a flatcar and a head like the smooth fist of a titan. A blue whale, an old shiny, leathery monster with barnacles on his gray underbelly and his eyes filmed with age and wisdom and myopia, with brown seaweed dribbling from one corner of his mouth, marks of the suckers of squid on his face, and a rusted piece of harpoon sunk in the unconscious blubber of his back. He rested on his belly in the pool, his back way out of the water and with his monstrous gray lips together in an expression of contentment and repose. He was not asleep; but he was asleep enough not to care where he was.

And he stank—with the fine old stink of the sea, the mother of us all: the brackish, barnacled, grainy salt stink of creation and old age, the stink of the world that was and of the world to come. He was beautiful.

The janitor did not freeze when he saw him; he froze a moment afterward. First he said, aloud, his voice matter-of-fact, "There's a whale in the swimming pool. A goddamn whale." He said this to no one—or to everyone—and perhaps the boy heard him, although there was no reply from the other side of the fence.

After speaking, the janitor stood where he was for seven minutes, thinking. He thought of many things, such as what he had eaten for breakfast, what his wife had said to him when she had awakened him that morning. Somewhere, in the corner of his vision, he saw the little boy with the paper sack, and his mind thought, as minds will do at such times, *Now that boy's about six years old. That's probably his lunch in that sack. Egg salad sandwich. Banana. Or apple.* But he did not think about the whale, because there was nothing to be thought about the whale. He stared at its unbelievable bulk, resting calmly, the great head in the deep water under the diving boards, the corner of one tail fluke being lapped gently by the shallow water of the wading pool.

The whale breathed slowly, deeply, through its blow hole. The janitor breathed slowly, shallowly, staring, not blinking even in the rising sunlight, staring with no comprehension at the eighty-five-ton miracle in the swimming pool. The boy held his paper sack tightly at the top, and his eyes, too, remained fixed on the whale. The sun was rising in the sky over the desert to the east, and its light glinted in red and purple iridescence on the oily back of the whale.

And then the whale noticed the janitor. Weak-visioned, it peered at him filmily for several moments from its grotesquely small eye. And then it arched its back in a ponderous, awesome, and graceful movement, lifted its tail twenty feet in the air, and brought it down in a way that seemed strangely slow, slapping gently into the water with it. A hundred gallons of water rose out of the pool, and enough of it drenched the janitor to wake him from the state of partial paralysis into which he had fallen.

Abruptly the janitor jumped back, scrambling from the water, his eyes looking, frightened, in all directions, his lips white. There was nothing to see but the whale and the boy. "All right," he said. "All right," as if he had somehow seen through the plot, as if he knew, now, what a whale would be doing in the public swimming pool, as if no one was going to put anything over on *him*. "All right," the janitor said to the whale, and then he turned and ran.

He ran back into the center of town, back toward Main Street, back toward the bank, where he would find the Chairman of the Board of the City Parks Commission, the man who could, somehow—perhaps with a memorandum—save him. He ran back to the town where things were as they were supposed to be; ran as fast as he had ever run, even when young, to escape the only miracle he would ever see in his life and the greatest of all God's creatures. . . .

After the janitor had left, the boy remained staring at the whale for a long while, his face a mask and his heart racing with all the peculiar excitement of wonder and love—wonder for all whales, and love for the only whale that he, an Arizona boy of six desert years, had ever seen. And then, when he realized that there would be men there soon and his time with his whale would be over, he lifted the paper sack carefully close to his face, and opened its top about an inch. A commotion began in the sack, as if a small animal were in it that wanted desperately to get out.

"Stop that!" the boy said, frowning.

The kicking stopped. From the sack came a voice—a high-pitched, irascible voice. "All right, whatever-your-name-is," the voice said, "I suppose you're ready for the second one."

The boy held the sack carefully with his thumb and forefinger. He frowned at the opening in the top. "Yes," he said, "I think so . . ."

When the janitor returned with the two other men, the whale was no longer there. Neither was the small boy. But the seaweed smell and the splashed, brackish water were there still, and in the pool were several brownish streamers of seaweed, floating aimlessly in the chlorinated water, far from home.

ABOUT GOLLANCZ

Gollancz is the oldest SF publishing imprint in the world. Since being founded in 1927 Gollancz has continued to publish a focused selection of bestselling and award-winning authors. The front-list includes **Ben Aaronovitch**, **Joe Abercrombie**, **Charlaine Harris**, **Joanne Harris**, **Joe Hill**, **Alastair Reynolds**, **Patrick Rothfuss**, **Nalini Singh** and **Brandon Sanderson**.

As one of the largest Science Fiction and Fantasy imprints in the UK it is no surprise we have one of the most extensive backlists in the world. Find high quality SF on Gateway written by such authors as **Philip K. Dick**, **Ursula Le Guin**, **Connie Willis**, **Sir Arthur C. Clarke**, **Pat Cadigan**, **Michael Moorcock** and **George R.R. Martin**.

We also have a strand of publishing in translation, which includes French, Polish and Russian authors. Gollancz is home to more award-winning authors than any other imprint, with names including **Aliette de Bodard**, **M. John Harrison**, **Paul McAuley**, **Sarah Pinborough**, **Pierre Pevel**, **Justina Robson** and many more.

The SF Gateway
More than 3,000 classic, rare and previously out-of-print SF novels at your fingertips.
www.sfgateway.com

The Gollancz Blog
Bringing you news from our worlds to yours. Stories, interviews, articles and exclusive extracts just for you!
www.gollancz.co.uk

GOLLANCZ
LONDON